JENNIE'S TIGER

JENNIE'S TIGER

A Woman's Pioneering Stand in an
Untamed Corner of Washington State

by Eva Gayle Six

To order additional copies of this book, contact:
Xlibris Corporation
1-888-795-4274
www.Xlibris.com
Orders@Xlibris.com
102689

This is the story of homesteading in the 20th century in northeast Washington state. It is based on a few pages of a memoir written by the real Jennie Wooding when she was in her 80's, long after her experiences at Tiger's Landing. Jennie wrote from memory, not from notes - because Jennie was, in fact, able to do very little reading and writing. Puzzling out Jennie's memoir and supplementing it with research made it possible to flesh out Jennie's story and present this slightly fictionalized version of an actual homesteader's experience.

TABLE OF CONTENTS

THE RAMBLING WOMAN'S PREAMBLE

Two wrenching bad things has happened to me in my life, and now I'm past 70 and gone blind, I believe I can tell you about the one of them and maybe I'll quit seeing it again and again in the dark. This first thing happened when I was a little past 20. The other one happened when I was past 50 and I'm gonna leave that one to someone else to tell you. It's still too fresh for me.

I've heard people say about things that happened to them long ago that it was like it happened to somebody else. I don't find that to be so. When I think back I feel like I was always the same person as I am now. I was just always Jennie. But I will have to say, now that I think about it, before this awful thing happened, both me and Wes must have thought that if you was good, then good things would happen to you. Because we was plumb knocked down by it - by how sudden it happened, and by the feeling that we didn't deserve it to happen. Afterward, we understood deserving don't have nothing to do with much.

It was in 1894. We'd been married 8 years. I can say those eight years was about pure fun. We'd knocked around the Arizona Territory trying to make one mine or another pay. In them days you could live off of the land, even in the desert, if you could think beforehand. We was just trying to make some ahead, kind of like gambling when you didn't have nothing important you imagined you could lose. What we cherished was each other and our two little girls, Naomi and Alma, and our baby Tommie. We figured that of course we could always keep them treasures safe.

Now Wes suffered on and off from the sore-eye. It kept getting frequenter, and the desert heat and dust made it worse, so we moved over to the West Sierra, in California, in the Green Horn Mountains - as always, chasing rainbows. We was going to do more prospecting, but we found so many folks was ahead of us and so many claims was already filed that there wasn't much left for us. So we went up high to logging country, around them big sequoias, to maybe see what was to be made up there. It was not much, at least not for us. So we set up a laundry for the loggers, and that did better than logging or mining ever did for us. We had quite a bit on the books coming from the loggers when the Panic of 1893 caught up with the mill. It closed, and so the loggers closed, and so we closed. Well, "on the books" didn't help much. But, still carefree as always, come September we packed up Naomi who was six and Alma who was two and the new baby Tommie who was 3 months and headed for my sister's place down in fruit country around Visalia. We thought we might find a orchard down there to dry on shares. We always thought a new place was going to do better, and besides it was always fun to visit any of my sisters, and most certainly Belle Golden and her husband Steve. So as we left the mountains we was somewhat disappointed we hadn't made a bundle, but the bank said they'd make good on the loggers' bills in time, so we was still hopeful. We was going on a jaunt. We didn't own no horses, but somebody needed a four-horse wagon took down and somebody else needed a two-horse team took down. Wes was blind just then from the sore-eye, even if it wasn't dusty in the West Sierra, so I was to drive.

We got everything packed in that spacious wagon: our clothes, our tent, our laundry buckets and gear, a big sack of weed fluff to put in Alma's and Tommie's diapers while we traveled, and Naomi's Sears Roebuck doll with the painted porcelain face and the eyes that was always staring. We was on our way, I'll tell you.

It was a high old wagon, and when you was up on the box, you was really up there. Wes was to ride up on the box with me and hold Tommie. We had meant for the girls to ride back in the wagon bed, but at the last minute we learned we had to take the extra harness for the two horses we didn't have, and besides, the girls wanted to be where they could see the 'horsies.' We hadn't had no horses for quite a while, since times started getting bad in '93, and they was quite the excitement for the girls. So off we went, all of us eager and hopeful as could be.

When it happened was when we was about 15 miles into the second day. We was in the foothills now, where it was up one hill and down another. We was out of the big trees, and there was mostly just grass on both sides of the road and mostly just rocks in the road. There wasn't no springs on that old wagon, and the jouncing we took was something. The girls might of been better off if we'd of put them in the back, tied on top of the load. We could think back afterwards and see lots of ways we could of maybe fixed things so it didn't end up the way it did.

We'd just came around a bend in the road on the top of a big hill when the horses got scared at something. Whatever it was, we never seen it ourselves, but them horses sure did. They reared up and then lunged down the road at a long run. There was just a wood foot brake on that old wagon, and when I put some extra pressure on it, it split right in two and the pieces bounced on the road. Then I braced my feet on the dashboard and wrapped the reins around my hands and sawed those horses' mouths with all of my strength until they was just a gore of blood, but to no avail. We started up another hill and the horses just lifted me from the seat. I was standing up on the dashboard then, when they started down the next hill. That loosened up the lines and I went back. I missed the seat, and I fell out. When Wes sensed that I was gone out of the wagon he grabbed the girls in one arm and he had the baby in the other arm and he started to jump out, but before he could, the wagon hit the left bank and threw him out. The little girls fell out of his arm and hit the wheel.

I seen them fall, and I jumped up and ran to where they was laying. Alma was sitting up with her head in her lap, looking like a rag doll. Only she was dead. Naomi was on her knees with her head throwed back. Her face looked pale, but only like she was a little sick. But when I put my arms around her and looked past her....there was pearly white, pink-mottled stuff on the ground by her side. I went kind of crazy then, and I picked up her brains and tried to stuff them back into the big gash on the back of her head.

Then I got some sense back, and I straightened the girls out and ran for help. We was about a quarter of a mile from a little mining town. I ran almost there, and then got the idea I should of took the girls with me, as if anybody could help them. Then when I was almost back to the wagon, I could see how dumb that was. I ran back to the town again and the livery stable was right at the edge of town. As luck would have it, their doctor was there, getting ready to take his horse and buggy out on a call. When he understood that the girls was dead and Wes and Tommie wasn't hurt, he made me sit down, and that's the first time I knew I was hurt. There wasn't no skin on my one leg from knee to foot, and my hands was cut deep. That doctor said the one thing that would make me sit still for treatment, and that was that my husband and baby wouldn't want to lose me too, to a infection. So he daubed me with a poultice and wrapped my leg and my hands in bandages; and instead of to the doctor's little buggy, the liveryman hitched his horse to a wagon to put my family, some dead and some alive, into.

The doctor drove me back, and we found Wes on the grass at the side of the road holding his two little girls, one in each arm, his head bowed over them, his tears just streaming down. Tommie was asleep beside him on the grass, and Naomi's doll in her blue checked dress was next to him, staring up. The team had ran around the next bend in the road and one front wheel come off the wagon and rolled off down in a gulch. The horses broke loose from the wagon and ran around still another bend in the road and they both piled up in another gulch. I don't to this day know what the folks there done with them horses.

I don't know if it was worse for me, seeing it, or for Wes, not seeing it. For both of us, the suddenness was terrible. When somebody's sick a long time and then they die, you can kind of get braced for it. But seeing them little girls set out with such fun on that trip, and calling to the 'horsies' and then in an instant being limp and dead, that's the worst thing there is. Like having your bones all of the sudden turn to jelly and slip out the bottom of your feet and you have to walk around with no firm frame in you.

I used to lie awake at night and wonder, in such a big world with all the sadness there was in it, if there was any as great as this one sent on to us. They say God is just, but for a long time I couldn't see why He should let anything so wrong happen to anyone as innocent as us. I didn't think I could ever get over it, but you know, you can't just die every time you want to, and we had our baby boy and each other to live for. And Wes and me was always in love. So we went on living.

Until the other thing happened, near 30 years later.

PART I
GETTING THE HAWTHORN
1900 – 1906

1900

JENNIE TURNED THE chunks of soggy cedar that stood upright in a row around the stove. She was hoping to dry some to feed the fire that was keeping the worst wetness out of the gray two-room shack where she and the three boys were put up for the winter, a winter now itself sputtering out. Spring was early here at Pilchuck, though not as early as down the hill at the Puget Sound. There, flooded green fields and soaked apple blossoms were already promising that within the month the rain would reduce from constant to frequent. Up here at Pilchuck the dark gray and the dark, dull green were relieved only by occasional droppings of fresh sawdust off the shingle wagons going from the mill at Sauk Slough to the railroad down at Marysville, by way of the road of black mud one step from the doorway.

Jasper, eleven months, was tied to a chair he could not drag to the stove or to the doorway where the teams of draft horses and wheels of flatbed wagons shook the shack. A sheaf of those shingles would have been useful on the roof; three battered pots were positioned to catch the rain coming through it. The puzzle was to keep Jasper tethered where he couldn't drink the yellow water from the roof or chew the tiles of black moss that sometimes came with it.

Tommie and Billie played in the bedroom, making islands and hideaways from the mattresses, bedding and garments stashed there on the floor. Periodically they went to the woodshed and brought in chunks of wood to replace what Jennie fed into the stove; then they had to sit by the stove to dry out. There they could smash their noses with two fingers up their nostrils, and pull their eyes down with two more fingers. Tommie at almost six could do this with one hand; Billie at almost four required two. Accompanied by their deepest growls, these monster faces made Jasper's face wrinkle and squint until he cried. As soon as their clothes stopped steaming, Jennie sent them back to their play in the bedroom.

She nursed Jasper and brought the boys back near the stove for slabs of bread smeared with butter and blackberry preserves. She ducked her way to the shed where crocks of milk were cooling. When the rain was this heavy, the days consisted mostly of keeping themselves dry and fed. If the downpour let up to a drizzle in the afternoon, they could go about something more fruitful, maybe start some churning or find some dandelion greens. Maybe she'd bake a couple of dried-apple pies to sell at the store. After he was laid off from the mill again because shingles were stacking up faster than they could be shipped out, Wes had left just a week ago to walk up to the Index mine to see if there was work there. Jennie wondered whether, with only one adult in the house, there might be room to take in some laundry from the mill workers and hang it between drips.

Just then the door opened inward with a screech. One boot then another ran across the scraper. Jennie went to greet the visitor, probably someone from the mill, just their luck, looking for Wes to go back to work.

Instead, Wes himself put his head around the door. "Hey, Girlie, need a drowned rat?" Jennie smiled at his joke, at his presence, at his handlebar mustache dripping from both ends, at the familiar way he turned his head to see her with his better eye. She wanted to hug him but stopped at his sogginess; she settled for taking his slouch hat before the brimful of water could pour on the floor. Tommie and Billie ran from the bedroom and threw themselves at Wes's legs. Jasper jerked at the twisted sheet that kept him in check and managed to move his anchor a foot. Wes untied him and picked him up. "Well, Boys, you're looking wise. What did you learn while I was gone?" The four scuffled on the floor; all five grinned. None of them thought about his being back too soon to signify good luck; they only cared that they could all see and smell and touch each other.

With two adults around, Jasper earned some freedom. Wes lay in the bedroom on a mattress and let the baby crawl on him. He lay on his back and raised the baby over his head, balanced him on his own feet, gurgled in his chubby neck, and finally held him against his chest while they both napped. Later, he chopped wood and milked the cow while Jennie fixed dinner, set the milk to separate, fed the chickens, and put the boys on their mattresses. She and Wes went to their own, and when the boys were well asleep, they consummated the welcome.

But sleep did not come at the end of the lovemaking.

"Jennie, there's no work at the mine till the end of May."

"And I hear nothing here before then."

"How much money have we got?"

"It's more than 75 cents; that's what we had when we hit this place." She smirked at how much they'd saved. "Spring's about here, and there'll be all the greens we want, and the eggs'll pick up. We'll be fine. We won't have to dip into the lard can."

"Jennie, be serious. It doesn't help to have you just try to cheer us up."

"Would it help to have me whine and wail?"

He smiled. "Okay. But let's take stock. Where are we headed? The only jobs I get put us where we can't even rent a fit house. About the time things get on an even keel, either my eyes go bad or the job shuts down."

"I was thinking about taking in laundry again. These mill workers need it just as much as them miners up at the Monte Cristo did."

"Jennie, you need space for that. In California, we could dry clothes outside. At Monte Cristo you and Ada rented a whole boarding house and had indoor hanging space. There's no such thing in this dripping shack. And even at best, it didn't do much more than keep us in grub."

"My trapping up at Monte Cristo was good and would have been really good if we'd stayed till the pelts was in prime. Wes, you're just down 'cause you've got a couple of months off. You've had worse before. Are you sure it's the money, or you just don't know what to do with yourself?"

"There's some of that, I guess. But I want to light someplace. Shifting around from job to job every few months doesn't let us get anything ahead. Every time we move it costs us, Jennie."

She laughed again. "Some times more than others. Wes, remember that time in the Sierra we was moving down in the fall, and we got that old coot who'd brought the load of fruit up and was going down empty, to take our stuff down. We thought we was making such a deal. And the damned fool got drunk the first night going down, and set his wagon afire. They doused it, and everything we owned was either burned up or mildewed. Do you remember the one single thing saved?"

"The sack of unmatched socks from the laundry. I thought I'd comfort you by telling you something, at least, was salvaged. And that's when you burst out bawling, because the sack of socks was saved."

At the shared memory, they turned together with a smile and a hug.

"You know, Wes, I guess if I cried about that it must matter more to me than I knew. We ran that laundry four summers, and was doing really good. Then everything went bad all of the sudden, and since....Naomi and Alma...it's never gone right again."

5

"Jennie, losing the girls was the worst thing that will ever happen to us. But it didn't cause us to lose our savings. The Panic of '93 did that, and it hasn't yet ended for us. McKinley can say it only lasted three years, but for us it's seven. So far."

Jasper whimpered in his box, and Jennie brought him into bed with them. He nursed lackadaisically and went back to sleep between them. The three of them fell quiet for a while, but the conversation couldn't be let drop. Wes picked it up. "I don't know how to make money if nobody else is. Jennie, even the railroads went belly up in California. If they can't make it when the stock market crashes and the banks close, how can Wes and Jennie Wooding?"

"That grub stake Uriah got to take you both to the Klondike sounded good."

"Thanks for the example. I got as far as Sitka when my eyes went bad and I had to work my way back down as kitchen monkey on the boats. I'll never know how clean I got the spuds, 'cause I couldn't see them. See, exactly what I mean. A good break does come along, and I cave in. So you spent the summer cooking for the harvest hands in Tulare County to earn fare for you and the boys to meet me up here."

"A hundred and twenty in the shade, and no shade. But it was work where I could have the little ones with me."

Wes rolled onto his back. "Jennie, you remember Knute Slettedahl, that was up in Monte Cristo when we were?"

"Sure I remember Knute."

"Well, he was at the Index this week, looking for work too. But he's been over on the other side of the state, in the Pend d'Oreille Valley."

"Ponder Ray?"

"That's how it sounds. It's a French spelling, he says."

"No deal. You've taught me some English spelling, Wes, but you ain't going to teach me French too."

"I guess it means something like "Hanging Ear," either something the Indians had, or put on, or something they did to somebody. Knute's been helping a survey crew there. He says it's going to open up to homesteading before long."

"Yeah, my pa tried that in Ventura County and Inyo County, but he couldn't hang onto it. I never could see much difference between our life when we rented or when we homesteaded - except maybe Ma worried more when we homesteaded."

"Jennie, I'm away from you and the boys about half the time now. Maybe we could make it work if I went out to earn wages while you ran the place. It wouldn't be much worse. And after the Proving Up, I'd be home all the time."

"What's it like there?"

"Knute says it's the prettiest place he's ever seen."

"Everybody says that about a place they've been that you ain't."

"No, he sounds really impressed. He says it's a really big river, with cedar trees along the bank, meadows in some places. They travel by steamboat, or else by horse. There aren't any roads, and it's brushy; you can't just take off through the desert in a wagon, like in Arizona."

Wes had been thinking over for three days what Knute had told him, and now enthusiasm boiled up. "Jennie, the survey isn't finished, so it's not officially opened up yet, but Knute says right now's the time to go squat there, because settlers will come in droves when it's announced, it's such good land. There's wild hay enough to cut for the winter. And he kept talking about how beautiful it is. He says he'd go in a minute if he had a partner or a wife."

"Do squatters get dibs on the piece they're on?"

"Knute says so."

"How would we get there?"

"That's a problem, all right. Where's that lard can?"

"Wes, this is going runaway. Let's sleep, and talk about it in the morning."

He put Jasper back in his box, and as Jennie dropped off, she knew he was still thinking.

IN THE MORNING THE RAIN was heavier than ever, splashing in the full pots. Jennie emptied them and the sound changed to drumming. The dog Si announced a visitor. Wes threw on pants and went to the door. Uriah Wooding was unexpected but welcome. Uriah and Wes were double cousins raised as brothers after Wes was orphaned at two. They introduced each other sometimes as cousin and sometimes as brother; the line faded for them.

Uriah's wife Ada had been Jennie's partner in the Monte Cristo laundry venture; they were good friends. Ada and Uriah were both prone to melancholy, and the cheer in the Wes Wooding household was a good antidote. This time, though, Uriah arrived with a wide smile. Wes hugged him. "I didn't know you were down from the cold country, Ryer. From the look of you, you made a strike."

"I did, a pretty good one." He took off his boots and came into the little room. Jennie by now was dressed and building up the fire. The boys slept while she made biscuits and chicory coffee. Wes brought Uriah up to date on all that had happened since he'd left him at the dock in Sitka, chiefly a report of shufflings from mine to mill and mill to mine. He went on to tell about the Pend d'Oreille.

"I didn't know there was still land to give away," Uriah said.

"It ain't to give away. It's to earn," threw in Jennie.

"But it doesn't have a purchase price?"

"True," she said, "but you got to have plenty of cash money: to get there, for one thing; then to buy windows, nails, well parts, and all such. You get just five years to improve the place enough to meet their rules. Then you get to keep it, if you have a house of such and such a size, if so much of the land is fenced, if a lot of it's cleared, if you've lived on it the whole time, and so on. They don't give it away."

"Tell me more about the way it works," urged Uriah. "Say you do finally get it, is it yours for good? You can leave it to your kids? You can sell it?"

"Sure, you can see it as an investment. Like buying that mine in Arizona was, and the place in Nevada was, like digging for gold in the Sierra was, like going to the Klondike was. And what those ever got us was the chance to move from one place to another. I'm tired of dragging these tads from pillar to post. And I'm tired of being just the thing the cat dragged in instead of really part of someplace." Her speech surprised her; she seemed sold on the idea.

Wes, too, forgot which side he was on. "Jennie, there's not any town or anything there to belong to. The place isn't settled at all. In Arizona and California and here in Snohomish County there's always a bunch of people around pretty close. This Pend d'Oreille place isn't even surveyed yet."

With the mouth of a jelly glass Jennie cut out another batch of biscuits and damped the stove. In her excitement she'd let it overheat. She held the oven door open a moment to cool it down, and put the biscuits in.

Uriah went on. "I did hit a little strike, Wes, and I'd like to parlay it into something before it dribbles away. What would this land be worth in a few years?"

"Who knows what anything'll be worth in a few years?"

"What do people do there?"

"Knute says there's a couple of prospectors, like lots of places. There's a guy with a little mill, but it's just for his own use mostly. You'd have to support yourself with the land. But that part he says looks likely. He was there through the seasons, and he says there'd be time to grow a good garden. Most of it's timbered, but you'd have a hard time selling logs to anybody, cause there's nobody there."

Jennie brought the biscuits and a fresh crock of preserves, wild strawberry this time, for the boys, now getting up. Tommie and Billie stepped out the back door to pee, and Jasper crawled to his mother's lap for breakfast. "Dammit, Boys," Jennie yelled, "I've told you to put your shoes on first and go to the outhouse. You'll kill everything I've planted around that door. You want pee burn on your chives?"

Uriah was dogged. "Let's go for it, Wes. We'll use my strike to get all of us over there, and you can pay me back when you're able."

"And if I don't get able?"

"Then I'll get some of your land, and I'll be rich before you." He sang the last words.

"Fat chance. Jennie'll think of a way to earn some money if she has to doctor mules for both those prospectors. I'll be a prosperous farmer while you're still sorting out your plow parts, Little Brother."

"Well, let's go over in the fall and take a look at it."

Jennie didn't look up from the diaper she was tucking in place on Jasper's chubby bottom. "You're out of work now, ain't you?"

Neither man got her meaning, so she clarified: "You'll go over right now, or I'll go myself."

JENNIE COULDN'T REALLY START PACKING, because Wes might come back and say they weren't going. She put in a garden as always, hoping she could reap before they left. When he came back in late May and said they were going, she sold the cow at once, to assure herself they really were going. Wes and Uriah had had time to put up the bare bones of two cabins and to stake out neighboring claims of 160 acres each, near but not on the river as their wives had directed, thinking of small children who could tumble down riverbanks before they could be grabbed. Most of it was timbered, but they'd selected as much meadow as they could and thought they had enough bunch grass for a cow and a team for each family.

"If we had a cow. And if we had a team," she said.

Work opened up at the Index mine, and Wes took advantage of the summer of wages. By August he could tell Uriah he wouldn't need a loan. Through the summer Jennie preserved in turn rhubarb, wild strawberries, cherries, apricots, wild blackberries, peaches, early apples, plums, pears, and fall apples, most of which she walked the ten miles down to Marysville to pick, hitching a ride back up with the shingle wagons. Crocked and crated, these would go to Pend d'Oreille with them. A crate of chickens, and slips and roots for the new garden would travel too.

In the second week of September, when the rains were starting up again, Wes hired a team and wagon and they loaded the family and goods. Tommie had nailed together a wooden cage for the dog Si, who would go along. Si knew their ways and they knew his. The striped cat, though, cared little for folks, and stayed behind where he knew the ways of the moles and the mice.

At Marysville they took the train to Everett, a one-street town where Uriah and his family would detrain from Seattle and they would all transfer to the train for Spokane. Wes and Uriah helped the station crew load their household goods into the freight car; Jennie and Ada settled the seven children into the passenger car. They left Ada's 14-year-old Alice and 12-year-old Ruby Belle in charge of Jasper as well as Ada's little girls, Mary, 7, and Ethel, 2, while they took Tommie and Billie back to the freight car to show them Si's lodging, and how to keep him and the chickens in feed and water. As the train jerked into motion, the two Wooding families occupied the center of the car. Teen-aged sophisticates from the Yesler neighborhood of Seattle, Alice and Ruby Belle had ridden in public conveyances before and were contemptuous of Tommie and Billie's frenzy, and embarrassed that Mary joined in. The three little ones bounced on their knees at the window and competed to spot sensations like white cows, flooded fields, wind-downed trees, and children limited to bicycles and shank's mare. When Jennie distributed fried chicken and corn muffins, they ate less than they dropped on floor, seat and clothes. They raced to the freight car to check the animals every 15 minutes. But eventually all were settled in for the night under coats and throws.

In the morning, in Spokane, they moved children, luggage, animals and rootstocks to yet another train and rode to Newport, a tiny village on the Pend d'Oreille River. Here Jennie did something momentous. She bought an iron cook range that would heat the house and cook their meals. Packing up and moving she'd done many times. But buying a range was what marked this move as a move into a new life. Now she would be a property owner, and this range was the first piece of that property. Once it was in the new house, it would not go from pillar to post, it would not be thrown in the back of a wagon that was going to yet another temporary space. It would be the hearth and the heart of the J.W. Wooding family, Permanent Residents.

The steamboat was scheduled to leave the dock at 8:00 a.m., but inquiry determined this was more accurately the hour at which the captain and crew would leave their beds, if they were feeling well so early. Still ahead would be the loading of mail, freight, provisions, and passengers. Both the Woodings' boat, the *VOLUNTEER*, and another, the *RED CLOUD*, had prominent newspaper advertisements declaring each *the fastest boat on the Pend d'Oreille*. Apparently this distinction, whoever owned it, was based on performance during a staged race when crew tossed coal, wood, and an occasional slab of bacon into the boiler; and gin, whisky and beer into themselves. On more mundane occasions like the transportation of passengers and freight, pace was a lower priority.

The *VOLUNTEER* proved to be neither the most beautiful nor the best engineered nor the safest nor the most luxurious boat on the river. She was 135 feet long and 15 feet high, plus an inconsequential little box serving as pilot house atop the second deck, and a single stack hardly taller than Wes. She had two enclosed decks. An outdoor deck surrounded the upper, passenger deck, where a spindle rail was the single attempt at adornment. Scraps of rusty tin spotted the roof of the second deck. Eventually the *VOLUNTEER* was fueled, the little stern wheel was revolving, and at somewhere near eleven o'clock the cracker box moved into the current of the Pend d'Oreille, headed downstream and north.

"Looks like this river runs the wrong way," she said, to try to jolly Ada a bit. Ada's response was the briefest semblance of a stiff smile.

The lulling motor and the lapping water meeting the lower deck soothed the children, and Jennie was able to give her attention to the river. The *VOLUNTEER* went around a bend, and clamorous little Newport was behind them. The shore's clutter of rafts, broken-up rowboats and general debris disappeared, caught at the river's first sharp bend.

With Jasper like a flour sack over her left shoulder, Jennie stepped onto the outside deck. It was neither cooler nor warmer than inside, and she could pretend she needed the isolation to keep Jasper asleep. A rocky narrow beach was backed by brush in vivid yellows and reds. Up a bank that was sometimes one foot and sometimes fifty feet high were cedars, firs, pines and tamaracks interspersed with golden birches, gigantic cottonwoods, quivering aspens, and flaming vine maples. Even with a cold gray sky the colors were stunning. What the locals called rain was falling; but to Jennie, coming off four years in the high Cascades, it was hardly a haze. Waves on the river were about four inches high, and in certain gusts were topped with a rippling skim. There were the mouths of sloughs occasionally, offering a glimpse of stiller water and quieter shores. In some places cedars with their trunks patched with chartreuse moss leaned over the water. A black beard moss hung from the branches of the tamaracks. On both sides of the blue-green river, the forest was everywhere and everything. Wes's "Hanging Ear" River changed from images of grizzly mutilations to a new vision of the big cottonwood leaves. "Look, Jasper," she whispered. "Elf ears." Creeks entered every little distance, each promising yet another world of shelter, solitude and wildness. She knew Wes had placed them on a creek; she hoped it had the promise of these.

With a thrill, Jennie saw a homestead appear as they rounded a luxurious bend of the great river, the smoke from its chimney speaking as nothing else could of the nest she sought. Fences of poles with their bark still on demarcated the garden from the corral from the pens. Not a stockade to keep out Apaches and marauders, as in Arizona; not a declaration of "stay the hell off of my property," as on Puget Sound; but a charming statement that "this is where I live and love." After a while the shores opened onto meadows that went back to the hills a few miles distant on the west side. There was the natural hay Knute Slettedahl had promised, and settlers were already making good use of it. Cattle and horses stood belly-deep where it was left to pasture; high stacks of winter hay already scythed lay in gigantic log barns. Homestead cabins were tucked snug against the hills, leaving the bottom land for the cattle, who wouldn't mind an occasional flood so much. All of a sudden the rain picked up and hammered on the roof. Jasper woke. She nursed him, and he stayed awake. Jennie went back inside with the others, but by this time she was in love.

Ada was getting out the lunch for both families, with an air of being imposed on by Jennie's self-indulgent reverie. Ada hadn't traveled well; the fun they'd shared at Monte Cristo was long ago. No doubt when she was into her own home she would become herself again.

THE TRIP HAD BEEN DESCRIBED as 50 miles long. In a straight line, it might be. But in actuality it was many more as the boat crisscrossed the river, dropping off an occasional passenger or piece of freight here and picking up one there. At a signal from the shore, the steamer would stop anywhere - anywhere a dog showed up at the bank, Jennie estimated. The official job of the *VOLUNTEER* was the delivery of mail. At some of the ports of call there were actual docks, usable at least in this season of moderately low water. More often Captain Cusick pulled the boat close to the shore, stirring the blue-green water to yellowish-gray, and the crew threw out a gangplank. At a few stops, the mail was merely wrapped in a packet, sometimes with a weight attached, and tossed to the addressee on the shore.

Another series of stops was less clear. The boat would go near the shore, a certain crewman would jump out, investigate something under the water, then climb back aboard. He brought with him the smell of water life like that of a tide flat. On about the fifth such stop, Jennie saw him draw something from the water and put it in a gunny sack tied to his belt loop. She recognized a man tending a trapline. "What do you take here?" He showed her a drowned muskrat, its fur shining and lush. "Sometimes beaver, sometimes otter." Jennie's mental account ledger gained a column on the side of supplemental income, the only overhead muddy sleeves and shoes.

Two other crewmen, stationed one port and one starboard, leaned far over the rail of the lower deck, close to the water, and watched for a drowned reveler who had fallen from the upper deck of the steamer *IONE* during last Sunday's excursion. It was the *VOLUNTEER* herself whose vernacular christening was *OLD BOOZE,* for the saloon on the upper deck, but she was innocent of at least this one mishap.

The boat now approached the other major settlement on the river: the village of Usk. George Jones, the owner of the competing *RED CLOUD*, had built a store and a creamery; Henry Keller had built a cheese factory, and Hamp Winchester a sawmill. The store housed an actual United States Post Office, and the packet here delivered would be distributed to settlers in this whole homesteading paradise. The town took up little room on the riverbank, most families living afield. But visible from the *VOLUNTEER* was an honest-to-goodness school, one of Jennie's sure standards for civilization. She had seen little of one in her own childhood, and her children were only now approaching the age for letters. This one showed what could happen in the wilderness, even Downriver. She touched Wes's arm and with her eyes led his look to the one-room log building with the generous windows that let the children see the world around them. They smiled mutually. A post office and a school would be all they needed of civilization, and the village of Usk proved it could happen even here.

Even this magnificent valley was narrow enough to shorten the day some, and in late September four o'clock signaled an overnight stop. Captain Cusick's farm was only another mile and a half downstream, at the mouth of Calispell Creek. There he would house some of the party, the fee for lodging included in their fares. But even his generous house, rebuilt after a fire a year ago and intended as a sometime hotel, could not handle the whole Wooding clan. Tommie and Billie were ecstatic at being assigned to sleep on the boat with Uriah, Wes, two crew members, and the other two male passengers. A quick supper from the baskets of traveling supplies was passed around, and Jennie with Jasper and Ada with her four girls went with Captain Cusick to his two-story log house. There they were met by the lively Ella, proud in her Mother Hubbard, the birth about two weeks away. Four-year-old Coral Jane, no more shy than her parents, pointed to her mother's belly and beamed. "That's our new baby." Her parents laughed delightedly. Jennie liked these river people. She had traded midwifery for goods for some years now, and found that not enough people indulged themselves in the joy of a birth. In fact, at that moment she saw Ada ushering her girls to their room, where they could all be scandalized in private. The Cusicks noticed, and exchanged another round of mirth.

Captain Cusick went to the barn to check on his cows and dairy hands. Jennie and Ella put their little ones to bed and went to the kitchen. Jennie helped Ella start some cinnamon rolls for breakfast for them all. "Mrs. Cusick, how long have you lived here?"

"Long enough to like it. And long enough to be called Ella. Do you mind being alone, Jennie?"

"I like to be alone, but I like better to be with Wes and the boys. I don't mind extra people, but I don't need them either."

"Then you'll be all right. There's more than enough to do, and something new and different all the time. I like being away from fuss and gentility. Here there's not upper crust and lower crust - just a lot of crust." She laughed at her joke. "Tell me where you come from, Jennie."

"A lot of places. I've gypsied all my life, all over the Arizona Territory, Utah, Nevada, California, some in New Mexico and Old Mexico, Washington lately. I don't mind any kind of work, and I learn pretty fast. I always got along all right, sometimes better than others, that's for sure. But what I'm looking for right now is a place to settle. I think it's time for it. I think for my boys to grow up in one place would be good. I ain't ever been really part of a place, and I'd like for them to have that feeling. I feel like I'm always looking at things through a camera, sort of, instead of being part of the picture. I guess I wouldn't change that, but I think the other would be nice too."

"Then you'll be fine here. Downriver where you're going, there aren't many women, and of course those half a dozen are spread out a lot. Some people think that's not a place a woman would want to go, but it can be fresh air, too. No Ladies' Auxiliaries or church societies, or whatnot. I think you're like me, and it'll be freedom for you."

"It's true that women can pen and peck each other pretty bad. I can ignore a lot of that nonsense, though. I guess you make your own freedom wherever you are."

The bread finished its first rising, and they shaped the rolls for the second rising. In spite of what she'd said to Ella, Jennie realized how much she did enjoy the company of a compatible woman. She had thought Ada would be that, but there was a chill growing between them. She didn't know how often she'd be able to get upriver this far, but she hoped a friendship between her and Ella Cusick would have a chance to flourish.

"Ella, when the baby comes, I wish I could get up here to help. I've delivered a good many babies, and I'd like to do yours. How often does Captain Cusick go down and up?"

"Every week. For Clarence and Coral Jane, I had Lucy Seymour from the Kalispel village. It's just across the river, and Lucy does a good job. But if Joe can make it work, it would be good to have a friend here to greet the new babe. I'll try to make that happen, Jennie."

In the morning the rain and clouds had gone, and though the sun was not yet over the mountains across the river, it lighted a blue sky striped with pinks. The world was getting bigger and bigger for Jennie. But fog was on the river to the height of Tommie, and his world was limited. He saw only gray haze, with the still, still water a deeper gray. They two had walked to the Cusicks' dock with the children's bedrolls, the kind of chore that had to be done but whose real reason was a chance to be out of doors while the morning was perfect.

A rowboat holding two dairy hands nosed suddenly and silently through the fog to the dock, down from the men's own homesteads above Usk. Tommie was riveted. One of the men tossed him the rope, judging him grown enough to secure a boat. Tommie looked at his mother, saw no interference, and looped the hemp through the hasp on the edge of the wooden dock. The man at the front of the boat eyed the inept knot, stepped onto the dock and redid it, reducing the sting of reprimand with a wink. Tommie watched, and would do it right next time. With a "Thanks, Sonny," the men headed for the barn.

"Ma, will we have a boat?"

"I reckon we'll need one." Tommie smiled at the rowboat, appreciating now what this much-touted homesteading could mean.

Cordwood was loaded into the boiler room, and Ella and her brood came along the path from the house with Ada and the other children. Ada carried crying Jasper, her shoulders implying that if she didn't remember him he'd probably be left behind. Jennie took him, with a commiserating smile at Ella.

As the *VOLUNTEER* nosed out to the channel, Jennie and her boys stood at the port rail and waved as long as they could see Ella and her three. Then they strolled unknowingly to the starboard side and were astonished to see yet another life. Two wood-frame structures and twelve tipis, some of canvas, some of reed mats, were scattered about. Women and a few men were arranging canvas over poles to make more. Children were carrying needed items to their parents. Jennie had had much experience with Indians. But these beautiful people were different from what she'd known. The women wore print blouses with close sleeves, and overblouses of yet another print, and loose raglan sleeves. Their skirts were a third print or stripe, and some wore long scarves loose in the front. But somehow nothing was inharmonious, and the garb was far more interesting than her own and Ada's dark, one-toned outfits. All the garments were as clean as Jennie's own - in fact cleaner, after travel on three coal-burning trains. Every woman had one or more pendants. Their hair was without exception done in long braids worn to the front over their chests; big, round shell ornaments hung from their ears. Little girls wore the same. The men's hair was loose, a more devil-may-care style. Some wore the commodious felt hats common to other Indians, one had a wide-brimmed straw hat, some were bareheaded. They had the sweetness and tenderness of the Owens Valley Paiutes Jennie'd grown up with, but not the defeated and unhealthy air of poverty. There was nothing of the angry and defiant look of the Apaches she'd known - and mostly avoided - in the Arizona Territory. The life of the Snohomish was so much like the settlers' that she'd hardly thought of them as another culture. These Kalispels were still living the community life that had taken centuries to build. Seeing her interest, Captain Cusick explained that they were starting a little early to set up their winter village. "They probably know something we don't about the winter coming up. Might be early snow." One tipi was so near the grassy river's edge that a person could almost step from bedroll to canoe. Sprawled in front of the tipi was a man about 25 with two little girls. His loose hair framed sharp cheekbones and a contented smile as he and the little girls watched the steamboat go by. A boy of 15 startled, then stepped into a blunt-nosed canoe and paddled it into the river. Dressed in only a breechcloth, he raised a three-pronged spear and thrust it toward the fish he saw. With a string tied to the canoe and to the spear, he pulled in a two-pound cutthroat. With a broad grin he held the trout over his head, stepped to the shore and pulled his canoe onto the grass. His brown torso rippled with his movement; Ada ushered her girls back to portside. Jennie and Wes applauded, and the boy again grinned and raised the trout, showing it off in their direction. "Their name means 'River People,'" said Captain Cusick. "They're related to the Pend d'Oreilles some way, but it's the Kalispels who live here. Between the fish in the water and the deer and caribou in the hills, life is good here for them. So they're pretty easy to get along with. Even as far downriver as you live, you'll get to buy huckleberries and fish and venison from them if you want. They can paddle down faster than this boat can go, and about as fast coming back up. These summer pine bark canoes are a wonder for speed. They'll change to dugouts when the ice comes."

Tommie and Billie noticed that most people were wearing no shoes. "They go in and out of the water so much they don't usually wear any. White people drown in the river all the time, but not the Kalispels. Whites' clothes are for land, and the water pulls them down real fast. Either keep your kids away from the river, Ma'am, or dress them for it." The boys stashed away that warning to use in later discussions of footwear.

As the Kalispel village disappeared behind them, Wes and Jennie moved to portside to join Ada. Captain Cusick was explaining the function of the milk separating station he had set up for the valley farmers to bring their milk to before shipping it out on the upriver steamer. Uriah appreciated the Captain's rampant entrepreneurism, and saw himself making his own fortune in the land of opportunity. Wes, like Jennie, was absorbed in the beauty of the journey.

The river became narrower and the banks steeper, the trees closer. The big Calispell Valley was gone; only occasional small meadows appeared, and just three man-made clearings with cabins in the whole day's travel. Mostly the shores were tree-lined, with more cedar and less pine. Signals and stops became rarer; homesteading had not yet affected this area as it had the upper river. They knew they were lucky to find any good land available in the new century, and the price of clearing their own fields was little enough. Wes, Jennie and Uriah smiled broadly. Ada looked more and more doubtful as the homesteads thinned.

As they came around into a huge bend that Captain Cusick identified as Devil's Elbow, he announced they should prepare to debark at Tiger's Landing. The *VOLUNTEER* blew three shorts and a long as it neared a clearing at the top of a 25-foot clay slope. The rain had stopped for the day, judging by the clearness of the sky to the west where the sun was angling above the hills to introduce an evening of moisture-shot sun's rays. A man came out of the log house that was there and waved a blue handkerchief in greeting. Captain Cusick added a full eleven toots, counting out the Wooding party arriving to triple the population. George Tiger was joined by Joseph Parker in a long gray beard. John Renshaw and his grown stepdaughter Nettie Phelps played a fiddle and mandolin rendition of "Foggy, Foggy Dew." Mrs. Renshaw, Orla, waved a white dishcloth, snapped a tambourine, and swayed in a near dance.

"They must think it's the Governor," observed Wes.

With both boat crew and riverbank hands helping, the household goods for both families, including two stoves, were at the top of the bank in not much more than an hour, and Captain Cusick took the *VOLUNTEER* on downriver to the village of Ione. Si for the first time in nearly four days was let loose to run, ecstatic in a world of new scents. George Tiger, reddening in the company of two ladies, gave a little address. "Mrs. Woodings both," he said, "I know your two houses are unfinished. I hope you'll accept my hospitality and put your families up in my cabin while you finish them. I'll go in with Joe Parker a while. One or the other of us is more often than not away anyway, and we can probably get along for a month or so." Joe Parker brought round a wagon and offered to take all those interested for a look at their new homes. Jennie, Ada and Alice went on the first trip. They came back in deep appreciation of George Tiger's offer. The traveling luggage was moved into his house, and the household goods into his little barn. The younger children had stayed, throwing rocks and sticks into the river. Si and George Tiger's dog Menlo swam out to retrieve. Ruby Belle watched from the top of the riverbank, the two toddlers in close check. Joe Parker was surprised at how charmed he was by the children. A bachelor nearly 50, Joe hadn't yet known he missed a family, but the sudden appearance of seven youngsters at Tiger's Landing, where there had been none, was intriguing. "I guess we'll need a school," he told Jennie and Ada. "I guess I've got room on my place, when it's time to build."

By now Orla and Nettie had laid sawhorses and planks with a reception supper for 16, 11 of them named Wooding. As the last of the potato salad, baked beans, and cold fool's hen was cleared away and molasses cookies laid out, the rain lightened and the music resumed, the musicians sheltering under George Tiger's entrance overhang. With the shower light enough to ignore, dancing broke out to "Ruby McClain." George Tiger and Joe Parker gallantly partnered with Alice and Ruby Belle. Orla Renshaw let Tommie tap the tambourine, and the clay of Tiger's Landing knew its first party. When the Renshaws prepared to drive away, Orla hugged each child and turned to her husband. "John, we'll have to see about a spot for a school if this is what people bring with them."

The Woodings were truly and fairly welcomed.

With the seven children settled and sleeping, and Wes, Uriah and Ada well on their way, Jennie stepped outside the jammed cabin for a moment to herself. She saw Si zag by with his nose to the ground, trying to realize the million plants, creatures and artifacts in this new world. Just now she herself was learning that the moon sent a pregnant glow over those mountains to the east before it rose over them. When it broke over the fir-serrated crest and back-lighted the streamers of cloud, it burnished the big river and she saw it was the most beautiful she'd ever seen, from the Gila to the Skagit. She was getting to know five new people who would be her intimate neighbors for at least six years. She'd never before stayed anywhere six years, rarely six months. Jennie the Gypsy she called herself. She'd told Ella Cusick, and she'd told Wes and she'd told herself that she was now ready for a change, ready for a settled home. She was tired of living in wagons and tents and rented shacks, she'd said. She was ready to build a true home for her boys.

But now that it was happening, she wasn't so sure. How could she be certain of something so unknown? Six years here in one spot at the end of the world suddenly was daunting. Did she really want a home that badly? Was that little unfinished cabin actually a home anyway? Damn it, Jennie, you're always afraid of something you want when it looks like you're going to get it. She was still standing there when the *VOLUNTEER* came by and ran with a soft thrum through the moon's spotlight. Captain Joe Cusick, for two days one of the most important people in their family life, sent a soft double toot to the people he'd brought to the end of the world, and headed back upriver to settlement.

In the morning Jennie and Wes, with Tommie and Billie pulling Jasper in their little wagon, walked the half mile to the shell of the house and took inventory. They decided which things they'd need right away - a floor, windows and doors, and chinking - and which things could wait - a porch, a second story, a summer kitchen, and furniture. The essentials would get them out of George Tiger's house, for his sake and their own, and it was getting harder to ignore Ada's air of martyrdom.

"We can't afford everything we need, Wes. There's still winter supplies to get in."

"We can afford the chinking. Renshaw says river clay is fine for that. I think the kids can do a lot of the hauling. We ought to be able to use our own timber for the floor. It's only 14' by 24'. There's just the cost of nails. I think we have enough cash left for that, and windows and doors."

"I know Uriah's going to Newport. I heard Ada complaining that he was going off and leaving her here. Let's ask him to get our stuff along with his."

"Jennie, what's going wrong between us and them?"

"From the time this trip started, she's been funny. Wes, he wouldn't bring her here if she didn't want to come, would he?"

"He might. Him and his everlasting investments. Free land. And I don't think Ada had any idea how unsettled this place was going to be. It's mighty different from Seattle."

Jennie remembered the old Ada laughing and bellowing out "The Irish Washerwoman" in mockery of the two of them when they were all under one roof and running the laundry at Monte Cristo. *When I was at home I was merry and frisky/ My dad kept a pig and my mother sold whiskey.* There was no sign of that jolly Ada now.

THE NEXT SUNDAY JOE CUSICK and the *VOLUNTEER* brought the two doors and three windows for the house, and a copy of the *NEWPORT MINER*. The page of local news for September 29, 1900, reported: *Two families, consisting of eleven people, went down the river last Saturday, where they have taken up homesteads. Their names were Wooding but we were unable to learn where they came from.*

In the week of interim, Jennie organized the children to move heavy, wet clay in the children's wagon from the river bank to both the cabins, where the two women and Alice chinked inside and out with wide channels of light gray that striped the houses horizontally. The children, even the toddlers, found the material good for sculpting, and the yard was slobbered with slopped-out mud shaped into everything from chicken eggs to a miniature *VOLUNTEER,* according to the sculptor's age.

At the same time, Wes and Jennie downed seven tamaracks from the intended garden spot, split them, smoothed them, and cut them to 14' lengths to run the width of the house. When a wagonload of clay arrived, Jennie would chink and daub. While she waited for the wagon to plod back to the river and take a load to Ada's house, she'd apply the adze to the half-logs Wes split. Both floor and chinking were ready by mid-October.

Wes's eyes were at least as good as they had been on the Coast, the air on the Pend d'Oreille being somewhere between the aridity of Arizona and the miasma of the Cascades. His carpentry skills weren't as developed as Jennie's, but together they managed. The most challenging job was hanging the doors and windows. Where Wes's measurements were imprecise, or where Standard Lumber Company in Newport was casual, adjustments were made with the plane or shim or, for one sensational mismeasurement, the saw. By November they could move in. Jennie gave George Tiger's house a grateful scrubbing, hoping she'd left it as clean as that meticulous gentleman had left it for her.

Joe Cusick explained that it was best to get the winter's supplies in by November, before the river's freezeup kept the boats off the river. Their order went out on the October 14th boat. The supplies came back from the little Usk store on the next boat, October 21st. The cabin was crowded with two barrels of flour, 100 pounds of potatoes, two backs of bacon, a sack each of salt, baking soda and baking powder, a round of cheese, a small bag of raisins and a pound of green coffee beans for Christmas, a 50-pound sack of sugar, 3 jugs of molasses, 50 pounds of cornmeal, 7 10-pound cloth sacks of oatmeal, 50 pounds each of red beans, white beans and brown beans, 3 gallon jugs of apple cider vinegar, a barrel of pickled pork, and - on Joe Cusick's own volition - a barrel of brined salmon bellies from the Coast. By return boat, Jennie sent with the mail to Chicago an order for two pairs of Arctics for Tommie and Billie; they wouldn't be able to wear last year's boots when the snow came.

The house was ready, the supplies were in. All that was left was the winter's wood and a woodshed to house it, an easy job for the two of them in the remaining time. Nights were cool now, but by moving Jasper into their bed, and bedding the other two boys together, everyone slept warm.

Jennie thought to ask Joe Cusick about Ella's confinement, to see if he'd considered transporting Jennie to help, as both the women would like. Good idea, he'd said, and when he left them on October 28th plans were made for him to come for her when the labor started, and return her when all was well.

The days of October were yellow and blue. The aspens turned brighter gold, then the tamaracks did the same. The wild hay was tawny. Ferns and grasses were every tone from pale straw to rich amber. The spurt of rain at the end of September never returned. The warm part of the day was short, but they were heated by the work they were doing: Wes and Jennie felling and bucking tamaracks, pines, and cedars; Tommie and Billie carrying the split wood and stacking it in the new woodshed, arranged by variety and size. Jasper had his own work, building stockades of wood sticks as high as he could, then destroying them and starting over. At the end of the day while Jennie fixed supper Wes would move the wood, which the boys could stack only four feet high, into tiers as high as Jennie would be able to reach in the winter. Nearly every night after supper they all went outside in the nipping cold to marvel at the sparkle of stars in the deep, deep sky. Jennie kept her midwife's bag at the ready, and looked every day for the special run of the *VOLUNTEER* that would take her to Ella Cusick.

On the regular Sunday run of November 5th the boat whistle coming into Devil's Elbow had a shriller sound. It turned out to be not the *VOLUNTEER* but the *RED CLOUD*, captained by George Jones of Usk. He stunned them with the news that almost a week ago Ella's baby had come. With labor progressing fast, Joe went to take the three children to his brother's house for the duration. Soon after he left, Ella's water broke and was immediately followed by a hemorrhage she couldn't control. By the time a hand came in from the barn and could go across the river for Lucy, the porch where Ella lay down, thinking to keep her house clean, was covered with blood. When Lucy came she found the afterbirth and a massive amount of blood surrounding Ella, but the baby only half emerged. Mother and child were both dead and Joe's life ravaged.

THE FIRST TIME JENNIE HELPED deliver a baby she was living inside Fort Thomas in the Arizona Territory with the Mormons, for fear of the Apaches. She hadn't yet had a baby herself, was just 15 and wouldn't be married for another year. Maybe with those Mormon women having a baby every year, and a man sometimes fathering three or four in a year, she hadn't learned enough reverence for birth. Always more where that came from, seemed the idea. By now she had delivered about two dozen babies and never lost one. She had perhaps come to take the process for granted. Probably Joe and Ella had. She understood why Sally the Paiute was so prayerful when she did the midwifery back in the Owens Valley; it wasn't an event to take lightly. Sobered, Jennie looked at Jasper in a new way.

Then, thinking of Ella's blood flow, she realized for the second time that day that her own monthly should have happened before today. Was she going to have a fourth young one? Maybe with the move and the new life she'd forgotten to be careful. It was still early, if she wanted to end it. But the thought of maybe having a little girl kept her from it. If it happened, it happened.

ANOTHER CONCERN REMAINED, ONE WES and Jennie had even less control over. They had come to the Pend d'Oreille knowing they were squatters, but they hadn't known when they chose the land and built on it that every alternate section across the continent had been given to the Northern Pacific Railroad, the railroads having convinced the Congress that rails across the continent and up and down its valleys would "develop" the country, would "ease life for the settlers." When Abe Lincoln had signed the Homestead Act 40 years ago, wasn't the point to give as much land as possible to ordinary people, farmers, the way Thomas Jefferson wanted way back a hundred years? The railroad lawyers agreed that while, yes, giving this land to the railroads might slightly profit owners and stockholders, more importantly it would bring those "little people" West and make land accessible for them. Wes was sardonic: "Oh, of course. They're doing it for us." John Renshaw explained to all listeners, "Sure, the poor railroads need more land. Half the land along all the railroad lines in the country goes to a few dozen Fat Cats who can stay snug in their mansions in New York and Chicago, and the other half goes to all the rest of us willing to give up five years of our lives." Jennie's reaction was, "Let's just hope they don't get our piece for their damned lieu lands. I hope to hell that survey gets done soon.

THE BOYS DELIGHTED IN WATCHING the ice grow on the river, and had to be kept under close watch so they didn't try to hop across on the floes. On a Thursday, four days before a boat was expected, the *VOLUNTEER* blew its whistle as it entered Devil's Elbow; by the time it put in at Tiger's Landing, the Woodings were all there to greet it. Joe Cusick himself came up the bank to greet them. He moved slowly, his gaze vague. Wes sympathized with the unmistakable look of alcoholic comfort. It was better than no comfort at all. Wes took Joe's hand in his own two. Jennie hugged him.

"The river's closing down," Joe said. "This'll likely be the last trip till spring. Waiting till Sunday looked unlikely, so I brought folks what I thought they'd need to get through the winter. Those Arctics didn't come, Boys. Ask your Ma to make you some moccasins. The Kalispels get along with those all winter. Here's your mail. The rest we'll hold at Newport till spring. If somebody gets Upriver, the Postmaster'll let him have anybody's mail he asks for."

Jennie didn't want it to be just a business call. "Joe, we're so sorry. I know there's nothing nobody can do, but we would if we could. Where's the children?"

"With my folks or Ella's. I'll see 'em quite a bit, but the ways I make a living don't let me be home much. Ella ran the home and the farm. There's no good answer, those kids'll never have the life Ella was giving them. But they'll be safe and healthy with my folks. I'll see 'em pretty often. Besides, a man can't raise two girls. That's the best I can do. The best I can do."

The Renshaws arrived, got their mail, and the isolation of winter closed in as the boat moved on. The little group waved goodbye to the *VOLUNTEER* and let their seclusion sink in. The Woodings walked the half mile home, Wes carrying Jasper. It seemed strange to be frozen in with no snow on the ground. Jennie feared for the rhubarb, horseradish, apple trees, onions and garlic she'd brought with her and put in in September, a chancy enough prospect anyway. She covered the plants with fir boughs, hoping to keep out the vicious frost that was threatening to go inches into the ground without benefit of snow's insulation.

That night, though, the snow came. Wes went down after supper to the creek to break the ice and bring water for breakfast; he came back with flakes spotting his coat. When Jennie awoke in the morning, she knew there were some inches by the way Si's bark and the sounds of birds were muffled. The rooster's ER-er-ER-er-ERRRR was softened. He wasn't clamoring for them to attack the day as usual; he was telling of his contentment in the coop full of hens in the world full of snow. Jennie understood, and moved over against Wes. She smiled at the fun the boys would have, and closed her eyes in comfort at the thought of having nothing to do over the next months but let the new baby grow and keep everybody fed. Ambition would have to wait till spring.

Nesting wasn't for Wes, though. Within a week he knew he had to think now about money if they were to have any in the spring to go on with the building. He decided to try the mines for work. There were mines being worked just 15 miles downriver at Metaline, but everyone there was prospecting. Wes and Jennie had agreed that was a bachelor's business. Besides, the fifteen miles included a vicious box canyon with a hard portage; you didn't just raft a few miles down and pole back at night. It was too wild even for steamboats. He'd just as well go forty miles upriver in calmer water to the Bead Lake Gold and Copper Mine, which Joe Parker said was working; at least half the year there'd be steamboat transport. As soon as the ice at the edge of the river was solid enough, it was a good walkway where snow didn't build up. Off he went, carrying fool's hen sandwiches and thorn-apple pie, a rucksack, snowshoes, and a good bindle roll.

The first day he got as far upriver as Yocum, where he stayed the night with Lee Bilderback, met the Jeff Honsinger family, and spent the evening in cards. He saw the Socialist newspaper *APPEAL TO REASON* there, and knew these folks' hearts were in the right place. He promised to bring the current copies back downriver with him. The second day he pushed himself to get to Joe Cusick's farm, but Joe was gone to Newport, a hand said. Wes stayed in the barn. The third day was easier. A Kalispel paddled him across the river and Wes returned the favor with a nickel. He walked on up the river to Furport, where he was lucky enough to find a pack train headed up to the Bead Lake Mine, mules going up empty for ore. He covered the whole seven miles in the luxury of mule back. The foreman let him stay in the bunkhouse, gave him a hot breakfast, and waited until the second cup of coffee to tell him there was no work. There were no animals going back down yet, but at least the trail was well broken. At Furport luck held again and he found a well-packed trail clear to the ferry for Newport, where he was sure there would be word of work somewhere. Had the boats been running, the mail delivered, and the *MINER* read, Wes would have learned before now of hiring at the Bossberg Mine over the mountains to the Columbia, as far in the other direction from Tiger's Landing as he'd come in the wrong direction. But it was only a few days lost, not the whole winter, and Wes was encouraged. He sat on a stump to watch the sun set and the early stars come out while he ate his last sandwich, then went into Kelly's Bar for a beer.

There he found Joe Cusick, who seemed to have been there most of the time since Ella's death. Joe bought Wes a beer, and had another himself. When he heard of Wes's need to get quickly to Bossberg, Joe perked up and insisted they take a look at the Pend d'Oreille, to see if a dash downriver might be possible. They left the noisy bar and stepped into the cold night. The smoke and spilled beer of the dim room were behind them; the full moon had risen and they stepped into its wash, brighter than the inside of Kelly's Bar. They walked across the railroad tracks and past the bars and "resorts" to the river. Joe looked at the ice, deemed the river close to safe, and said they'd take a look in the morning, night being too dangerous for running anyway. Kelly let them both sleep on the floor.

While Joe slept late in the morning, Wes went to the Newport Mercantile to buy Arctics for the boys. The price alarmed him, and he settled for one pair, big enough for Tommie. He went to the post office and got mail for everyone within two miles of Tiger's Landing. Back at Kelly's, Joe was breaking his fast on beer and pickled eggs. He had about him the mock exhilaration such fare provides, and the two went to the river. Wes knew little of riverboat navigation, much less of the whimsy of winter ice on the Pend d'Oreille. He couldn't encourage or discourage the slightly sober Captain Cusick. Joe decided to try for it. Wes was eager to get home and not at all sorry to miss the 50-mile hike to get there. With Joe as Captain, two stranded homesteaders as crew, and Wes as fireman, they loaded the foredeck with enough wood for the whole trip, and the *VOLUNTEER* made a sprint downriver between floes. Joe's strategy was that the faster they went, the better they could outmaneuver collisions and the less time they'd spend in jeopardy. With no commercial or postal commitments, he meant to be at Tiger's Landing by dark. The boiler room was the warmest place Wes had been since leaving home four days ago, and an occasional shared nip with Joe completed the luxury. Concern about the sharp floes dimmed. The homesteaders were oiled enough to accept passing by their homes and spending the night at Tiger's Landing, and it was a jolly crew that entered the Devil's Elbow at four in the afternoon, with just light enough to dock and walk safely. The 'steaders would put up in George Tiger's empty cabin, but first Wes and Joe jollied on to ask Jennie to spread dinner for them all. As always, Jennie's joy at seeing Wes overrode her disappointment at no job and, in this case, only one pair of winter boots for two boys. She built up the fire and went to work.

Eager to get to Bossberg before the possible job was taken, Wes spent just the one night, saw Joe and the *VOLUNTEER* off, and said goodbye to Jennie and the boys. He'd be back in a few months with some money for spring development in his purse. John Renshaw allowed that, yes, he could sketch Wes a reasonable map for the trip. It would be about 30 miles for a crow, but he couldn't know for sure which trails between the Pend d'Oreille and the Columbia would be broken. He asked about Wes's snowshoes, advised him there would be many mines in the Gillette Mountains to check out, and wished him luck.

Two days after Wes left, an exceptional freeze put bigger floes on the river, and froze solid Renshaw Creek, where the household water came from. Jennie went the 20 yards each night to sweep off any snow, enlarge the hole, and take back two buckets of water. Possibly Tommie was big enough to do it, but to end each day with a few minutes under that night sky was something she didn't want to share with anyone.

Two days later the cabin's chinking, not yet fully dry, froze hard and began to fall out. A desperate trip to the riverbank showed the clay also frozen hard. Day by day they stuffed in and stuffed in again paper from the packing and rags from the cleaning. Tommie and Billie loved the task, especially the outside part, and giggled as they tried to keep Jasper from picking out either the old or the new chinking. That entertainment lasted all winter.

THANKSGIVING WEEK, GEORGE TIGER RODE his winter-shod horse to Newport on the river ice, bought two turkeys at the butcher shop, and brought them back to share with the neighborhood. Thanksgiving Day, George was early at the Renshaws,' doing his part in the preparations of the meal. When Jennie arrived with the boys, he casually handed her a letter from Wes that he'd brought back from Newport. Jennie took it and stuffed it quickly into her pocket. "You aren't going to read it, Jennie?" he asked.

"Not right now, George," and she moved abruptly across the room to take over mashing a pot of rutabagas from Nettie.

After the afternoon of festivities and after helping Orla and Nettie clear away the feast, she took the boys home. When they were soundly asleep and Jasper safely in his box, she waited till the fire was burned down to ashes, put on her coat, and went through the trampled path to George's cabin. The arrival of a woman alone at his cabin was a first-time event for the bachelor on the Downriver banks of the Pend d'Oreille. He blushed as he invited her in.

"Trouble, Jennie?"

"Not like you mean, George. But I have to ask you to keep this secret, what I'm going to ask you to do."

"Nothing easier than keeping my trap shut, Jennie."

Jennie sat on George's single chair and took a couple of deep breaths before she asked her favor.

"George, would you read this letter to me?"

"Jennie, I'd be glad to. Is that what you're fussed about? Shoot, lots of people didn't get to go to school. Why is it so particular with you?"

"I haven't felt it much before now, George. When Wes is away he always writes to me, and he knows I'll find somebody around to read it to me. I guess he didn't think about it being different this time."

"How's it different this time?"

"We're here to live for good now. And Tommie's getting old enough to notice things. I don't want the boys to ever know this. And if I keep it on the q.t. from them, I'll have to keep it from others. And the Renshaws - they're all college people. I'm sure as hell not going to let them know."

"Fair enough, Jennie. It'll never leave this room." And he read her letter to her.

"Dear Jennie and Boys,

The trail was broken up the mountain to Middleport, up above where you are. I spent the night there in a trapper's shed. I got to Aladdin the second night, both days' walks pretty easy, thanks to a broken trail and short days. Had to stop early, when it got dark. Slept again in a farmer's barn. This one wasn't much help in routing, though. He knew just the north-south market road of his own valley. The map I had from George and John was better.

From Threeforks, the trail was pretty clear with only a few trees across. Ran into soft snow there, and put on the snowshoes. Made me think of those evenings in October, you shaping the yew into frames and weaving those strings of elk tendon, and me reading you *David Copperfield*.

At the bottom of the range I had a few miles of compacted wagon road and I could walk without the snowshoes, faster going. I found an empty cabin with grub, stove and wood. I made tea from your kinnikinnick leaves; not bad. Left the overhang with more chopped wood than it had when I got there. The fourth day of walking I got to the Bossberg mining area, where I tried my luck at the Bonanza, then the Young American, then the Bossberg mines. Nobody was hiring, and they all wondered where the bad information had come from. God-damned *MINER*. I kept asking where they thought there might be something, but the only real help I got at Bossberg was to be rafted across the Columbia. One place after another, they sent me to the Napoleon Mine, then north to the Scotia, the Hidden Treasure and the Red Lion. Then west to the Kelly, and south to the Knob Hill and the Flag Hill at Republic. Enough of Wild Geese, Jennie! I'm here at Republic, and I'm taking work with a pack train going west as far as the Okanogan River. The one place I'm pretty sure of finding work is the Monte Cristo, back where I started from in the Cascades. I've come about 400 miles, and I guess I have about twice that to go. I'm resoling my boots here and I think I'll get there by New Year's Day, if luck like this pack train holds. Love to you and the boys. Hug them all for me. Wes."

BY DECEMBER THE SNOW ON the ground was a foot deep on the level and two feet beside the paths Jennie shoveled to the woodshed and the toilet. They hadn't got an outhouse dug in the fall, so she built a seatless chair that she placed weekly over a new spot; at the end of the week she moved the chair and brushed leaves or snow over the used spot. After using it in a couple of heavy snows, she built a framework for a tarp. She kept the wood chopped ahead in case of a heavy storm, and Tommie and Billie kept the porch and the woodbox filled. There was no preserving or gathering to do in the winter. She bought her milk from the Renshaws, the boys going over the trail to their house daily. Jennie was a lady of leisure.

On Christmas morning they were awakened by shots, the neighbors across the river sending holiday greeting. They took some pies and went to the Renshaws once again for a dinner in the afternoon, joined by George Tiger and Joe Parker. Nettie Phelps played a pump organ, her stepfather the violin and her mother the guitar while they all sang "Silent Night" and "O, Christmas Tree." It was a moonless night, so the guests left at dusk while they could still find their ways on the trails through the woods to their own homes.

1901

WES HAD BEEN away many times, and he was always in her mind, always something missing. This year, though, was better; her own life absorbed her and his absence was less an ache. With no adult sharing her life, she could nap when she wanted, start a job and leave it unfinished when she wanted, go to bed when she wanted, or wake up and stay in bed to drowse. Tommie and Billie could fix themselves a breakfast, and Jasper was still nursing, still sleeping with her. At dark, somewhere around five o'clock, she could put them all to bed and have some hours of sewing and reflection by the lantern before finding her own sleep. She had never been so rested in her life. With snow surrounding them, there was little she could do toward building the farm. She made a few pieces of furniture: a bed, a table for eating from, a table for preparing food, some shelves for the kitchen corner, and a couple of bedframes. She could do it at her own pace, in her own time.

At seven and five, Tommie and Billie were perfect playmates. The single pair of Arctics was never a reason for dispute. One boy would go outside and the other would watch through the window calling out instructions, "Make a big snowball, big as me." "Now put another one on top." "Come to the door, I'll bring you Ma's hat to put on it." When the inside boy needed very badly to put his hands on the project, the first boy would come inside and give the boots to his brother, and the brother would go outside to play in the snow. They thought keeping the paths open to the woodshed and the privy was part of the play. Most days they could keep the main trail open, and going to the Renshaws' for milk was an adventure, including as it did crawling across the log Jennie'd felled for a bridge. On days of heavy snowfall when Jennie had to break the trail herself or when she needed to go out to chop wood or shoot a grouse, one or both of them would cheerfully mind Jasper, entertaining him with forts built of firewood. They'd build the fort with Jasper in the center, and when it was as high as he could reach, they'd let him smash it down to rubble. If a deer was near the house they ran to hold him up to the window to see.

With the river firmly frozen over, the settlers on the other side were not so distant, and Jennie met Frank Schmaus, a German bachelor whose visits were as abrupt as his conversation. The first time she saw him he knocked sharply before anyone knew he was around. "Hello, Missus. I shot a deer, and I trade you a haunch if you make mincemeat out of de odder one for me, and put some of it in a couple of pies for me. I can make pies, but dey ain't so great."

"I could use a little bit of venison, but mincemeat takes apples. I've got some I dried over on the Coast before I came, but I mean for them to last the winter."

"Okay, I'f got some dat ain't dried, sitting in my cellar. Carl Harvey's got a tree down der below de Z Canyon, and I give him some tanned hide for 'em."

The deal was struck with the haunch reduced to half a haunch but with enough untanned back hide from a deer thrown in for moccasins for the boys. Frank Schmaus wouldn't come in for chamomile tea, but she did manage to exchange names and invite him to come back. "Sure, Missus. I got to bring de apples and de hide, don't I?" And he was gone.

The tanning took two weeks. Jennie cut the hair short and turned it inside; then the boys delighted in pulling and tugging and rolling and rubbing it to softness. Each night they'd roll it in damp cloth and start again the next day. When it finally would stay soft without more moisture, Jennie built a fire outside and they played Indian and watched through the window while it smoked on a pole frame. They were excited when Jennie took it down, more excited when she made patterns of their feet and cut the leather to fit. She made the moccasins to cover their calves, and now they could both play in the woodshed. One day as she opened the cabin door to call to them, she overheard them plotting a prank. To foil it, she went out the back door, waded waist deep in the snow to come up behind them where they were on the woodshed roof rolling a large snowball to drop on her when she came for wood. When she spoke from behind them, "Hello, Boys," they erupted in giggles and yelled "Foxy Grandpa, Foxy Grandpa!" As she laughed with them, Jennie was stabbed with loneliness for Wes, for the evenings when he read them Foxy Grandpa in the funny paper so that Foxy Grandpa was a real person, one who liked to play jokes on little boys, the kind who would sneak up behind them in the snow and top their joke. Wes brought everything to life.

Jennie's favorite game of the winter was keeping food on the table. She'd had no garden that first year, of course, and no root cellar yet, but meat was easy. At the hole she kept open in the creek's ice she could catch in 15 minutes enough cutthroats for a meal. The grouse she shot with the old 10-gauge were called fool hens for their habit of sitting still no matter how long it took to go for a gun, load it, aim, and fire. Si, dog-of-all-work, saw himself as a hunting dog; whenever he spotted one of the birds he set up a barking several tones shriller than his normal one. The abundance of game was tiring. Once when Jennie told the boys she didn't intend to wade out again in the snow that day to shoot a bird they didn't need, they protested, "Ma, Si won't keep barking at them if you don't go out and shoot them." The birds weren't even good for trade, because everybody else could shoot all they wanted too. Jennie didn't care to shoot deer, with no way to preserve it; even a wintering-over goose was too large for her little family to eat in a week. She did occasionally trade with a neighbor for a small chunk of venison, as she had with Frank Schmaus, or with an occasional Kalispel who would come down in a winter dugout. Ducks were on the river, but Jennie went there only a few times; controlling the boys at the water's edge was too chancy. Once during a warm melt at the end of winter Joe Parker shot a bear and shared it all around the neighborhood. The chickens never laid well after their journey, and quit altogether in the short days of October; she missed eggs. They'd bought potatoes and onions at the Usk store, and fortunately a barrel of sauerkraut. She'd thought that exorbitant, but that and some crocks of pickles from Pilchuk, and some carrots and turnips from the Renshaws were all she had for vegetables. When she came in September there were still thorn apples on the hawthorns. They had dried on the tree and Tommie and Billie could shake them onto a blanket and fill gunny sacks with them. They made a pie or a syrup for pancakes that were better than no pie or syrup. And she had her canned fruit from Pilchuk. So the boys were fed well enough, but she looked forward to the next season when there'd be more variety. That first winter was just enough challenge to be interesting, but not a thing she wanted to repeat.

In March the ice went out of the river, in fact on a particular day in March, in a particular hour. Jennie was amazed at the quickness of it. Around six in the evening, dinner over, she was rocking and knitting for the new baby when she heard loud cracks and booms. It took her a while to think of the possibilities: no one would be felling trees after dark; there was no mining in the neighborhood; it didn't sound just like guns. She went outside and listened; it was coming from the direction of the river, for sure. Then she remembered George Tiger saying that some years when the ice went out it made a good show. She guessed this was it. She checked the boys: sound asleep. She checked the fire: a bed of cinders, nothing to catch and flare up. So she put on wraps, lit the candle in her Palouser, and headed for the riverbank. As she neared it, the snapping grew louder. A quarter moon sent some light through thin clouds and she doused the lantern. White chunks of ice glowed in the black water. She could see other watchers here and there along the bank, but distant enough that she didn't have to share the moment with them. They seemed all to feel the same; there was no conversation, no hailing or calling. No one bothered to add feeble human voice to the din. For a month there'd been a pileup of huge floes of ice growing higher and wider below where Renshaw Creek entered the river. Now it was exploding as the chunks cracked off one by one, slammed into one another and dropped into the fast current below the clog. The pile was 15 feet high in spots, and chunks from the top splashed down with a thunderous boom. They sped downstream, faster and faster as they spun away from the dam, still ramming into one another and resonating to the top of the valley on both sides. Within a scant hour, the ice had cleared, floes from upriver were drifting by serenely, and the blowup was over.

THE RIVER'S GRAND UPROAR WAS echoed a few days later by a petty community skirmish. Orla Renshaw had not forgotten the suggestion she'd made at the Woodings' welcoming party, and she wasn't going to let things drift. She put a note on the wall of the Ione store advising of a meeting at George Tiger's house for the purpose of organizing a school district for the Downriver area. Since September Orla had been learning the state requirements of a school district, investigating how the Usk and Newport schools operated, and reading of schools in New York and Europe. She came to envision one where the children grew up to be knowledgeable, skilled, self-confident persons who could meet any kind of life and live it productively and happily. If they loved school they would love life, her books said. By April Orla was bursting with her plan for such a school at Tiger, had picked out a perfect site, already cleared, on a corner of the Renshaw homestead, and had written to her brother in New York City (the famous political cartoonist Homer C. Davenport, Orla couldn't help mentioning), to secure book donations for such a school.

When 26 adults, several like Jennie with children in tow, showed up at George Tiger's house for the meeting, Orla was in seventh heaven as a hostess. She greeted each person at the door, apologized for the lack of seating, or even elbowroom, and absolutely bustled as she arranged George's nightstand as a lectern.

Jennie was astonished to see so many people present. "It must be everybody from 10 miles up and 10 miles down." George opened the meeting and told the story of the seven young Woodings coming to Tiger's Landing and opening his eyes to what was needed. He admitted the winter had gone by with no action, and he was afraid those Wooding boys would grow wild if they didn't get inside a school pretty soon. Tommie and Billie shrank in their chairs with blushes and smiles when so many grownups turned their way and laughed. Jennie was touched to her heart. This was what she'd had in mind in coming to the Pend d'Oreille. During all the years of drifting - four days making photographs in some little Utah town, four months in an Arizona mining camp - she hadn't meant anything to anybody. Now here were all these people coming together to make a school for her children. True, more children would come soon, but George had just said hers and Ada's were the ones that started it all.

George, briefed by Orla, said the first "order of business" was to state where the boundaries of the school district would be. That brought quiet, as everyone realized their school, their community, they themselves, would be part of a bigger system. They would be meeting official expectations, would be governed by a State Superintendent of Schools, for Pete's sake. Jeff Honsinger rose. "What I want to say is the kids at Yocum need a school too. I guess they could get six miles down here when there ain't snow on the ground."

"The survey's getting done," offered Uriah. "Sections are an easy way to show where something is." They figured out where children lived. They amazed themselves with the immensity of what they created: a School District that ran from the Idaho border on the east, 30 miles west to the Tiger Divide, to the Canadian Border on the north, and to the blue slide on the south: 780 square miles!

"For us, Ma?" whispered Billie.

Orla's next "item of business" was the election of School Directors. When Joe Parker suggested "Jennie Wooding, who started it all," Jennie's palms began to sweat and her legs to weaken. If she took on that job, she'd have to sign things and read things. Wes wasn't here to cover for her. Jeff

Honsinger was seated next to her. "Jeff, I can't do it." Jeff had never seen her frightened, and knew it must be serious.

"Jen says no, but Wes'll do it."

Laughter erupted. "Sure, push him in when he ain't looking." "Jennie, what'll he say when he comes home and finds out you got him elected?" Someone imitated a train whistle.

Orla pointed out that Wes was seldom in the area. They mistook her point, and gave him the one-year term. Art Youngreen accepted the two-year term. Orla suggested a woman on the Board would be a good idea. They elected Christina Carpenter to the three-year term, and the Board of Directors was full.

Her lips a bit stiff, Orla reminded George that she had something to say, and an offer to make. "Sure, Orla." And he sat down.

Orla's glow returned as she described in rich detail the school site she had chosen. She described extra large windows, bright curtains, cucumbers and sunflowers growing in pots on the windowsills, music lessons given by herself and her family, maps and globes, and happy children learning twice as fast as their parents had, because they'd be so happy in their beautiful school. She described the spot she'd selected. "John and I are honored to offer that acre for the Renshaw School." She beamed on this final flourish.

It had taken Orla a whole winter to come to where she was, and she shouldn't have expected them to understand in one evening. The offer was not met with the cheers she expected.

She assumed everyone would be as delighted as she was with the vision of the children happy in their school, learning all the useful skills and having a good time doing it. She was met with silence. No one knew what to say to Orla, so they said nothing.

Uriah couldn't say in front of his sister-in-law that they didn't want the Socialist influence that might accompany the gift from the Renshaws. Pearl Mellott didn't say, yet, that they didn't need Orla's Eastern ideas. Renaldo Greenamyer didn't point out that there were no youngsters in the Renshaw household, so what did they know about schooling kids? Jeff Honsinger didn't remind her that his children were a long way in the other direction. Blessed silence continued a bit longer.

Hoping to end the embarrassment for the wife of his longtime friend, Joe Parker stepped forward with a counter offer. He had an acre, also cleared, "if you maybe want the school farther south for the youngsters from Yocum and up that way." He might as well have slapped Orla in the face.

Then they all began talking, hurling at their neighbors their own educational wisdom. They'd all been to a school themselves, at least for a while, and every soul was certain his own school, even if he'd hated it at the time, was a model for all time.

George, bearing the double pain of seeing the school plans in jeopardy, and his home the site of discord, used a small pan and a big spoon to gavel order. "We'll have to vote, I guess. We aren't going to agree this way."

The vote was 18 to 8 to accept Joe Parker's offer. Pearl Mellott sent the final shot: "We'll have our plain old country school open by fall, and these plain old country kids will learn plenty in it."

The first public meeting at Tiger's Landing broke up in anger. Jennie went to Orla.

"Orla, it's a good idea and I voted for it. The time I spent in school was so boring I was glad I couldn't go no more. I'd love to have something like your school for my boys. I guess sometimes the best idea ain't the most popular one. But, Orla, it's still the best idea." Orla let Jennie hug her, but couldn't speak. Nettie and John escorted Orla home, and Jennie took her boys home. In the morning she sent a gingerbread and the last of the quince preserves over to Orla when the boys went for the milk.

JENNIE'S FIRST SPRING TASK WAS to build a summer kitchen on the back of the house. When the new baby came, she'd be more comfortable. All the boiling and cleaning for the birth could be better done outside the main house. And later in the summer she could heat all the water for canning and preserving without making the house miserably hot and steamy. To get a head start, she hired a man coming through from Pinckney City meaning to meet the steamboat. He hadn't known of the once-a-week schedule, and had to kill four days waiting for his transport. Jennie gave him room and board and $1 cash for felling a cedar on the other side of the forty, and cutting it into shingle bolts. She and Si dragged them home over the summer. The tree was a quarter mile away, and that was the hardest work of the whole season. Putting up a pole frame and splitting the shingles was easy, and she could do it in spare moments. The summer kitchen was ready early, and she added a counter to make a year-round laundry space.

Going to the creek for morning water in a soft rain in late April, Jennie saw a pair of brilliant wood ducks paddling downstream. At noon there was a kingfisher working the creek. A flock of grosbeaks chattered to her evening chores. There was still snow in the creek bottom and among the trees, but no longer in the clearings. She went to the tools in the barn and laid out saws and clippers. The next day she and the boys attacked the hawthorn trees near the watering hole, wearing leather gloves against the thorns. She sawed the hard wood and the boys pulled the downed little trees to a pile for burning. Jasper sat or lay in the little wagon and hugged Si whenever the dog came near. In an afternoon they tamed a path to the water hole; the rest they would leave as a barrier to the creek until Jasper and the new baby were older.

The next day they began clearing the brush and slash that remained between stumps of trees they had downed last year when they built the cabin. This space would be her first garden. Beginning at once, she kept three stumps burning all the time. The smell of cedar, hawthorn, and cottonwood smoke became the smell of home. One evening going in to fix their dinner, she noticed that the chives and rhubarb she'd planted with little hope last fall were poking up. She began sending the wagon with the boys when they went to get the milk so they could fill it with manure from the Renshaws' barn. They loved the excuse to wade the creek with the wagon. In another week chickweed was volunteering in the dirt ball that clung to the horseradish she'd brought from Pilchuk. By late April there was enough to have a mess with their dinner every few days. Nettles and then dandelions followed, and they had greens on the table every night. The taste of spring, the taste of spring!

Evenings while she sewed, Tommie and Billie cut a third of the remaining potatoes into pieces for planting. When she could tell which patch of ground would drain well, Jennie spaded between the stumps. When she had the sod off and the soil stirred, the boys used whittled sticks to plant spuds, careful to turn the eyes up. As he turned two, Jasper found his first useful task, carrying little piles of seed potatoes in a can from his wagon to his brothers. Orla Renshaw gave Jennie some hops and she planted them to vine over the porch. Soon the garlic, onions and horseradish were up. Orla said it was safe now to plant the cabbage and Brussels sprouts seeds Jennie'd brought from her Pilchuk garden. She found morels and coral mushrooms in the woods and set the boys to gathering them and slicing them to dry on a screen she rigged above the stove. Food would be a lot more interesting this year.

With both harvesting and planting going on at once, and the birth just two months away, Jennie threw off her winter lethargy and was rarely in the house during daylight. One cloudless, warm day in May Tommie and Billie said they were both going for the milk. Ten minutes later she heard Billie wailing along the trail. As he came in sight he howled, "I hurt my toe-oe-oe-oe! I hurt my toe-oe-oe-oe!" Jennie could tell the wound was not life-threatening, and the rhythm of the wail struck her as funny. She couldn't go to him for laughing, and he ran to her continuing his complaint, "I hurt my toe, oh, oh, oh!" She gathered him up, laughing, when he reached her, and chorused the "oe-oe-oe's" with him. Soon he was laughing with her as they sat on a stump and inspected the assaulted digit, holding it out away from their clothes. A half inch, including nail, was missing from his left big toe. He confessed he hadn't gone with Tommie at all but had gone into the woodshed to cut some wood for whittling. They continued to rock on the stump with his toe in her mouth. The blood didn't stop, so she carried him to another stump where she had seen some of last year's puffballs. She exploded a few on the toe, letting the powder stanch the blood. She carried him into the house, pulled out her doctor's bag, and applied witch hazel, took some stitches, and wrapped the toe in cloths. For weeks, they could set each other off laughing with "I hurt my toe-oe-oe-oe" in Billie's funny little sing-song.

On the first boat in March, three more letters came from Wes, together with the now superfluous Arctics. The last-written said he'd be home in June; in May she began meeting the boats. Finally on June 17 he was there. She ran up the plank to greet him dressed in the same Mother Hubbard she'd worn for each of her six pregnancies.

Seven months was a long time for such little boys to remember their Pa, but Wes had developed a knack for speeding up reunions. He had them show him around the place and each stressed his own part in making the farm. "Pa, me and Ma built this chicken yard." "Pa, me and Tommie cut and planted all these spuds." Jasper rode on his father's shoulders, not exactly remembering the man who was carrying him, but liking him if the rest of them did.

Coming through Newport on the way home, Wes had taken time to subscribe to the *NEWPORT MINER* and *THE APPEAL TO REASON*. The latter had been available in all the mining camps he went through, and he was accustomed to reading it. The former he considered a businessmen's rag, but it carried the closest thing to local news there was, and might list work closer to home. The next boat brought both journals, and evening reading sessions resumed. Jennie and the boys all loved the sound of his voice whatever he read, were just as happy with *THE APPEAL* as with *OLIVER TWIST*. In the early years of their marriage, Wes had made the sessions into reading lessons for Jennie. He'd taken her beyond the third reader she'd finished in her last school in Flagstaff, but when Tommie got old enough to notice, she wouldn't allow the tutoring in front of him.

"Jennie, there are good reasons for it. It doesn't warrant shame."

"I know, and you know, but he don't have to know. He'd never look up to me after that. He thinks all grownups can read, and it's best that he does. When he goes to school he'll just take it for granted that he should learn everything the teacher says. If he knows I can't read, maybe he'll think that's passable."

"What school would that be, Jennie?"

"There'll be a school."

WHEN JOE PARKER WAS APPOINTED the first deputy law enforcer for all the Pend d'Oreille Valley north from Tiger to the Canadian border, the *MINER* editor enthused, *"Joe is all right. No better appointment could be made."* Jennie thought it was a good sign of coming civilization, though she agreed there seemed no need for a lawman just now. She well knew, though, from life with Arizona and California bandits, that being remote could be dangerous. And as more people moved in, as they would when the survey was completed, there were sure to be bad apples. Hy Maggott objected on the grounds that it was a step toward taxation. "Soon as there's salaries, you and me's got to ante up."

"Hy, you ain't paying taxes any more than the rest of us, 'cause you ain't Proved Up yet. And if and when you do, you'll be able to afford to pay, 'cause you'll be able to sell your timber and pay your fair share of things around here, with the rest of us."

****

JENNIE WAS WAKENED ON JULY 1 by a sensation of being squeezed low down, below where the baby rested. By the time she was fully awake the squeeze had stopped, and she lay in a suspension of time and place, wondering what had happened to her. Then her mind wandered to the rooster in the chicken coop and the snipe in the creek bottom, both predicting the dawn. She moved close to Wes to enjoy his warmth but not to wake him. The sun was up enough for the full contingent of summer birds to make their music when the clench came again, stronger this time. Of course. She snuggled closer to Wes, waking him now. "We'll have the new baby by tomorrow morning,

Wes." He took her in his arms, and they lay silent for another half hour, as a couple of pains came and went.

For the first four babies, Jennie had always been close enough to travel to her mother or one of her sisters for the birth. When Jasper came, in Pilchuk, she was too far away from them and she didn't want a stranger to help, nor did she want to pay one. Wes became the midwife, under her clear instructions; he'd declared it wasn't much harder than helping a cow or a mare, but a baby was a lot more gratifying than a calf or a foal. Nettie and Orla had only one birth between them, and it had been attended by a doctor in New York City. Ada she didn't trust to follow instructions and keep her head. Wes knew he was It again, in fact had come home from the Monte Cristo in time for the birth.

For some days, Jennie had been scrubbing her clean house and putting clean bedding ahead. She prepared a box of necessaries: a rubber sheet, some herbs for pain, string and scissors, lye soap for scrubbing Wes's hands and her body, clean clothes for Wes, swaddling clothes for the baby and a cradle she'd made during the winter. When they left Pilchuk they hadn't brought any baby things, believing Jasper to be the last of the line. It had been a pleasure during the winter to make new things and even to have the time to tat some lace and embroider some flowers.

Jennie got up, lined her underpants with her monthly cloths, and went out and shot six fool's hens, in order to have the next two days' food ahead. She skinned and cleaned them, threw the crop, throat and stomach to the chickens, and put the birds to stew. She fixed breakfast for the five of them, and sent the boys out to their chores and play. Again she gave a special scrubbing to everything, and set pails and pans of water on the stove. The stove would burn high through the day, thankfully in the summer kitchen. By now the pains were closer together and growing stronger. She pulled the sheets off the bed, laid the rubber sheet on the tick, and put on fresh sheets. She laid folded sheets across the center of the bed, and put a pile of four more at the ready.

Wes fed everybody a lunch, cleaned up, and sent the boys back outside. Jennie bathed and refilled the water vessels. About three o'clock she got into the bed, bare and sweating. She propped herself up with pillows behind her back, dropped her head to her chest, and with each pain began to push with all her strength. She had Wes scrub himself and put on the clean clothes. He let her clench his hands, he rubbed her back or shoulders or arms. Jennie had never known another man who by choice took the lead in assisting at a birth, but she thought it made very good sense. With no one else could she relax so completely. No one else knew her moods and sensations so well. No one else cared so completely about her and the baby. If she wanted to yell, he didn't panic, just gave her support.

He brought her a mirror - cleaning it first - to let her check to see whether she was open enough for the head to come through. She was. She pushed some more, and the head showed. Another hour of pushing and it began to emerge. She wouldn't use the mirror anymore now; at every birth she'd attended, there was a fearful moment when the head came out, looking blue and lifeless, when she thought the worst. She didn't want to see that this time. When enough head was out that he could put his hands on it, Wes began a very gentle pull. The shoulders cleared the opening, and the baby shot out like a fish escaping a trap. Wes caught it, wrapped it in a blanket and deftly cleared its nose and mouth with a finger. He pinched the cord, tied it with the boiled string, and clipped it with Jennie's boiled scissors. With a long piece still attached, the baby lay on Jennie's chest and she made her last hopeful check. No, it was a boy. But the thrill of the healthy baby's strong cry took away any disappointment and it stayed away. Four fine boys it would be, and the little girls a sad, sad memory.

She slept till supper time, when Wes brought her some fool's hen broth. In celebration, the boys had dug some new potatoes, pulled some green onions, and picked and shelled some peas. She ate enough to reward their pride. Then she slept through the night, Wes bringing her the baby only twice in that time.

She was up to fix oatmeal for a simple breakfast, her mind on naming the baby. Wes liked David. She did too. Wes admired famous people, hence the firstborn boy, Thomas Alva. Jennie favored names from their families, hence Jasper Allison after her father, a mean-spirited, self-centered coot who didn't deserve the honor. She had hoped to name a little girl after her mother, but since that hadn't worked out, she suggested her mother's maiden name, Harum. So David Harum he was.

When Ada's Ruby Belle came by to ask if the baby was going to come soon, she was delighted to find him already nursing. Word came back from Ada later that day, with a serviceberry pie, that the Wooding name was done proud by the first white baby in the north Pend d'Oreille. She said it couldn't be helped that it wasn't a girl. The next day she dressed all four of her girls in their frilliest best and paraded them over, ostensibly to see baby boy Davey.

A WEEK LATER WES READ to them of the Miner editor decrying the "dummies" who would sell their homestead property for $1 to lumber companies or railroads. Jennie was aghast. "Throw away a chance like this? Wes, this is heaven we have here. Why would anybody not hang onto it, especially after all the work?"

"Some of them can't take it, aren't Stickers. But a lot of them meant to do it in the first place. They're just shills for the lumber barons."

"Well, the newspaper's right to call them 'dummies'. They aren't apt to get another chance like this."

"It doesn't mean 'stupid,' Jennie. It means 'silent.' The lumber company has probably given them the money to Prove Up in the first place, and maybe now they'll give the man a job, and the company gets land the law didn't mean for them to have."

"Well, hooray for the *MINER* for once."

In the same issue he read of work at the Bead Lake Mine near Newport, and in the morning he was gone. A letter came back on the next boat saying he had a job, and at least it was only 40 miles upriver and not across the state. He asked her to send certain garb, and she had a bag ready for the boat when it returned upriver that same day. She included a note asking if he could buy a cow for her. She said she had to have it with all these boys. Jasper had been taken off the breast sooner than he might have liked, and buying milk for three boys was expensive. The next Sunday's boat brought a letter from Wes saying he'd bought a cow, got it real cheap because it was a little hard to handle, though he didn't think she'd have too much trouble, and it would be on the next boat. Jennie and the four boys met the next boat. Wearing the harness Jennie had made him out of some wornout pants of Wes's, Si pulled Jasper and Davey in the wagon, She left the boys all at the top of the bank and went down to claim her cow. They seldom saw Joe Cusick anymore; he might have tolerated a mean cow better. But it was a disgruntled Captain Flanders who led the balky cow out of the lower deck. Jennie asked if a letter accompanied her. "If you want to stand right there on the bank all night you might get one tomorrow. Your husband forgot to give it to me till after the boat took off. So he wrapped it around a rock and threw it. Well, he got the rock to the boat, and dented the flag pole, but the letter fell off into the river." The cow was cranky too.

Jennie followed the four boys home along the trail, sometimes leading, sometimes pulling the cow. This was an animal not to be trusted, and if she kicked, Jennie wanted the boys far ahead out of range. By the time they reached the shed, the cow's nature was clear, and the boys were sent into the house. Only Jennie was to be in close quarters with this animal.

Heeding Wes's warning, she had prepared in the shed a stall, manger and stanchion for the cow. That should make any cow milkable, she thought. But as the cow entered the shed, she began to kick. She had alienated Captain Flanders by kicking three holes in the walls of his lower deck, and she planned to continue here with the same conduct. But Jennie didn't plan to build this shed twice, and she took the cow back outside and tied her to a tree. She spent an hour building a set of wooden hobbles, time that let the cow relax a bit after her unnerving boat journey. But upon reentering the shed, the cow began again to kick violently. Jennie took her back out and again tied her to the tree. At this point Jennie had to go in the house and nurse Davey. When she was ready for a fresh start, she brought out with her a five-gallon pail for the evening milking, put it in the stall, and led in the cow. When the cow saw the container, she again let fly. Even though she had no calf, she did not intend to share her milk with anyone. Jennie was just as determined that she would. Jennie couldn't come close enough to put on the hobbles, and earned bruises from knee to ankle on her left leg to prove she had tried. On a hunch, she took the cow back outside and tied her to the tree. No kicking. She brought out the bucket. No kicking. When she put the bucket under the cow's bag, however, the cow promptly put a foot in it and tipped it over. Jennie took another break, built a milking stool and, sitting on it, held the bucket between her knees. Here the cow couldn't see the bucket, so she didn't kick at it. This uncomfortable position was the only way the cow could be made to produce. Contrary to all Jennie's experience with milch cows, this one preferred to be milked outside - enclosures set her off. After a day at loggerheads the cow didn't give much milk, but enough for dinner and breakfast. As the week went on, production increased only slightly, and Jennie decided to continue buying butter from Orla. Churning was a chore for households with extra hands anyway, and besides Jennie'd rather be working in the garden or building onto the place than pumping a churn.

During the next week Jennie fenced in a corral to contain the cow when no boy was around to herd her out of the garden. The cow leaned into it and pushed through handily. Any bad habit an animal could have, that cow had in spades. Jennie added another tier of rails to the fenceposts, but didn't fool herself it was a permanent solution. When summer progressed and the lush grass loosened her bowels, the cow seemed to delight in swishing her shitty tail into Jennie's face. Jennie got three clothespins from the porch and attached them to the tail and attached the tail to a tree branch when she was milking. She hoped it was uncomfortable.

That summer Jennie continued to clear more land for next year's garden, piling slash for fall burning. She chose a spot for a root cellar, across Renshaw Creek in a hill steep enough for a dugout. Using small logs for supports, she built a solid door and then a gas exhaust on the roof. The location required a bridge across the creek, and she used ropes to drag logs into place for the stringers. Now the boys' wagon could cross the creek, laden with cabbages to winter in the root cellar. When they made bunch grass hay she realized she needed a hay barn. Tommy wasn't tall enough to hold the poles in place so she bartered some knit goods with Hy Maggott for help. On the day before they started, Jennie's new shoes arrived on the boat and she started the first day of construction in them. By the time she went in to fix the midday meal she was limping. "You got a hitch in your gitalong there, Jennie," Hy observed. She told him the right shoe was fine but the left one was impossible. "And three weeks to reorder from Chicago ain't soon enough." Hy offered to wear the offending shoe through the afternoon for her to break it in. Sure enough, three hours later the shoe was well stretched. They were sitting on stumps and trading back when they heard a steamboat whistle. "Distress signal, Jennie. Somebody needs help." She grabbed Davey and all of them ran to the Landing.

The help needed was a kind no one could give. Lydia and Jeff Honsinger's little girl Ethel had drowned in the river, and those on board the *VOLUNTEER* were a search party hoping to recover the body. Jennie handed the baby to Hy and went aboard. Jeff wanted to tell the whole story to Jennie. He'd bought a little metal boat from Monkey Wards....they were almost back home... eddy...tipped over and all went in...nobody could swim...he could touch bottom...he thought he grabbed hold of her, but her red hair looked just like Lyd's.....they never saw Ethel again...but they just had to find her to bury her...Lyd couldn't stand thinking of her in that cold water. Family and neighbors lined the decks on both sides to watch. There was no need for Jennie to leave her boys. They were going as far as Dead Man's Eddy below the Metaline Falls, and if they didn't find her before then, they'd wait till she came up there. The boat moved on.

"Hy, Davey can wait a little while, but these boys are learning right now to swim." They spent the long evening in the water, and Tommie and Billie took as naturally to the water as she herself had back when she had to herd hogs across the Owens River. Hy allowed that maybe two was a little young, is why Jasper cried when they tried to get him to paddle from Jennie to Hy. She agreed he could wait a little while too.

THEY HAD SPENT THE FIRST winter without a proper privy. Now Jennie was determined to have one. When Wes came home unexpectedly in October, he found her standing with a shovel in a four-foot-deep hole and wearing a pair of his overalls. "Jennie, who's dead?" he teased.

"Wes!" She climbed out, brushed herself off, and threw her arms around him. "Wes, are you here long enough to build an outhouse? "

"Nice welcome. I know what I'm needed for, don't I? Truth is, I may be here long enough to fill that outhouse, Jennie. Bead Lake's closed for the winter."

"Wes, I wish you could stay home. You can't imagine how wonderful last winter was. It's so quiet, so peaceful here. The only thing missing was you. Stay home with us."

"Long enough to build an outhouse, yes. But, Jennie, we've got to keep at the improvements, and that takes cash. And we've got to buy a horse to help you with the heavy work around here. But there's good news. An Englishman named Jordan was down here looking for gold. He wasn't lucky with that, but he says he's found cement rock about six miles downriver from here

"What's cement rock?"

"It's used in a new building material. There's not any cement made in this whole state, but this Jordan's an engineer, and thinks he knows what he's doing. So till deep snow he's hiring men to clear land and build houses, a store, a bunkhouse and cookhouse and a mill. He's going to dig ditches, dam Cedar Creek, and build a flume around the big hill he's named Mount Jordan, after himself. He's determined to have his plant and a town right off the bat. I can do any of that, if my eyes hold, which they usually do in the fall."

"And if this Englishman's money holds, which it might."

Wes helped with what harvesting was left, and through the fall was able to come home three times; the boys knew him better than they had the previous winter.

By Christmas the town of Cement was built and the men who'd put it up in three months were laid off. Wes spent Christmas with the family and left for the Coeur d'Alene country where he heard mines were hiring.

1902

THROUGH THE SECOND winter, Jennie prepared for the second spring. More settlers were moving in, encouraged by word of the survey about to be finished; she moved fencing to a higher priority. She made pointed fence pickets by the dozens. They were extra work, but maybe they'd look more homelike to the inspectors. She split shakes as time allowed, for when they might be needed or traded.

In March the first chicks hatched, another sign to Jennie that this homesteading idea was going to work. To deter skunks, badgers and raccoons, she built a stick fence around the chicken yard. Tommie and Billie could drag little hawthorn and alder trees that Jennie felled and limbed. She loved that each stick had a different shape, and that they all went together in harmony, for a rustic little fortress. With Si's help the boys could also drag a log vee over the trail to make it look more like a road. Someday they'd have a horse and wagon, surely, and a road would go further than a trail to make the place look like a "year-round home" when it came time to Prove Up. George Tiger said she had nothing to worry about; he was astonished at how homelike the place looked after less than two years. His place, he said, was still just a prospector's cabin; hers was a true family home. Encouraged, she ordered fruit trees through the *MINER* to be sent down on the boat. One day while she was working outdoors a spring rain came to one side of the clearing while sun continued from the other side. "Look, Boys, our 'stead's plated with silver."

Now turning three, Jasper was charged with keeping the new trees watered. He could use a little tin pail to fill lard cans set in the wagon, then direct Si to haul them to the trees. There, he could climb into the wagon and lean on the side of a lard can to tip it into the depression around the tree. He kept a dozen young fruit trees watered through the summer. The clearing Jennie and the boys had done the previous summer let her plant potatoes, onions, turnips, rutabagas, cabbages and squashes for the next winter. Vain about the size of cabbages she'd grown on the new soil – some up to 20 pounds – she put in triple what they'd need, planning to sell some to the settlers she knew would be coming this year.

Having fought all winter with the contentious cow, Jennie determined to do better. She'd had to milk the beast outdoors, rain or snow, wind or cold. The new pointed picket fence didn't discourage the cow from going her own way. Jennie answered an ad in the *MINER* for a milch cow for sale or trade, and sent ten squares of cedar shakes with Captain Flanders. The cow came on the next boat. In the meantime she had arranged to ship the old one downriver to Harris Page, in exchange for a dozen good layers. They'd never even named it, sensing it was an impermanent boarder. When the boat came with the new cow, Captain Flanders looked happier this time until he caught sight of the cow she planned to send onto his boat. "Is that that same old kicky cow I brought down here in the fall?" Only then, when she was leaving, did the cow gain a name; whenever they referred to her thereafter, she was Kicky Cow. The new, well-mannered cow, immediately named Patience, was led off the boat and put in Tommie's care. Jennie led Kicky Cow down the bank to the water's edge. But the gangplank and the low door at the end of it didn't please the cantankerous animal. She balked. Joe Parker, on his way downriver to visit Joe Bettencourt, didn't care to have the boat delayed. He gave her a punch with a stout stick and she made a sprightly jump onto the deck and into the room, where they heard a battering sound until the boat rounded a bend a quarter mile downriver. To their satisfaction, the Woodings never saw Kicky Cow again. Word came back months later that Harris Page milked her once, turned her out for the summer, and butchered her in the fall.

IN APRIL, THE NEWS WAS so big that Wes came home from the Coeur d'Alene. Townships 42 and 43 were open to settlers! Until the entire survey was finished and passed on in Washington, D.C., the Woodings of Tiger's Landing had been mere squatters. Now they could file on Hawthorn Lodge, as they had named their home on the Pend d'Oreille.

In May the news was still big, but now it was bad. When George Tiger and three others went to Spokane to file their claims, they found they had indeed selected lieu lands, lands given outright by the U.S. Congress to the Northern Pacific railroad. Everyone downriver was distressed, knowing they had only a 50-50 chance of being on one of the alternate sections open to homesteaders instead of to the railroad barons. Not that it helped much, but everyone was on their side. Even the pro-business *NEWPORT MINER* reported gleefully: *It is said that at the land office in Spokane a few days ago the N.P. land agent appeared to file on lieu lands in the newly opened district down the river. Mr. Agent wanted his filing accepted in advance of six settlers who were before him, but was told that he would have to 'go way back and sidetrack' and take his turn, the same as others.* The line of petitioners cheered.

Despite popular support, when the next group, Wes, Uriah, Charles and Arthur Norman, Joe Parker, and five other neighbors went in to make application, they found they were wholly or partly within lieu land limits. They were rejected. They appealed on the spot, which appeal would be taken to the general land office at Washington, already swamped with such petitions. Entry would be delayed at best. At worst, they would be denied, and their months or years - in Joe Parker's case 18 years - of residency and labor would be discounted.

Wes, Uriah, and five others went together to hire a lawyer to present their case. The *MINER* commented, *No doubt they will hold their lands, but they shouldn't have the expense and trouble of an appeal.* Fair-minded people thought the NP should have checked on occupancy of pieces before they chose them for their lieu lands. Wes said, "It's theft in the first place for them to get half of what was intended for farmers, and to add this insult to it is the worst kind of arrogance." John Renshaw suggested no real mental process was involved: some bureaucrat 3,000 miles away just hop-scotched across a map without regard for either human beings or railroad owners.

The confusion didn't affect new settlers who'd waited for the formal opening, and they came now by the scores. "Hey, Jen, you seen the rag city?" asked Jeff Honsinger. George Tiger's big field looked like a Civil War encampment, with sometimes 200 white tents of settlers who'd come down on the boat, some now headed up Tiger Pass, some looking for pieces closer to Tiger's Landing. Every good piece, and many bad ones, were claimed; Jennie was glad she'd sent Wes and Uriah over when she had. The two winters of isolation with her boys had been lovely, but she knew they'd be the last. Her mind, like George Tiger's, went to building a town.

Uriah's went to building an empire, and he arranged for his two single sisters to come to Tiger to take out homesteads, to make a united 640 acres in the Wooding name. Instead, soon after they arrived, his sister Ida married Nels Hansen and his sister Julia married Arthur Norman and lived on homesteads in their husbands' names as the law required, but at least adjoining the two Wooding claims.

THE SCHOOL DISTRICT WAS ORGANIZED, the directors elected, but still there wasn't a proper school. The Parker faction had won, but Jennie'd forgotten what they'd won. Pearl Mellott's snippy vow of a school ready by fall hadn't materialized. For a three-month fall term Tommie and Billie had been cooped up with other children in George Tiger's cabin. Now, a year later, everyone still seemed to think the topic too hot to reopen. The Miner editorialized *...let the schoolhouse be built and for the love of Mary and her little lamb swallow the rag and turn attention to the erection of a building.*

Jennie staked out an acre of land across Renshaw Creek. Remembering last year's battle, she went tactfully to Joe Parker to determine his plans.

"Jennie, I feel bad about what happened last year. There's people that'll not be friends for a long time. Sure, we won the vote. But I don't know as it's worth it. I want there to be a school, but I don't want to be crowing about it being the Parker School on Parker land. I said I'd give land, and I sure will if it's wanted, but now I wish there was a way out."

She tried the Renshaws. Orla said, "Our land wasn't wanted, and our vision for the school wasn't appreciated. Parker's land is way too far upriver. Imagine the Youngreen children and the Page children going all the way up there. But it's true we don't have any youngsters, and I think we'll just stay out of it."

Jennie went to George Tiger. She drew in the clay a map of the area, showing the homes with children in them. "George, you and us are right in the middle. Kids could come half upriver and half downriver to school."

"Jennie, you know I'm more than willing. But I don't think the riverbank's a good place for a school. Any land I have to give away, a kid could skedaddle from the teacher's desk to the water in half a minute. That's why I didn't offer last year. They've met this last term here in my house, and I've worried about it the whole time. Mr. Melgaard's had to keep them all together every minute; he was afraid to let them go to the outhouse, almost."

"George, how about we call a meeting of the directors when Wes is home, and me and Wes offer that piece of ours that's across the creek, full of hawthorns? That way, I won't get to clear the whole damn thing myself; everybody'll have to help. The commissioners say they're going to put a road by there some day. And it's far from the river. We can even leave a circle of thorny hawthorns around the outside of the playground to sort of pen the little buggers in."

She wrote to Wes and he came on the next boat. The school directors met at George Tiger's house, at three in the afternoon to accommodate Wes.

They didn't announce a public meeting this time, figuring correctly that everyone was tired of bloodshed, and decisions were what they'd elected the directors for anyway. They agreed they had imposed too long on George's hospitality. George offered to take care of the courthouse papers when he was next in Newport, and Wes went back on the same boat. The Woodings now had only 159 acres to improve.

On a windy, cool day in April women and children gathered at the hawthorn patch with saws, clippers, and plenty of gloves. Everyone had long sleeves and scarves or hats. Hair was wrapped, and hats tied on. No amount of protection was enough, though, and Alice and Ruby Belle kept the tender-skinned littler children at Jennie's house. In spite of all this protection, blood was still too common. Mary Wooding was charged with keeping clean water and cloth strips, witch hazel and calamine at the ready. For a week after, women with scratched faces and hands would greet each other with proud comparisons of their red badges of accomplishment. Husbands and brothers would tease about cat fights.

The hawthorn trunks were no more than six inches across, somewhere between trees and bushes, but they were one of the hardest woods in North America. Christina Carpenter brought a sharpening stone, and made it available to all. As at Jennie's place, the women did the sawing, the children the hauling. With 14 women and 24 good-sized youngsters, they cleared the acre and piled the brush in a day. The burning would have to wait for a windless day, and with the brush out it was clear they had chosen a windy knoll for the school. Ethel's hair ribbon bobbed vigorously as she stood still and watched Ada arrange the baked beans, pickled beets, fresh bread, rhubarb swizzle and sugar cookies for the lunch.

The first week of May was perfect for burning: little wind, occasional showering. The nearest families - Greenamyers, Underwoods and both Woodings - kept the fire going. Smoke or the smell of smoke was with them everywhere they went. By the middle of the month logs from various ranches had been delivered by the Carpenter and Youngreen teams. Men, women and children met on a warming day in mid-May to build the one-room log schoolhouse. No one ever acknowledged it was because of Orla's suggestion of last year, but the school was given ten twelve-pane windows, paid for by subscription, and more light streamed in than into any of their homes. Jennie hoped it would stream into the little minds. The caulking, too, was more carefully done than in any of their homes. They had tacitly accepted Orla's challenge to a better school than any of them had known.

On the day of construction, both John Renshaw and Uriah Wooding were in Colville at the county courthouse serving as jurors, for $2 a day cash, easy earnings for a 70-mile round trip on horseback. Wes, on the other hand, gave up two days' pay to come home for the event.

IN THE FALL, THE CABBAGES were almost as big as those of the first year, and Jennie sent word to several neighbors that she could sell some. The only response she got was the offer of some excess cottage cheese in barter from Orla. Frank Schmaus made a visit about then, and she tried him. "Shoot, Missus, eferybody can grow cabbages here. But I tink if you made sauerkraut, you'd get some takers, sure." He talked her through the instructions, and offered the loan of two crocks. Frank loaned her a cabbage grater too, and for a week she grated cabbage and salted it. She tended it for two weeks, daily removing the slime that rose to the top of the crocks and replacing the cloths on it, weighted with rocks so the juices rose above the cabbage. When it was delectably golden, she sent her message around again. This time she sold 100 pounds of sauerkraut for 40 cents a pound, cash. She set to work with new enthusiasm to remove more stumps, planning 200 pounds for next year.

Mike Mouchand bought some. Mike was new to sauerkraut, and assumed it needed long cooking, since Jennie'd told him there'd been none in the making. He approached his stove to check on it. At first touch the lid he had placed firmly on the pot jumped to meet him, and a full pan of sauerkraut exploded on his face and around the room. When he showed up at The Landing with blisters to the tip of his nose, he was questioned. He said he didn't mind the burns so much, but to lose the last of his sauerkraut was hard. When Jennie heard of it, she rowed some sauerkraut and some salve across the river to him.

1903

BY NOW, THE fourth winter, Jennie was known as a nurse and midwife, and some families were calling her Aunt Jennie. Christina Carpenter, two miles north toward Ione, was a nurse too, even had professional training. Mrs. Carpenter had the advantage, too, of a horse to ride to housecalls. But there was plenty of work for both, Jennie was a good walker, and between the two of them they kept the sparse population healthy. People noticed Jennie's talent, and she was glad for the income. Gradually she built up a supply of medicines, some - morphine, aspirin, carbolic acid, ipecac - brought with her or sent on the boat from Spokane; some -yarrow, tansy, lemon balm, parsley - grown in her own garden; and some - Solomon's seal, Oregon grape, mullein, chokecherry bark - gathered in the woods and fields.

IN JULY A MISSIONARY FROM the United Brethren came downriver looking for sites for services. Wes happened to be home with a bout of sore eye. "Missionary? To us heathens in the wilds, huh?" George Tiger was accustomed to opening his house to transients of all kinds, but this one was ambitious. "I think we'll need something larger," he sniffed. George Tiger directed the evangelist to Wes, the most accessible of the school directors. Wes allowed the use of the schoolhouse, but smiled at the irony of one of the Landing's leading Socialists donating land to facilitate revival of doctrine he thought better left to die. As Brother Smithens left Tiger's Landing on Sunday afternoon to try his luck downriver, he was clearly disappointed by the attendance, and especially the take. The only one who had even invited him for a meal was congenial George Tiger, who offered venison jerky and cold biscuits.

LATER THAT MONTH THE FIRST big party in the Downriver's short community history was held at the head of the box canyon and its impassable rapids, at the new house of John Bettencourt. Bettencourt's Landing was the last steamboat landing downriver, due to the rapids. Though he hadn't kept a calendar, John had been in a cabin there since about 1880. No one, not even Kalispels, had lived on the land before him. It never occurred to him it wasn't his. The roar of the canyon was to him like the whisper of the aspens to Jennie. But when the survey was completed, he had cooperatively filled out the forms and paid his $16 filing fee. Because of his long tenure, John had no waiting period, squatters always having first claims. Even the railroad had no idea of wanting land in such a tight canyon, and his claim was unchallenged. In July, Joe Parker and Elmer Hall, the first settlers of Tiger's Landing and Ione respectively, went the 50 miles to Newport as witnesses to John's improvements. Finishing at the land office, they went to Kelly's Bar and toasted President Teddy, who had signed the Proof. Then they toasted Joe Cusick who had brought them upriver, then the clerk at the land office, Kelly himself and each of his employees, each other, and John Bettencourt's good dog Grover, keeping guard back at the property.

Four days later, John Bettencourt's housewarming was a symbol of homesteading success for Downriver residents from Blueslide to Metaline. He was the first, and the rest would follow shortly. Folks downriver of John used the long portage trail around the falls, some afoot, some on horseback. Folks upriver of John came in every kind of rivercraft floating. The *VOLUNTEER* picked up the more affluent passengers within 15 miles upriver and brought them down; Capt. Cusick would enjoy the party all night and take them back the next day. Wes built a raft big enough for his family and Uriah's to float down; they would walk the eight miles home the next day, saving a dozen $2 fares. George Tiger and Joe Parker went in a pine bark canoe. The Pages went in a dugout canoe, giving rides to friends below them. The tally was 17 rowboats, 14 rafts, 12 bark canoes, and 6 dugouts.

Even Ada was outgoing on the trip downriver. Her girls were decked out to her satisfaction. Alice, now 18, had a fluffy red organdy dress and a straw hat with silk poppies she'd brought back from Seattle. Ruby Belle, nearly 16, chafed because though her dress too was of organdy, she was still made to wear it above her ankles with dark stockings, like her little sisters. Ada's pride was that at this party she'd show the locals what her girls were destined for, and it certainly wasn't life as homesteaders' wives. Her vanity brought out her best humor and she sat on a chair on the raft and joined in banter and laughter. Jennie hoped maybe the bad times were past, and Ada would be her old self.

John Bettencourt's new house was twice the size of his original cabin, but couldn't begin to accommodate the party, which overflowed into his big meadow above the river, south of his big, sound, hardy orchard. Each woman who saw those trees became speculative, wondering whether hers would look that good in a few years, and in the meantime what John would trade this fall for some apples, prunes, or pears.

Every musician in the Downriver came to this Housewarming. There were seven guitars, a dulcimer, three banjos, six harmonicas, two jew's-harps, and two squeezeboxes. Wingy Charleton came with a tambourine to replace the fiddle he'd played before he lost his left arm to a pulley in his hayloft. There were a set of spoons, and four fiddles including Nettie's. Hy Maggot called out "The plumbing section's here" when Rufus Walton arrived with his cornet. As always, the heart of the body was John Renshaw, this time with a mandolin. Jennie declared there was nothing like a mandolin to keep feet from sitting still. Tommie spent the night at the knee of one or the other of the musicians, hoping for a chance to play spoons or tambourine.

John had set up sawhorses and planks in the barn, and each woman arriving added her offering for the supper. John's good well provided the only acknowledged drinks, though the frequency of trips by men to check their watercraft might have suggested otherwise. It was good that John's barn was large, and good that the summer's hay was not yet in. Children, as sand came in their eyes, were taken up to the loft to soft little piles of last year's hay and bedded down. Only then could parents completely ignore the threat of the river and the roar of the Box Canyon and concentrate on their own festivities. The floor of the barn was for dancing. The women had the advantage of light summer dresses, most having recently sewn a new one for the Fourth. The men owned just one suit each, usually of a medium serge too cool for winter and too warm for summer, worn with a starched collar and a fancy tie. The proper respect for John, his home, the neighbors, and the occasion could not be shown in flannel and denim. Finery was called for.

In Alice's head the excitement turned to giddiness. She had not before tonight met Charley Gilmore from Sullivan. She knew the name, of course, and knew that her father and uncle did business with his father, but Charley lived three miles downstream and on the back side of the river. There was nothing in local etiquette that prevented her dancing with him, though, and since he was the lightest and nimblest of partners, she didn't stop after "The Blue Danube" and "Rye Waltz," but continued through "The Prairie Queen" and "The Military Schottische" to "Rockaway" and "Fireman's

Dance." By then she realized that she was a young woman and he a young man, no longer girl and boy, as they had been when they arrived at the party. When some people tired of dancing and drew blocks into a circle around the gigantic bonfire John had stacked, Alice and Charley were still tripping and whirling. After "Breeze" and "Old Zip Coon," she began to think that being in his arms without dancing would be nice too. Ada, of course, had kept a close eye on all the girls, but when she traveled up to John's new outhouse, she came back to find Alice missing. She glanced around the field but didn't see her. She went to the bank and looked down on the river and boats, but didn't see her. She went back to Uriah and the little girls, but they knew nothing. She didn't even stop to upbraid Uriah for not keeping an eye on Alice for the little time it took Ada to go to the privy, but followed the trail to the orchard where she'd seen other young couples strolling throughout the evening. It was not comforting to find the hat with the red poppies abandoned beneath a pear tree. Then she began calling, not in the sweetest or calmest of voices. Ada was not one to mind disturbing the peace of any strollers or spooners, and went from one tree to another searching and calling. Finally Alice, alone, stepped from around a fine big Spitzenberg tree. Her cheeks were redder than the apples' would ever be. Her hair was mussed and her dress was crushed. But her mother's obvious ire did not erase her smile. "What, Mama?"

For the rest of the night, through hours of dancing and feasting and more dancing, Alice was kept close to her mother's side. But the smile seldom disappeared. When Ada went to the table to fill her plate, she took time to attach Alice to Jennie for safekeeping. "Aunt Jennie, how old were you when you married Uncle Wes?" Jennie knew the answer wouldn't please Ada, but had to admit to sixteen. The wise little smile broadened. "Will you make me a special dress, Aunt Jennie?" Ada returned and Jennie went back to the dancing. She told Wes what was happening. "Yes, well, a pretty red dress will do that." They hoped Ada wouldn't make too much trouble.

"Jennie, you were younger than she is, and here we are sixteen years later, still in love and still dancing our legs off." And dance they did, till the sun was over the hills across the river and the musicians, who'd by now taken turns to make music for sixteen hours, finally tired out. It was light enough to see their way home, and there was no excuse for prolonging the party.

Remains of the supper provided breakfast, and John's house was considered well warmed. Over the next week John disassembled the rafts and piled the pieces with his winter fuel. He smiled and was specially warmed whenever he put that particular wood on his winter fire.

****

WES HAD COME HOME IN time for the Housewarming, and stayed on to help Jennie put the second story on the house. George Tiger was busy at Colville and Newport trying to persuade his senators to do what they could to have the new game license repealed when they went back to Olympia. They couldn't. George was sure his Caribou Lodge would do the area more good if there were no limits on what guests could shoot. "There's more fish in the lake and more animals in the woods than all of Spokane could take anyway." In August he went to Spokane to receive a consignment of silvers to put in Sullivan Lake to supplement the cutthroats, and said he'd be staying at the Lodge till snow flew. The Woodings saw their chance to ask him for another favor.

The Woodings again camped in George's house, all the furnishings of their own lower floor covered with sheets, blankets, and canvas tarps borrowed around the neighborhood. Jennie and Wes went onto the roof and dismantled it. Tommie, Billie and Jasper whooped and ran from the house as shingles dropped, then ran back and collected the dropped shingles and stacked them near the barn for patch material, or for new outbuildings as the need arose. Those broken in removal would serve for kindling. The house would have new ones that Jennie and the boys had split during the winter. Davey, now two, separated out as many nails as he could and collected them in lard cans. Wes warned all four boys under pain of a tanning to keep their damn shoes on. Jennie and Billie chorused "I hurt my toe-oe-oe-oe!" The old roof was cleared away in two days, and construction of a second floor began, divided into two rooms, a dormitory for the boys and a bedroom for Jennie and Wes. The grownups' room would be at the south end with a window looking onto the winter moon, through the branches of a big cottonwood. And it would have a door! Summer evenings and mornings they would hear the wind in the leaves and birdsong at dawn. Winters they would hear the snap from a tamarack fire in the downstairs stove. The ladder would be in the boys' room, and Wes and Jennie would have their love nest undisturbed. They had two blessed nights there, but as soon as the second story was roofed, Wes was off for Bossberg.

****

HERE SHE WAS ALONE AGAIN. Wes had left an hour ago, headed on foot to the American Mine for a winter's work. He'd already be well up Tiger Pass, his traveling pack on his back and his boots well oiled. Jennie knew his mind was on her and the boys. Hers was surely on him. Though the hill was thickly treed between her and the trail, she felt him there.

Her aim today was a honey tree over near the valley edge, just below the road Wes was taking. Tommie and Billie had spent the summer locating a likely honey tree. Wes had made them a little box with a sliding lid. They would put a slice of sugar-soaked bread in the box and let some bees come for it. Then they'd close the lid long enough for the bees to want to fly, and open it again, then follow the bees' zigzag as far as they could. At the spot where they lost sight of the bee, they'd repeat the lure. Little by little over the summer, they'd found a perfect tree - one they said Ma could knock over and rob by herself. Today wouldn't be the robbing day, though, just a scouting day. She sure wasn't going to take those little boys' word sight unseen. So here she was with four-year-old Jasper, hiking a half mile across the valley bottom, just by coincidence in Wes's direction. Davey she left with his older brothers, but Jasper's cheerful company was welcome, and his work at the place wasn't enough to be missed. They could afford this outing that was part work, part lark.

They were off very early. She wanted to beat the sun that would pour down on them where Uriah had cleared some acres. To keep Jasper moving when there were so many birds and bugs and flowers and fungus to look at was a challenge itself. Jennie wished she had the time to just look at things, to savor the morning cool, to listen to the birdsong, to tell Jasper a little tale or two. But to get to the tree and back before midday meant she had to be the stern Ma that kept her thoughts on the job and not on the fun. Being torn that way made her impatient; thinking of Wes made her sad. Maybe she wasn't as attentive to what was going on around her as she might have been.

At that moment Jasper made her smile as he answered a raven on a fencepost. He could imitate about any bird, but the ravens' caws were his favorite and hers too because there were so many variations. When this raven gave an indignant "Quaaak!" Jasper gave it right back to him with a hint of mockery. It should have flown off then, but it didn't. It wanted to hold its ground. There were two more exchanges between boy and bird before the bird finally flew off to the field to the north. There his compadre was involved in something on the ground. Jennie realized she'd been seeing this for quite a while without it registering. Now that she gave it some attention, she supposed that the haying in progress in that field had left some dead killdeers or rabbits.

Jennie and Jasper went on, to the valley's edge.

Still in August there was an active spring coming down off the hill, wetting their feet. They went a little slower, and she took his hand to steady them both as they placed their feet on clumps of grass and tried to avoid the black muck between. For Jasper it was fun, and his giggles were contagious. When they reached dry ground and a big enough rise, Jasper pulled away and ran ahead to where the stumps and pasture gave way to birches and alders. He danced ahead of her, then turned north where he was out of her sight for a moment. She smiled at his fancy and turned to walk toward him, resting for a moment on her hawthorn walking stick when she moved into the shade. Early as it was, the sun had warmed her; she was sticky under her clothes, and her chest was mildly pounding. A rest felt good. She gazed to her left, up the hill, and took in the bracken, marking it as a place to come back to for spring fiddleheads for the pot. Hazelnut trees here were lush, but there were plenty closer to home that she knew had no worms. She turned her eyes to the copse straight ahead of her, where the alder and birch shaded another spring with hummocks of grass around black mud. With her breathing slowing and deepening, she took a relaxed look to the right and down to the ground, expecting the uncropped bunchgrass and taller thistles that grew there. She did not expect to be magnetized by huge blue eyes that looked as if they had been watching her for some minutes. The blue eyes were in a smooth, tawny head that matched exactly the cat's long body and tail. The cougar was all blue and gold, with a look of deep calm about it. Jennie knew to keep eye contact for her safety, but the big cat's serenity would have kept her mesmerized anyway. The animal made no offer to move, nor did she - until back into her consciousness came Jasper, now ten yards up the hill past the cougar and still unaware of it. He'd pranced on past it. As Jennie's eyes went to Jasper, so did the cat's - but as if in curiosity, not malice. She looked back at the cougar, and he back at her. She knew she should now continue eye contact with the beast and back away - and nothing could have been easier.

Except that it wouldn't solve the Jasper problem. Jennie didn't want to use her voice to warn Jasper or give a command, because she didn't know what introducing a new element would do to the balance that so far maintained. She had the walking stick, and raised it high in both hands so the cat would be daunted by her height.

Jasper now had stuck his foot between hummocks and was mired past his ankle in the black mud. His head was down and he was trying to extract himself without drawing his mother's attention. He'd had enough warnings about this kind of carelessness. He knew that if she saw his plight she'd scold him for clumsiness. Instead of calling for help, he remained silent, hoping she wouldn't notice. Jennie was grateful his predicament was working for them, keeping him quiet so the two sets of magnetized eyes - hers and the cougar's - kept their contact. She thought that as long as that continued the cat would not pounce. She knew he was capable of springing 30 feet from a dead stop, and she was only 15 feet from him. Fortunately, Jasper was further, probably 50 feet. On the other hand, what good would it do that he couldn't get Jasper till the second leap?

Jennie felt the dampness down her back and on her palms. How long could this impasse go on? Slowly turning sideways, she faced the cat and began to edge to her left, towards Jasper. The cougar wasn't bothered. He seemed now to have almost an amused look, as if he understood her dilemma and wondered how she would get out of it. She wondered too. But she continued to move calmly toward Jasper, remembering to keep her face to the cat and to slightly edge toward her left shoulder so the distance between them increased. She reached the swampy ground. How to maneuver between mounds without looking where she was stepping? She couldn't risk getting stuck too. Jasper was still engrossed, still believing he could solve this himself without drawing Ma's displeasure. Her walking stick was a lifesaver; it was now a support, resting in the mud but keeping her on the hummocks. She still had no idea what she would do when she reached Jasper. She was close enough now that he couldn't fail to acknowledge her. As he looked up, he had no defense ready at the lip so she had time to give him a signal - a hand over her mouth - that he was to be quiet. Having lived for his four years with both the possibility of danger and the certainty of discipline, Jasper gave no thought to disobeying. He stayed quiet and his eyes went back to his mired foot. Still balancing on the stick, Jennie bent her knees and brought her head down. The cougar brought his eyes down with hers. Did he realize this squat made her more vulnerable? Probably. But he still didn't spring.

A new problem now arose: how to keep her long skirt from slipping underfoot and tripping her. If she sprawled on the ground, surely then the cat would spring, even if he wasn't very hungry. It would be instinct. But still no action from him. She pulled the back of the skirt up between her legs and tucked it into her waistband at the front, as if for horseback riding. Jasper had now found a cottonwood limb suitable for a digging stick - he'd still like to extract himself rather than have his mother rescue him like a baby. Just then Jasper had success and she was able to rise back up with him in her arms with his back to the cat. She reinforced the command for quiet by putting one hand over his mouth and holding his head firmly with the other so he didn't turn to look. He was facing directly over her shoulder, exactly away from the cat. It would be better, simpler, if he didn't know it was there. Jasper knew something was giving his mother's silent orders an urgency, and experience had taught him to go along with whatever she or Pa said when there was that certain tone about their directives. Jennie abandoned the walking stick and again eased her way from hummock to hummock with Jasper in her arms until she was on dry ground. She still faced the cougar, but was farther from him, perhaps 30 feet instead of the original 15 - but that meant farther from eventual escape. Ahead of her the swamp deepened, so she had to go back the way she'd come; she did the same controlled sideways step, but now to her right, till she was well past the cougar. Then she walked forward. When she could no longer see him, she changed to a more natural forward gait. She lengthened her steps, but didn't break into a lope or a run, because she didn't know if the cat might have moved to watch her departure. She finally put Jasper down so he could walk under his own power, but she kept his hand in hers. Jennie peeked occasionally back over her shoulder as they walked the 300 yards across the field into Uriah's wood, where she would be safe, out of the cougar's vision if he was watching. Only then did she speak to Jasper, to tell him it was ok now to let go of her hand, to walk as fast or as slow as he wanted, to talk in a normal voice.

"What was it, Ma?"

"A cougar. Not a really big one, probably about two years old, and thank goodness not very hungry. I think he ate something back there where those ravens were, but I missed the signal. You did just right, Jasper, and got yourself out of the mud and kept your mouth shut when I told you."

They went on to the house, Jennie congratulating herself, too, on handling the danger herself. She missed Wes, and loved Wes, but she could handle things on her own. Maybe after a meal she'd rig up that new stump puller that one person was supposed to be able to work.

1904

THE WINTER OF 1903-4 was harsh. Snow was on the ground the first week in November and stayed there till mid-May. New Year's Day broke at 35 below. The littler boys' tender skins were kept in the house. Tommie and Billie came back in to brag how fast their nose hairs froze. Families with more than one cow were out of hay by January. Most stock animals stayed alive on lichen and moss; those that didn't were butchered when they were found soon enough, and fed the coyotes, cougars and wolves when they weren't.

Deer and caribou came down to the valley, out of the deeper snow. Meat was even more abundant than usual, and worthless in barter. Every household had more jerky than it could use in two years. Wes was home for three months because the dry cold set off his sore-eye and he couldn't see in the dark of the mines. He sawed cordwood for the riverboats, split shingles for trade, and cut fenceposts and rails for the homestead.

Jennie was freed to sew a wedding dress for Alice, of ivory silk Ada had ordered from Chicago. The heat of Alice and Charley's every meeting was clear even to Ada, and by January she knew she'd best not make them postpone the marriage any longer. With the choice of groom out of her control, she turned her energy to the ceremony. Alice and Charley would have been happy with a wedding at either family's home, but Ada needed something else. The log schoolhouse wouldn't suit, she felt, but the four-mile journey to Ione somehow, she alone believed, would lend a flavor of hauteur to the event. In Ada's mind the difficulty of moving everyone in the depth of a hard winter added importance to the event.

Alice made a sketch of the dress she envisioned, a modest style appropriate to the three-room board-and-batten home of the Justice of the Peace in Ione, Washington. Ada was not satisfied, and always referred to the "gown." She visited Jennie more than daily, always with the intent of glorifying said gown. She would come in stamping snow from her shoes, breathlessly implying she'd just come from Alice, who'd changed her mind about some detail. There should be hand-strung bugle beads around the collar. There should be a train. No, there should be a veil with a train. There should be a tatted waist girdle. All these things were within Jennie's capability, but outside Alice's wishes. Neither mother nor daughter could confront the other, and Jennie bore the brunt of every point of variance. "Wes, Ada manages to spoil everything, don't she? Why can't Alice and Charley have what they want?" Wes talked to Uriah. Uriah had no interest, either in the wedding or in Ada's bullying.

Wes and Jennie remembered how free they had felt when they married. Jennie was 16 to Alice's 17, but she had never been in the clutches of a mother trying to live a life vicariously. By 16 she'd been away from her parents for eight years, a nanny to her sister's three children. Wes was 26, had been prospecting in Arizona for 10 years. It never occurred to them to consult anybody about their marriage plans. Now, they were sorry for Alice and went ahead, walking a fine line assisting the bride as asked, but carefully avoiding the role of parents, in hopes of protecting what remained of their friendship with Ada and Uriah.

The full dozen Woodings and the half dozen Gilmores crowded the ceremony; it helped when Tommie and Billie were stationed outdoors to keep the steadily falling snow from piling up on the porch and walkway. Because the wedding was "out of town" as Ada liked to say, she couldn't be expected to spread a wedding meal. They all walked to Ellamae Swartley's boarding house for a piece of a small sheet cake Jennie had made, and a sip of egg nog she'd asked Ellamae to mix up while the rest of them were at the ceremony. Cake, milk and eggs had all been packed in sawdust on the way in to town to keep them from freezing. The trained gown was a bother wherever it went, its pretension turning what could have been a delightful family festivity into a self-conscious and strained gathering. "'Tis ever thus with Ada," Wes whispered to Jennie. They were glad that Alice and Charley planned to live downriver, below the swirling box canyon.

******

BECAUSE WES COULD BE HOME with the boys it was easier this winter for Jennie to walk the six miles each way to the store at Cement and come home with her groceries on her back, but the cash to use there was scarcer. It was convenient, though, to have a store so close, rather than 35 miles away at

Usk and to have to depend on the grace of a riverboat crew to fill her order. While she was sitting at the Cement Store to chat before starting back, Frank Schmaus came in. "Chesus Christ, Chennie, it's fresher'n hell out dere." She agreed that it was. "Vy you don't open a store at Tiger's Landing, Chennie? Dis is a long damn hike." On the walk home, she wondered if Frank's idea might be more than conversation. She tried it on Wes.

He was open to the idea. "I worked in a store once back in Arizona - I believe that store is where we met, my Girlie - and I could do it here. But I'm not ready to leave the Coeur d'Alene. The Union is too important, and I'm not leaving it when things are moving forward. But I don't know that there's anything to running a store you couldn't handle, Jennie. Which just leaves the idea of how the hell to buy one. Frank didn't say he wanted to sponsor it, did he?" And that was the end of that.

IN MARCH JENNIE REGRETTED SHE was the local doctor. It was the end of the hardest, longest winter anyone, including Joe Parker, remembered. The boys didn't mind: at nine Tommie still enjoyed snowmen and snow forts and snowballs, and at two and a half Davey could play a junior version. But some people had trouble getting through the winter. When April came with snow gritty around the cabins and the lovely white dressing long off the trees, and the landscape was unremitting grays and blacks, dull greens and dour browns, it seemed to some as if the fresh spring green would never come back.

Jennie stepped out one evening to throw the supper dishwater onto the chives and saw Cora Nesbit coming up the trail. Cora and her husband Willard had taken up a relinquishment a mile and a half up Tiger Mountain, where the winter was two weeks longer on both ends. Jennie had delivered Boyd two years ago, and tended the frail baby a half dozen times since. Some people weren't made for the hardscrabble life, and Cora and Willard were two of them. They could see ahead about twenty minutes, and went into the winter with little stored. Cora couldn't shoot at all, and Willard not much better. They couldn't dress an animal, had none of the skills needed to keep a little family healthy through the winter. The last time Cora had come for her, Jennie accompanied her home, wanting to see how life was in the Nesbit home. It was even worse than she expected. Cora was one of those people overwhelmed by everything. Dirty dishes were on the table and mush was caked on the makeshift counter of wooden boxes. The smell of the diapers Boyd was wearing was gagging, and a fetid pile of pale yellow baby shit topped the dirty diapers lying in the corner.

As Jennie and Cora entered, Willard only nodded. Freed from child tending, he went out without speaking. "He's going to split some wood. We ran out at dinner time." Boyd was whimpering on the floor, his face dirty, his eyelids swollen, his mouth rimmed with black. Cora picked him up, embarrassed, and made an effort to clean him. She wiped his snotty nose with the dishcloth, then his ringed mouth. "Whenever the stove's cool enough he wants to eat the coals. I don't know why." Jennie knew why. The malnourished baby might have been even more sickly by now if he hadn't been able to find the bits of nutrient the charcoal supplied. Jennie stayed till the wood came back in, then she built up the fire. She washed the baby, noting his sunken chest. She washed the diapers and washed the dishes, in snow she brought in and melted. Willard had gone right back out after bringing in a minimal amount of wood, and Cora sat at the table with her head in her arms. If these people had lived the long winter in this sordidness, it was a wonder their melancholy hadn't straightout killed them by now.

She asked Cora if the baby was still on the breast. "No, I didn't do so good at that right from the beginning, so I gave it up." She showed Jennie a simmering pot of a flour and water slather that was her milk substitute. Jennie said her boys would come up each day with a quart of milk, but if Willard could get down to pick it up, it would help. She knew he wouldn't, of course; he wouldn't want to be seen around the Landing getting handouts, and also three miles was a long walk. Apparently Boyd wasn't worth either embarrassment or exertion.

Now Cora had left again, with some milk and some beef broth.

A couple of hours later all the Woodings were in bed, and Jennie was telling Wes of the scene at the Nesbits. "Jennie, you're right. If they manage to raise that baby, it'll be with a lot of help from the neighbors." When they heard the knocking they knew it was Cora yet again. Jennie went down.

"Aunt Jennie, Boyd's crying and crying. Could I take some more of that milk up tonight?" Jennie fixed a basket with the milk and the leftover supper biscuits and more berry leather than the boys would have liked to see go out of the house. She promised to visit again tomorrow and opened the door for Cora. She had hardly closed it when she heard the girl scream. Wes shot down the ladder and the two of them ran to Cora, who was staring up the hill. The wavering red glow in the sky was clearly from her cabin. Cora could only stand and scream. Wes went back in, dressed, and left. Jennie led Cora back in, seated her in the rocker, and built up the fire.

The younger boys slept through the commotion, but Tommie and Billie wanted to come down. Jennie took them back up, told them there was a fire at the Nesbits', and they must stay in bed. She pulled a chair up beside Cora, gave her some chamomile tea, and rocked her. "Aunt Jennie, where will we live? Where will we live? We're in debt for that old cabin, and now we can't even live in it."

Wes came back after three hours, his face black. Cora was asleep in a bedroll by the stove, Jennie in the rocker. Wes asked her to go outside with him.

"Jennie, Boyd is dead, and we don't think Willard will make it."

She put both hands over her nose and mouth. "Wes, what do I tell her?"

"Just what I told you, I guess. We took Willard and Boyd in to Christina Carpenter, since Cora is here. The cabin is too hot for us to figure out much right now. Willard was outside, and he doesn't look so bad. I guess it's his lungs that's doing him in. You think every breath will be his last. The baby was inside, and she mustn't see him."

Her temper flared. "Why the hell was Willard outside? Who did he think would watch the baby?" Her voice had raised, and Cora came to the door.

"What is it?" But she knew, only clung to the last moments before hearing it said would make it so. It was Wes who went to her, took her in his arms, and told her as gently as he could.

"Cora, let's go in and sit down."

She screamed and began to struggle against him. She screamed again, her wild eyes on the hill where her grief lay. She kept screaming as Wes tried to lead her back into the house. She fought him to get free, intending to run up the hill to her horror. Wes put her over his shoulder and carried her into the house. She screamed some more, and the four boys started down the ladder. Jennie sent them back up, told Tommie briefly what had happened, and ordered them to stay upstairs until further notice. Tommie took his brothers into their parents' big bed, and they held to each other, imagining what they'd do if their house caught fire, how they would save everybody.

Cora was not subsiding, she was worsening. She wouldn't drink the warm milk with laudanum that Jennie held to her mouth. To the screaming she added kicking and then resumed beating on Wes's chest. When Jennie, strong enough a match for a half-starved woman as well as for a Kicky Cow, spelled Wes, the beating on her breasts hurt her, and they reluctantly tied

Cora's hands with soft cloth strips from the doctoring bag. Cora could take no more comfort from Jennie than from Wes, and the screaming continued. The boys covered their heads and Davey cried. Jennie tried again, this time planning to pinch Cora's nostrils and pour the laudanum down her throat, but Cora twisted free and bit her. Nothing they could do would calm her; her screams now tortured her throat.

Tommie was sent to tell George Tiger of Cora's condition, and to ask him to take her to Dr. Phillips in Newport. "Tommie, tell your folks that Willard's gone." George was at their house with horse and sleigh by the time Tommie could walk home. They wrapped Cora in a quilt, bound her feet, and tied the quilt around her. Jennie piled in beside her to give comfort, and off they went. After clogging the river for nearly four months the ice had gone out just the week before, lengthening Cora's nightmare and leaving them eight hours of trying to find a trail around trees, through creekbeds, and up and down hills. By dark they were at the doctor's house, and he helped her to some quiet with a shot of morphine. The next morning, talk of sending her to the mental hospital at Medical Lake finally brought Cora to her senses and she joined the ranks of those who live their lives sane enough not to be locked up. There was no point in her going back to Tiger, and they put her on the train for Yakima, where she said she had folks. The sheriff paid for her ticket out of county funds, but sent along a letter to her family asking for reimbursement.

While Jennie and George drove back home the next day, he described the situation at the Nesbits' as he and the others who went to help had pieced it out from what Willard told them before he died, and from what they found. Willard had apparently gone back out to the woodshed to split more wood, and Boyd had got out of his bed and gone to the stove, stirring up the blaze enough to catch afire the gunny sacks nailed around the stove for warmth. Willard had finally sensed the smoke and gone into the house, shutting the door behind him. He picked up the baby, but was overwhelmed by the smoke. Blinded and confused, he couldn't work the latch to get back out. He climbed out the window with the baby, but was seized with dizziness and dropped Boyd inside. Before he could reach back in for the child, he collapsed on the ground. They found the baby inside, nearly incinerated.

THE HORRIBLE WINTER WASN'T OVER yet. On March 24 the boys came home from school and said Melvin Greenamyer was sent home sick from school. On March 25 word came from the Normans that they needed Jennie to tend Hattie, who'd been kept home sick. Jennie went, and found the little girl feverish with a red, sore throat. She guessed scarlet fever. By the next day Hattie's face was a mask of bright red rash with a white circle around her mouth, proving Jennie right. She diluted some sulfurous acid, gave the girl some drops of it, and wrapped her in a wet sheet. She knew she could depend on Ida Norman, Uriah's sister, to nurse the child carefully, and left enough medicine for her to have some every few hours. The Normans' house was more spacious than most in the area, and she could ask that Hattie be kept in a room by herself, to protect her brothers. She hurried to the school and asked Mr. Deshler if he'd consider closing the school to contain the illness. Unclear whether his salary would continue, Mr. Deshler suggested they not panic, but wait a few days. By the next day 17 of the 26 children were absent, including Tommie and Billie. Jasper, accustomed to running over to the school for recess and lunch hour play, didn't get out of bed. Five of the children still attending wore asafetida bags around their necks, little drawstring sacks made by their mothers and filled with lumps of gum-resin. The odor in the heated schoolroom, not unlike a room full of rancid garlic, weakened Mr. Deshler's resistance to school closure.

Wes was gone back to the Coeur d'Alene region, and nursing the three boys was a fulltime job. Jennie sent for Nettie Phelps and Ruby Belle, both too old to likely contract the disease, and both reliable as messengers and helpers. The girls took word to the infected families that they would have to nurse their own, with instructions on what to do. Jennie sent warning that keeping up with the laundry for the sheet packs would be the biggest challenge. She would send to both doctors, one 50 miles upriver and the other 35 miles across mountain, for more sulfurous acid. Nettie and Ruby Belle reported that all families were cooperative. The school directors agreed to close the school for the remainder of the term, with Mr. Deshler continuing his salary, but spending his free days chopping wood for the next term's heating. Only the Greenamyers suggested a different treatment. They said they knew from Mrs. Greenamyer's grandmother that the best treatment was to withhold liquids, and not urge food.

At home Jennie's only help was Davey, too young to have used the school's communal water ladle. He now spent most of his days outside, hauling water from the creek in the old wagon with Si in the harness. She made beds downstairs for herself and the three sick boys, and let Davey have Si upstairs with him for company at night.

The day after he left, George Tiger came back from Newport with enough sulfurous acid to allow each sick child in the area to be treated every four hours for a week. When Joe Parker came back from Colville with an even larger amount, Jennie made some into an ointment, and allotted some to burn for inhalation. Nettie and Ruby Belle distributed the medicine and the instructions. Jennie told them she'd call, if need be, on the families with the sickest children. It turned out Jennie's own family was almost the worst. Christina Carpenter, whose little boy didn't catch it, increased her visits; her, Nettie's and Ruby Belle's horses were seen on the road all day long.

In their sickness, Tommie and Billie had to be kept from cuddling in one bedroll. Jennie compromised by letting them lie foot to foot, touching but perhaps not reinfecting each other with their breath. Billie's rash was never as serious as Tommie's, his fever never as high. Within a week, he could help with the nursing, taking a special pleasure in burning the obnoxious sulfur. Tommie's and Jasper's cases were not so mild.

Jennie sponged them several times each day and night, and gave them aconite in hot water to bring the fever down. She made them teas of Oregon grape root, chamomile, mint, dried elderberries, wild ginger, venison - anything to tempt them to drink - and had water always at the ready. Tommie did whatever was suggested, and slept most of the day and night. It took two weeks, but by late April he wanted to go outside. She made him wait. They were all tired of the darkened room, but Jasper still needed it to protect his eyes.

On the first day of his affliction, Jasper had come in from feeding the chickens burning hot. His throat was red and swollen, his tongue furry. He was the only one to vomit. From that first day he seemed to be in his own world, uninterested in his family, watching something in the near distance. When Billie asked what he was watching, he said "little dancing circles, with little diamonds in them." Bathed in tepid water, he remained burning hot. He was unresponsive to Jennie's nursing, except to resist her. He wanted no food or drink, had to be forced to take liquids. The tension between them built up. Whenever she approached him, she was braced for trouble. Whenever he saw her coming, he turned his back. He slept little, and usually woke with a headache. Light was torturous. He was irritable and quarrelsome. After three weeks the fever was down but his urine was cloudy, and she tried harder to get him to drink, increasing the opportunities for confrontations. The last straw was when he refused medicine. Exhausted and worried, Jennie found herself dashing from the house, cutting an alder branch, and giving a licking to a sick child. "It's good for you, dammit!"

By now, many of the cases were mending, and she asked Ruby Belle to come stay with her. She wasn't afraid she'd repeat her fury, but she could see they all needed help. To both Jennie's relief and her chagrin, Jasper relaxed with Ruby Belle and took the medicine from her. Shamed, Jennie went about finishing up the little nursing Tommie needed and visited some other households. She found nearly every child recovering, still sleeping much and eating little, but clearly headed for a normal summer.

Though not the Greenamyer children, the ones who had been deprived of liquids. Melvin was out of danger, but extremely weak. He had been sharing a bed with Thelma, to ease the nursing. Thelma died on May Day. All Jennie could do for the Greenamyers was suggest that they bury their four-year-old girl at once, with only a family funeral, to prevent starting another cycle of illness around the area.

When Wes came home for a brief visit a week later, he asked why she hadn't sent for him. "I guess I was too busy to think of it. Wes, I've used so much water bathing those boys over and over, and washing sheets, and trying to sanitize the house, I hope there's some left in the creek." Ruby Belle went home and Wes took over the nursing, reading or telling a story any time someone asked for it. Jennie slept for most of three days. Then Wes went back to the Coeur d'Alene, this time to the Terrible Edith.

The spring had a late start, but by mid-May the aspen were prancing, and the freshly chartreuse tamaracks were waving their branches like the fronds of giant ferns. The cottonwoods were dropping their sweet, shiny husks that perfumed the whole outdoors and sneaked into the house on their shoes. Late afternoons the sun would sit on the edge of the mountains and slant through the wet air to sparkle on Renshaw Creek.

IN THE SUMMER, JENNIE TRAINED Patience to pull the plow, and cultivating became easier. She wondered she hadn't tried it sooner, in planting time. "Pull the plow" is all it was, of course; no cow, not even the personification of this one's name, could be expected to cultivate with traces. Tommie or Billie led the cow with a rope, and kept a feedbag on her to keep her out of the vegetables. Jennie guided the plow, a 16" footburner she'd made over the winter. Plowing with Patience was easier than milking with Kicky Cow. Jennie built sideracks on the wagon and taught the cow to haul to and from the riverbank. Patience took them to dances and parties all over the area. Si might have been miffed at being replaced as the family team, but instead he chose to supervise, trotting importantly at the cow's hooves.

****

JENNIE WAS STIRRING A POT of rhubarb sauce to keep it from scorching when Tommie and Billie came racing down the road from the river and ran gasping into the kitchen. "Ma, Ma, there's a big bull pine washed up at the Landing. Let us make a dugout, Ma. Let us make a dugout." A dugout would be undeniably useful, handling a heavier load than the pinebark canoe, or even the rowboat. She could take a load of vegetables down to sell at the Cement store, and paddle back with money in her skirt. She thought over the various dangers involved for the boys: being on the river bank, using sharp tools, keeping a fire. They were eight and ten, and had their heads on straight. Jasper didn't, but no doubt they'd cooperate in excluding him. It wasn't just that he was only five; since the fever his judgment seemed impaired. If there was a way to hurt himself or them, he'd find it. But she couldn't put them all under glass. She sanctioned the dugout. "But just you two, not the little boys."

There was only one axe for the two boys, but when they kept at it long enough to get the log squared off and the ends trimmed, George Tiger was impressed and gave them free loan of his tools, so long as they were cleaned and returned to their places in his shed after each work session, even counting morning and afternoon separately. Joe Parker got interested in the job, and showed them how to shape and smooth the keel, one boy with an adze, one boy with an axe.

Then he and George Tiger rounded up Hy Maggot and Charlie Lucas and the six of them turned the log back upright. The boys were on their own for the rest. They notched out the top and cut it away, one boy with an axe and one boy with a saw. Then the part that was even more fun: they set a fire in the notched-out hole and had an excuse to stay long hours at the riverbank to tend it, taking turns watching the fire and shucking their clothes for a swim. As the summer advanced and the days were warmer, there was nearly always a naked, long-limbed boy paddling between the shore and the island half way across the river. When the fire had burned a large enough area, they each used an adze to chip out the charred wood, much easier than removing green wood. Then they set another fire and did it all over. The dugout was on the bank all that summer, and sometimes they let the Norman boys help with the work. The Wooding boys' dugout was the summer camp of Tiger's Landing that year.

The hard part for Jennie was keeping Jasper, who still hadn't learned to swim, home from the river. Since his sickness, whatever she disallowed, he wanted. Whenever he was out of sight for long, she was terrified that he had gone to the river. Not that he wanted to help. There was no job he seemed to settle into with inclination or satisfaction. All work was punishment for Jasper. Davey at three was more help than Jasper at five, and much happier. Jasper preferred to play idly alone, imagining personal friends. Prime among them was Mr. Pute Watey, who lived up a tree. Now she had to worry about Jasper's climbing beyond safety. When he grew up, he told them, he was "going to get a black cowhide and make me some black cowhide whiskers, and be a man by the name of Jackson." He never again, after the scarlet fever, had the contentment of being a boy or of being himself. He had strange fears. He came in one day crying and said he'd seen an ant nest on fire over near the Renshaws'. When Jennie saw it across a draw, she almost thought he was right. At closer look, she saw it was covered with bright orange tamarack needles from last fall. The snow had come so early they hadn't had time to lose their vivid color, and retained it under the snow. It was radiant, and she wished Jasper could have been delighted by it instead of frightened. Tommie and Billie took care of one of her concerns, at least, when they picked him up by his arms and legs and threw him in the river, claiming it was high time he learned to swim. Too proud to let them know his terror, he paddled around keeping his head above water until he learned to swim and on the third day he swam within two strokes of the far bank, protesting to her anger that "You just said not to swim across the river - and I didn't." He had a new way now to chafe against her.

On a still day when the smoke was vexing, mixed with low cloud cover, stillness and summer heat, Tommie and Billie again came racing in from the riverbank. "Ma, Ma. Mr. Tiger says we can't use his tools any more. Ma, we aren't done yet with the dugout. Ma, he's mad at us."

She went straight to The Landing. "George, what've they done?"

"They've been real good all summer, Jennie. But when I went out this morning there was an adze hanging there with mud on it, an axe on the floor with mud on it, and a saw missing. It's a lot to expect boys their age to do it right all the time, I know. But that was the deal and I figured you and Wes would want them kept to it."

"You know we would, George. I'm just here to see how we can make this right with you." Ignoring protests of "But, Ma, we didn't," she set the two about cleaning the two muddy tools and putting them away. But they didn't find the saw. She doused the fire in the dugout and disallowed them the riverbank. They searched through Wes's tools with no results. They dug through sawdust in the woodshed without success. Over three days they scoured every spot, indoors and out, where wood was handled; no luck. The next day she saw them through the window with their heads together watching Jasper where he sat on a stump petting a barn cat. An hour later they came in jubilant, with the saw. "It was up Jasper's tree where Pute Watey lives. He says he was cutting a limb off to make a tree house." They were quickly reinstated into George Tiger's graces and went on with their work. When Jennie talked to Jasper about it, he said Mr. Pute Watey did it. Jennie was left with worry. She couldn't afford to have an untrustworthy boy, but it appeared she had one.

Buckets stood at all times beside the dugout, for fear the fire would burn too deeply. Now with the work near the bottom of the canoe, the concern was greater. When Jennie stepped into the house to check on some cottage cheese hanging to drip over the sink, she saw Jasper move furtively away from the kitchen stove. She stepped back, but peered to see why he was sneaky. He slipped out the back door, headed for the riverbank, and she saw him pull her box of matches out of his overalls pocket. Ordinarily she would have taken the matches at once, but this time she wanted to see his intent. She followed him to the riverbank, and saw him pile leaves and wood chips in the canoe to start a fire. Before he could, she stepped forward and took the matches, expecting a struggle. "Give me those, Mister, and no lip." But he didn't seem to mind very much, as he didn't care very much about anything now.

She didn't tell Billie and Tommie about his second misdeed, but she kept him close to her. It wasn't difficult, as he seemed content to sit in the small old wagon and pet a cat.

Jennie had known some crazy people in her life. Religion had been mixed in it in most cases, but not in all. What surprised her about all of them was that they didn't seem crazy all the time. They were often just very quiet, very withdrawn. Then they'd break out into something outrageous and sometimes violent. Old Bert Berkson back in Visalia hung around their laundry day after day, seeming to have nothing to do. He didn't talk to anybody, just watched Jennie and her sister Belle work, or sometimes not even that, just watched the distance. It scared her to see Jasper look that way. When Bert did finally break out and start taking his clothes off, the Sheriff had to take him to the asylum. Jasper didn't do much of anything that would exactly draw the neighbors' attention. But he also didn't seem to want to be part of anything. He was remote from the rest of them. Petting a cat seemed harmless, but the way he did it spelled danger to Jennie. She wanted to get closer to him, but the more she tried the more he pulled away.

WITH ONLY A YEAR TO go before Proving Up, Jennie worried whether she'd improved the place enough. There was the house, now with two stories, the little barn, a shed, the root cellar, the bridge across the creek, the corral, the outhouse, a mile of fencing, the blacksmith shed, the worked soil, the clearing. Would this tally up to the required improvements? When Wes came home briefly from the Terrible Edith, he told John and Orla he hoped he'd be able to make Proof.

"Why wouldn't you, Wes?"

"Well, I'm worried about the fulltime residence requirement. Two times when I've come home, Jennie was visiting at the neighbors." They all laughed. This was his way of bragging about how close to home she'd stayed for four years, she who had been the Rambling Woman. No inspector could claim the place hadn't been lived in. And it surely was improved.

Not satisfied, though, she thought around for another project. Not sure the family needed it, and not sure she could sell the product, she built an icehouse near the creek, just to increase the value of the homestead. George Tiger's sawmill kept going through the fall, and she traded him pies, jerky, fruit leather, sauerkraut, spuds, squashes, dried mushrooms, salted trout, knitted socks and gloves, and one grand turtleneck sweater, for boards. Frank Schmaus showed her how to build the icehouse with double walls, 6" apart and filled with sawdust for insulation. She had enough shakes on hand from previous winters to roof it. She didn't have to trade for the sawdust; George was glad to have Patience haul it away. The roof was on by late December, when the best ice was ready for cutting. That first winter, her learning year, the creek produced all the ice she wanted. With Patience now for hauling, she could go some distance from the house. At the mouth of Renshaw Creek where it entered the Pend d'Oreille, the ice that year formed a foot thick and smooth all across. She took her oldest work boots and drove nails through the soles from the inside, to walk on the ice. Tommie and Billie could work with her, but she wouldn't let them ruin their shoes. As a result they fell down a lot, probably more than required. They loved to pretend to lose balance, slide across the ice, wave their arms for balance, and yell "whoooaah....whooaah..."

Jasper and Davey sat bundled in the wagon. Davey would laugh on cue at his big brothers. Jasper just sat. The little children's wagon was not big enough since Patience had replaced Si as the farm team. For the summer's haying Jennie had built a wagon box. When Wes was home he made it a set of snow runners. For the ice harvest, Tommie and Billie made three scrapers, wooden blades on wooden handles, and the three of them cleared the ice of snow. They waited for a night when moonrise was before dark so they could see. Frank told them to work after dark, when the sun didn't warm the surface. The ice clear, they used Wes's crosscut saw to cut lines across the mouth of the creek, a foot and a half apart. Then they went the other direction, again a foot and a half apart, cutting the ice into blocks. Getting the first one out was tricky, but a peavey did the job; then they could easily pop out the others and slide them across the ice toward the sled. They did only a small load, took it to the icehouse, and made one layer. The next day they brought more sawdust and covered the layer. Through four days Tommie and Billie were sent to keep the snow off the ice patch and let it refreeze. A cold snap gave them clearer, finer ice the second time. They put two feet of sawdust on top of that second layer, and Jernnie decided she had enough for the first venture. They called the job done. Just as well, as the first week of January brought a quick thaw, and the ice was never useful again.

No one but Jennie recognized that at Jasper's age Billie or Tommie would have been part of the crew. They left him to sit in the wagon and pet a cat.

1905

JENNIE'S WINTER PROJECT made the summer surprisingly lucrative for one like her, content with modest fortune. Miners and industrialists couldn't lure Dame Fortune down the river, but She came floating in full regalia to Jennie Wooding, who neither invited nor expected Her.

Dutch Jake's annual picnic in 1905 was held on Midsummer Night's Eve, which fell that year on a full moon, thus plaiting three strands of excitation. Jake always threw his picnic before or after the Fourth of July so as not to compete with that festivity, more a family affair.

Dutch Jake Goetz was the owner of The Coeur d'Alene, the most flourishing beer hall, chop house, music hall and gambling establishment in Spokane. He had named it for the Idaho mining district where he had made the strike that financed his more pleasurable businesses. For this year's picnic Jake had chartered the steamer *SPOKANE* and ordered a lumber barge with a 60-foot canvas canopy lashed to the front, to be pushed ahead of the bow of the big sternwheeler. Dutch Jake's guests included the dealers, pit bosses, rakers, croupiers, waiters, cooks, dishwashers, showgirls, bartenders, bouncers, janitors, maids and handymen from The Coeur d'Alene, as well as Jake's business associates and the higher rolling of his customers, and nearly every politician and policeman in Spokane, only a skeleton crew having remained in town to enforce a degree of law and order. In the early years of the picnic an aide had asked whom to invite. "Infite? Neffer mind infite. Effrypotty velcome." Dutch Jake was averse to exclusiveness.

Jake's 18-piece band that paraded daily through downtown Spokane to drum up business for The Coeur d'Alene was given double pay for the two days of the picnic, their talents being required; half of them would play at any one time, providing constant music during the whole event. Also on duty were what the Spokane *SPOKESMAN-REVIEW* called *risque showgirls,* joining other entertainers: minstrels and interlocutors, an Irish tenor, a comedian, a skirt dancer, and a trained bear.

Dutch Jake's guests would entrain at Spokane, ride an hour to the dock at Newport, and cruise 50 miles downriver to the little town of Cement where they would dock for what might remain of the night, and return upriver the next day. Dutch Jake secured the necessary permits and licenses for 350 picnickers. The *MINER* reported at least 500 partaking, and no lack of food and drink for them all.

The barge provided 750 square feet of dance floor, the 9-piece band played on the *SPOKANE's* generous bow, and the non-dancers crowded into the upper-deck salon and filled both outdoor decks. The barge's two rails supported a half dozen eight-foot firs decorated with streamers. Bunting emblazoned the rails of both barge and boat; flags flew fore, aft, and atop. Decreasing the dance floor by about 100 square feet was the veteran of all his parades and picnics, Dutch Jake's cannon, to be fired as the *SPOKANE* left the dock, as she passed each Landing, and whenever the spirit might move either a crewman or an imbiber.

Dutch Jake provided 75 kegs of beer for the gentlemen, and for the ladies four dozen bottles each of spruce beer, ginger beer and root beer as well as tubs of lemonade. He provided a picnic prepared in the kitchens of all three Newport hotels, with some supplies coming by train from as far as Chicago to the east and Seattle to the west. Local truck farmers, hunters, butchers, fishermen and provisioners large and small had been making deliveries for days. Their bounty was turned into cole slaw, platters of sliced hothouse tomatoes on beds of watercress from local streams, crisp cucumbers and onions in vinegar, three kinds of potato salad, platters of roast beef, corned beef, grouse, duck, goose, chicken, turkey, mutton, ham, smoked Spirit Lake bluebacks and salted Chinook salmon. There were vats of beans baked with generous molasses and mustard, and six kinds of bread and rolls with fresh sweet butter shaped into tiny cannonballs. Local breakfasts had seen few eggs for the past three weeks as they were saved up for their yolks to be deviled and forced through pastry tubes into their serrated whites and presented on beds of kale. There were endless pickles: pickled beans, cucumbers both sweet and dill, onions, and green peppers; pickled red peppers, green tomatoes, zucchinis, and fiddleheads; pickled coral mushrooms, morels, carrots, and baby corn; pickled beets, peaches, cauliflower and broccoli. It wasn't that fresh summer vegetables weren't available. It was that Dutch Jake loved pickles and assumed everyone else did too. He had in addition ordered sauerkraut from five different establishments, spiced with five different condiments.

Dessert alone required two tables: the hotels had gone beyond assiduous to competitive in the production of lavishly decorated and exotically flavored cakes. White cakes, yellow cakes, chocolate cakes, marble cakes and spice cakes were filled with lemon custards and raspberry jellies, frosted with creams and drizzles, and decorated with butter creams in every color, representing all flowers known to the gardens of Washington and Idaho. Most popular of all was the shortcake made with giant Hood River strawberries from local farms, the *SPOKANE*'s modest galley providing fresh biscuits every half hour and cream whipped on the spot every twenty minutes. Washtubs of ice deplenished Newport's icehouses and kept food and ladies' drinks cold. The beer kegs were stored in the river and towed by short rope until a new one was to be tapped; an open keg didn't last long enough to need continued cooling. There was no ice cream; Dutch Jake eschewed excess.

As the *SPOKANE* moved away from the dock and into the current, the band played a number unidentifiable in the din of the whistle that shrilled nonstop until the boat rounded the first bend. The cannon had been shot off six times by then. As the whistle and the cannon finally quieted, locals on the dock who had come to see the fine affair off could make out the departing strains of a German polka from Dutch Jake's homeland.

The *SPOKANE* moved slower than the current down the river, allowing the picnic to roll into full revelry by the time it passed the town of Cusick, where Joe and his cronies cheered and answered the cannon with gunshots in admiration of Dutch Jake and his carousers. Across the river, Kalispel drums encouraged them further. The *SPOKANE* moved on. By the time she reached the Blue Slide, three obstreperous drunks were tied up in the engine room, just out of reach of the bear. Dutch Jake had no patience with those who couldn't hold their liquor.

It was a strict rule on picnic excursions not to put in at any landings on the way downriver. Experience had shown that it was impossible to keep the crew out of the beer, so the risky landings and departures were kept to a minimum. So when the *SPOKANE* rounded Devil's Elbow to the tune of "Money Musk" and blew four toots, as on an ordinary passage, Jennie and the boys were curious enough to head for Tiger's Landing.

Jasper was the first there, in time to see a vision round the bend a mile upriver. The decorations and the dancers seemed afloat, the low barge invisible in the sparkles of the river. Jasper saw people dancing on the river, surrounded by bright ribbons and giant trees. Then the boat came into view: three tiers of people, each on top of another, all in fine dress, the men with flat straw hats and the women in fluffy, gauzy gowns, and all looking his way and cheering. Then his mother and brothers arrived.

Most of the merrymakers suspended their dancing and dining to watch the challenge of the boat navigating to the dock. When the connection was safely made, a cheer went up and the cannon was shot off once again. The Wooding boys cheered and waved to the Captain, Art Flanders, who lived just across the creek from them when he was home. "Jennie," yelled the Captain, "Jake's running out of ice. How about that icehouse of yours? Can you spare us some?"

Leaving Davey and Jasper to watch the dancing, Jennie took the older boys, most of the *SPOKANE*'s crew and their freight dolly double-time to the icehouse, piled the dolly with ice still laced with sawdust, and brought it back to the *SPOKANE* in less than an hour. As they wheeled the dolly, a loaded wheelbarrow, and their little rusted wagon up the landing plank, the boys chanted:

"It ain't a lot, but it's all we got.

It's all we got, and it ain't a lot."

Beautiful ladies from Dutch Jake's variety show were smitten by the four barefooted little boys in homemade shirts who so cheerfully were giving up their summer's ice cream for the sake of the party, and the Wooding boys could tell often and long of the kisses from ladies who looked so beautiful and smelled so fine. Smothered in pink organdy, white dimity, and sky blue chiffon, hugged against bosoms revealed above beribboned and belaced scoop necklines, Tommie, Billie, Jasper and even Davey awakened to a new vision of the World of Women.

A bill for hospitality can be presented to no better person than an inebriated host, and Jake's payment assured that Jennie would always have ice at the ready when a boat arrived. The new icehouse was not only justified, it was lucrative, and Jennie was working out in her head contracts with the Sunday Excursion Boats. The boys could learn what ice cream was another year.

When the *SPOKANE* passed by the next morning, headed back upriver and south, she slipped by Tiger's Landing with no fanfare, many of the male passengers, half the crew, and most of the musicians asleep on the various decks and the barge. Jennie and her crew were busy emptying the icehouse of sawdust and dumping it on the raspberry canes.

IN SEPTEMBER, THOUGH, THE WES Wooding family was not so fortunate. Uriah, George Tiger, and Arthur Norman all made their Final Proof and secured their deeds. Wes and Jennie had come at the same time as Uriah, three years ago, but Wes had been in the Coeur d'Alene at the time they filed, and he wouldn't be eligible until spring. Jennie, of course, a married woman, couldn't claim to be a head of household. That gave her another winter to worry about whether she'd done enough to Prove Up.

BY THE TIME OF HER fifth garden, Jennie had built up four acres, and could sell all she could harvest to neighbors or at the store at Cement. When word came from the mining camp downriver at Metaline that they'd take all the potatoes she could send in the fall, she could see the need for more help, and she put out word she was in the market for a cayuse. A week later two Kalipsels came swimming across the river on two ponies and leading a third. They gave her her choice. She worked each of the three for about a half hour, walked them, rode them, tried them in wagon traces and with the plow, and most importantly watched them stand still, then made her clear choice: the smallest and youngest one. He wasn't fully trained and would require less retraining, had more of his own nature intact. She had $15 cash set aside for the deal, and the Kalipsels accepted if she'd throw in a knitted baby's cap for the older man's papoose.

Within a week Jennie was as fond of Shorty as of any of her nieces. She hadn't realized how much she'd missed horses. She hadn't had one since they left California 11 years ago. Before that her life had been full of horses. As a tyke she'd ridden, with her sister, when the only way to mount in the desert was for one girl to hold the horse's head down, and the other to crawl up its mane and settle on its bare back and pull her sister up. There they'd stay herding cattle until noon when they'd go home, slide off for lunch, and crawl back up again for the afternoon. She and her seven siblings were Pa's crew of cowboys when he broke wild horses for sale. He'd form the kids in two lines in front of the corral and chase the horses toward the children, who waved their arms and hooted to channel the horses into the corral. At seven she and the other children rode bareback droving the family's herd from the Owens Valley of California to Ventura County to homestead, then back again a year later when Pa lost interest in Proving Up. At eight she'd left Pa's pitiful place to go with her sister and husband, an itinerant photographer, to travel in a horsedrawn combination darkroom and gypsy wagon through California, Nevada, Utah, Arizona and New Mexico. As child-of-all-work, she hitched and unhitched the horses and groomed them, standing on a box till she was tall enough to reach the mane to comb it. It was an interesting, ever-changing life, suited to her nature. But she was, after all, a little girl with no mother to caress her. Her sister was not unkind, but was absorbed in her own children. It's possible little Jennie might have turned into a sad child except for the horses. In times of loneliness or low spirits she could lie on a horse's sturdy back, fondling its silky ears between two fingers and petting its sleek neck. This was her life for eight years, till at sixteen she married Wes. For the first seven years of their marriage, she was the chief wagoner, drayman and hostler. She'd loved horses like humans. But since the bust of '93 they hadn't owned one. There'd been rental teams, of course, but you couldn't build a friendship with a hack. Now she knew what she'd missed.

For a week Jennie left the garden to the boys while she made friends with Shorty, built him a stall in the little barn, and moved him in and out of the corral and from tethering spot to spot. Shorty was an ornery little cayuse, and Jennie was a firm handler, but there was something about her need for a horse after a dozen horseless years that permanently gave Shorty the upper hand; he could tell when he'd win a battle if he just held out. He became trained to her expectations, but there was for the 18 years she owned him something of independence and stubbornness about him. She finished his training so that he was a reasonably reliable saddle, wagon, plow and pack horse, but he was never an easy horse for anyone but Jennie.

THE TERRIBLE EDITH CLOSED DOWN for two weeks, and Wes came home. He brought with him a two-month-old puppy, part of a litter out of the mine mascot. "Different ones of us took a puppy, didn't want to leave them to the coyotes." Since he'd presented the puppy with the four boys looking on, it didn't matter whether Jennie thought they needed a second dog or not. Si was sure they did not, and had nothing to do with the newcomer. The puppy was passed among the boys until bedtime, licking their faces, cuddling against their chests, riding like a baby in their old wagon, drinking the milk they brought him. When night came, they asked to have the puppy in their bedroom "so he won't be scared." When that wasn't allowed, each offered to sleep in the woodshed with him. Wes stayed with the *APPEAL TO REASON* and left Jennie to make arrangements. No, she said, a dog sleeps outside, and a dog learns to take care of himself. "But, Ma, he's not a dog, he's a puppy. He'll be scared."

"He'll get over it, too."

"He'll cry, I bet."

"Well, we'll be in here and we won't hear him."

But they did. The puppy had nestled in Wes's vest since he'd left his mother and litter, had never known there was anything as awful in the world as an empty dark barn. His howls began the minute the door was closed on him. Any dog but Si, and any woman but Jennie, would have softened. When Davey tried to sneak down the ladder to go to the rescue, he got swats that sent him back to bed. It was Shorty who solved things. They heard him break out of his stall and heard the puppy cries stop. When they reached the shed, there sat Puppy under Shorty's legs, whimpering only a little as he remembered the horror he'd endured for all of ten minutes. "He's got to learn, dammit." She reached to return Shorty to his stall.

"Ma, let Shorty stay with him. Shorty'll take care of him." At that moment, two coyotes gave their imitation of seven wolves, and she could only yield. "But none of you're staying out here." It was a lame face-saving, and they had to be careful not to smile at each other on the way back to the house, so as not to queer the deal. When she crawled in bed Wes observed, "Glad you won that one, Girlie."

When Shorty was put out to clean up the fall garden refuse, Puppy followed him closely, the only one in the family who didn't have to keep respectful distance from the dangerous rear hooves. Billie gasped in fear for Puppy the first time he saw him jump up and pull on Shorty's tail. But Shorty tolerated it a while, then turned around and gently nosed Puppy away. Puppy waited till Shorty appeared to forget about his tormenter, then pulled again. It became their play all through that fall.

Wes spent his time home cutting cordwood to sell to the steamboats. Having Wes home, working within earshot, coming in for meals with them, talking with her in the bed at night and loving her in the morning, was Heaven.

When he left, he'd be on one of the last boats of the season, and even letters would be unreliable. There were enough intertwined farm roads in the county now to constitute a passable wagon road, so the winter mail could now be sent by sleigh downriver to the post offices at Ione and Cement, if snowfalls allowed. This progress was a mixed blessing. Folks at Tiger's Landing had to take themselves to their designated post office to pick up their own mail. When the boats were running, the Captain would drop off mail at any Landing, but that was sometimes little more than half the year, considering low water time and freezeout time. A ruinous thing had happened last winter to a homesteader who lived far from a post office. His insurance payment was due in December. He got it ready in November to go on the last boat, since he couldn't count on mail service again before March. But the freeze came early again, the boats stopped prematurely, and the payment didn't go. His house burned in January, uninsured.

Jennie's love of the mail was more personal, centering on Wes working in the Outside.

When she couldn't touch him, the letters were next best, and she believed she could usually get a scent of his pockets off the paper, his tobacco especially.

THE NEXT TIME SHE WAS in the Cement store, she asked what it took to get a post office. "How come there's one at Cement and one at Ione, a mile away, and then there ain't one till Ruby, 12 miles away? That's a long way for folks in between to hike on snowshoes." No one really knew, but thought it had to do with how many people wanted one. They knew there'd been a try for one between Ione and Tiger's Landing, to be called Page, but it was turned down because not enough people asked for it. A lot of them wouldn't sign a petition for it because they thought it would encourage too much settling, and they liked things the way they were. "Yeah, I like things the way they are, but I'd like 'em better if the damned mail was easier to get," Jennie rebutted.

She struck quickly. While Wes was home, she had someone to watch the boys and get meals on the table. She had transportation now, and could get around to the neighbors. She had Arthur Norman draw up a petition for her. She gave thought to her traveling appearance. "I oughta look like somebody who could represent the U.S. Government." She pirated from two dresses and made a riding skirt. Sitting aside rather than astride was not her usual way; she'd never wanted to put out the cost of one of those side saddles. But for this occasion decorum and dignity had a high priority. So bareback it would be. Just a bridle on Shorty was a little risky, but she was sure she could manage to stay on in the unfamiliar, awkward, back-straining posture. He threw her only once, and that was right in the yard, when Puppy ran out in front of him. She dusted off the riding skirt, steadied the hat she hadn't worn since their arrival five years ago, gave Shorty a talking to, and was on her way.

She decided her northern limit was the Youngreens and Carpenters, so as not to infringe on Ione's territory. She went only eight miles west up the Tiger Hill Trail, because there was already a post office at Middleport, on Lake Thomas. She didn't want to step on anybody's toes. When she went south as far as the Blue Slide, she ran into a complication she hadn't foreseen. They hadn't thought of it but now that they had, they'd rather have one of their own, and asked to see how a petition looked. She went last, on Saturday, to the folks east and across the river, so that Tommie could be out of school and go with her. She rowed and he held the rein on Shorty, who swam. Then Tommie rowed back home, instructed to be at the riverbank before dinner time, so he could row back over for her when she yelled. She went downriver as far as the trail that headed up to Sullivan Lake, and found that the people there, too, thought a post office was a good idea. She quit while she was ahead, amazed to find that the four families and six bachelors that were in the area when the Woodings settled just five years ago were now 33, coming to 61 names on the petition. Starting soon after the Woodings moved in and showed that this was a fit place for families, various bachelors had gone out to find wives and bring them back, sometimes with ready-made families. The finished survey had brought lots of new families, and the filled post office petition went off to Washington, D.C.

Without waiting for official notice, which would doubtless come after snow flew, the neighbors got together again for the construction. George Tiger, always ambitious for his "town," insisted they make it big enough to hold a store, even though no one was proposing to start a store. He donated the logs and the land, and the neighbors erected the Tiger Store and Post Office on the bank of the Pend d'Oreille where the riverboats would bring the mail.

To Jennie's surprise, approval of the petition came back almost at once, asking her to submit three possible names for the new post office. "I ain't about to ride that route again, George. Let's just us pick out three names." They sent in the obvious one, Tiger's Landing; Devil's Elbow for the big bend of the river that brought the boats to George's landing; and Hawthorn, a reference to the tough little tree they all loved and hated, and which gave its name to Jennie's homestead and the school. The Government, the return letter said, liked brief names; the post office would be called Tiger, and it would open January 1 if a qualified Postmaster could be found. Within a year there were post offices Downriver, called Yocum, Blueslide, Crescent, Sullivan, Big Meadows, and Metaline. "You mean they heard about my petition way down there? People sure don't mind stealing a good idea when they hear one." Wes thought it might have had more to do with increased population.

1906

THE GOVERNMENT WAS able to get the post office open only three weeks later than they'd promised. In late January a month-long thaw opened the river channel, and an interesting little man, Emmanuel F. Yoder, entered their lives. He'd worked elsewhere for the U.S. Postal Service, his wife had recently died, and the reclusiveness of the Tiger position, combined with the chance for some still unclaimed land, brought him down the river. He was full of regulations and devoid of humor, though not of human warmth. Self-importance wasn't a common thing among the settlers, but they had tolerated worse faults in each other, and they accepted his as what came with the territory if you invited the government to your front door. They toted up the bank and installed in the log post office the ornate postal boxes of brass and glass that came on the boat with E.F. Yoder. They thought everything was ready for delivery.

And everything was ready except the boat crew. Now, the boat crew didn't have to live with Emmanuel F. Yoder, and they didn't have to condone his loftiness. On his trip downriver, he had unknowingly insulted Purser Charlie Barker by not looking directly at Charlie nor offering to help when instructing "Please have dose crates unloaded at de United States Post Office at Tiger."

It turned out Charlie was again the Purser on the *SPOKANE* when it came down three days later. The mail for Tiger was bagged and well labeled and laid in the baggage room next to the mail for Ione and Cement. Charlie understood perfectly what was intended, but Charlie's pride in his professional stature was just as vigorous as Emmanuel's. When the *SPOKANE* reached Tiger's Landing, there was no other reason to stop than to deliver the mail. Charlie told Captain Flanders, who didn't deal directly with freight, that he could move right on to Ione. There the Tiger bag was unloaded with the Ione bag. When questioned, Charlie said, "Oh, I think that's that big shipment George Tiger's expecting, and he gets his mail here at Ione, doesn't he?"

A similar thing happened on the next delivery. On a hunch, Jennie put on her riding skirt and she and Shorty went to see what they could do about the situation. She came back with the mailbag, and delivered it to the Tiger Post Office. She did the same for two weeks, then one day went in early to arrive before the boat. "Charlie, you're being a horse's ass. I don't care if you like our new Postmaster or you don't, but I got other things to do than ride this horse eight miles whenever I want my mail." Thereafter the mail was delivered to the riverbank at Tiger's Landing, but not up the bank to the Post Office; that much Emmanuel F. Yoder, alone among Pend d'Oreille Postmasters, would ever after have to do himself.

WES WAS HOME AGAIN IN February, the Nabob mine in the Coeur d'Alenes not proving out too well. From the minute she saw him coming off the *RED CLOUD*, hunched against a sharp snow-spitting wind, Jennie knew there was more bothering him than the stopping of wages or the loss of eyesight. With the crackle of tamarack in the banked stove drifting up to their room, he told her about his qualms. Word had come of a man in Idaho, at Caldwell way up the Snake River near Boise, being blown up by a bomb planted in his gatepost. "And, Jennie, they have the dastard that did it, and he claims he was hired to do it by the Western Federation of Miners, in fact by Big Bill Haywood himself." True, the victim, Frank Steunenberg, had done some despicable things himself. "He was the Governor of Idaho six years ago when the state troopers put all those miners in a bullpen, brought in federal troops, and some miners got bayoneted. He was a union buster of the worst kind, after he was elected because people thought he was pro-Union. A blood-dripping wolf in sheep's clothing. But he was also a family man going home to his wife and children, and nobody deserves to have that happen to them. His little girl was watching for him out the window and saw it, and she was the first one out of the house to get to him."

"Oh, Sweet Jesus, Wes."

"This Harry Orchard skunk who admits he did it is pure slime. But Big Bill Haywood is an idol to me. If there's anything to the story that Big Bill is part of it, that makes me wonder about what direction Unionism is going. I want to see a better deal for working stiffs, sure, but I don't want to be part of a thing like that to get it."

"Caldwell's a long way from Coeur d'Alene, and longer from Tiger's Landing."

"But it's the same Union. It's the only defense guys like me have against the mine owners. This isn't like the gold panning you and I used to do in California, Jennie. That just took a pick and a pack and a pan and a spade, and you knew you had some chance at finding something for yourself. This silver and lead mining is different. It takes big capital to get it out of the ground; you need tunnels and tracks and hoists and explosives and concentrators. So men like me are just paid stiffs. The Owners can put us in tunnels that are waiting to fall in on us. They can pay us anything they want. They can hire too many men when the market's best for them, and lay us off any old time. They can work us 16 hours a day in wet tunnels till our lungs wear out, then throw us away and get a new guy. They can get away with anything at all, because they can borrow money at the banks or from their Fat Cat friends back East. I want like bejesus to even up the battle."

"How can you do that?"

"By all the miners working together. And the United Federation of Miners was connecting us all together from Arizona to Colorado to Montana to Washington. And it looked like a great thing for all of us. Jennie, I've been believing in it, and recruiting for it, and I guess evangelizing for it. Oh, I'd heard a little about miners using dynamite to blow up a mine here and there, but I didn't think it was the Union, just some renegade members, and I could see how frustrated a man could get with the owners bringing in scabs. Jennie, when they took a train and blew up the Bunker Hill concentrator, people lined the tracks to cheer them. It was a war, really, and both sides fought dirty sometimes. But now this is just plain murder, right at a man's home. No matter how good the idea of the Union looks, I can't be part of that."

"Maybe you're jumping ahead of things. If this Orchard guy is coward enough to do something like that, wouldn't he tell any kind of a lie to save his hide? I wouldn't judge Big Bill too fast. Is there gonna be a trial, or what?"

"Lord knows how long that'll take."

He talked for hours. She came to see that while she had just one life, the one here at Tiger's Landing, he had two: this one that she knew about; and the one in the Coeur d'Alenes where he'd been earning money to bring home, but had also been working for his old dream of all people with an equal chance. She listened through the night and came to see that Unionism was his religion. This quandary he was in was soul-wrenching. He talked on and she listened on. Finally a log fell in the stove downstairs and brought them back to the present, and the thought of the morning's duties told them to get to sleep.

His conscience too confused, Wes didn't go back into the mines.

IN MARCH THEY FINALLY PROVED Up, as easily as Wes had expected. His brother-in-law Arthur Norman and his brother/cousin Uriah went with him to Newport as witnesses. They testified that the family had been in constant residence (how constant, only Jennie knew), that five acres or more were cleared, and that the following improvements had accrued:

two-story log house, 14' X 24'	$150
root cellar	6
7 acres fenced	65
outhouse	3
chicken coop with stick fence	3
barn	50
toolshed and smithy	10
bridge over creek	8
woodshed	5
10 fruit trees	5
200 strawberry plants	2
icehouse	28
Total	$335

They got their Proof back in two weeks, signed by Teddy. When the weather warmed in May, it was time for a celebration, held inside and outside the $50 barn. John Renshaw and Nettie Phelps provided the music, all the neighbors provided the midnight supper. Jennie's elderberry blossom wine of a year ago christened their homestead Hawthorn Lodge. The area already sported other proud names, and there'd been a christening party for each one. Besides Hawthorn Lodge, there were other botanicals: Wildwood and Uriah's Cedar Valley; the topographic: Fairview, Lakeview, Bellview, Hillside, George Tiger's Devil's Elbow, Lost Creek, Pleasant Valley; the homesick: Missouri Hill and The Euclid by some people from Ohio; and far up the valley side The Acme and the Royal Crown.

At the Wooding celebration the hawthorn trees that surrounded their namesake were blossoming, and the cause of much teasing. Hawthorn in bloom can, in large numbers, give a strong scent, ultrasweet and putrid, remindful of fish slime on a surface where the fish lay overnight. Whenever a movement of air stirred the aura, there came an affectionate josh. "Think it's time to move that outhouse, Wes?" "Ain't that Davey out of diapers yet?"

Frank Schmaus chipped in, "I'f had sauerkraut go bad, Chennie, but it don't touch yours." Months and years after the night of dancing, though, when they remembered the party some thought of the music, some of the stars, some of old friends, some of the food, but everyone thought with fondness of the surrounding glen of ivory blossoms with their gentle putrescence.

Jennie fed everyone breakfast of cornmeal mush with honey, fried eggs, warm frothy milk, and coffee from beans the boys had spent yesterday roasting and grinding. When the light was good enough for them to find their way, people hitched up their wagons and yelled their goodbyes. The boys slept in, Wes taking their early morning chores. Coming in with a load of wood, Wes saw Jennie at the sink with a look of more content than is common on early morning dishwashers. "Pretty proud of yourself, building up a valuable piece of property, eh, Jennie?"

"Proud of myself, building a home."

Stunned, they both realized they had reached this point with different expectations. "Wes, you ain't thinking this is something to sell, are you?"

"Well, isn't that what we'd been waiting for, to Prove Up and use the place to get a better one?"

"Maybe" was all she said, wanting to mull a while on that. He went over to the river to help put together a raft of posts for Uriah, and she went on with the dishes. She could see that neither of them had realized they'd drifted down different channels of the stream. She tried to remember the conversation back in Pilchuk that had brought them here. Had anyone said anything about what they'd do with the homestead if they got it? Had she really meant to give up the gypsying for good? At what point in the six years had she come to think this was permanent? At what point had Wes come to see it as disposable property? She'd been here six years, day by day tending the place and making it grow, just as she had the boys. Like a child, could you fail to love it after that?

Billie was the first down the ladder. "Billie, remember that house we lived in back in Pilchuk?"

"Nope."

She hadn't thought of it before. Except for Tommie, Hawthorn Lodge was the only home the boys knew. The idea of a home as something rare, something to be hard won, was something they didn't know. She guessed she was glad for that. She could see how different their childhood was from her own. Ma and Pa moved their brood from one rental farm to another every year or two. When she was with Anna and James and the kids in the photographer's wagon, they stayed put anywhere from a day to six months. It might sound adventurous, but it didn't have the richness of earning and building and loving your own place. And now she needed to mull that over.

When Wes came back, he'd been talking to Ben Harshberger about land Ben had bought in Utah, on the Colorado border. "Ben says there's some for sale next door in Colorado between the towns of Bedrock and Paradox. There must be some kind of a joke in there, Jennie." But she wasn't in a mind for jokes.

Three days later Ben was back downriver and Wes brought him to the house for dinner. Now that they'd Proved Up, they could sell off poles from the place. They'd have a bigger piece of money than they'd ever had at one time. Ben cruised 80 acres and gave Wes a figure he could expect to get for a year's worth of thinning. They subtracted the wages for two men to help with the logging, and Ben said he'd look for a piece for Wes and Jennie when he next went down to Utah.

When they were alone, Jennie asked if he was sure this was what he wanted to do.

"I believe so, Jennie. How about you?"

"Maybe not."

Neither of them wanted to battle it out; the differences were too deep. She resigned herself to the move, and planted the entire garden in potatoes to sell at the Bella May. She wouldn't need a harvest for the larder; she'd be starting all over next spring in Colorado. The poles started going in 60-foot rafts upriver to the train at Newport, brands on their ends to show which settler got the money, destined for their job as utility poles in places where they had telephones to break into everybody's quiet and electricity to put a glare in every corner. The only good she could see in the coming move was that Wes would not be in the woods. His eyes weren't any better in a mine or on a farm, but there were fewer things to watch out for that could fall on a man and maim him.

IN JUNE THE *NEW VOLUNTEER* brought Ruby Belle home from school in Seattle. On her first morning she came to Jennie's kitchen in tears. "Aunt Jennie, when I get here I love it so much, but the time here is spoiled by thinking about the next term. I wish Mama'd give up on this high school idea. She thinks I'll marry somebody in Seattle that's better than who is around here, but I don't see 'better' the same way she does."

"Ruby Belle, have you seen Jimmie Mansfield since you've been back?"

"Aunt Jennie, you knew!"

"Everybody around knows, except your mother. And I guess she knows, but won't allow it's possible. She's still hoping somebody in Seattle will catch your eye, and you'll end up better off than she is."

"Better off how? No one I know in Seattle has as many cedar trees as Pa has. No one there can watch the stars or the river the way we can. What does she think is 'better'?" When Ruby Belle's tears were dried and she'd shared a chuckle over the latest E.F. Yoder story, she went home. Jennie thought some more about the dispute between herself and Wes. Maybe Wes's idea of 'better' was different from her own. She'd been thinking it was the way only of men to be cursed by always wanting to do better and have more. But here was Ada making her own family unhappy with the same notions. Ruby Belle was right. Jennie had seen most of the West, and there wasn't anywhere better than the Pend d'Oreille Valley. On the other hand, there weren't any men better than Wes, sore eyes and all. Why did it have to be a choice?

ON A MORNING IN JULY when the river fog hadn't lifted by midmorning Tommie went out to get Shorty to load him with tent, cooking gear, and fishing poles for a stay up Tiger Hill at Nile Lake for himself and Billie. They'd lined up customers for cutthroat. Only the new buckskin cayuse, Doll, was in the corral. He checked the potato field, since Shorty sometimes pretended to confuse spring and fall and would nibble away where he shouldn't. No Shorty. He assumed Shorty and Rover (which Puppy had grown to be) were off somewhere together until Jasper came in from the Landing road with both Rover and Si. Still, he was sure they'd just missed him in the fog. "Well, let's try Doll out. See if we've taught her anything." They strapped the wooden pack saddle on Doll. In the kitchen Davey was trying to convince his mother that five was old enough for a fishing trip. Tommie put his head in. "We're off, Ma. Shorty's not around, but he'll come home when it gets dark."

He didn't. The next morning, mentally scolding the absent boys who had taken her only transportation, she used as a crew the two little boys who were left to her: Davey five years old and Jasper absent-minded. The three of them split up, and walked all the fenced acres, checked every homestead within two miles, and inquired at all the tents by the river where disappointed would-be settlers were trying to decide where to go next to find land. Jennie had reluctantly spared the older boys from field work to allow them their outing, but now that she needed the little ones to search for Shorty, she was sorry she had. On the third day Tommie and Billie were back with 200 cutthroat in lidded buckets and barrels full of water tied on the horses. They delivered the fish and picked up the search again. They didn't find Shorty either, and Jennie was sure she'd lost the wily little cayuse that gave her a chuckle a day. Then Wes came to tell her she was about to lose more than that.

"Jennie, Ben Harshberger writes that he's bought us a place in Colorado."

"He bought us land we ain't seen?"

"I asked him to, if it was going fast. Look at all the poor out-of-luck folks over at the riverbank. They didn't get here fast enough, and the land's all gone. I don't want that to happen to us in Colorado."

"Wes, what if it ain't any good? What if it don't have water on it, for instance? How do you know what it looks like?"

"Ben's a good scout. I trust him to find us a good piece. So I think I'll go down there and start getting things ready for you and the boys."

She could feel her Paradise slipping away. For 14 years they had chased rainbows through Arizona, California, and Washington. Now for just six years they'd been working in one direction, and had built the best home Jennie'd ever stepped foot in. She knew for a certainty there wasn't anything better than what they had right here. To have a home as good as this one, and to have made it with your own hands, it couldn't be any better than this.

"Wes, why do you think Colorado will be better?"

"Jennie, this is just a little backwater. With what we can sell this place for, we can set up really well down there. Ben says there's lots of cattle country there, people getting rich in it."

"What's it look like, Wes?"

"Like everyplace else, I guess."

Her anger rose. Did this idea of leaving their home come from his disillusionment with the Union? Did he just want to get further away from that? "How many places have we lived in, Wes? Was any of them better? Is this going to be better just because it's in a state we ain't tried yet?"

"Jennie, we've only traded off some poles from this place and already we've got the land there all paid for. Think what we can do with the sale money." She wondered to herself what influence Uriah had had in this.

When she didn't answer him, Wes said, "I'm going on Wednesday's boat, Jennie."

So it was done. She packed a trunk with all Wes's clothes and the things they could do without for a few months: Naomi and Alma's still staring doll, the photograph collection, all Wes's books and everybody's winter wraps. They'd be in Colorado before cold weather. She couldn't remember ever going ahead with something that felt so wrong. She talked some to Tommie and Billie about it. They didn't want to leave, especially, but they thought maybe a cattle ranch would be fun, too.

June was a painful time to say goodbye. The wild roses and the mock orange came into bloom. The cottonwood fluff on a breezy day flew horizontally through the air like a slow fleet going north. As she went about the late chores during the long, gentle evenings, the sweetness of the cottonwoods was a caress. When five acres of potatoes came into bloom at the same time, she couldn't believe they were going to give this up.

She tried to think of things she could give away to Ada's girls or to neighbors, but she couldn't make herself give up one more thing. It was good the boys were old enough to take care of the chores, because her heart wasn't in it. She moved slowly, with head down and eyes often closed when she stood still. She thought she'd pay goodbye visits, starting with Orla and Nettie. But she could see her despondency was a burden on them, and didn't try again. Most days she tried looking for Shorty, going a little farther afield each time, always with no luck. She planned the uprooting. Si was too old for another move; maybe Uriah'd take him. Rover could go. It should be easy to sell Doll and Patience, with so many settlers coming in. It looked as if she wouldn't have to make a decision about Shorty. The rowboat she planned to give to George Tiger; his was getting dilapidated, and they owed him a lot. She'd let the boys try to sell the dugout and keep the money for their own. The crop should get them to Colorado and help them settle in. A move never was profitable; so many things had to be replaced. Would there even be a house on the new place, or would they be starting again from scratch?

Part of her trouble was that she didn't have enough work to do. She had no winter wood to get in, expecting to leave as soon as she sold the potatoes. A single crop was easier than a diverse one, and for the first time she could find herself caught up on garden work. Nothing was ready to butcher yet. There was no point in building anything new, as she had every other year. She spent some time cutting and drying herbs; those they'd need wherever they were. She made no move toward finding a buyer for Hawthorn Lodge and its 159 partly logged-off acres. For one thing, it would be so easy they could do it at the last minute. For another, buying and selling land seemed to be to Wes's taste, but it sure as hell wasn't to hers.

At the end of July the *NEW VOLUNTEER* brought a letter from Wes. She took it to the bench outside the post office, above the river. She sat to slowly puzzle it out, and braced herself for his summons. But no! He was coming home, bringing the trunk. It would be a while yet; he was blind again. The dust around Paradox was even worse than that in the Owens Valley. The good luck was that he'd been able to back out of the deal on the land, and when he could get home he'd have most of the money from the poles. Ben Harshberger was putting him up, and was sorry about everything. And the last line: he wanted to stay put in the Pend d'Oreille, and he'd talk about it when he could lie in bed with her and listen to the aspens.

She went first to George Tiger, who was home just now. He could see her joy as she reached his doorstep. "Jennie, I'm glad. For you. For me. For the town." She went next back to the post office, and told Emmanuel Yoder the news, and that he was free to spread it to anyone he thought would be interested. Emmanuel thought that would be about everyone. She was embarrassed to go to Orla and Nettie's after they'd let her cry on their tablecloth, but she had to tell them. John picked up his fiddle, and the women took her hands and pulled her into a ring-a-rosy. Last, she went to tell Uriah, as Wes had asked her to, but he wasn't in. Ada said she was sorry for Jennie, that to get out of here was all she herself thought about. As Jennie walked the mile home, she pondered on what she could have said to that. Orla and Nettie and everyone reached out to Jennie so, but Jennie didn't know how to send the favor on to Ada.

Then a rain started, a special boon. They wouldn't have to carry water to the spuds this week, and her valley would keep its midsummer vibrancy a while longer.

JENNIE WAS AT THE RIVER to meet the boat one afternoon in August, in case there was another letter. As the boat entered Devil's Elbow, she could see a tall man, not Wes, waving his arms on the upper deck. Then she could see his hat was in his hand and he was swinging it around his head; then she could tell that he was yelling as loud as he could toward the Landing. After a bit she could make out her own name. He kept it up till the boat landed, then ran down the gangplank and straight to Jennie, still waving his arms and hat. "Jen, Jen! Hey, Jen! Ora found your horse. Ora found your horse." It was Jeff Honsinger, from six miles up the river; he'd taken the boat down expressly to bring her the news. "Ora found your horse. And if you come up he'll go with you and show you where he found your horse." Jeff Honsinger was a big, raw-boned, loose-jointed, loud-spoken fellow. You usually could hear him before you could see him. His exuberance made him loved on both banks of the river for ten miles in either direction.

"Come on, Jen, let's go. Ora found your horse. Come on up and get him." He was ready for her to start the hike back upriver with him straightaway.

"Jeff, even for Shorty, I can't run off and disappear. I'll get the boys set up and come up on the evening boat and stay over."

He waved his hat again. "Jen, Ora found your horse. Hallelujah! See you later." And he turned and started up the river bank, holding the hat ahead of him to push brush out of his face on the narrow trail. She heard one last laugh, and "Ora found Jen's horse" as he went out of sight in a red willow thicket.

Jennie caught the *RED CLOUD* on its way back upriver; she never left the lower deck, scanning the riverbank for Shorty. By the time she arrived at Yocum it was too close to dusk to start the search. In the morning 17-year-old Ora, even more gangly than his father, was slow to rise and slower to dress; he dragged through his chores. He was slow at everything but his breakfast. By the time they were ready to go, the August day was already heating up. Lydia Honsinger went to prepare two jars of water for them to take, but the boy rejected it. "Ma, we don't want to have to lug all that." Ten minutes out, the valley rose, and in another ten minutes Ora wanted water. Jennie ignored him, kept climbing in the lead. She knew he wanted to turn back, but she kept going, meandering on up, slow but sure, under and over and around logs and through brush. "So thick," she told later, "it'd barely let a hummingbird through." About a quarter mile from the top they saw fresh tracks and signs of a horse. But no horse, and still no water. The only water they knew was down a draw in Lost Creek, just as far down the other side of the hill as they had come up. Ora wanted to go down; Jennie tried to dissuade him. She wondered herself how you could be so parched when the air was so humid, but she kept quiet about it. Not Ora. He complained constantly, and nothing doing but that, instead of following the horse tracks, they had to go down to the creek, still crawling over windfalls, through brush and around nettles, just as thick on this side as on the other.

There were no signs of the horse down here in the draw. Mosquitos were drawn in hordes to their sweaty foreheads and necks and gave Ora yet another thing to bellyache about. Jennie'd had enough; she led the way five miles back to Lydia and Jeff's, intending to walk another five miles down the riverbank to home. Lydia interfered. "When did you tell the folks you'd be home?"

"I told them I'd be home when I seen that horse, to know whether he was Shorty or not. I'm gonna come back on a day that ain't so hot."

"Hooey. You're here now. You'll stay all night and you and Ora are going to go and get that horse. Ora'll be haying in a couple of days, and there's no need for you to catch that cayuse and lead him all the way back down by yourself. Ora, you'll get yourself out of bed and be off when it's cool."

The next morning Lydia set them on their way at five o'clock, each with a rucksack with a bottle of water with a little mint tea added. No nonsense from Ora this time. They went back over the same route to where they'd seen signs of the horse the day before. They followed his well-beaten trail into a brushy valley. "And there he was," she told at dinner, "standing right by a nice little stream of water as if he'd been there all his life." When Jennie spoke to him he pricked up his ears and started right for her. He took the salt she'd brought and licked her hand until she pulled it away. Apparently Shorty the roamer had wandered into the vale and couldn't find his way out. He had lots of feed and water, but was pretty well eaten up by flies. By ten in the morning they were back at the Honsingers, having gone no more than a mile and a half from the house. Easily Jennie could have done the job the first day without Ora's help.

"Lyd's fixin' a good dinner, Jen, you've got to stay." She did, and afterward they sat on the porch watching Shorty at the nearby hitching post.

Jennie at last felt she could politely leave. "When I was younger, I could jump on a lot bigger horse than Shorty, but I don't know as I can now." Lydia offered to get a chair, Jeff suggested leading the cayuse to a stump. Suddenly Jennie felt all the relief and joy of having restored to her Wes and Hawthorn Lodge and Shorty all in one week. She threw her cape over Shorty's back and with one leap hopped on. Jeff's loud voice shrilled, "She's on. Lyd, she's on. God, Lyd, she's on," his arms swinging and flopping in the breeze like a bird fanning his wings for takeoff. Jennie laughed all the way home at the memory.

When she got there, Rover was tickled to see Shorty. He ran to him, smelled him, jumped up to put his paws on the cayuse's nose. Shorty nuzzled around the dog. The first boy Jennie saw was Tommie, and she threw her arms around him and swung the big 12-year-old off the ground, her head thrown back in laughter. Then she headed for the icehouse, deciding what needed doing if she was to have ice to sell. It was her place again to build on.

WHEN SHE SAW WES ON the deck of the *NEW VOLUNTEER* she knew he couldn't see her, and she knew by the shake of his head that he needed her help. The Army Engineers were still blasting to make the Box Canyon navigable, and the sound of the detonations added to his confusion. She went up to him. Their hug was long and still. Then she took his arm and without appearing to assist him made sure he got to the ground safely. The boys took his luggage, and they all climbed into the wagon and drove home. The boys toured him around the improved icehouse and showed him how fast they could sew potato bags shut. They knew they weren't moving to Colorado, but they wanted to hear stories of the cattle ranches just the same. They sat by the creek under the alders and watched a kingfisher work the water while Wes made up stories of Colorado that, strangely, had little boys named Jasper and Davey in them. Tommie and Billie smiled indulgently, gratified at this acknowledgment of their maturity. They remembered when they were the little boys in the stories Pa told.

When they came in for dinner she greeted them: "Well, we've sure as hell got enough spuds. I shot this fool hen today, and here's some sauerkraut Frank Schmaus sent over when he heard we wasn't going after all. We'll be eating this year like we did the first year, when there wasn't no garden."

"Doesn't George Tiger have anyone to run that store yet? This year we have cash, if we just had a store to spend it at."

Jennie could usually see an idea whole, and she did now. "One time you said I could run a store, Wes. What's it take to get into one?"

"By God, you're right, Girlie. Some of that pole money could go to set up a store instead of for dusty land in Colorado. People come here to get their mail, and they'd get their groceries and dry goods and hardware, if it was here. Jennie, that's damn smart. You and George Tiger know how to get a town going, don't you?"

Jennie was sure Wes knew more about mercantile merchandise than she did, so she worked on the potato shipment while he rode Doll down to the Cement store to let Hiram Hatler tell him where to order merchandise, how to keep accounts, and what to charge. "And watch out for credit, Wes. You can't help out everybody that needs help, or you'll end up needing help yourself."

JENNIE AND WES WERE IN bed with the window open, the cottonwoods and aspens whooshing outside, the cedar he'd cut down scenting the room. From the south window they could see the moon rise over the mountains to the east. Wes lay on his back, hands clasped behind his head, elbows out. "Jennie, as soon as I started out of Spokane on the train, I knew I'd had enough of starting over. You were right, Girlie. If gypsying ever is good for anybody, it's for young people. From there on I was pretty much in a funk. It was hotter than hell as I went south, and I'd think about you here in the trees, the boys playing in the creek. Jennie, this is Heaven. I want to keep us here, and keep us together all we can. We've tried about everything there is to make a dollar, and this funny old farm is paying off better than anything else did. We're finally pulling out of '93." He rolled toward her, and found her cheeks wet. He kissed them and wiped them. The moon was going up past the window now, and the sky was a clear, dark blue. Stars were starting to sparkle.

From the barn Shorty whinnied in agreement. "Shorty had a sad summer, too. He says he's going to stay home from now on."

IT WAS DAUNTING TO DEAL with the big merchandise firms in Spokane. The *RUTH* brought a cash register and two display cases, all they could afford. Neighbors turned up half a dozen odd tables to hold goods. Tommie and Billie made sawhorses, and crates and barrels held the rest. The *RED CLOUD* brought a collection of buckets and tubs, shovels, rakes, hoes, coulters, wheelbarrows, nails, hammers, crow bars, cultivators, lanterns and horse tack. The *NEW VOLUNTEER* brought yard goods, thread, overalls, work shirts, gloves, socks, and work caps. The *SPOKANE* brought cheese, flour, saleratus, salt, white sugar, brown sugar, molasses, nutmeg, pepper, cinnamon, beans, coffee beans, tea, and cocoa. Homesteaders brought in seasonal turns pork, veal, beef, sausage, venison, bear, strawberries, potatoes, cabbages, squashes, turnips, rutabagas, parsnips, root beer, birch beer, and five kinds of herbs for teas. They managed to cram it all into the 20' X 30' room, along with E.F.Yoder's United States Post Office. Money went out in large amounts and came in in small amounts, but it did come in. And Wes was right. She hadn't had to worry about her lack of school skills: she knew dollars and cents and could use a scale; she could read the names of things on the labels, if not all the fine print; and she could always look at the picture on a can. For the first year Davey was with her in the store, and the other three came there as soon as school was out. It was hard convincing them that the storeowner's children didn't have the privilege of free candy. After their own efforts were closed down, they taught other boys to snitch the candy, taking a share for the information. It took her almost till spring to catch onto that.

"DAVE" THE
JUVENIL-
PACKER·OF·THE
PEND·O·OREILLE·
·VALLEY·

PART II
GROWING PAINS

1907 – 1915

1907

FOR SEVEN YEARS Jennie had been thinking she'd Prove Up and then luxuriate in free time, finally put trim board around all the windows, put in more flowers just for the looks and the smell, take on all the fancy sewing she wanted, like those plaid shirts with big flat collars the boys in town were wearing, and just generally be a Lady of Grace secluded in the Hawthorn Lodge. But the store changed that, tying her there for hours each day. There wasn't always a lot being sold or traded, but there was always someone hanging around, expecting at least conversation. "Wes, I'm trapped there - every lonesome galoot in the country knows they can come and chew and chaw at the store."

"Jennie, if you weren't such a good conversationalist, if you didn't look so truly pleased to see them, maybe they'd stay in their cabins. In fact, Charlie Lucas told me he left his chicken house half cleaned the other day and came down to the store because he couldn't bear to think about poor Aunt Jennie maybe being all alone."

"Horse pucky," she replied.

She thought it over. The first year, that first blessed winter snowed in in Hawthorn Lodge with the boys, had been a revelation. Maybe people were made for a lot more isolation than they realized. Now Hawthorn Lodge was Proved Up, and she could sit on her laurels, stay home and polish them. But instead here she was in the center of what could be called a town, chewing the rag with everybody who strayed in. Did people ever do what they really wanted? Know what they really wanted? Maybe they were like the boys - going for candy and more candy, when even they knew they'd feel better without it.

But it turned out, tethered as she was, that she met a lot of folks she otherwise wouldn't. The woods were full of people who came out only to buy their flour and lard or trade their cabbages - or, increasingly, to buy some coffee or sugar, luxuries they couldn't resist when they were right in front of their faces. "Wes, five years ago people used wild honey for their pies; now they buy sugar. They used beet root for coffee; now they buy it year round instead of just for Christmas. Are we going to make them all go broke?"

"Wes and Jennie Wooding, exploitive capitalists, huh? I wouldn't worry about your Christian soul, Jennie. If anybody's getting rich, it's Parker Brothers Wholesalers, not us."

With Davey in school now, Jennie was briefly alone in the store for the first hour of the day, as a rule. She appreciated the time to get the fire going, dust off the hard goods, and see what was running out. One damp morning a man she hadn't met came in. He had high boots laced over tan canvas pants, a six-button double-breasted black shirt, and a broad-brimmed black felt hat. He was neither miner, woodsman nor farmer. He spoke with an educated sound. He bought enough staples for three months, called his dignified dog, and rode off in the direction of Tiger Hill with the goods in leather pack bags. "At this rate, we'll be well acquainted in 15 years," she told Wes.

"That's Frank Darrow, Jennie. He came here from Chicago. He has a place up near Middleport. Lives alone. They say the house is lined with books. He's supposed to be Clarence Darrow's brother or cousin. You know, that lawyer that defended Big Bill Haywood and some Wobblies? John Renshaw thinks he came out to Idaho to help his brother with the case, but then got kind of fed up, disillusioned with both sides. Like me, come to think of it, huh? Anyway, he does live kind of like a recluse. If you get an opening, Jennie, I'd like to know him better. If he lugged a house full of books up that hill, he must be worth talking to."

"Sounds like he knows how to live the way he wants, anyway, not just drift with whatever comes along."

John Renshaw didn't mind the changes that were coming, even made a major contribution to them. Flush with money from pole shipments from his own and his stepdaughter's claims, John Renshaw built the grandest building Tiger had yet seen. John told the *Miner* that it was an *amusement hall and meeting space for Socialists,* but locally it was already dubbed Renshaw Hall. On Saturday, February 2, the Socialists threw a dedicatory dance with music by the Renshaws and five others. Enthusiasm was high for both the political statement of a finished Socialists' Hall and for the food, dance and music. To Jennie's surprise, the party broke up before morning light. When people had finished their midnight supper, Jennie blinked when she saw Alice, up from Metaline for the party, pick up her empty deviled egg plate, wave it to signal Charley across the floor, and show signs of heading for Uriah's house to spend the night. How will they see to get home, Jennie wondered. But Alice knew her own business, so Jennie went to help her by gathering little Ira from among the other sleeping babies. She walked out ahead of the Gilmores, carrying a load of quilts and child, and looked around for their wagon, expecting to have to walk from rig to rig to puzzle out the right one in the dark. And of course she could see it plainly by the skinny crescent moon far over by the west wall of the valley. She hadn't realized how many trees had been taken out in eight years, how broad and bright that left the landscape. Not only could Alice and Charley pick out their wagon, they would be able to see the rutted trail all the way home. She waved them off and went in to Wes. "I think I'm getting foggy in the upper story. I went outside, thinking I knew what I was going to see, and all of the sudden it's a different place. Remember how you couldn't see the river from here when we got here in ought ought?" She pulled him outside to show him the transformation. "Where'd all them big cedars go?"

"They went to buy this fine assembly hall of John's."

"And are we glad or are we sorry?"

If Jennie had reservations, she was alone. Renshaw Hall was kept busy, and one particular use brought her around. Professor J.B. Miller, teacher at the Hawthorn School, had organized the Hawthorn Literary and Debating Society, which met weekly in one crowded house or another. Now it could meet in Renshaw Hall, which always came complete with music, so the evening could finish out with dancing. The Society's legitimacy was ensured when they received a challenge from the Tamarack Club of Blue Slide to debate the topic "Does Power Bring Justice? Is Might Right?" Jennie didn't dream of joining the debaters, but she loved to listen to her neighbors suddenly become silver-tongued. When Charlie Lucas, who had been covered in soot when he cleaned the stove in the store that afternoon, stood up in a suit and tie and used words like "political equality" and "economic democracy," she was thrilled. "Ain't they scholarly!" she said to Wes.

Without Jennie's encouragement, Tiger Town continued to grow. The *MINER* bragged that ten copies of the newspaper were now delivered weekly to Tiger, and found someone to send in a column of local events. For the quarter ending at New Year's, 1906, the post office register showed 172 entries. "My god, Wes, what all are people sending and getting?" Nearly everyone was now able to take cedar poles off their land, and they came to

Tiger's Landing to wait for the boat to ship them upriver. Former itinerants like Wes Wooding and George Tiger could stay at home, the profit in cedar poles surpassing what they could make in distant mines. Several bachelors found themselves with the wherewithal to gain families; Joe Parker made up for lost time by marrying and importing a widow with two half-grown daughters. He told John Renshaw he just wished he'd done it sooner and got two spreads, the way John had.

George's barn collapsed under snow that winter, and he realized he was spread too thin. He hired a couple, Robert and Flora Cross, newly from England via Iowa, to work full time for him. Flora would cook for George's work crews and Bob would do whatever was needed, starting with sawing boards for an early start next summer on a new barn.

But even all this excitement wasn't enough for Ada. The winter school term finished on February 22 and four days later she and the girls took the first spring boat out. She declared they were probably going to make their home in Seattle, where Uriah was waiting for them. Ada's frustration had nearly reached the pitch of madness in the past three months. After she browbeat Uriah into the move, he went ahead in early December, and she'd been trapped by the ice until now.

Wes made a change of course too. He announced to the Miner reporter, who reworded the declaration: "It's too goddamned muddy to slide poles, and that's going to be it for this winter for me." He turned his energies to a new venture: he would build a packtrain business to transport settlers' goods up Tiger Hill to the homesteads. Jennie hoped he'd charge fair rates - fair to himself.

Excitement continued even through the growing season. In June the Tiger Wideawakes took the *NEW VOLUNTEER* downriver to beat the Ione Skippers 11-3 in 7 innings. In July they played the Blue Sliders in an unscored game. The steamboats gave reduced fares to spectators traveling to the games. "Wes, imagine grown men taking off a work day to play a game." But she didn't too often keep the boys from watching the practices.

In July a jury in Boise found Big Bill Haywood innocent of the murder of Governor Steunenberg. Wes didn't learn of it until late August when the *APPEAL TO REASON* arrived. Miners from Idaho to Arizona had celebrated all through the night when the decision was announced, but the *NEWPORT MINER* hadn't mentioned the trial at all. Wes proposed the paper change its name to the *NEWPORT PLUTOCRAT*. He organized a belated celebration in Renshaw Hall and John's mandolin had never been more joyous. "Jennie, I'm not going back to the mines, and I'm not going back to the Union. But it sure feels good to know I wasn't any part of a bombing murder. It raises a cloud off the whole thing."

With so many amenities, Tiger was the chosen site of the third annual Settlers' Picnic of the Pend d'Oreille, held in August. The Pend d'Oreille Navigation Company sold half price tickets from all points to Tiger and return. The whole county was invited, whether they were *members of the craft* or not. The *IONE* and the *NEW VOLUNTEER* were both needed for the crowds. The picnic ground near the Landing was the center of festivities with a platform built there and decked with bunting for speeches and recitations. Music and dancing filled Renshaw Hall and spread into the street, where a second band played. The Cusick Indians and the Usk Reds came for a baseball game, and families of Kalispel players came in canoes. The settlers bet among themselves during the baseball game, and the Kalispels gambled at stick game after it was over. All day George Tiger wore a look of euphoria, Jennie and Wes took turns to keep the store open, and Emmanuel Yoder rented all three of the rooms at his hotel.

In October Ada and the three girls came back on the *IONE*. Uriah was gone to Alaska again when she got to Seattle. She'd waited seven months for him to come back, and had run out of money. Ada moved into the homestead and took temporary work hanging wallpaper in the Cottage Hotel for E.F.Yoder, a public declaration that Uriah was not her breadwinner. She would try to put together a life for herself and the girls in the backwoods Uriah'd brought her to and then left her in. Within a month the mistake was apparent. Ada's misery had not abated in Seattle, and her second try at Tiger wasn't working either. In November she sent Mary to live with Alice downriver in Metaline, where she could attend what was supposed to be her last year of school and where she could help with Alice's babies. Ruby Belle, now 18, stayed at the homestead with 8-year-old Ethel. Ruby Belle refused to leave the place she loved, and especially Jimmie Mansfield, who was working hard to make it possible for them to marry. She was practicing for the same thing by making a home for Ethel. Ada astonished everyone by taking a job cooking at Murphy's lumber camp at Blueslide, where she would stay through the week, coming home just weekends. "Wes, does she need money that bad? Why would she leave the girls spread around and go be alone in a dirty, wet lumber camp?"

"Jennie, I can hardly figure out my own marriage, much less anyone else's."

"But it seems like we oughta do something for them before it gets worse."

"How could it get worse? They don't want anything to do with each other, but they're caught in this marriage. Go talk to her if you want, but I doubt it'll help."

Jennie decided it might even hurt. She wasn't sure if she was being prudent or cowardly, but her policy would be to stay out of Uriah and Ada's business, and help the girls as she could.

1908

JENNIE'S LIFE WAS becoming a river rapids. There was no time to cogitate, calculate or consider. Uriah and Ada's life was coming apart, sharp rocks tearing at the bottom, and people falling out of the boat. The town at Tiger's Landing was changing so fast it couldn't be steered, and certainly the depth of the changes couldn't be gauged.

In January, with the boats frozen out, Wes took a day off from logging to run the store while Jennie took a sleigh load of supplies downriver to Box Canyon. Her pet, Shorty, didn't work well with any of the other horses, but she insisted on hitching him up with young Kit, lengthening the trip by a couple of hours. When she got back, 17 cords of wood was stacked outside the store. "What's that for, Wes?"

"The Harpers needed supplies to get them through till spring, and they don't have any money. We'll sell the cordwood by summer, and come out even."

"Who we gonna sell it to? Everybody can cut their own. Who's gonna put out cash for it?"

"Well, then, we'll use it in our own stove. We have to keep the store warm. And Aubrey Harper has to keep his family fed."

"With four boys, we can get our wood cut cheaper than trading beans and flour for it, Wes." She knew he was morally right, but she knew, too, that Parker Brothers Wholesalers wouldn't take payment in cordwood.

Fortunately for business, Wes found other pursuits, and left running the store to Jennie for a while. The Downriver Socialists began their campaign of 1908 in January, with a story in the *MINER* and enticing posters penned by Wes:

> *J.J. Miller of Colville and Lee R. Bilderback of Yocum will*
> *address the people of Tiger at J.B. Renshaw's Hall on Tuesday*

evening, Feb. 28th, on Socialism. Come and hear what these men have to say. Prove all things and hold fast to what is good, just and right, but reject the evil. All are invited.

The hall was filling up on what would have been a dreary, soggy, overcast night. Both the convinced and the curious were filling the hall with enthusiasm that was in some cases for Socialism, but in more cases for a social evening. As some were seating themselves on John's backless benches and others were still hitching their horses and filing in, they heard the excitement of sleigh bells coming from the south. Jeff Honsinger was arriving with a sleigh load of folks from upriver at Yocum. The chatter and laughter of welcoming was just beginning to die down when bells from the west stirred it all up again; Wes himself had gone up Tiger Hill to bring folks from Middleport. As they greeted friends and neighbors they didn't see often enough, they folded robes and blankets and took them inside for seat cushions.

The meeting was a success. Renshaw Hall always came with music, and the altruistic speeches appealed to both Socialists and Christians, and many people present were both. Sharing one's goods was a popular notion for all, if not consistently practiced. Jennie listened and understood a little better why she had 42 cords of wood ricked outside the store. The Socialists elected officers, including Wes as Secretary. He circulated a petition, which met with enthusiasm, to create a voting precinct called Tiger.

School Board elections, too, were due. Joe Parker came into the store while Jennie was finally getting around to removing Valentine post cards from the store window, and again asked her to run. "Jennie, you've been oil on troubled waters all along, and maybe if you were on the Board there'd be less smoothing necessary." Jennie kept her eyes on the embossed ivory lace, the cherubs, hearts and forget-me-nots while her own heart choked her.

She was scared more by Joe's friendly request than she had ever been by wild horses or a mountain lion. She put Joe off, and talked it over with Wes. "Nobody here knows I can't hardly read, and you know I don't want them to know - especially the boys. I don't belong on the School Board, acting like I know what a school should teach, and how the teacher should do it. I've gone to just a few months hit or miss in some dinky desert schools." The amount of evasion and fibbery necessary to keep her secret was all she could handle now. "I can't sit there at School Board meetings and look like I know what I'm doing. Wes, how can I get out of this?" But she couldn't think up an excuse, she surely wouldn't tell the truth, and elected she was. At the very first meeting, though, she found her footing when the question of teacher replacement came up. The only applicant for the newly-instituted spring term was a woman. Phil Mellott proposed waiting another year to add the spring term, so they'd have until fall to find a man. Jennie told him, "The hell with that, Phil. This woman's got nothing but good recommendations, and the spring term is a good idea. Maybe with more time in school, some of these kids can get through the 8th grade exam before they're 16." Joe Parker was delighted to see her slam two strong points at Phil Mellott before Phil could come up with one. (though Joe did have to admit that the oil on these particular waters was briskly thrown). Mrs. Lena J. Roberts, Widow, became the first woman teacher at the Hawthorn School, and several children were unhappy to learn of a third school term, starting immediately.

Mr. and Mrs. J.W. Wooding were surprised to find themselves becoming People of Substance. In addition to being Secretary of the County Socialist Party, Wes was elected President of the Old Settlers Club. His stature was noted when the *MINER* ran a piece of doggerel by someone in the Upriver facetiously identified as Frederick Wilhelm Guggenheimerschmidt, who had apparently stayed at E.F.Yoder's hotel on a bad day. After describing various fictional deprivations, the poem concluded:

So von und all, both big and schmall, ve vent to Mayor Wooding
Und he fixed us oudt mid limburg cheese, und der landlord make a pudding.

Silly as it was, Wes was pleased by the honorific.

WHEN THE MOST IMPORTANT CHANGE, for good and for bad, came to the Valley it was "Mayor Wooding" who represented Tiger. There'd been talk for some time of a railroad coming down the valley. It would surely bring prosperity to all, it was said, with lower freight rates and faster, more frequent and more dependable year-round runs than the steamboats could offer. More settlers would come and *help to make the country what its resources warrant,* crowed the *MINER.* In March no announcement had yet been made, but there seemed no doubt the Railroad was going to happen. The only dispute was over whether it would go down the east side or the west side of the river. It had been taken for granted that it would go down the east side since the builder, Mr. F.A. Blackwell, owned most of the timber on that side and was building the railroad for the purpose of extracting it. "Fine by me," said Jennie. "I'd rather have the filthy thing over there than over here." But she was in a minuscule minority, and west siders decided to put their oar in. A committee was formed, and Wes was chosen to represent the Tiger area, since he was now seen as a leading businessman and an officer in two important organizations. More relevant, he was a clear speaker and thinker, and he was, actually, a pretty good choice if you believed in the coming Railroad Prosperity.

While Jennie once again prepared the garden without his help, Wes put in a frantic two weeks gathering right-of-way costs and computing the probable tonnage to be shipped on a Westside route. An Eastside Committee was doing the same.

While the Eastside had more timber to send out, the Westside could claim more agricultural tonnage as a certainty. However, Wes found little consensus among homesteaders on the issue of right-of-way costs. In fact, there was little consensus in his own family. Wes was sure the Railroad had to be progress, and urged that the homesteaders not be greedy for fear they'd queer the deal. Jennie was content as things were, and hoped high right-of-way costs would discourage the whole venture. She tried to get Wes to explain to her what "progress" meant, but he only assured her that there would be more people and more money. Jennie had seen the Railroad come to the Owens Valley, to the Mojave Desert, and to the Imperial Valley in California. In no case did she remember anyone prospering from the Railroad except the capitalists who built it. In fact, the Imperial Valley farmers were worse off once the Railroad could monopolize shipping and keep the rates as high as they wanted them. But Wes had caught the fever and did everything he could to please Mr. F.A. Blackwell and associates. Mr. F.A. Blackwell himself, with his son Russell and several other nabobs representing "Eastern interests," debarked from the SPOKANE, specially chartered for the group, and put their well-shined shoes into the gray clay of Tiger's Landing on a late March day. Only months later would the settlers learn that on this same visit Mr. F.A. Blackwell had purchased the entire Pend d'Oreille Navigation Company and all its steamboats. As he intended, Blackwell got a bargain; the owners, Joe Cusick and his brother Fred, could see that the steamboats were about to become white elephants. At the meeting in Renshaw Hall (whose primary function was never revealed to Mr. Blackwell) the Westside Committee pressed its case. Mr. Blackwell, not yet having softened the owners of rights of way on either side of the river as much as he believed he could, assured the Committee and the listening crowd that his would be a "pure business decision" and that the losing side would also have good service, with a system of good ferries and boats. "And I suppose Mr. Blackwell will be on hand to help load all those hay bales and cedar poles twice," said Charlie Lucas. But the committee had to be satisfied and wait for the survey crews to do their work on each bank.

In April Ada was finished with the cookhouse work at Blue Slide. She came back to the homestead but lasted quick. She hated the place and saw nothing she wanted to do there. When Flora Cross was laid up for some weeks when she was thrown by her horse, Ada found work as her replacement, cooking for George Tiger's crews for a month. In May she announced she was moving with the three girls to Alice's house in Metaline. Ruby Belle asked to stay at the homestead. "Mama, we ought to have someone in the house to keep an eye on things."

But Ada has heard some gossip. "And let you see that Jimmie Mansfield without anybody around. No, Miss. You'll be where somebody can keep an eye on you," Ada snapped.

"She's probably right about that, anyway," said Jennie.

JENNIE REMEMBERED A BAKING SUMMER day when she was 16, down in the A.T. James and Anna had by now bought and settled on a little farm outside Safford, north of Bisbee. All Anna's children were in school now, and Jennie had more freedom than she'd had in years. Wes Wooding was working in the Safford store. For months they met and talked there, then began arranging meetings. Jennie would slip out and go to Mrs. Anderson's Boarding House where Wes lived, and they would go walking or horseback riding. On one ride, he asked her to marry him. Soon after, they hired out together to bring Peter Anderson's cattle in from the hills. They pretended to themselves that this was only a working arrangement, that nothing would happen that shouldn't. When they stopped for lunch they found a little protection from the blazing heat under some palo verde bushes in a dry arroyo. They took off their hot and heavy chaps and vests and took a break from the heat. Removing the garments was somehow a trigger, an invitation to intimacy. When she turned away from his eyes and sat on the ground with her back against a tree, ostensibly to eat, he laid his head in her lap and looked up into her eyes. The kiss that followed wasn't the first, but it was the first that should have waited until they were married. Had Wes's horse not whinnied, making them think someone was nearing, perhaps there would have been more. But more waited until night. They had told themselves they'd bring the herd down in one full day, there'd be no need to stay over in the hills. And probably they could have, but the fleshly attraction was too compelling. They decided they weren't sure they had all the calves, though they heard no bawling from any calf or cow. Stay over they did. They still didn't admit what was happening. They made a fire and made bedrolls on either side of it with saddle blankets and their outer clothes. She lay down in hers, her skin excited. Her mouth went dry and she felt her nipples rubbing against her bodice. When a pack of coyotes began to howl, Wes used it as an excuse to move near her "for protection." Jennie had slept outdoors in the Southwest Desert more nights than not in the past eight years, and coyotes bothered her no more than did the glowing moon and shining stars. Coyotes were part of the night music she drowsed off to night after night. But she didn't laugh, and she didn't reject his "protection." They rolled their two bedrolls into one, and then they became one. They were married two weeks later by a Mormon Justice of the Peace, his two wives serving as witnesses. Naomi was born two days shy of nine months later, and Jennie always privately hoped she was a product of that stunning Arizona night.

Jennie had no bad memories at all, no regrets or shame, about that night. But she knew they were lucky. Ruby Belle shouldn't be left alone in the house; Ada was doing at least one thing right.

ADA WAS READY FOR THE move to Metaline, but delayed her departure when she heard of a coming wedding at Renshaw Hall. "That ought to be a fine one," she told the girls. "Let's wait a couple of days, and go to it."

Nettie Phelps was to marry Charlie Lucas, a complete surprise to everyone, including Nettie and Charlie. They had known each other for almost ten years, just as they had known the clay of the landing and the thorns on the brush. They had agreed on all things political and discussed no other things. Even they didn't know what brought about romance, if it could be called that. "But Jennie, I'm about to turn 30, and if I don't want to just drift on the way I am, I'd better make a change. Nothing's wrong with Charlie," Nettie explained when she invited Jennie to the wedding. Charlie told Wes, "She's got a house she makes mighty nice, and she's no nonsense. Why should I keep on batching?" Justice of the Peace E.E. Emery said the few necessary words to allow Nettie her change and to let Charlie move into her comfortable home, and everyone went to Renshaw Hall for a party. If Nettie was different in any way that evening from her usual straightforward self, it was that she only danced and depended on others to make music. Ada went home disappointed. "It wasn't any different than any other party. She didn't even have a new dress. I'd think the Renshaws could afford something better."

THE SURVEY CREW REACHED TIGER by mid-June, and by July the property owners were groveling, offering free right of way through timbered land if the railroad would cut the timber, which they'd have to do anyway, and leave it stacked beside the railroad bed for free shipping. Some with meadowland asked as much as $50 an acre. There were very few holdouts, notably Arthur Norman, the brother-in-law whose land abutted Uriah's to the south. Arthur, like Jennie, was inclined to hold with the plan he'd been building for seven years; he wasn't eager to tear his homestead in half in order to help Mr. F.A. Blackwell make a fortune. He tried in court to have the survey moved away from his homestead, but of course without success. Both Jennie and Arthur were somewhat mollified, though, when they learned that the railroad bed as surveyed would cut across only a small corner of each property.

Wes continued to give his energies to the Socialist Campaign and to the Westside Railroad Committee (He saw no conflict between the two.) but he did find time in June to go south to the Calispell Valley to move 300 head of cattle north to Metaline. A concentrator for ore had been floated downriver past Tiger's Landing in December on its way to the mines in Metaline. This was producing a mining boom, and the railroad promised another. Whether the tracks went down the east side or the west side, the Metalines would have the butcher shops for both booms. Wes had been buying and selling cows here and there, but in amounts he could handle alone and ship on the steamboat. But on his last trip to Metaline he'd impulsively arranged a deal requiring him to provide 300 head of cattle. He'd seen a notice in the *MINER* by a rancher in the Calispell Valley who had that many cattle to sell, and when the offer to buy in Metaline was made, he figured he'd just as well make the middle profit as anyone. He guessed he could find the cash somewhere, or anyway Jennie could.

"That's funny you'd come up with that just now," Jennie said when Wes told her of his plan. "I was just thinking the other day about that herd you and me brought down for Pete Anderson down in the A.T. before we was married. Remember that?" They were sitting on the porch, the little boys in bed and the big boys playing cards with their cousins at the Norman house. It was high water season and with so many trees gone, the murmur of the Pend d'Oreille reached clear to the house. Wes smiled at her, took her face in his two hands, and his kiss said that he surely did remember. Two more kisses and they realized there was no reason they couldn't go early to bed. An hour later they resumed the discussion of the trail drive. He rolled toward her.

"How many hands would I need, do you think?"

"Well, it's going to be a lot different going through timber and brush. In the desert you can see the cows. You and I did fine with 100 head, just the two of us. And time for hanky-panky. Here, with that many head, you'd need a good half dozen horsemen, probably ought to be eight, to keep an eye out so some frisky heifer don't take off on a side trail."

The next day Wes left on a scouting trip to work out the route. Then he went to the settler who'd declared 300 head ready for market. But it seemed that in the time it had taken Wes to get to the Calispell Valley the man had sold 100 head, and Wes had to visit ranchers throughout the Valley, locating a few here and some more there. He got mostly yearlings and long yearlings, though he tried for just heifers and steers; to make up the contingent, he had to take a few old cows, anything but new calves. When they got moving, he'd want to go fast, not take time every few miles for mothering up.

This venture would have to succeed, and succeed by the beginning of July. The money Wes took in his pocket to pay for the cattle was that set aside for the next payment to Parker Brothers Wholesalers. He assured Jennie there was no reason to worry, it was a simple transaction: he'd pay for the cattle in the Calispell, and Clyde Avary in Metaline would buy the whole herd and parcel them out to butchers and work camps. Jennie's job was to find him a crew while he was gone on his scouting trip.

Easier said than done. The Woodings owned a total of four cayuses, counting the impossible Shorty. They could mount just Wes, Tom and Bill. Everyone else would have to provide their own animals, which narrowed the pool. It was the middle of farming time, with weeding, haying and harvesting all going on, narrowing the pool further. Thank goodness Uriah and Wes had brought their two sisters to the Pend d'Oreille, shortly after their own arrival. Both women had found husbands at once which was, of course, their plan, if not Uriah's. Ida was now married to the former Cement schoolmaster Arthur Norman, and had two stepsons and a nephew between the ages of 12 and 15 that could be let go to help Wes out. Julia had no sons, but her husband Nels Hanson was a favorite worker in the area. Nels agreed to put aside his own work for a week and, in gratitude for favors Wes had done him, go on the cattle drive. To round out the crew, Jennie persuaded Hy Maggot to give up his spot on the stump outside the store and work off some of his bill inside the store. Hy agreed. Jennie had to admit that Wes's comradely way of doing business sometimes paid off.

When Wes came back, two days later than expected because of having to replace a third of the merchandise, the crew was still ready to go: accommodating in Hy's case, willing in Nels's case, and awed in the boys' cases. Not once since they had arrived at Tiger's Landing as little tads had James, Charles, William, Bill or Tom traveled as far from home as 30 miles. None of them had ever seen a cattle drive, or even seen 300 head of anything, including people, in one place. None of them had slept away from their homes as long as five days. Now they were asked to do all these things and they felt highly honored.

The trip south to the Calispell was undemanding and the boys believed they were born cowboys. Had they been a more worldly kind of youngster, they might have swaggered by the time they dismounted at Joe Cusick's ranch where Joe had a fenced field Wes could use for a few days. Jennie had sent a pot of beans and some raised bread for the first night's supper, and after they'd eaten, the boys remounted and rode around and among the cattle, curious how the animals would behave, what would be expected of themselves. On that first peaceable evening it didn't seem to them that 300 cattle behaved much differently than two or three; they sometimes lay still and chewed their cuds; they sometimes chose to run to the far side of the field where Joe's fence stopped them.

Six hours later the five boys were in the deep sleep of adolescents when Wes called them awake. They had ridden hard the long previous day, but as soon as they realized what this day held they were on their feet, breakfast eaten and bodily functions accomplished, horses saddled and bedrolls tied on, ready for action.

Hy Maggott was to be the lead rider; tied behind his horse was a Judas cow, an elder from the miscellaneous stock who was willing to lead her associates to slaughter. Wes wanted the drive to go as fast as possible. "Clyde Avary's paying me for 300 head whatever they are, within reasonable limits; he's not paying by the pound. What they lose this week they can gain back on his bunch grass." So Hy went at a good pace and the rest of the cattle followed. Wes, Tom and Bill were on one side of the herd and

James, Charles and William on the other. Their chore was to keep bolters from going up side trails or to retrieve them if they did. Nels, with the best combination of good eyesight, quick responses, and clear judgment, brought up the rear.

Any straying animals that the other six missed he would gather in. Organization was clear. They were sure of their assignments. They'd be home well ahead of schedule.

But as soon as they left the big meadow and entered timber and brush, the job changed. The cattle could duck around bushes and go under windfalls better than could a man on a horse. Never mind Wes's request for speed, the challenge became to hold back so the front animals wouldn't go too fast; there was a limit to how spread out they could be and still be under surveillance. The nimble agility of the five boys was a boon. They could be on and off their horses, they could duck and dodge, they could lead a horse through a thicket, better than the men. But while they were on the ground they couldn't keep an eye on an errant cow any better than anyone else, and while they were lithely going down, around and under, two more cows were straying away. The work was a constant frustration; it seemed that invariably a red heifer was taking off to the left on a side trail while a black steer headed for a gully full of windfalls. Hy was forever yelling for help as some piebald long yearling sprinted ahead of the lead cow. It was impossible to keep the herd, spread out as it was through numberless game trails, headed on the route Wes had scouted.

Homesteads were in general to be skirted. Wes had secured permission from several farmers to put down segments of fence and replace them after the animals had gone through. But he couldn't do this too many times or he wouldn't get to Metaline this summer. They didn't want to pick up any homesteader's cows that might be interested in seeing where everyone was going, though they could later be returned if the unbranded animals could be matched to the right owners. But what couldn't be undone was the ruin of this year's garden; the season here was too short for replanting. Wes was the everlasting good neighbor, and he would take this herd over any mountain before he would harm someone's livelihood. One thing did work for them: since the snow melted two months ago, the cattle had been feeding at their pleasure on the rich grass of the Calispell Valley; and unlike the Arizona cattle of Wes's experience, they had never known thirst; they lived in a world of profuse springs, marshes, creeks, ponds and lakes. It was not difficult to keep them moving, because they knew there'd be more water in a little way.

But it was difficult as all hell to keep them moving where the men wanted them to go.

On they moved through marshes and meadows, woods and underbrush. The dusk of June went on till 10 o'clock, but at last the boys were let off their horses and ponies and the cattle settled down for the night. "Be glad we picked the dark of the moon, Boys, or these critters would be chewing all night. As long as they can see, they munch." Wes had hardly said that, it seemed to Tom, than he was saying, "The sky's coloring, Boys. Let's get ready to move 'em on before they move themselves without us."

Nels came back from counting the cows. "We only lost one, I believe, Wes. Not bad in this kind of country." Wes was less satisfied than Nels with the tally. "One a day will about wipe out the profit. Let's peel our eyes sharper." Each of the five boys was privately sure he was the one who'd let the stray get by him. Today he'd come up to the mark, though. There wouldn't be a missing cow tonight, by golly.

That night, though, there were two cows missing, this in spite of the fact that Wes had spent more than an hour going back for a brindle heifer who'd decided to return to the Calispell by herself.

The boys showed less eagerness on their fourth dawn, got out of their bedrolls with less enthusiasm and onto their horses with less alacrity. Their muscles were not more comfortable, as Hy had promised they would be "once you get used to it." The trail got no easier. In fact, as they moved north the underbrush became denser and stouter. Few animals were put out on range here to wear it down, and there had never been Kalispels here burning the underbrush to make clearings for their camas or huckleberries. There was an almost solid covering of currant, ash, serviceberry, buckbrush, and an ungodly amount of hawthorn whose thorns they agreed were measurably longer and sharper than those at home. This was the day they were scheduled to arrive in Tiger for a break before heading on north to Metaline, and they were only halfway there.

It had been a shorter day than the others, and after their supper they sat around their small fire, and while Hy played his harmonica Nels told them stories of growing up in the wheat fields of North Dakota. Perhaps it was this unaccustomed relaxation that put them all, even the men, into such a deep sleep. Before they woke, the dawn broke and the cattle woke.

"Son of a bitch! Son of a bitch! Get back here, you bunch of buttheaded scrags!"

Wes was running toward the herd at the same time he was trying to put on his high laced boots. He'd have been dressed faster if he'd simply sat down and put them on in the usual way. But what took away his judgment was the sight of his 297 head of cattle heading at a dainty trot back south toward the Calispell Valley. The outfit of eight got themselves onto their earnest mounts. These were not experienced cow ponies. These were good-natured cayuses accustomed to trying whatever job was thrown at them, jacks of all trades, but absolutely masters of none. The same could be said of the horsemen. They accomplished nothing more than to chase the herd back south through the same brush that had lashed the riders when they came north, at a faster pace than if they'd been left alone. No one had thought there was a lot of order to the drive of the last three days, but this was a complete rout. After a couple of hours at a run, the cattle began to slacken and to veer east toward the river. Soon they could see open grass below them, and sped up. The riders, even Wes, were beyond caring. As the brush opened up and the slope gentled, they felt only relief. Wes could see down to Jared's Landing. Bid Jared hadn't been too adamant when he more discouraged than refused Wes access to his land. His garden was well fenced, he had two brothers living with him to help defend the homestead, and his own animals were off on range. The trading post and the post office were not Bid's responsibility to replace if they were damaged. Besides, these weren't wild-eyed stampeders, they were just homesick cows who wouldn't mind a pause for a good graze. Wes decided to impose on Bid's friendship.

Bid, his wife Tina, and his brothers helped settle the cattle and move them into a field of stumps near the house. They found space in the various outbuildings for the cowboys to lay down their bedrolls. Tina passed out plates of fried cutthroat, fried potatoes with lots of pepper, and chard thinnings dressed with bacon grease saved from breakfast, followed by rhubarb crisp and heavy cream. Then they lay down for the night in order to wake early and not make the same mistake of letting the cows see the morning before they did.

Wes sat up with Bid, working out the next day's strategy.

"If it was November, the river'd be down and you could move 'em along the shore."

"Yeah, Bid, but it isn't. It's June and the river's as high as it gets."

"If that railroad right of way was cleared, it'd be a snap."

"Yeah, Bid, but they haven't even decided where it's going to be."

"If more people had their roads cleared...."

"Some do, Bid, and I wonder if that's not my best bet. We could keep these critters bunched up better and control them some if we did come to somebody's spread. They didn't do too much damage to your place. Think I should risk it?"

"I think it's the only way there is to keep those brush splitters behind you, Wes. Moving along in the bottom land should get you to Tiger in two days."

After their four hours of sleep, the boys were ready for a better day. The formation that had been planned could now be maintained fairly well and even William felt things were more orderly. By deep dusk they were at the Blue Slide, as far back north as they had been when the herd took charge of itself and turned south. Ahead of them, though, was the roughest terrain they'd yet had to cover. About a hundred years before, a gigantic slide of bluish clay had come down off the mountain, narrowing the river and shaping a formidable hump that was now covered with thick cedar and thicker brush. There was no semblance of trail going up and over, and no room for one to follow the river. Settlers without exception used a boat of some kind to execute travel around this point. "If it was November, I might risk swimming them around, but not in June for sure," said Wes. So Bid Jared's prediction of two days to Tiger failed too. They camped on the south side of the slide.

When morning light let them look for deer trails, they found that none came down the main part of the slide, which ended in a 50-foot cliff; the deer couldn't drink there, so they didn't approach. Animals always went down either the south side or the north side. So the cattle drive had to go far enough up the hill to find the game trails they were so dependent on. As the crow flew or the cattle might have swum, they moved about a mile north. In reality, they covered 15 harsh miles to get around the Blue Slide. By night, though, they were at Yocum, and spent the night at Jeff Honsinger's place.

They came riding into Tiger on the afternoon of the eighth day. The herd was bawling, giving generous warning of its arrival. By the time Tom, Bill, William, Charles and James entered the village, a good dozen children, including several young siblings and cousins, awaited them. Everyone from the store turned out. At first they had heard just the din coming from the woods. Finally Hy emerged, and then 294 animals trotting with their heads down until they sensed open pasture; then they looked up and began to run toward the green grass of June. Jennie ran to open the gate. A half hour later every cow, heifer, steer and calf was inside the Woodings' fence, and the riders went over to the store where Wes met his payroll by passing out bottles of birch bark beer. The five boys who had made the successful trek to Calispell and back couldn't have been prouder. Their fatigue was washed away by the drink, and they only looked forward to the next day when they would have to drive this herd right through Ione, where there would be lots more folks to watch, probably even some girls their own age. William forgave the cattle for their noise, because it drew a crowd as well as did a circus calliope. The boys took well to lionizing.

The road above Ione was well established by now, and Wes had the cattle on to Metaline in two days and was back with the cash only three days late. Jennie sent it on to Parker Brothers Wholesalers. It wasn't the first time it had been late, but so far they'd only complained, without any specific threats. She hoped they'd got away with it.

******

WEST SIDE GETS RAILROAD TRUMPETED the *MINER* on September 24. Wes was proud of his part in attracting it. Jennie was happy for him. He came home with $50 cash and a contract from the right-of-way agents for one acre at the edge of the east 40, the 40 where they lived. He hadn't asked exactly where on the 40 that would be.

"But, Jennie, how much could it hurt, one acre out of 160?"

George Tiger was ecstatic, sure this was finally what was needed to put his town on the map. He threw a party at Renshaw Hall, and touted Wes as the hero of the day.

AS FAST AS HE COULD get there after he heard the news, Uriah came home to Tiger in the fall after a year in Nome, where he claimed to have made a "fine strike." He and Ada lasted in the house together about a month, then he moved to Metaline with Alice and Ruby Belle. In fact, he went on the *SPOKANE* with the ton of potatoes Jennie had grown for the boarding houses. Even Davey was in school now, and she'd sewed most of the sacks shut herself, sitting on the bench outside the store with Rover, where she could bask in the September sunshine and watch the low, slow river while she did it .

Afternoons after school the boys were allowed an hour of play before they began their chores. The river was a constant attraction for Tom and Bill with their dugout and their fishing gear or the chance to help unload a steamboat or make up a raft of poles. Davey was not yet allowed to go down the bank alone, and had to content himself with throwing sticks for Rover. Sometimes he sat at his mother's knees, holding the potato sacks for her to sew. Jasper was most often by himself, often up the tree with Mr. Pute Watey, where he could gaze down at the creek, hypnotized by the dartings of water spiders.

On a particular drowsy day, Jennie was pleased to see Tom and Jasper come up together from the riverbank, Tom a slender shape beside the pudgy Jasper. "You been in the canoe with your brother, Jasper?"

It was Tom who answered. "I needed help getting it in and out of the water, Ma, and Bill's off someplace."

"Off where?"

"I don't know. Probably up at Mike Mouchand's."

She knew Bill was fond of Mike Mouchand, but she was surprised to learn he'd rather visit him than play around the river. "Why would he be?"

"He likes to look at Mike's guns and traps and gear."

At that moment, Clarence Bauer on his Blaze came galloping down the Landing Road. "Aunt Jennie! Aunt Jennie! Bill's shot! Come quick! Bill's shot!"

She didn't move. Tom realized why, so he asked for her, "How bad is it, Clarence?"

"It's his foot, only. But it sure bleeds. It just pours blood, Aunt Jennie." Then she could move. She dashed into the store, grabbed her nursing bag and told Emmanuel she'd be gone for a while. She hiked her skirt up from behind, tucked it into her front waistband, and leaped on the horse behind Clarence. As they rode, he explained the particulars: Bill had taken a bunch of boys up to visit Mike, to see his new .22 that he sent for from Chicago. When they got there, Mike wasn't home, but Bill thought Mike wouldn't mind if he took some boys in to show them.

By now they were at Mike Mouchand's cabin a mile up Tiger Hill. Clarence's brother Phillip was kneeling beside Bill, using his flannel shirt to stanch the blood. She grabbed it from him and tied it around Bill's leg above the ankle. She elevated the leg and took a second boy's shirt to press on the wound. Philip explained, "He didn't know it was loaded, Aunt Jennie." Bill closed his eyes and looked frail. He knew looking too weak to defend himself was his best bet. Anyone 12 years old should know better than to say he "didn't know it was loaded."

"Well, at least he got the same foot. He may just lose the rest of that toe he chopped when he was five." They tied a makeshift travois behind the horse, propped the foot on a pile of hay from Mike's barn, and Jennie rode the horse slowly back to the house. The wound wasn't immediately life-threatening, but it could be crippling. They'd go on the morning boat to Dr. Phillips in Newport and see if he could save at least part of that unlucky big toe. She sent Jasper to find Wes to tend the store for a few days, starting now, if he could get away. She cleaned the wound, and made Bill a pallet by the stove.

Dr. Phillips had no trouble sewing up the four-toed foot, but he wanted Bill to stay in town for a week to watch for infection. "A little limp will be likely." Then they took the downbound *SPOKANE* to Tiger. Searching the bank in eagerness to be home, Jennie closed her eyes halfway across Devil's Elbow, lowered her head and smiled with exasperated fondness. "Good God, Wes." The store must be half empty, from the amount of cordwood stacked outside.

****

EVER SINCE THELMA GREENAMYER DIED the year of the scarlet fever, Jennie had had a special feeling about her mother, Elzena. Whenever Elzena came in the store, which was at least twice a week, she brought back the memory of the sick children's red faces and the white circles around their mouths. Jennie and Elzena weren't the only two women in the country who'd lost children, one way or another, but because they had in some way experienced Thelma's death together, Jennie felt a connection to the woman. She and Elzena never spoke of it, but for Jennie at least it was in the air whenever they were together.

One hot day in late August Elzena came in with two dozen eggs to trade. "The days are starting to shorten, and you won't be getting a lot of eggs. How about cash for these, Jennie?"

Jennie usually traded for flour or yard goods. (She knew some customers had figured out that their chances were better with Wes, and would wait till he was behind the counter.) Seldom did anyone ask her for cash and when they did Jennie had a clear but kind way of refusing, something along the lines of "I wouldn't have much luck trying to pass your eggs on to Parker Brothers Wholesalers, would I?" But she asked Elzena why she needed cash.

"I heard about one of them Spiritualists. There's this one comes around to all the towns in the area: Priest River, Newport, Usk, and all. He's got a wagon with all his gear, and he takes it on the riverboat, and he goes to people's houses that live out a ways. He'll have a ghost show right in your house where you think there could be a ghost, and you can have people come to watch and charge them a dime and get enough to pay the Spiritualist. But you have to send him half of the money ahead of time. So I got to get me some cash together."

"You've got a ghost, Elzena?" Saying the words as if she allowed there might be such a thing as a ghost gave her a strange feeling.

"We do have. We hear her. She knocks on the wall between our room and where she used to sleep. Sometimes she moves things around; I'll find the cream on the table when I ain't moved it in from the porch. She'll hide Melvin's things. He right now don't know where his school bucket is. She ain't being mean. She just wants to let us know she's here."

"You think Thelma's in your house?" Jennie nearly choked on the words.

"We know she is. And we'd love to see her. With them Spiritualists - Mediums, some call them - you can sometimes talk to the ghost and find out what it wants to make it rest easier. I guess mainly I'd just like to see her." She caught the last word short of a sob. In the 14 years since Naomi and Alma died, Jennie'd done this same thing herself many times. But even her empathy for Elzena didn't persuade her to extend the cash for such a purpose. Elzena left with five cents worth of cheese.

Wes was away buying cattle, and Jennie wasn't sure she would have talked to him about it anyway; he might have just made fun of Elzena, and Jennie's own feelings were too confused to want that. She thought through her repugnance for Elzena's superstition, and found that while that was real, it wasn't the whole story. Elzena was ignorant, surely, and she had let that ignorance cause the death of her child. She wasn't especially generous or kind, even when she expected generosity and kindness from everyone else. She was rather childish, and maybe a little lazy. No, on the whole Jennie really didn't care much for Elzena. That didn't mean, though, that she would hurt her. Or that she would deny her any comfort, even if it was a sappy kind of comfort. Though not any sappier, really, than Joe Cusick's drinking after Ella's death. Elzena could go on believing in visits from The Other Side, and could go to all the seances she wanted to, and why should Jennie Wooding care?

The cottonwoods behind the store were gold against a bright blue sky that frosts had cleared of haze when Elzena brought in a letter to go on the mail boat. "I've got the money for the Spiritualist. I was kind of shy to tell Renaldo about it. Afraid he'd be too tight. But he said he'd like to see Thelma. He took the money from the pole sale, and we figure we can pay ourselves back if we eat more fish and fool's hen this winter and sell our table pig and steer."

Wes was home now and Jennie told him of the coming event.

"Thelma the Thumper, huh? You going, Jennie?"

"Wes, I believe she'll ask me. But I think I've figured out how I feel about it. This Other Side stuff is hogwash, sure. But it's harmless. It might turn harmful, though, if Elzena was getting some comfort from it and if somebody made her see it was hogwash. I'm going to make it my business to try to keep people away from this seance who might make fun of it."

"Well, that's me, then. It's maybe not awfully harmful, but it's taking meat off the Greenamyers' table and giving it to a couple of con artists."

"It's not going to hurt the Greenamyers to eat fish instead of pork."

"I hate the idea of scammers coming through in a wagon. We're honest people here, and we work honorably for what we want. I detest this kind of stuff. You're right. People like me should stay away. I'd have a hard time keeping back a smirk. And I'd like you not to take the boys."

"Maybe she won't invite me."

But she did. And she made Jennie into a kind of confidante, one always available to tell of the latest communication from The Other Side. Having received the deposit of the pole money, Professor Carl F. Roth and Mrs. Roth sent back a pamphlet telling how Elzena should improve her "receptivity" so that when they arrived and held their seance, her chances of a visit from Thelma would be greater. Their pamphlet explained that scents from The Other Side were one of the most effective ways Spirits let the Worldly know they were around. Within a week of learning this, Elzena had three times come into a room and smelled substances that were not in the room: vinegar she used to rinse Thelma's hair; lemon she used to bleach Thelma's muslin dress; cloves she gave Thelma for sore gums. She said she'd be thinking about something else altogether, and come in the room and smell the thing that meant Thelma was nearby. Also the thumpings had become louder and the snatching of belongings more frequent. "Melvin can't hardly lay nothing down."

"Wes, she's completely convinced these buncos are real because they sent her a photograph of a ghost they say they conjured up, supposedly a little girl that drowned in a horse trough when she was four, the same age as Thelma.

Elzena showed it to me. It's just a big smear of white against some wallpaper. In fact, it looks like an acid burn like Jimmy Hildreth used to bawl me out for when I helped in the darkroom. But to Elzena it's a little girl's dress."

"Are you going to be able to carry this off, being her friend and support? Sounds like you're getting more disgusted with it."

"Just let me blow off some steam. Yes, I'm going to see it through. I don't have any choice, really, and if the neighbors think I'm nuts too, they can just think so."

The seance was announced for November 7 at the *Greenamyer domicile,* as the *MINER* described it, adding: *We failed to get our credentials in time to go to see the ghost. It is to be regretted that so valuable an opportunity was lost.* The sarcasm was wasted on the Greenamyers, if they even saw it. In addition to the newspaper notice, Elzena invited everyone she ran into. Jennie interceded where she could sense skepticism, or worse. She explained to the Renshaws, for instance, her campaign to preserve Elzena's credulity. She told Charlie Lucas to lay off. There were still plenty of people planning to attend. Ruby Belle came up from Metaline on the *NEWPORT,* though perhaps with more interest in Jimmie Mansfield than in Thelma Greenamyer. Miss VanSlate, the Yocum schoolteacher, came down on the *IONE* for what was generally called "the ghost show."

"Fine thing for a schoolteacher to be interested in. I'm glad I ain't a Director where she teaches," Jennie told Wes.

"I thought you didn't know what a teacher was supposed to teach."

"I know she shouldn't teach that little dead girls flit around the house and make mischief. Or that we don't stay in the ground after they plant us. Maybe I'm mad on account of Naomi and Alma. I like thinking about them being part of the earth, the soil, the grass, the trees, and all. I don't want to think about them wandering around looking for us, trying to "communicate" with us. When we die we get to be part of some Big All, we don't go on being our little selves."

"It's no stranger than thinking that we stay in the ground until some Resurrection Day, and all spring up and hug each other. And then we get all separated out, the good and the bad, and the bad ones get tortured forever and the good ones get bored forever. You've always been very live-and-let-live about that, My Girlie. Why is this any sillier?"

She couldn't answer. But with loyalty trumping clear-headedness she showed up at the Greenamyer house on Saturday night an hour early to help set up, as Elzena had asked her. She was grateful for her first task, washing up the dinner dishes and putting the milk into its flat pans to separate. It kept her from having to meet the Professor and his wife. But then Elzena, Renaldo, and the Medium and his wife came into the room. Both women were wearing white. The men were in suits and ties. Jennie helped them move some unneeded furniture onto the back porch and place the dining table in the middle of the floor, put a fringed cover over it, and place six chairs around it. Then Jennie was stationed inside the front door with a muffin tin. To her horror, she was to collect a dime from each onlooker; those to be seated at the table didn't have to pay. "You're used to handling money," Renaldo said.

My god, she thought, this is worse than being right in the ghost show; this'll look like I'm making money off it or sponsoring it or something. But she'd said she'd follow through, and she would. A solemn look was appropriate to the evening, so her lack of enthusiasm looked natural. As people came in she collected their dimes, made change where necessary, and kept her eyes down. Finally Mrs. Rolf came over and told her they were ready to start. She took the tray of money and told Jennie to stay near the door in case there were latecomers. She could let them in and collect their money after the "Session." She herself would be in the kitchen, "to make sure no wrong Spirits show themselves, just little Thelma." The participants would sit at the round dining table, alternating man, woman, man, woman. Elzena had rung in three of the neighbors to fill out the group. There was no knowing how they felt about Spirits from the Other Side; it was pretty hard to say no to a neighbor who asked a favor. There were onlookers crowded into the living room and overflowing into the bedroom. A few were seated; most had to stand. Mrs. Rolf instructed them all to be completely quiet and to move as little as possible "so as to make no distractions for Professor Rolf." It seemed to Jennie that not having the onlookers present at all would give Professor Rolf a still better chance; but then, of course, there wouldn't have been any dimes to collect. Mrs. Rolf turned down the wick on the single lamp in the corner of the room, and the only people clearly visible were the three women at the table in white dresses and Mrs. Rolf herself. Then Mrs. Rolf went into the kitchen, and the six participants closed their eyes, joined hands and put their clasped hands on the table. Soft, rather eerie music played by a violin and an organ in the manner of a hymn came from a windup Victrola Jennie had seen in the kitchen. After about a minute, a knocking came from the kitchen. To Jennie it was obvious that Mrs. Rolf was making the sound, but no one else seemed to think of that. There were soft gasps from the onlookers. The Professor reminded them to be quiet. The knocking was repeated, and the onlookers contained themselves. Professor Rolf asked, "Are you trying to reach someone here?" There was one knock, followed by three more. "Please knock once for yes, and twice for no." He asked again, "Are you trying to reach someone here?" There was a single knock. "Will you tell us who you are?" No response; the ghost seemed uncertain. "Will you give us clues?" One knock. At this point Professor Rolf's head jerked up and back and his eyes opened, though they seemed to be glazed over, not looking at anything in the room. The music became slower and eerier. Then the Professor spoke; Jennie could tell it was the Professor because his lips were moving. The voice, though, was like that of a very young child.

"I've got a kitty."

Elzena sobbed once, and looked all around her. The men on her two sides each put a calming hand on her shoulder.

Now the Professor's head came down, and he said in his own voice, "What's your kitty look like?"

His head went back up, and the voice changed again. "He's a yellow kitty."

Elzena cried out: "It's him. It's Dandelion! Dandelion's with her!" Once again the men seated Elzena.

At this moment the lamp went clear out and an indistinct white figure moved quickly from the kitchen, around the table, and back into the kitchen. As it went by her, Elzena reached out to touch it, but it was already far past her. Elzena stood up, and made to follow the shape. The two men stopped her. She was now sobbing noisily, a mess of grief and hysteria. Jennie had never seen anything so deliberately cruel. She forgot all the protocol of a seance and left the wall where she'd been standing. She went to Elzena and took her in her arms. "Jennie, it was her. It was her. She really was here."

Mrs. Rolf had reentered the room and was lighting the lamp. Professor Rolf, his face glistening with sweat, was still in his chair, his shoulders sagging and his head lolling back again. Mrs. Rolf went to him, mopped his face, and gave him a drink of water. The other people at the table directed their concern to Professor Rolf; only Jennie and Renaldo cared for Elzena. Jennie asked him to get a cool cloth while she supported Elzena and guided her into the bedroom. The onlookers in that doorway crowded aside reluctantly, peering curiously into Elzena's face. Jennie wondered if they'd come here to see the ghost, or to see Elzena in agony. Either way, they got their damn dime's worth. She stayed until Elzena was in a shallow sleep. Jennie had suggested they let Melvin stay at her house, with Wes and the boys. Thank goodness they'd taken the advice.

When she got home, all the boys were sound asleep and she could talk softly with Wes. "Wes, I'm sick to my stomach. You shoulda seen Elzena. People used to think the Apaches did awful things to people. At least they did them because they was their enemy. This tonight was just to make a buck. The Apaches tortured people's bodies. But you can torture somebody's mind just as bad. Renaldo tried to hold himself together, but I know he was hurting bad too. What do you think this Professor and the Mrs. Professor are made of? What scum! And I was a part of it."

"You knew going into it it was wrong, Jennie. But there wasn't anything you could do. You decided not to tell Elzena it was a fake. And you were so right about that. What if she went through all this, and then found out it was a trick?"

"But she thought and I thought she'd get some comfort out of it. I don't see she did. She's right where she was, except she had to go through the loss again. It was like having Thelma die again tonight. That figure she believed was Thelma ran by her. She couldn't touch her. Hearing what she thought was Thelma's voice just tormented her. How is she any better off?"

Jennie hoped Renaldo was as much comfort to Elzena as Wes was to her. They slept through the night wrapped together.

The next day Jennie saw Elzena and Renaldo come to the Landing to see Professor Rolf's wagon loaded on. The Greenamyers seemed respectful and even warm; there was no hint of disillusionment. It looked as if the Rolfs had pulled off the hoax, with Jennie complicit.

It was a week before Elzena came into the store, then she gradually resumed her usual frequency. She never once mentioned the seance. There were no more stories of thumpings or snitchings. There was no acknowledgment of or thanks for Jennie's help at the Session. Apparently the ghost had left on the boat with the Rolfs.

Wes made a game of reading the notices for Spiritualists in the Spokane *SPOKESMAN-REVIEW* whenever he came across a copy. *Know your destiny* was a common enticement. *No fraud, no deception* seemed to protest too much, he said. He was especially delighted by *All callers this week will receive an Egyptian lucky bean.* Several were self-proclaimed business psychics or specialists in mining. "Where were they when we needed them, Jennie?" Eventually he saw a 10-inch advertisement for Professor Carl H. Roth.

*If you are contemplating marriage Professor Roth will tell you
whether your coming union will be for your best interests or
not; whether your wedded life is to be 'one grand, sweet song' as
GROVER CLEVELAND said of his, or whether discord will
be your lot.*

"I guess the grieving mother business fell off. Maybe we should have
them back to help Ruby Belle and Jimmie. But what I want to know is why
that fat old plutocrat Cleveland is supposed to be good bait."

Jennie never got as much fun out of it as Wes did.

ON A COLD SATURDAY MORNING in early November with the river fog vaguely
promising to burn off, Wes took Bill and Jasper with him to the Landing
to braille up some poles to send upriver. Ice could come any day, and the
job was urgent. Some youngsters whose mothers weren't Jennie Wooding
had been out of school lately, finishing the jobs that had to be done before
snow flew, some even still bringing in wood. Snow had held off, and the air
didn't feel like snow now either, but the calendar counted for something, and
this might well be the last day of open trail. The Wooding pack train went
twice a week as far as Middleport, and settlers beyond that point mostly
got theirs up the other side from Colville.

The orders had been prepared the day before, and in the early morning
dark and fog Jennie, Tom and Davey were loading three cayuses with winter
supplies. What the homesteaders up the hill had failed to order they would,
for coming months, have to do without or come down for on showshoes.

The Porters on Lake Leo had lost all their chickens in May to skunks and
wanted all the eggs Jennie could send. She'd distributed six dozen, probably
the last of the season, in the cloth bags of flour, and made sure those bags
were on the outside of the load on Old Mose, the least cantankerous of the
three animals. Shorty carried mostly boxes of tinned food that wouldn't
easily break open if he decided to brush off his load on trees, or if he decided
to kick or lunge during loading or unloading. Two kegs of liquor for a
couple of bachelors on Coffin Lake were nested in sacks lined with moss
and sawdust, and they went on Kit.

Tom at 14 was as tall as his mother, and they stood on either side of an
animal. One would heft up a 100-pound box or gunny sack and the other
would hold it in place while the first one secured it with strap or rope, well
inspected the day before. The boys were always sent off with their gear in

good shape. They didn't need to be making repairs on the trail, especially if they were to go the ten miles up and the ten miles back down in one day. Davey was as proficient as his brothers, but he couldn't change his seven-year-old stature. He understood a diamond hitch as well as anyone, but his mother and brother had to hold the pack items in place while he stood on a box to execute it. He knew to put a wad of soft moss on the scab on Old Mose's back before putting the blanket on, and he knew to make all the blankets smooth so a crease didn't rub a new sore. He was invaluable at keeping the animals calmed while the bigger folk did the loading.

Jennie checked off the list one more time, and the boys put their lunch and coats on top of the load. With temperatures mild in the 40's they'd already worked off the need for coats, but they'd need them on the way back down in the late afternoon. They started off with Shorty in the lead, the only place he'd stand for. They started off single file: horse - boy - horse - boy - horse. But the animals were so used to the trail that as soon as they were out of their mother's sight Tom and Davey were walking side by side. Whenever the trail came near the water, they stopped for a drink from Renshaw Creek, still coursing down to the valley, smaller and quieter than in May but still clear and good. Just a few yards up the valley wall they stopped and turned to look back. Through the thinning fog they could see the lanterns in the nearest cabins. By the second switchback they could see all the valley except the river itself, still banked in fog. At the third switchback the sun was coming over the mountain. At the fourth switchback they stopped to sit on a couple of cedar stumps and eat their biscuits and berry preserves. An hour later they stopped and ate their slabs of green tomato pie under a golden tamarack hung with black horsehair moss. The horses grazed beside the trail, and Tom and Davey lengthened the break, lolling in the brief fall sun playing paper-rock-scissors to decide who'd do all the chores left in the day: who'd unload Shorty, who'd unload Kit, who'd unload Old Mose, who'd ride which horse down, who'd unsaddle which, who'd haul water and who'd brush which animal, and on and on, deciding in advance things of no imminent importance or in fact of any importance at all. They reached the last stop, on Thomas Lake, about two o'clock. They unloaded the three animals and were ready to head back down with a scant hour of light left. "Your folks musta let you get a late start," said Day Gandy. They blushed, but didn't explain why their day was running so late. They didn't need any grownups to tell them it wouldn't be fun to unsaddle the horses and feed them in the dark, and they knew for themselves that a November day didn't allow the leisure of the long July days when they'd enjoyed this trip so much more. As the light went, they finally began to hurry. It would be faster to ride down, but the homemade wooden pack saddles were not made for boys' backsides. After less than a half mile, Davey got off Shorty and walked ahead, hoping to inspire the suddenly glue-footed cayuse to speed up, since he wouldn't allow any horse but himself to lead. Tom felt discomfort in the same place Davey did, and maybe more of it. He got off Kit and walked in front of her. Old Mose, the slowest of the three, brought up the rear. After another half mile the boys were impatient. Tom especially was ready for home. He cut a keen willow, fell in line behind Shorty, and tickled Shorty's belly with the branch to urge him on. Shorty ignored it. After five or six ineffective little tickles, Tom gave a sharper lick. Shorty put his ears back, raised his head, and snorted. He stopped dead for some moments, then continued on at the same slow pace. Tom stepped up his urging. This time Shorty snorted, reared, and when he came back down he kicked back hard, and took off down the trail at full speed. Davey was ahead and around two curves, knowing nothing of the rear action, when Shorty galloped by. He looked around and found himself alone. He waited a couple of minutes, then realized there must be trouble. He ran back uphill to find his brother out cold on the trail, his face a bloody mess, and the other two cayuses waiting patiently for direction. He went to Tom's head, put his own arms through Tom's armpits and heaved him into a sitting position. "Tom, can you get up?" No response. He dragged him onto a hummock. "Tom, can you wake up?" No response. He dragged him onto a stump. "Tom, wake up, 'cause I can't lift you. Wake up." At last there was life. Tom grunted a bit, wiped tentatively at his nose, and with much help from his little brother, staggered up to lean against Kit. Kit was only 13 hands high. If she'd been a full-sized horse, the task might have been beyond the little boy. As it was, he tugged his half-conscious brother onto the saddle where he slumped over Kit's neck. "Can you sit up, Tom?" Tom could not. Davey made a cushion of their coats, tucked it under Tom, lashed him to the saddle and walked alongside to lend balance. They moved slowly, but they moved. Old Mose gave up the grazing that had interested him more than the mishap, and followed along. The trail by now was fully dark, and it was Kit and Old Mose who were in charge of finding the way home. Tom did nothing, and Dave just leaned into Kit, propped up Tom, and went wherever the cayuses led him.

Shorty, believing himself the most offended by the whole affair, headed straight for his stall and his buddy Rover, and was out of sight there when

Jennie came home from the store and built up the stove for supper. She didn't expect the pack train back before dark, and sensed no trouble. Wes had sent word that he and the other two boys would keep working at the river as long as they could see on the water, which would be another hour yet. She was even a little relieved to find that both work parties were late, and she'd have a few blessed minutes to herself. Figuring she had more time than anyone else, she took her lighted Palouser and went to the barn to milk Patience. She found Shorty standing in the corner of his stall with his pack saddle still on. She looked around for the rest of them, and was trying to figure out an explanation for Shorty's solo appearance when she heard Davey calling to her. She took the lantern and went toward the sound. The Palouser didn't throw its light very far, and she was almost upon them before she could see them. The light and shadow playing on Tom's face made it look even worse than it had to Davey. The blood was crusting now, and she couldn't see what was underneath. "Jesus Christ, Davey, what happened to him? Tom, say something. Say something." The sound of his mother's voice brought Tom around some. He tried to get off Kit, but was tied on and slumped over the side. She caught him and supported him while Davey undid the rope that held him on. They dragged him off and away from the horse's hooves. The amount of blood was frightening, even for Jennie. The memory washed over her of Naomi and Alma lying dead near the horses' legs and baby Tommie lying nearby in the ditch. There had been a second accident four years later, with her driving again, when four-year-old Tommie had been caught in the reins and his arm broken and his neck nearly so, and again the horses standing nearby. Tom had got away with two close calls, and she hoped this would be another.

"Davey, we ain't going to reharness these horses. I just saw John Renshaw go by with his wagon. Run get him before he can unhitch, and have him come and take me and Tom to the doctor in Ione." John came, and they went the four miles to Ione with Tom's head in her lap and her heart in her throat. But the doctor was gone to Spokane. They went two miles back south to Christina Carpenter's. "Christina, I'm too shaky to sew this boy up. Fix his face for me, will you?"

Christina was of course obliging, but she had no catgut. While John Renshaw held the nose in place Jennie washed away the blood and Christina went to the barn and pulled a few hairs from the tail of a white horse and came back to sew Tom's nose. "White won't show as much if some gets left in." In the time it took John to stir up the fire, boil water and sterilize the horsehairs, Jennie had cleaned the wound and satisfied herself that, as usual, the injury wasn't as dire as it appeared. Tom was quite conscious by now. He moaned some, but didn't cry out. It was just as well that he had no mirror. While she sewed, Christina distracted him with the story of the time she was out looking for a strayed cow in the dark, and a cutbank at the creek collapsed under her. She'd cut her nose on the rocks, just like Tom's. "I was all alone, and I used the same kind of horse hair on my own nose, looking in the mirror to sew it up. See, Tom, no scar at all."

TOM FULLY EXPECTED TO BE lionized at the store and around the Landing. He looked pretty bad now that the bruising was in full bloom, and he should be allowed to tell of his and Davey's exploit while everybody admired their staunchness. But when Ada heard of the mishap, she spread poison. "Jennie and Wes think it's a lot cheaper to work those boys like black slaves than to hire a man. I guess this will show them a child's a child." When Pearl Mellott came in the store, she asked if Little Tommie was all right. Tom, sitting by the store fire for a day of recuperation, stiffened. He hadn't been Tom for so long that "little Tommie" didn't rankle considerably. Pity wasn't what he wanted; he deserved the rough joshing that he'd seen men give one another after injuries.

Jennie heard Luella Underwood bring up Billie's shot foot. In her version, Billie wasn't snooping around where he didn't belong on his play time, he was hired out to clean Mike Mouchand's cabin for him. "Wes, there ain't a grain of truth in what she says, but it hurts. People are looking at us different."

Was there any truth in what they said? Were they building good men, or just using free hands? She found herself, one afternoon in the store, taking the shipping tissue off some lemons and smoothing it out to take to the outhouse, the softest wiping paper available. It would be kept in a box beside the hole to be periodically taken for burning, so as not to fill up the hole too fast. Both were tasks Davey had done when he was three. When she realized she was doing work a child could do, she stopped; she couldn't namby-pamby them just because the neighbors were gabbing. But maybe there was something to what they said. She tried to think it through to the bottom. It made her mad that here she was doing exactly what everybody'd said was so great, and now all of a sudden they turned on her like badgers. Wes said, "Pride wenteth, I guess. We maybe were too cocksure the boys could handle it." They looked for ways to reduce the risks but there was, as

Wes pointed out, no way to make boys grow back down. But the snow still held off and for the two remaining weeks of open trail they hired Harold Mellott to run the pack train. Ada sniffed that they'd maybe learned their lesson.

1909

RUBY BELLE AND Jimmie stood it until January. Then they eloped and took the steamboat south to Newport, a train to Spokane, spent the night in carefully separated rooms, and took another train north to the county seat at Colville in order to avoid the 35 miles of snow-covered hills between Tiger and the county seat. They stayed one night in the Pinckney Hotel and returned south and north by the same route, having been gone a total of six days. Only Ada was disappointed in the marriage; the rest were disappointed only at not being able to plan a wedding breakfast or dinner since no one knew when the bride and groom would be back. But uncertainty didn't stop Jimmie's brothers and Ruby Belle's cousins from planning a humdinger of a chivaree.

A few days later the newlyweds were back and had gone to bed in their new home near the riverbank. Ruby Belle's happiness was considerably marred by thoughts of her mother's disapproval. "Jimmie, I feel wicked. We're married, and legally we haven't done anything wrong. But I feel like the town thinks we're wild and loose. Are we outcasts?"

"Ruby Belle, I don't see how we can be. We never did a thing before we were married that your sisters couldn't watch." She'd been happier the two nights in the hotels, away from everyone she knew, but now that she was back in Tiger she felt like a scarlet woman. Jimmie was hard pressed to help her relax and feel like the mistress of her house.

An hour after they'd gone to sleep they were wakened by a stump exploding outside their bedroom window. Ruby Belle let out a shriek, and dissolved in tears. Jimmie tried to reassure her that it was just some rowdies welcoming them with dynamite, but she put the pillow over her head and tried to disappear into the covers. For half an hour he comforted her while they listened to tin pans being banged with blacksmith tongs, guns shot off, and any kind of improvised drum being thumped. Seven or eight dogs among the more reliable barkers had been brought along. Mary and Ethel had whistles of remarkable shrillness. The wedding trip to the county seat had allowed good time for sending out invites, and even Alice and her in-laws had come up from Metaline, as well as several friends from Ione who loved a good rouser. All of Tiger was there, including two trumpeters who had left home their musical craft but not their noise.

At last Ruby Belle was coaxed into her clothes, and they invited the partiers in for coffee. Jennie had brought a carrot sheet cake. Jimmie's father, correctly assuming Jimmie was unprepared, had brought cigars and candy to pass around to the guests. The Renhaws replaced the trumpets with fiddle and mandolin, and dancing continued till dawn.

Though neither of her parents was there for fear of encountering the other, Ruby Belle was made welcome as an adult, and Ada would have to come around or be the outcast. When Jimmie went outside to milk after the guests had left, he saw his father-in-law over across the field with a tripod, surveying and platting what was to be the extension of the Town of Tiger, and the next step toward his fortune.

****

THE CONTRACTS FOR RAILROAD GRADING had been let in December, and now nearly every man in the Valley was applying to work when the construction came to his own neighborhood. Everyone had plans for how to benefit from the boom. Uriah was turning all his timber into railroad ties, a crew of six men working steadily for him. Wes thought he saw a way to get rid of the 300 cords of wood now stacked beside the store. The steamboats, he said, would be making extra runs to bring materials and laborers to the worksites, and would need extra wood for the boilers. "Says you and everybody else, Wes," Jennie pointed out. "There's cordwood stacked along the bank from Newport to Metaline, hoping for a sale."

"Well, when the trains start running in the fall, they'll use wood for their boilers."

"And in the meantime, Parker Brothers won't mind waiting? Looks like we'll lose the ice business, too, when the boats shut down. The railroads always got their own icehouses."

In February Uriah announced he was clearing land for a hotel. This astonishing new venture was unlike anything he'd undertaken before, and it seemed to Wes no coincidence that Ryer had thought of a new hotel just when Ada had taken over management of E.F. Yoder's Cottage Hotel. He was stepping on George Tiger's toes, too. During his ten years of trying to build the town, George had surveyed and platted the half mile near the river, closest to the Landing; now here was Uriah tripping in from Alaska to plat the next half mile west, beside the coming railroad.

Uriah's father had died in January over at Pilchuk. Jennie was fond of the old fellow with the long beard who'd raised Wes and who liked to help her in the cabbage field. Uriah and Wes had gone for the funeral, and both came back reflecting on the shortness of life. Their father had never found time to realize the ambitions of his early years, and now in their late 40's these two sons realized they should take inventory. In Uriah this, combined with the bitterness of his disintegrating marriage, resulted in the spurt of industry and investment. In Wes, it reinforced his wish to better the world. He gave his Socialist activities more time than he gave the store, even when he was in the store. The *MINER* poetized again on life at The Landing:

If you want to get your money's worth,
Just come to Tiger town;
You can get terbacker, bacon and beans,
And sugar both white and brown.

There ain't no preacher at Tiger town,
But Socialists galore;
For they read the APPEAL TO REASON
At the Tiger grocery store.

******

IN MARCH JENNIE RODE THE train five days to visit her parents in the Owens Valley of California. The mud season was the one time she didn't love the Hawthorn and Tiger and all the Pend d'Oreille. With the snow gone or filthy, the roads impassable, floors impossible to keep clean, and with the ground too cold and wet for planting, she thought it the perfect time for a visit to the parents she hadn't seen in 13 years and likely would not see again. She wasn't regretful, either, to leave the discord that seemed to be on all sides. There was the Ada and Ryer mess, now expanding into a business competition. Zach Zimmerman had announced plans for a second grocery store, to include a butcher shop, which would threaten Wes and Jennie's business. And now there was another school dispute. Of the three School Directors, two were up for re-election, and three people were seeking those slots. Somebody would end up feeling his neighbors didn't appreciate him. The vote came out a perfect three-way tie and the decision would be tied up for months while the County Superintendent made the choice. The outcome was a constant topic of conversation among people coming into the store, and it was not to Jennie's liking to have to guard her tongue for fear of showing favor or disfavor toward those who would soon be her colleagues. She packed her bags in impatience that served as discretion. She was in no hurry to get back.

While she was in California, Wes had the *MINER* sent to her so she saw the Tiger columnist note that *We're in bad need of a director here at the Hawthorn School. The only one we have is in California.* Two more weeks and Wes was quoted as saying that if his wife didn't come back soon, he was going to California and bring her back. The next week she smiled at the news that *Miss Smith is staying at the Wes Wooding home.* She recognized Wes's teasing about replacing her, and packed her bags.

When she got back the Zimmerman store was open in Ryer's house, Ada and Ryer were occupying separate rooms in The Cottage Hotel, and the school directors numbered three, including Jennie. Two thousand dollars worth of cordwood was stacked outside the store, and Parker Brothers Wholesalers was threatening lawsuit.

BUT JENNIE WAS BACK AT The Hawthorn. Thank goodness it was spring; her way of consummating her return would be to put in garden, to put seeds into the ground where they'd turn into what was needed to nourish a family. The ground was ready, and she was ready. She hurried eagerly through the morning cleanup, found Wes's old canvas coat, and put on the broad-brimmed hat someone off the steamboat had left in the Store. She walked out on an April day that promised the last of the snow would be gone in a few days. The drier parts could be plowed now, though other spots would take more time to drain. She spotted a patch of chickweed and started pulling it to put the first fresh greens on the table. Her basket was half full when she saw the first stake and wondered what the boys were cooking up now. They'd have to think again if they thought they could put a shed in the middle of her garden. She looked ahead of her and saw another stake, and beyond it another. Gradually she made out that there were two rows of stakes running in a straight line north. She turned, and they ran as far as she could see to the south. There were some moments of bewilderment almost like dizziness while the strangeness sunk in, before she could start to figure out what was happening. My god, the railroad survey is coming right through my garden! We can't let them do that. We've put manure and compost on this plot for eight years. It's built into mighty good soil. Dazed, she followed the rows of stakes north, sometimes in mud, sometimes in melting snow, occasionally on dry ground or green patches. She was just starting to comfort herself that she could build a new place for spuds, which would grow about anywhere. After all, the first year's garden had been pretty darned good - this soil here at Tiger knew how to grow things. Then an even more horrifying thought hit her, and she ran back south, past the house, to the orchard. Truly, they planned to take out her fruit trees - the ones Jasper had watered with his wagon, the ones she'd trapped moths off, the ones she'd pruned every February, the ones that were at last ready to produce enough fruit for a family. My God, how did we let this happen? She ran to the house to find the contract Wes had signed. It didn't say they were going to take out the garden and orchard, did it? She snatched the paper from the apple box that served as her filing cabinet. When Bill came in the door to find a pair of dry socks, she forgot her deception about reading and thrust the hateful paper at him. "Read me this!" She'd looked at it before, had seen the $50, had understood the 19-37-43 that located The Hawthorn for all the world, had made out the word *corner*. She'd thought she understood what would happen. And Wes hadn't objected to anything. Bill read it through twice for her, and she saw that the horror of the contract lay in its vagueness. Why had they signed it before they saw the survey stakes? Fifty god damned dollars! To tear the heart out of The Hawthorn? Maybe they could still stop it. Maybe the Railroad could lay over a little and go closer to the school. She began seeing flaws in the plan the engineers had made. "Bill, ain't it too wet going through that swamp just north of us? We ought to help 'em find a drier route."

"Ma, they'll fill in the swampy parts. If they move this stretch a few yards west, it'll mess up their route clear from the Blueslide Tunnel. Trains don't turn that easy; the track has to go real straight. I think it's pretty well set, Ma."

Not bothering with a saddle, she rode astride to the Landing. She burst into the Store. "Wes, the Railroad's gypped us. Fifty god damn dollars for my garden and fruit trees. Fifty god damn dollars for ten years of our work. Fifty god damn dollars."

Sitting at the stove, Charlie Lucas and Hy Maggott decided they'd lounged long enough, tipped their hats to Jennie, nodded to Wes, and vacated the premises. They didn't know where they stood, exactly, on the Railroad question, but they knew Jennie was in real pain, and that she didn't need bystanders just now. Wes closed the store early and they went home to get their bearings, she to grieve over what could not be undone, he to help her see that her world would go on.

In the morning, she took the boys' milking chore as a way to be out of the house and alone. The animals in the barn were a comfort too; Shorty and Si and Rover didn't know anything about Railroad issues - they just knew she felt bad and they were sorry. A lot of nuzzling went on in the barn that morning.

By the time she had cornbread in the oven, she'd calmed down enough to work out a new plan, and sent an order on the morning boat to Newport for a dozen new trees. It was late in the season, and only eight trees came back on the *RED CLOUD* the next day. She chose her cherries, apples plums, and pears so there'd be fruit over six months. They were out of plums, though, and there wouldn't be more till next year. Jennie had the rootstocks in in a day, and worked off some steam by hauling the water herself, with Shorty's help. The best slope for keeping the trees' feet dry happened to be where they'd be across the tracks from the house, but the creek wound by the site and hauling water was just as easy there as anywhere else.

She marked off the part of the garden that wouldn't be displaced by the cursed Railroad and worked for weeks like a demon, sentencing Wes to still more time in the store. Here she was after ten years, breaking sod again. She had the garden plowed and the early things in by early May. She unharnessed Shorty, put him out on range, and had a sense of harnessing herself when she went back to the store and let Wes out to look for beef to buy and then sell on the hoof to the Railroad camps. But again he wasn't the only one, and so far the Railroad wasn't gaining him much.

JENNIE FOUND OTHER REASONS TO hate the Railroad. In May a foreman was killed at the Blueslide Tunnel when falling rock crushed his head. After the fact, the whole south end of the tunnel was lined with cement to prevent accidents. "Why don't anybody shut the barn door *before* the horse gets out?" Jennie said when Wes read her the report in the *MINER*. Two men had been killed building the railroad grade near Ruby when rock fell 35 feet on them from the top of the cut. "The bosses didn't know mudslides come in March, I guess," she said.

"They knew," said Wes, "but two men - especially with names like Otto

Blad and Gus Nelson - are cheaper than a late completion date. They've got to start hauling stuff on that Railroad in order to pay for it. Jennie, 15 other men quit on the spot, but the hiring halls in Spokane replaced them by the time Blad and Nelson were put into the potter's field in Newport. See, if we had that One Big Union, it would be every worker in the country out in sympathy, not just 15." Jennie knew, again, that Wes was right, and that he didn't have a snowball's chance in hell of seeing it happen.

BY JUNE THE SNOW WAS off all the surrounding mountains except the highest, Hooknose and Abercrombie far to the north, and Jennie put in the corn, squash, and other warm weather things. The school term was over, and the older boys were working with Wes in the woods. Nine-year-old Davey was running the pack route by himself, neighbors be damned. Jasper had no taste for it, so he became her store and homestead helper. Whether he minded that his little brother had the job of a man while he had the job of a boy, no one knew.

By the middle of the month the Railroad grade had come close enough that she could walk to the work site. She'd had no idea how huge the job was. A dozen whitetops were set up on the river bank: a cook tent, bunk tents, a hay tent, an office, a laundry (She could forget about a little business she's been thinking about.), and a small infirmary. Eighty mules worked quietly until meal time, when all 80 cut loose with brays heard from one side of the valley to the other. Local men had their horses there as well. The camp would get to Tiger soon, and everyone there hoped to turn a fat profit provisioning the men or working on the crew. Locals were given first shot at jobs, using their own plows, scrapers, wheeled fresnoes, wheelbarrows, picks, axes and #2 shovels. The Railroad provided tools for the imported labor, which was most of the 2500 men spread along the 45-mile roadbed. Shay engines, side delivery graders, and a train crane were all working. Horse or mule scrapers were moving tons of dirt. The size of the work area was astounding. She had imagined the route would be about 15 feet wide. Instead, the scrapers and horses and mules needed room alongside the actual roadbed to dig dirt, to fill low spots, and to lay gravel either dug near the job or brought by rail car as far as the tracks extended. The real job, she could see, was laying the bed and cutting the ties. Laying the tracks would be easy.

By the middle of July the tracks were catching up with the grade, were now laid as far as Usk. Jennie heard that Joe Cusick's piece of the railroad pie was his liquor business with the workers, who were always ready for some liquid comfort to replace the families and home comforts they missed. This market replaced Joe's trade with the Kalispels that had been closed down when Joe's settler neighbors petitioned in May to have his license withdrawn because he incited so much wildness across the river. Joe knew when to respect a backset in the river, and kept his license by keeping his promise to sell only to Whites. The Swede crews were his favorite, the Italians and Greeks were pretty good. The Montenegrins and Bulgarians were Muslims, though, and didn't use alcohol. That was just as well, Hy Maggott noted, because they could raise as much hell sober as the Kalispels could drunk.

By August the grade contractor was pulling out of the county and the track-laying contractor hired some of the same crews. When a crew of Montenegrins was camped a mile down the tracks from the Wooding house, their music was audible in the evening after equipment quieted and mules were stabled. One night when the moon was close to full, the four Wooding boys sneaked down to watch. Even Tom at 15 felt a thrill with a trace of fear when he saw the men in turbans and pleated skirts holding hands to dance in a circle around their fire. Something like a gigantic mandolin made a sad and haunting music that accompanied their plaintive singing. Bill whispered, "Is that what they wear where they come from?"

"Well, I don't guess they bought it special for this job."

"It's a dress, but they sure don't look like women in them." Jasper saw a fierceness in the bearded faces.

"Why don't you get yourself one for school, Jasper? Maybe kids wouldn't call you 'Lardass' if you covered it up better."

"Yeah, they could call him Jillie Girl."

The reconnaissance ended in scuffling, and when one of the dancers seemed to turn toward them, they skedaddled for home.

FRANK DARROW, BACK FROM VISITING friends in Ruby, brought with him a Railroad story that amused him so much he broke his habit of aloofness and sat at the stove at the Tiger Store and told it three times over two days, to share the joke.

"It seems a Swede Foreman, Ole Bakke, one morning gave a directive to a Bulgarian crew ballasting and surfacing the track bed at Ruby. One of the Bulgarians claimed to know enough English to serve as interpreter and he passed the order on. But nothing happened. Ole tried again, and the interpreter passed on the second, sterner order. But the men still refused to go to work. Now, Bakke had already had his frustrations with crews that didn't speak English. A Greek crew had one time filed a formal complaint with the contractor stating that they didn't want a 'whiteman' as their foreman. The contractor backed Bakke in that incident and fired the whole crew." Here the Tiger Store listeners interrupted with a discussion of what exactly a "white man" was and whether foreigners could be allowed to define the term. Darrow eventually got to go on with his story. "That made Bakke pretty sure of himself, and he now fired the Bulgarian interpreter for not conveying orders. The interpreter said something to the workers that I won't repeat here (with a glance at Jennie), but it provoked the entire crew of 56 Bulgarians, beards swinging, shovels and picks menacing, to attack Bakke. Bakke realized it wouldn't matter whether the Railroad bosses supported his authority or not because by the time they heard of his plight he'd be punctured pulp. He ran toward the supply shack but he heard the mob gaining on him, every man shouting a shrill threat that didn't need any translation. The train crew by now were through unloading the steel rails they'd brought up, and the train started to move, headed back south. Bakke saw his last best chance, and jumped in the nick of time onto the engine. The engineer, Skinny Betz, and the fireman, Heinie Bohm, were too busy with their own work to notice him, and didn't see him swing out with one arm holding to the engine and the other gesturing triumphantly. The train was creaking and straining as it gained momentum, and they didn't hear him yell back to the Bulgarians, either. Not that it mattered; Bakke yelled in Swedish, the trainmen knew only English and German; and the Bulgarians knew none of these. But they clearly understood what Bakke meant, and they didn't like his hand signal one bit.

"Now from Bakke's position, it appeared he had left the swarm behind, and was safe with his own kind. But the Bulgarians got a different perspective. The engine and the coalcar that blocked Bakke's view were followed by six empty flatcars. The Bulgarians didn't hesitate, and before the engine picked up full speed, they jumped onto the flatcars so they were now on the same train as their quarry. Bakke still believed he was safe, and that he would soon get to a town where there would be protection and law enforcement. But before long the fireman saw a bearded man creeping across the top of the coal car and yelling over his shoulder to his compatriots. The engine was now coming up on the Usk depot, and Skinny slowed the train so Bakke could jump off and make a dash for safety. It took the Bulgarians a minute to figure out what was happening, so that Bakke had locked himself inside the station before they could jump off too.

"The Bulgarians started beating on all sides of the building, peeking through the windows, still shaking their fists. When they saw Bakke use the telephone, though, they realized authority wasn't on their side. They didn't mind hurting a foreman, but they knew better than to damage Railroad property. They left off their hammering and sat on the ground with their backs against the building and ate their lunches. I guess they intended a sitdown strike until their grievance was addressed.

"But in less than an hour an engine arrived from Newport pulling just a caboose, loaded with Constable Mills, a full posse, and enough rifles and pistols so they could impress the fine points of labor law on the insurrectionists."

"Volunteer Goons," observed Wes.

"The Bulgarians wisely accepted their arrest, but then on the advice of a grader who knew as much law as Bakke knew Bulgarian, countersued the contractor. Only two workers and the interpreter were fined, but all 56 were fired. In addition, the interpreter and the two others were rewarded for their countersuit with court costs of $43.95. The management-prone court, which understood nothing of Balkan honor codes, found Bakke innocent of wrongdoing."

Instead of laughter, Darrow was met with a spirited and angry discussion of labor practices and prejudiced courts. Darrow, too, would have liked a better ending for the aggrieved, but if no one else did, he got a good chuckle out of the backwoods case.

THE LAST OF THE CREWS moved on north of Tiger just as school was ready to open and everyone was ready for life to get back to normal. "Though 'normal' ain't going to be the same," Jennie grumped. The new teacher, newly widowed Christina Carpenter, was staying temporarily at The Cottage Hotel while a teacher's cottage was built next to the school. Frank Darrow gave Mrs. Carpenter a copy of The New Practical Arithmetic for the 20th Century, and she and everyone else were proud to have the lessons made out of it. One homesteading widow advertised for a youngster to stay on her place to do chores, and used as bait the *excellent school at Tiger*. Wes told Jennie he knew she didn't have to worry about what kind of School Director she'd make. "Here we are with the best school around. Everyone knows you'll back the teacher every time, Jennie, and raise hell with families that let their kids lay out to work. Who says you have to be a scholar to run a school?"

On November 8 the first train ran. The youngsters from Tiger got a free ride to Ione. Jennie remembered how thrilled she had been with the same ride when the train came into the Owens Valley. She was less thrilled now, though, with the cinders, smoke, and shake of the train that went by right outside her door, so close she'd had to tear down the summer kitchen to make room to walk between the embankment and the house. After just one pass of the train, it was clear why only poor people lived next to the tracks in any town. The cinders falling onto the roof didn't build confidence. Black soot covered everything in the house. If they'd used wood in the firebox, as Wes had counted on, it wouldn't be so bad. But F.A. Blackwell had a coal business in Spirit Lake, and that proved more profitable for him, if less so for the homesteaders. The gigantic rick of wood next to the Woodings' store looked more and more like a white elephant.

THE NOVEMBER ELECTION WENT TO Wes's liking. The County went dry outside incorporated towns. The only precinct in the Pend d'Oreille Valley to vote wet was Ione, 14-27; their saloons and "resorts" (as the whorehouses called themselves) depended on it. In Metaline Falls the vote had been dry, and the saloon and gambling hall owners were disappointed. Both towns immediately began plans to incorporate so as to be eligible for liquor licenses, but found they had to wait one and two years, respectively. Wes steamed that they'd probably get around the law, and ruin the young working men, but for the time being his side had won.

With his mixed feeling of triumph at the vote, and apprehension that it was only a delaying tactic, Wes was ready for a fight, preferably off his own turf. There was that same dilemma - wanting to fight valiantly for the right, and at the same time wanting to keep peace in his backyard. He found the right ticket when the *INDUSTRIAL WORKER* out of Seattle began asking for participants in the Free Speech Fight shaping up in Spokane. The ones in Butte and Missoula had been successes, and this one in the bigger town seemed promising. It looked as if Wes could participate without angering any neighbors. As it turned out, he didn't even have to go to Spokane to do his part.

The Spokane Police Chief had announced that he could and would jail 500 demonstrators. The plan of the Industrial Workers of the World was to bring to town so many protesters that they couldn't all be jailed. In November alone 600 were crowded into the jails, and they still kept coming. The Mayor tried to work an agreement between his hard-nosed police chief and the workers for whom he had some sympathy, but things had gone too far by that time. The IWW headquarters in Chicago asked if the locals would like a celebrity to attend, and pointed out that Elizabeth Gurley Flynn, "The Rebel Girl," was still in Montana and could come on to Spokane by the next train. The locals jumped at the chance, knowing Flynn's effectiveness. The innocent and proper look of this black-haired Irish lass from New York was her best protection, and police knew the best way to incite a mob was to lay a hand on her. But when she arrived, the unmarried Flynn was several months pregnant. Free love among the Socialists was already a sore spot with the public, and the locals weren't sure if she'd be more help or more hurt. To Flynn, they suggested that her safety might be insecure. She insisted on speaking, though, and it was clear her image was only enhanced by the breath of madonna. The crowds leaned toward her as she marked the air with jabbing hand gestures, they frowned when she was serious and laughed when she joked; they brought bystanders to join the crowd. The police responded to her popularity by jailing her along with twenty-five others at the same demonstration. Knowing what could happen to Free Speech people in jail, local Union leaders bailed her out the next morning and chose a new strategy: to use her only for fund raisers in small outlying towns. Lee Bilderback at Lost Creek (as Yocum had been rechristened) and John Renshaw at Tiger were delighted. They tossed for the honor, and Renshaw Hall was to welcome the kind of celebrity for whom it was intended, F.A. Blackwell not quite filling the bill.

Wes joined John Renshaw and Lee Bilderback to form a welcoming committee when Miss Flynn, one of the first visitors to do so, came into Tiger by train. Coming from the south, the train was visible for about a mile. "What's that on top?" asked Lee.

"It moves. Maybe a bear?"

"How would a bear get up there? More likely a cougar."

"Too big for a raccoon."

As the train slowed, the animal on top stood up. It was a man.

"My God, he looks like he rolled in cinders."

"If he rode up there from Spokane and then went through that Blue Slide tunnel, he'd just as well have rolled in cinders."

As the unpaid passenger let himself down the side and jumped to the ground, they saw a large pistol in a shoulder holster. When his feet touched the ground, he pulled out a blue bandana, dipped it in the snow beside the tracks, and wiped the soot off his face and hands. As the train came to a full stop he swung into the car he had been riding on and they saw him approach a young woman, lower her luggage from the racks, and take it off the train for her. The welcomers had been intrigued enough by the topside traveler to forget about their official visitor, but now they realized the pretty woman in the long red wool cape was the famous rabble rouser. She set an unadorned broad-brimmed felt hat on top of her thick wavy hair and pulled on a pair of supple leather gloves. Wes wondered how this much dignity and grace came to be in a girl he knew was only 19. As she stepped down, the drape of the cloak drew their eyes to charming ankles. They could see why she was such a favorite speaker, and she hadn't yet said a word. As soon as he was assured the local committee would take care of his charge, the informal bodyguard disappeared in the direction of the riverbank. Miss Flynn explained, "Headquarters doesn't send money for bodyguards, so when one of the boys figures I need protection, he's on his own for expenses. Hence the outside accommodation."

"Where's he headed?"

"I believe the committee asked for a home stay for me. He doesn't want to crash in on it, so he'll see if he can find a shed or a boat on the riverbank to hold off the snow. Jake's used to this kind of travel." John Renshaw excused himself and hurried after Jake, offering him dinner at his house, and shelter in Renshaw Hall.

"Anyway, being out of Spokane is a vacation for him. He's been arrested six times for taking part in Free Speech Fights. If he did sleep on the riverbank, he'd be better off than in the Spokane jail. A favorite trick of the coppers, after they've beaten a guy up with their billy clubs, is to put as many of them as they can into one cell and turn the heat up as high as it'll go. Then after a couple of men faint, they take them all out and put them in an unheated cell for the rest of the night. At least on your riverbank the temperature would be steady. In your Hall, he'll be in luxury."

"Did that happen to you, Miss Flynn?"

"No, I was in with women who... had... another kind of charge against them. Then the local Wobblies bailed me out after one night. I don't want to tell you about that one night, but I wasn't treated any worse than the other women; actually better, come to think of it. My trial for conspiracy came up pretty soon and a jury said I was innocent. The prosecutor was pretty mad, because everyone knew I was perfectly guilty of speaking on the street. The jury foreman told him, 'She ain't a criminal, Fred, an' you know it! If you think this jury, or any jury, is goin' to send that pretty Irish girl to jail merely for bein' bighearted and idealistic, to mix with all those whores and crooks down at the pen, you've got another guess comin.' And I think my being pregnant made everyone kind of protective. They didn't want my baby to have a toothless mother."

While they talked, they escorted Miss Flynn to Wes's house. "Here's my humble trackside homestead, Miss Flynn." Wes showed her her pallet by the stove.

She spotted Wes's stash of magazines. "Mr. Wooding, I see they aren't confiscating the *APPEAL TO REASON* in Tiger yet. Those Spokane coppers do, you know, when they find them at the IWW Hall or anywhere around." After they commiserated on the lack of freedom in the big town, the men left her alone to settle in.

When Jennie came home from the store, The Rebel Girl turned from the stove and greeted her with a handshake. "I'm pleased to meet you, Mrs. Wooding. I'm Gurley Flynn. I thought with an unexpected guest, you'd accept some unexpected help. Your cabbages were irresistible, and I'm trying an Irish stew with Western American venison. It may be new to all of us, but it'll be tasty."

"You ain't exactly unexpected, Miss Flynn. Wes and Lee and John made sure everybody in the Valley knew about you. Feathers in their caps, I gather. You're giving a talk at the Hall tonight, I hear."

"Yes. I'm supposed to raise money for the Free Speech Fight in Spokane. The Union tries to help out people who leave their jobs to come take part. And they put up bail as often as they can. You don't want to stay in jail too long. Head thumpings can be for keeps sometimes."

"What's a Free Speech Fight, exactly?"

Miss Flynn looked at Jennie so long before answering that Jennie thought she'd said the wrong thing. Then she said, "Mrs. Wooding, it's a breath of fresh air to hear you ask that. I'd forgotten there were people busy with just living, and not fighting a war all the time. I've been doing street speaking since I was in high school. I don't even have a home, not one of my own. I stay with my parents in the Bronx sometimes. With this baby coming, I've been trying to imagine how I'll live now."

"What do you mean 'in the broncs'?"

"The Bronx is part of New York." She laughed with delight. "I really am in another world! Mrs. Wooding, you're a revelation."

Jennie reddened. If she read books, she wouldn't make gaffes like that. But Miss Flynn's sharp blue eyes weren't mocking, they were admiring. Jennie tried to save face. "Wes does more of the politicking for us. I care about it, but as you say, I'm pretty busy with four boys and the farm and the store and the nursing." She paused. "And, truth be told, I keep kind of a grudge against the government. It seems like no matter how much you talk about it, they're going to run things to suit the rich anyway. Wes and his kind think the government's supposed to be run to help most of the people. I don't know how he can read so much and still believe that'll happen. I have to admit I stay out of it because I'd just stay mad if I didn't."

Before they spoke again, each woman spent some minutes thinking about her own life and comparing it to the other's. Neither was sure enough of her thoughts to say anything.

Jennie stirred the woodstove and started drop dumplings to go on the stew. "So, what's a Free Speech Fight, exactly?"

Miss Flynn leaned forward as if she were on a platform in front of a crowd. "First thing, remember that the 1st Amendment says people can 'peaceably assemble' and that they have 'freedom of speech.'"

Jennie didn't remember, because the Constitution hadn't shown up yet by the third reader. But she had grown up assuming the two principles, whether she'd ever heard of them or not. She pretended she had read what she wished she had.

Miss Flynn continued. "What the Industrial Workers of the World want to do is talk about their ideas on the street. That's the only way they can get more people into the Union, and the Union's the only way they can make working conditions better. But in Spokane, as in Butte and Missoula, the cops have decided Wobblies can't speak in public. In other words, people can speak freely there *if* they don't say what the cops don't like. The coppers are paid to develop their political opinions. Bankers back lumber and railroad barons, and all three want labor to stay as cheap as possible. The whole idea of a strong union is poison to them. So they pay the cops to haul Wobblies to jail and beat them up. We keep on bringing in more and more speakers until they have to give up because their jails aren't big enough. And that's what a Free Speech Fight is." Gurley was setting the table. The dumplings sat ready for the broth when Wes and the boys would come in from the chores. The women sat while they waited.

"Ain't you afraid, Miss Flynn?"

"Only sometimes. I understand everyone calls you 'Aunt Jennie.' May I?"

"Sure, Gurley." Jennie grinned. "You know, that feels funny to say. Wes calls me Girlie sometimes."

"It's the boys in the Union that call me Gurley. That's my middle name. They mean it as a term of affection, and it truly works. I feel a warmth in it every time I hear it." She stirred the stew, tasted it, took some thyme from a cheesecloth bag hanging behind the stove, and stirred again. "Aunt Jennie, I haven't talked to anyone about this yet. I wanted to try it on a woman first. At the Spokane jail there's only one room for women. So I was in with a couple of prostitutes. They bring them in all the time. It's kind of a silly exercise, because the women will go right back to work the next day. I wondered why the cops would keep arresting them when they say they need more room for Wobblies. The women were nice to me, gave me an apple and a blanket. But then I heard the one named Flossie complain to the jailer about my being housed in with them. So I started paying attention. And it turns out what they didn't like was that they couldn't have johns come up to them there in the jail."

"That can't be."

"That's what I thought. But I pretended to be dead asleep with a pillow over my head, and they decided I was safe. So a jailer would come and get one and they'd be gone a while, then she'd come back, and then she'd go out again. They both came and went all night. Jennie, the Sheriff is actually running a brothel right there in the Spokane County Jail."

"Even in Ione they have to keep the resorts all together over by Muddy Creek. The cops know it, and they don't try very hard to stop it, but I never heard they made money from it."

"They probably do. Through payoffs to ignore it all. But this is beyond that. This is actually using public property to exploit those poor women. I'm sure the largest share of the fee goes to the cops."

"That'd puke a railroad boss."

"I wondered how you'd react. I'm not going to bring this up in Tiger. I'm going to stick to my standard stuff, but when I'm back in Spokane, I think I could make good use of it. I think the wives of those same cops and barons would react just like you did, and maybe realize that only Free Speech can clean up business like that. It could be played as a labor issue - which it is, with the cops taking an unfair rakeoff - or as a moral issue. I'm guessing in Spokane or in Tiger the moral issue would be stronger."

Jasper came in with the milk, and the others soon after. Bill came in the door in time to hear Gurley tell Jennie that she wasn't going to talk about Flossie and her job troubles tonight, but stick to her regular, "the hiring halls and the sharks and the perpetual hiring plan." At dinner, Bill asked, "Miss Flynn, I know what a shark is and a hiring hall, but what's a 'perpetual hiring plan'?"

"They're all related. The sharks run the hiring halls, and an out-of-work man can come into Spokane and give his last dollar for a job. He might decide that's worth it, and that's fine, if he gets a job. But there are lumber camps and railroad crews and mines where he'd last just a week on the job and then be let go. By that time his replacement would already be on the way from Spokane. So, actually, there are three crews in perpetual motion: the one that's on its way to a new job, the one that's working for a short while, and the one that's on its way out of the job. The hiring hall makes a lot of money and gives a share of it to the employer. The employers can give the workers any kind of miserable working conditions they want because the men think that if they accept whatever's thrown at them, they might be able to keep their job."

After dinner Wes and the boys went directly to Renshaw Hall to arrange benches and build up the fire. Gurley asked, "Aunt Jennie, I wonder if you have some red thread. My cape lining got snagged when I stepped on the train."

"You bet, Gurley." She went to her sewing basket, then turned back. "Sure, and I wouldn't mind a few minutes off my feet. Could you be doing the cleanup while I darn your darlin' cape?"

"Sure and I would," she laughed. "Jennie, when did you get to be Irish? You sound just like my folks."

"I was just talking that way to tease you. But my folks do some of that, and my older brothers. They weren't born over there, but I guess it can stay in a family. I left home so young I lost it. "

"Where do I put this dishwater?"

"Outside the door on the chives. Gurley, this lining is done nice. Who sewed it?"

"My mother. She's very proud of my work, so she made that red cloak to be like a flag. Most of the people who call us Reds or Communists hate us. But my mother would love to see some of those ideals come about. When I wear it, though, I don't think so much about politics as I do about my mother sitting, after working all day, sewing that lining in and still able to make her stitches invisible."

"Here you go."

"Aunt Jennie, this is amazing! I can't even find the spot you darned. Sure, and you've got the gift in your fingers, just like me mam." The four boys came home. Tom and Bill helped Wes escort Miss Flynn to Renshaw Hall, and Jennie stayed home with Jasper and Davey.

1910

BY THE END of January the winter's snow pack was deeper than most years', and they thought it would take care of last year's drought. But the heavy snows of February didn't come. Instead, the melt started early, with the ground still frozen so that much of it ran off instead of soaking in. "Look ahead to carrying water for them spuds," Jennie warned. But the harm would be much greater than to Jennie's garden. By mid-March snow for skidding was gone, and John Olmstead and Wes closed their wood camp up Tiger Hill. The Forest Service regularly published precipitation measurements for the Kaniksu Forest Reserve, which the backside of the river had become. Each month was more dismal than the last. "I guess we wouldn't know it was dry if we didn't have a Ranger to tell us," said Hy Maggot. "Good thing I paid my taxes, or I wouldn't know that grass was crackling underfoot."

"One good thing, though," Jennie allowed, "the soil's drying out early. It's warm enough to plant right now." So she put in the May things in April and the June things in May, thinking to beat the late August freezes at the other end. But one year was enough, she told the boys, of lugging tools and carts eight feet up, over, and eight feet down the railroad embankment, so she built a shed on the garden side. Rover was up and over with her every time, and she realized he didn't consider the garden his responsibility any more since he couldn't see it from the house. She knew everything from ground squirrels to whitetails to bears would raid it. Maybe this division of the homestead wasn't going to be so easy to get used to after all.

The railroad's effect on the house itself was certainly not getting any more comfortable. The house and all its contents got a shaking every few hours. Jennie made rails for the dish shelves, like she'd seen on the riverboat. She was disgusted by the coalsmoke and ash covering everything, including their clothes that hung on pegs. Cinders from the locomotive and sparks from the rails and brake shoes were more than inconvenient, they were downright dangerous.

The boys loved night passings of the trains, when they had a fireworks show, but Jennie didn't think the entertainment worth the risk. She had Tom build a platform on the roof and they took a barrel of water up there with a dipper and a stack of gunnysacks to dampen. Out of poles they built a ladder for each side of the pitched cedar shake roof. After each daytime passing of a train, a boy went up to check for hot spots. At night she and Wes traded off.

The Railroad was not even trying to clean up its mess or soften the scarring. Brush was still stacked for burning, or not even stacked, just left strewn along the right-of-way, and drying out fast. Wages, she knew, were not going to be wasted on that. Pits where gravel and dirt had been dug out were now covering themselves with weeds instead of grass, and the weeds grew more fuel that dried out faster than grass.

A private loss that she didn't tell people about was when she had to put a curtain on their bedroom window. The headlight of the train poured in, and startled her awake. Once it happened when she and Wes were making love, and they dove under the covers. It might have been funny, but it wasn't to her. So her sequestered nest was no more; the stars weren't there if she opened her eyes in the night, and the moon never passed by.

Finally she surrendered. "Wes, how about we build a new house for us and maybe find a renter for this one? Things here can't ever be made good again. We oughta just give up. We can go on the other side of the tracks, still near the creek, where we're next to the garden. I already put the new fruit trees over there. It's true we'd be moving toward the road, but it's a lot quieter, for Pete's sake, than the railroad. I know we've put 10 years into this place, but it's not what we meant it to be anymore." No one, not even Wes, knew what it cost her to say this.

She had no trouble convincing Wes. The Socialist was getting a kick out of becoming the prosperous property owner, and the idea of a new two-story, milled-board house with a well and porches fore and aft gave him a chuckle. What made Jennie smile was remembering that first winter with the boys in the old log house, with baby Jasper pulling the chinks out every chance he got.

They walked out together to pick a spot, or so she thought. She soon caught on that they were walking out so he could show her the spot he'd already chosen: on a rise a scant 30 yards from the county road. She thought maybe he didn't understand what the little wagon road would likely turn into. "Ain't it a pretty busy spot?"

"Jennie, you always say you want to be a recluse, but I notice you spend a lot of time with folks. Half the people here call you Aunt Jennie. From the store, you know every single person in the country. You've delivered three dozen babies here, and doctored about everybody at least once. Let's just admit you like to be in the middle of things, and build where we can see folks pass by. And a few years from now when we're shipping by truck, it'll be a lot handier."

They asked Tom what he thought of it. "Good choice, Pa. Lots less snow to move."

Well, it had been her idea to move, hadn't it? But she hadn't meant to completely desert Hawthorn Lodge. Well, what did she mean, then? You can't move a log house. At least the new spot wasn't on the main street of Tiger, and she gave up arguing with Wes and herself.

The ground was still frozen, so they couldn't dig for a foundation, but they began in late March to clear the spot. Once decided, Wes wanted to go full bore on the job. As soon as they'd cleared the site and moved the harvested poles to the railroad pole yard, Shorty, Kit and Mose began hauling boards from Cass Hacker's sawmill at the south edge of town. The windows and doors came by train this time. Tom had finished his 8th grade exams almost a year ago, and now was a third hand on the job. The whole thing was up by the time Mary and Ethel came home from school in Seattle, and Jennie had a surprise party for them in the old house, her private farewell to the Hawthorn Lodge. She was resigned to the new place, but leaving the old one was hard. She kept finding reasons not to start moving things to the new house, a fortunate delay as it turned out.

Alice and Charley had moved up from Metaline, and on May 8 all four of Ada's girls joined Jennie and 25 other women and children in a day of maintenance work at the Riverside Cemetery. Cattle had been moving through the graveyard, attracted to the lusher grass there, and had been knocking over gravestones. When the crew got there, they found the brush had leafed out early, and almost immediately begun to wither; it was as dry now as it should be in August. They stacked what they cut, but didn't dare burn it as they would in a normal May. Mary said it seemed as if the whole county was one big brush pile. Jennie concurred. "Between the Railroad right of way and the way the Panhandle is getting the trees out, nobody's been taking time to clear slash. And now can't nobody burn till fall."

When Jennie opened the cursed curtain one morning about a week later, she saw magenta clouds resting on top of the hills, and stretching clear across the valley. Everything looked like a photograph tinted with a fireside-red glow, like Jimmie Hildreth used to do to some family pictures. She stood and watched it, long enough that she felt cool standing there, and reached for a sweater. She watched some more, but it didn't fade. She got dressed, checking the window after each garment. It still was the hot pink of fireweed. The rest of them got up and as they all went through the morning chores they watched the sky, still putting on its show. It wasn't now the morning mountain pinks; those had faded. The dawn was well over, but there was still a coppery, amber look to the air and to everything the sun touched.

Walking over to open the store, Jennie smelled cedar smoke. So that wasn't an overcast that was dimming the sun. And her eyes weren't burning because she was short on sleep. A smoke-dimmed sky was not new to the settlers, but surely no one would dare burn in this dry spring. She looked up to the hills on both sides of the valley; she couldn't see to the tops, and she couldn't see any mountains to the north or south. Not only Old Hooknose and Abercrombie were hiding, but little Pennsyltuck and Jordan, just five miles away. It was like ought two, when 60 families moved in within a year, all burning stumps and slash to clear spots for their houses. Or the years right after Proving Up, when they were selling their poles and burning the residue, and you seldom saw the sky from April on.

Grandma Olmstead was the first person in the store that morning, bringing for trade a basket of morels in a lining of moss.

"What do you make of this air, Jennie?"

"I wish I could just enjoy looking at it. But I believe it says there's fire too close."

"What do you hear about the comet, Jennie? When's it coming to our parts?"

Wes had read to her and the boys about Halley's Comet, and about the chances of its being seen out West. "This month, I believe. You're not worried about the gases some say it brings, are you, Grandma Olmstead?"

"No, no, I don't mean that. I know better than that. Nobody's going to get poisoned, for gracious sakes. No, I want to see it because I saw it when I was a little girl, back in Wisconsin, in 1834. I'd like to be able to say I saw it twice. Old Mark Twain says he was born the year of it, but I was big enough to remember it. We all took chairs outside and watched every evening for a month or so. And he says he's going to die this time it comes, and I plan to hang on a while yet. No, I'll outdo him on both ends, and I want to get to brag about it."

The smoke continued and increased as the days went by. "Wes, I don't think Grandma Olmstead's going to get to see her comet. I ain't seen stars in a good while."

"We may see worse than a comet. Every time I feel a breeze I watch the hills for flame. If we get through this year without fire, we'll be mighty lucky."

They weren't.

On Friday, May 20, they knew it was actual. For more than two weeks they'd thought it might happen, knew it was happening elsewhere, tried to believe the winds would change all their known patterns and skip their little world. But on this morning the dawn sun was a deep red ball, and by midmorning towers of smoke were coming over Tiger Hill, billowing 200 feet into the air. People working outdoors wore handkerchiefs over their noses and mouths. About noon Joe Parker tried the new telegraph line that had got this far north with the railroad. At Newport they knew of several fires throughout the county, and the smoke at Tiger could be any or all of them. No, the state fire warden hadn't even realized there were towns that far downriver, and he didn't have fire guards or firefighters to send that far afield.

All work stopped except that of hunkering down for the inevitable. Joe Parker became a commander. He recruited strong girls, Ada's Mary among them, to man the windlasses on the riverbank, cranking up the creaking, rusty cables bearing bucketload after bucketload of water to be used by whoever came to the riverbank with a container of any kind to fill. Wagons pulled up with galvanized wash tubs, copper boilers, and every bucket of every kind the family owned. Drivers filled them with all the water available, and took it to their houses where they damped down gunnysacks, quilts, and canvas tarpaulins. The Wes Woodings, the Renshaws, and others near the creek had a shorter haul. Jennie sent Davey to the riverbank with a pair of leather gloves for Mary. "She won't have thought of that," she said.

Jennie was the foreman at Hawthorn Lodge. She chose which things would be wrapped in canvas and buried in the yard. Each of them made a stash of clothes and extra bedding. "But keep in mind, we hope we'll be sleeping here tonight." Wes's books went in, and Jennie's collection of photographs dating back to 1878, when she'd joined James Hildreth's traveling photographer's wagon. From the barn Jasper brought ropes and leather tack, stacked it in the yard and covered it with wet canvas. They moved the furniture out piece by piece and stood it in the creek. She sent her wealth of laundry tubs to the roof of the house and had the boys carry water one bucketful at a time up the ladders to fill them. She had them wet down the outbuildings. With pickaxes and shovels, and with some small fires, they finished clearing a thirty-foot-wide firebreak they'd been making around the house, the shed, the privy, and the barn. She had them take out any segments of fence that might give fire a route to the house.

They conferred about the new house, and decided they'd have to sacrifice it. They couldn't protect two, and the old one was where they still lived, where all their belongings were, and which Jennie's heart could never entirely abandon. The new house had some lumber and some labor in it, but it hadn't been their home and their hearth. The newly finished house on the county road would have to take its chances. Then, too, while she hated giving that damned Railroad any credit, the eight-foot dirt and gravel embankment was between them and the fire, while the new house sat exposed on its rise, daring the fire to come to it.

By noon Wes was smoke blinded and could help only with tasks he could do by touch. By touch he put hackamores on the cayuses and led them to the river and tethered them on long ropes. "Too much brush around the creek," he said. He cursed himself for never piping water into the house; it had seemed so easy, with four boys, to bring a few buckets of water a day from the creek. Now here he was feeling a path from the creek to the house, hauling four buckets at a time in the boys' old wagon. It was Jennie who thought of tying a damp cloth over his eyes for some relief. As he passed by with a bundle of braided rugs Bill ribbed, "You look like you're going to the firing squad, Pa."

"Nay, Fool, I'm smelling my way to Dover." They both smiled at the reminder of Lamb's King Lear that Wes had been reading them.

In the late afternoon the wind picked up as it did most afternoons, and the flames and smoke intensified. The threat looked more immediate. Joe Parker and George Tiger rode up into the hills in the direction of the fire to make sure all settlers up that way were safe. They brought several children down to share the comparative safety of the river bank settlers; their parents stayed to defend their homesteads.

At sunset the wind died down, and the fire stalled on the other side of the west ridge. The eerie red ball returned. But as darkness came on, the glow of the fire reflecting on the clouds and the smoke billows showed clearly that the hubs of hell were just over the hill. No one slept that night except Davey, young enough to put all his faith in the grownups and succumb to the long hours of labor. He rolled up in a blanket and slept near the door. The rest of them sat outside on stumps and liked to imagine they were holding off the holocaust.

On Saturday, May 21, the fire crested and started down the hill toward Tiger Town. The settlers on the hill turned out to be the safest of all. The fire stayed in the treetops as it came down in some swaths; in others it flash-burned the underbrush and left the trees unscathed. These settlers, too, had protected their homes, and while they had less water with which to fight the fire, no homestead was burned out, thanks to the large clearings that had been inspired probably less by a concern for fire safety than by a desire to see the sky and grow gardens.

Then the fire landed fiercely at the valley's edge where it burned more deeply and slowly and started across the quarter mile toward Tiger Town.

It didn't come in a solid wall, but sent curious fingers across, whimsically missing some homesteads and hitting others. Still their luck held. What managed to jump the firebreaks around each home was effectively beaten out with wet gunny sacks or spades.

At the Renshaw house the mandolin, the violin, the tambourine and all small instruments were wrapped in canvas, boxed, and buried. John spent an hour of precious time building a pole frame in the house around the organ and draped it with wet, well-wrung canvas. "Even if the house catches, the old harmonium might have a chance."

By midday tendrils of fire were touching the logs that had been taken during the past year from the Underwood place and piled in a huge deck along the tracks for delivery to the Panhandle mill in Ione: seven hundred thousand feet by the inspector's estimate when he put his blue chalk on the log ends. Bill Underwood had received his payment, so the loss would go to the Panhandle, who could afford it better than Bill. What the logs represented to the settlers at Tiger was a gigantic pile of fuel running north-south for a quarter mile along the west side of their town, the side where the wildfire was approaching. If those logs were ignited, brave Tiger Town would likely go with them. And who was to protect the logs? Households scattered any distance at all from the business district had to give their first loyalty to their homes. Only those few living near the landing road between the railroad and the river chose to protect the logs. Plus Joe Parker and George Tiger. "Go on home, Joe. You've got a family in your house."

"Martha and the girls can handle it. They know I've got to meet my sheriff's duties first." Using the same methods every family was using at its home place, half a dozen men tried to beat out firebrands and cinders as they fell on the massive wall of logs.

Hy Maggott realized, "These are Panhandle logs. Shouldn't they be here protecting them?"

"Yeah, but who's gonna quit whacking firebrands long enough to go tell them?"

"Anybody know how to use that telegraph in the station?" Precisely as Charlie Lucas said this, fire downed a telegraph pole and the line was out. "Pretty precarious, ain't it?" he observed.

"Who can go to Ione and tell the Panhandle?"

"Try the Wes Woodings. They're close by and they've got six; maybe they could spare somebody long enough to go."

The river again became the travel route of choice. Tom and Bill were too important to the family's own firefighting; the mission offered too much chance for misjudgment to be entrusted to Jasper, so it was nine-year-old Davey who took a small raft he and his cousin Charles Norman had built in the previous week's play, and set off for Ione. High water for the river was still a month away, high water for the creeks running into it was two weeks behind them, and the challenge was not great for a boy who'd spent his life by the Pend d'Oreille. He poled along the shore, and was at the Panhandle millpond in less than an hour. An hour more and he had the thrill of riding into Tiger on a handcar with the first crew of six men. They had doused their clothing in the millpond before they left, and they draped wet gunnysacks over their heads as they neared the Tiger blaze. As they came to Renshaw Creek they slowed and let Davey roll off the car and onto the embankment that was shielding his homestead from the flames. Davey's reward was in the glory. The handcar would shuttle back and forth to the Panhandle until 40 men had been reassigned from the saws and the planer and called in from their off shifts. Ten men from the railroad would join them, and the full crew of fifty would be no more effective than the six Tiger businessmen had been. But it did allow Tiger people to protect their own buildings. By dark the massive log deck was shooting flames so high into the air that people four miles away in Ione didn't need a boy to come tell them there was trouble at Tiger. At some points, as the high wind that was fanning the fire mixed with the wind created by the burning trees, the roar was loud enough to be heard in Ione.

They thought they'd worked before, but that Saturday night was the test of their lives. From the doomed log deck the flames lapped up into the stands of cedar and white pine still awaiting the Panhandle logging crew.

The wind got so strong empty buckets were not secure and went rattling by as if trying to find their own way back to the river for a refill. Wes said it was like tornados back in Kansas. He swore he felt the ground shake.

When the flames surrounded the Joe Parker house south of town, Joe was no longer at the log deck. He was with the $2000 worth of cordwood still stacked outside Wes's store waiting for a customer. It was unclear why Joe should risk his own property to protect the most famous White Elephant in the area. By the time George Tiger was able to get Joe's attention and show him both the pointlessness and the futility of his efforts, Joe couldn't get through the blazing tornado to his house. He feared the worst, and went down the river bank and followed the shore south to where his house should be. At first he thought he'd gone on by it in the smoke. He went back north a ways. He did this three times, and finally realized the house was no more. And he saw no one. Joe was overcome with guilt and fear; the helpful, comforting woman and her two little girls that he'd brought to the wilderness had trusted him. He sat in the sand with water up to his waist and sobbed. Every few moments he took a look at the top of the bank to see if they weren't somehow coming through the fire to safety. After a half hour, either Joe's devotion to his duty or his inability to live with this kind of grief sent him back to Tiger. There were, at least, still living people and standing buildings there, a semblance of a normal world. He joined the men working with shovels and buckets; all their faces were as black as his own, and no one saw that his agony was worse than the fatigue and fear they all shared.

When dawn came on Sunday, May 22, the sky had yet another trick: it was a ghastly yellow. The log deck and the cordwood were still burning, but daylight lessened the horror. They could see what they still faced. They could see that there was a world still around them, with homes and businesses still standing and people still alive. Through the night each person had lived in a tiny circle of roar and flame, smoke and heat, sweat and dirt. Now with daylight the circle included some fellow humans, some signs of success. They couldn't yet stop to eat, but they grabbed water every few minutes, straining it through their teeth so as not to swallow cinders and firebrands and ash. They didn't dare remove the wet gunnysacks from their heads, but they could hold up their faces and make human contact.

Around noon Hy Maggott saw some people moving up the railroad bed from the south, stepping around the smoking ties. As they got closer, he saw they were three women. "Where's Joe? Joe Parker! Ain't that your family?" Martha and her daughters had buried what they could, and sensibly abandoned the house in good time to get to the sloughs a couple of hundred yards south of their house. They'd taken Joe's boat out into the center and while they needed to douse a few flying firebrands, the fire was less violent at this distance from the Panhandle log deck. They rowed south till they were well away from it, walked through the green forest to the railroad tracks, and walked back down the tracks to Tiger Town. Martha told Joe she never for a moment considered the house more important than their lives.

By afternoon most of the fuel around the town had burned or been cleared away by the crew. A firebreak between the buildings and the log deck at one end of town, and another between the town and the cordwood at the other end, had been cleared. Exhausted youngsters and women relieved each other at the windlasses, and water kept coming. There are worse places to fight a fire than beside a big river. The businesses and stores were soaked, but they hadn't burned.

At the Wooding homestead, as at many others, there was time now to eat a cold breakfast. They went two by two to the creek to wash their faces, always leaving someone at the house to guard against new outbreaks. Everyone moved slowly, raising their feet barely enough to propel them across the blackened earth. Jennie asked Tom to take her hand and they climbed up onto the embankment to look across to the new house. There was no miraculous reprieve. It was hard to believe how completely the entire structure had disappeared. Everything was the same color of black; grass and foundation were indistinguishable from one another. Sparkles in the ashes showed where windows had exploded. Their ambitious spring's work was gone, but she still believed they'd made the right choice. Hawthorn Lodge was intact.

Black trees, black bushes, black grass, blackened people were left. It took two days for the shock to lift and voices to sound normal. During that time goods remained buried in fear of a new blaze. The log deck and the cordwood smoldered on; the air remained full of smoke, and lanterns were needed day and night.

It turned out all the Northwest was smoky, and would remain so through the summer. Fires burned somewhere in the Pend d'Oreille Valley constantly. It was unclear who was responsible for firefighting, much less fire prevention. In July the bigger lumber companies and the Forest Service made a pact to fight fire jointly, and agreed that from now on all slash would be burned each fall and each spring. But of course nothing could change fast enough to help before the horrendous Big Blowup in August that killed 200 homesteaders and firefighters from Newport to the Rockies and across Idaho and western Montana. As at Tiger, people used their own tools and worked where they were personally threatened. The lumber companies reassigned their regular crews to fight fire on their holdings. The sky was darkened over six states, and the sunsets were red clear to Cheyenne, Wyoming.

Rain never came. President Taft asked all Army forts in the Northwest to shoot their guns simultaneously at 8:00 each morning in an attempt at rainmaking. The Navy guns in Puget Sound and along the coast, where shipping was hindered by the smoke, were to join in, but the Generals and the Admirals could never quite coordinate their schedules, and the master plan never developed.

Jennie richened her soil by tilling in the ash, and planted a new garden. Having their fire early in the season was more luck for the downriver settlers than those upriver would have. When their fire came in late August they couldn't put in a second garden, and many had to be housed in Newport like beggars through the winter. Others were killed, maimed or permanently crazed.

A strange phenomenon developed that summer and fall. In past years, social events were mostly saved for the winter, when crops didn't fill everyone's days. This year, though, saw the beginning of the Odd Fellows Lodge in Ione; the card parties and dances so common in bad weather continued through the summer; the Sunshine Club continued to meet monthly, including once *at the home of Miss Mary Wooding,* Ada's presence in that home being by now more or less ignored by all. A Grange was organized at the Tiger School, which had miraculously been spared by the fire. "Hawthorn all around it was better than a firebreak; it's too damned hard to catch a passing fire," surmised Jennie. George Tiger hired more men than he could afford to build a two-story dance hall. Why the town needed a second hall was not clear, but several families were able to rebuild sheds and barns on the strength of George's payroll. In another act of largess, George platted 45 lots on his land and donated all the "streets, avenues, roads and alleys" to the public. More than ever, George saw that the homestead system, which kept people separated on their individual acreage, kept towns from developing. He sold the lots within the Town Plat for $1, virtually giving away his land and his money to give the dazed homesteaders something to rally around. With logs for rollers and a team of eight horses, George Tiger moved four frame buildings a half mile west to be near the railroad, all the businesses except the log store. If the Tiger community didn't materialize, it wasn't George's fault.

A new post office was built near the tracks. A tiny railroad station came next, the same shape as the big ones at Dalkena and Ione, but scaled to the size of business expected at Tiger. Everything now faced the tracks rather than the river, except the old log store that couldn't be moved.

Soon after Lost Creek's fire in July Jeff Honsinger, riding one horse and leading another, had come up the county wagon road to pay Jennie a call. "Jen, we're clearing out. I brought you Old Star. We don't want to take him with us down to Oregon, and we're moving out. Ain't no shame to it. We can rebuild, but we want to do it where you can look out the window at something besides charcoal and ash. And, truly, Lyd's pretty shaky. She ain't got over being scared, and she don't want to start over on everything, with the ash to fight too. She says she can't smell nothing but singe."

For the second time, the Woodings began the second house. There was no work that didn't leave the worker black from head to toe, and even Jennie allowed her men to put on blackened clothes from the day before. Work was quiet now, too. A general silence was over all crews, whether building, logging or farming. "It looks like a whole town of coal miners," Wes noted. Fall rains helped, washed some of the ash down into the grass that had grown through the summer. As things gradually came to look normal so did the people, and then they began to sound normal and occasionally laughed and teased a little. George got his dance hall built in time for a grand opening in December, and hosted a dinner for everyone. When the snow came, it brought a blessed disguise.

1911

THE USUAL RUGGED winter jollity never developed that year at Tiger. Instead there was a gentle kindness among neighbors. There was a softer tone to the teasing among people who came into the store and to joshing on the job. Everyone had suffered great fear and great loss, and everyone wanted to save others from more. Everyone was somewhat fragile, and knew the neighbors to be the same, so no one was rough, even in play.

The towns downriver from Tiger had not suffered, the worst fires had missed them, and now they seemed to come into a wild adolescence. They were able now to sell liquor within their newly-incorporated town limits. The Metalines' gambling trade and Ione's "resorts" flourished. Proximity to the Canadian border made the area prime smuggling territory for Chinese laborers, opium, and now, with State Prohibition, alcohol. Miscreants of any stripe could make a quick escape to Canada, and were drawn to the far downriver.

But upriver, where fire had taken away so much the settlers had built, things were the worst. When the fall rains deepened the gloom, some were crazed. Isaac Brown at Lost Creek beat his wife and chased her and their children out of the house with a long-bladed knife; they ran to the neighbors for protection where Brown, in pursuit, was shot dead by Floyd Pennington, with whom he had emigrated from Kentucky. Even Joe Cusick was jailed, having threatened to kill his wife of one month with a gun. William Moon was one of the lucky ones; recognizing that he was suffering from delusions, he asked to be locked in the county jail; the Sheriff took him to the mental hospital at Medical Lake instead.

When the spring melt came and the snow mixed the ash underneath into gray sludge and revived the scent of scorch, things were not better. One Frenchy, who for years had withstood the loneliness and hardships of homesteading alone, *became violently insane*, the *MINER* said, and was taken to Spokane by Deputy Sheriff Murray. Clyde Brewling on the other side of Tiger Hill murdered his housekeeper and cremated her on a pyre of pitch pine logs. Sadie Hanky of Blueslide hung on longer than most; a single homesteader, Sadie had been struggling alone to clear her land in spite of chronic ailments, for seven years. But now she spent one year in Medical Lake and then sold out for $1 and left the country.

The crimes of poverty increased too. A home in Newport was burgled of its home-canned food and three sacks of potatoes; the burglar tried to peddle the fruit around town. Someone broke into the meat market, stole a beef heart, and tried to sell it at the Midway Restaurant, where a suspicious cook called the sheriff. When a recent and desperate young widower left his home overnight to deliver his children to relatives, burglars wiped him out, moving the dresser drawers to the sidewalk where they could more conveniently empty the contents into their conveyance.

But at Tiger people found less harmful ways to forget the devastation. They found what comforts they could to make the blackness more bearable. The lectures that winter at Renshaw Hall and the dances in George Tiger's new Hall, the Grange meetings, the Sunshine Club meetings, the card parties in homes, and all the other gatherings, while subdued, eased the pain of loss, lessened the depth of despair.

All Wes's notorious cordwood was gone. The part of his store merchandise that survived went almost entirely to needy neighbors; as usual, Wes's books didn't balance as well as his pack horses. Parker Bros. big wholesale house hadn't wanted the wood, and they surely didn't want the pile of ashes it had become. In addition to the lost cordwood, Wes and Jennie found themselves with $1500 on the books and, still standing in the woods, $2000 worth of additional, uncut cordwood for which there was no longer a market, all accepted in trade for groceries long since eaten.

"Wes, I think I can make more running the farm, selling more stuff from the garden. And I'd be a damn sight happier out from behind this counter. The town is over at the railroad now, and I feel like I'm in the hoosegow here, sometimes. And you could get more time for pack trains and cattle business. Let's quit losing money here and get us some freedom." They decided to sell.

With Zimmerman's bigger and better store open, the business wasn't worth much, and the old log building, from which the business district had moved away, had always belonged to George Tiger. They got enough to pay just half the wholesalers' bill. "Jennie, you'll come up with something; you always do." Jennie doubted that, but her disappointment at the financial loss was less than her considerable relief at being freed of bondage. She didn't know exactly how she'd be spending her days, but it was going to be where there was sky over her head.

STEVENS COUNTY WAS BEING SPLIT and a new county, made mostly of the Pend d'Oreille Valley, was forming, and friends suggested that Wes should join the mob running for the new, salaried county positions. He was well thought of, admired and liked. He liked jawing, and that was half the job, wasn't it? He'd lost much of what he'd been amassing, but who hadn't? That wasn't a mark against a man. But Wes was more comfortable as just a supporter of his party's ideas, and didn't relish public life. "I don't want to traipse around talking people into voting for me."

With the newly formed county, the seat of legal business moved from 35 miles west in Colville to 50 miles south in Newport. While the county seat would now be further for flying crows, it would not be over a 3300' mountain pass, and the train ride to Newport would be more comfortable than a horseback ride. Joe Parker and Wes both thought there was still too much traveling involved. Wes said, "With a serious courthouse down there, they'll be wanting to have meetings all the time; a man couldn't get his plowing done." Jennie didn't point out that in the past 11 years he'd been available for plowing exactly three times.

The downriver country did pretty well in the election: Ione produced the Auditor and the Engineer; Metaline Falls the Prosecuting Attorney and the Coroner. Tiger got the true plum: the Sheriff of Pend Oreille County would be B.F. Gardiner, the Idaho & Washington Northern section foreman for the Tiger-Ione stretch. Joe Parker hadn't sought the sheriff job, sticking with his decision to take care of family business for a while. George Tiger didn't try either; he was busy transporting trout fry to Caribou Lodge, after the *MINER* announced to the world that the fishing at Sullivan Lake didn't seem to be what it had been. They did not comment on their own story of the previous June when they reported that a "party of workmen" for the Railroad had fished in Sullivan Lake for two hours and taken 395 trout. A week later the paper reported that F.A. Blackwell himself, with a party of "Eastern interests," had gone fishing. Apparently the assignment of the first party had been to find a suitable spot for Mr. F.A. Blackwell to impress his friends, or potential backers, or whatever they were. Using one employee to prepare his hooks and two more to clean his fish, Blackwell was able to take 28 trout in 35 minutes. The *MINER* had shared his pride when they reported that he had sometimes had two fish on at the same time and that his Eastern friends were much impressed by his sportsmanship.

Since the Railroad came two years ago, schedules and maps had been dropping the *d'* from *Pend d'Oreille*. Most people ignored the change, if they even noticed. They would write whichever came to mind - or to hand. Now the new county became officially *Pend Oreille*, and they tried whenever they could to remember.

The new new house by the county road had just about twice the space as the old one, and the tables, shelves and bedsteads Jennie'd made the first couple of winters weren't going to fill it. She let it be known that she'd take furniture in trade on unpaid bills. Never in her life had Jennie lived with polished wood. There was none in her mother's succession of rented shacks. There was certainly none in Jimmie Hildreth's photographer's wagon. She'd never known she missed it. As she and Wes moved from place to place in Arizona and California, she'd sometimes taken with her what the wagon would hold, and just as often nailed together some wood to meet their needs, as she had here at Hawthorn Lodge. She took for granted the way the rough wood caught on a dustrag or put splinters in her hands. But real "furnishings," as Ada would have called them, with carving on legs and fronts, with brass drawer pulls, with a sheen that reflected lamplight, were not something she'd had or needed. But when Pearl Mellott rowed across with a pressed-wood straightback chair, Jennie began to see something in it. Christina Carpenter had moved into the new teacher's cottage, and brought Jennie the whole suite of bedroom furniture that was a sad reminder of Frank. Jennie told Wes she was coming to like pretty things. "Jennie, we're in danger of turning bourgeois. Maybe you'd better turn down some of these things, before I'm drummed out of the Socialist party." Elzena Greenamyer brought the round dining table that had accommodated the seance. "You know, Wes, every time I look at one of these things I'll have some kind of memory of the person that give it to me. I used to kind of laugh at women who bragged about 'mother's pie cupboard' or 'Aunt Julia's sofa,' but I'm coming to see that a piece of furniture can stand for a person or a happening." George Tiger brought back from Newport a beveled mirror with a four-inch frame trimmed with something like gold.

"George, you ain't got a bill at the store."

"No, but I can give a present to a friend, can't I?"

Esther Underwood brought an oak dresser with a hinged mirror. "Aunt

Jennie, back when you delivered Claude and when you brought Florine through the scarlet fever, I didn't have near enough to pay you. I may not owe the store anything, but I owe you a lot."

The fun of arranging the new house was short-lived, though. Parker Bros. Wholesalers of Spokane didn't know anything about what J.W. Wooding et ux. of Tiger might or might not have done for their neighbors, or how loved they might or might not be in Tiger, Washington.

Unreceptive to Jennie's suggestion that they accept periodic payment, Parker Bros. got a lien against the 159 acres belonging to J.W. Wooding. Jennie was frantic.

"Damn it, Wes, I want to hang onto this place. I don't give a hang about the store; in fact, I'm glad to be out of it. But the homestead's different. We've worked too hard to get it. Where would we traipse off to next? And we thought we was going to be able to leave the boys something. We can't let this go. We can tighten our belts somehow, and Bill's about to go to work full time; that'll be four of us."

Once more, Wes's past generosity came to the rescue. He'd carried Mike Fox on the books when Mike needed it. After Wes's stake, Mike had done well, now had a profitable little sawmill near the riverbank, and had finished repaying Wes a year ago. Wes approached him on taking over the Parker debt and accepting payments over time. "Wes, I couldn't say no. I owe it to you and I'm happy to be able to make up to you what you did for me."

Wes took the good news to Jennie. "I'm sure we can do this, Girlie. With the hills filling up now with this second wave of homesteaders, the pack business is good. With the railroad and the cement plant at Metaline Falls, there's plenty of need for beef and potatoes. Long as we keep at it the way we've been doing, this will be just a short setback." Jennie didn't have as much bravado, but she appreciated the reprieve.

THE TIMING WAS TRAGIC FOR Bill. If it had come two years earlier or two years later, his whole life might have been different. Alone of the four boys, Bill loved learning. They were all quick at their lessons, and they liked well enough to go to school, where friends were. But when they found themselves with extra time after finishing a lesson, Tom would carve a whistle or help a younger child with his lessons, Jasper would draw a picture or just gaze out the window, and Davey would get permission to go outside to split some wood, haul some water, or talk to a horse someone had ridden to school. Only Bill went to the back of the room and read an unassigned book.

Bill had come this year to admire Ray Harting, who had taken the Tiger School as his first job after finishing not only high school but the two-year course at the normal school at Cheney. The young man did an excellent job with the lessons for all the children, and furthermore he taught the older ones a bit of German, and took the whole school on nature walks where he taught them the Latin names of flora and fauna. He took over the Tiger Literary and Debating Society and brought it even greater popularity. He published a neighborhood newsletter. Ray had brought with him from Cheney a Remington typewriter and a box of carbon paper; he made the first four copies of each edition and taught the 7th and 8th graders to type so they could make additional copies. Ray was a great success, in what was becoming a long line of excellent Tiger teachers.

Bill came to wonder if he could do what Professor Harting did.

On a windy March day with the snow melted back to the edges of the schoolground, Bill stayed after school, he said to set up the folding stage for the Easter program. He couldn't speak what he had in mind when he came in, nor all through his task. He was still shy to bring up a difficult subject, and was almost out the door when he turned back and asked, "Professor Harting, do you want me to come in on Saturday and put some fresh paint on those blackboards?" As he said it he wondered who'd take the pack train up if he stayed here.

"No, Bill. If you have free time on Saturday, put in some extra hours getting ready for your 8th Grade Exams. How's that science coming?"

"It's not my best," he mumbled, slouching back into his desk. But Bill had reason to be more confident than he sounded. At the end of the 7th grade he had passed the state physiology and geography exams with high scores. It was true he preferred history and literature, but there was no reason to doubt his ability to pass in all subjects.

Ray knew this better than Bill. "You know, Bill, I have to take my certification exam in May too. Usually only half the people taking it pass. Maybe I'm the one who'd better study on Saturday." He let the silence that followed that remark continue, sensing that Bill had something else to bring up. Chitchat would only delay the real conversation.

Finally Bill got to it. "Professor Harting, how did you get to go to high school?"

"I guess I was just lucky, Bill. My folks lived in town, and my dad had a pretty good law practice; he didn't need me to help make the living. So I could just walk to the high school, same as you walk to this school."

"I wish there was a way for me to do it."

"Have you asked your folks about it?"

"No. But there's no high school here. I couldn't just walk to Newport or Colville very well."

"I hear there's a girl from Metaline Falls who boards in Spokane and goes to high school there. She comes home on the train for vacations. And there's somebody from Ione who stays with her grandmother in Newport. One family even had the mother and the youngster rent a house for the term and she went with him."

"My ma has to stay here and work. And we can't afford to board me. And we don't have any relatives closer than California. Out of luck, I guess."

Ray shuffled some papers. "To tell you the truth, Bill, I've been thinking about this very thing. I believe I could give the 9th and 10th grade subjects. That would get you half way there. And I hear Ione is thinking about having a high school. Maybe by the time you got through 10th grade, you could ride your horse into Ione for school, or maybe stay with a family in exchange for work."

Bill left full of dreams.

He brought it up at supper. Jasper and Davey of course had to say they couldn't see why anyone would stay in school longer than they had to. Tom wasn't too far from that opinion, glorying just now at 15, at the end of his first year as a working adult, in freedom from school hours and disdain for children's play. But he said he'd help hold up Bill's end of the pack train if need be; Tom rather liked the idea of himself as the generous older brother.

Wes and Jennie were flabbergasted. They truly had never had the idea come into their heads before. No one in Jennie's family had even finished the 8th grade. Wes had, but never considered going further.

"But things are different now, Pa. The law says now you have to stay in school till you're 15 or pass the 8th grade exams."

"Which isn't the same as high school."

"No. But if I want to be something, I'll have fellas all around me who went to more school."

"What do you mean 'be something'?"

His chin went down on his chest. "I don't know. Maybe a schoolteacher like Professor Harting."

All chewing stopped. After a moment of astonishment Davey whooped. "My brother a schoolteacher? I don't know if I'd be proud or ashamed. Can't you make a living with your hands?"

Wes was the only one to understand what it was to love to read a book, to see a world beyond the immediate. But he hadn't found any problem with just sitting down and reading one. He didn't see why you needed to go to a school to do it. Jack London didn't need to. Big Bill Hawyood didn't need to. And he knew plenty of people who did do it and who came out still not able to see beyond the ends of their noses. At the same time, Wes was the one most able to allow that somebody else - even a boy seated at his own dinner table - might have a different truth inside him.

"I guess we can keep this table set with you going on part time. Ray wouldn't necessarily expect you at the school all day, long as you kept moving ahead in your lessons, would he? You could take the pack train weekdays while Davey's in school, maybe, and study on Saturday and Sunday?" The dream was getting closer.

"Yes, Pa. I'll do my full share here, and I'll study nights. Professor Harting will work it out with me."

Again the elder brother: "Better make sure you pass, first. Those questions aren't easy. Quick: what are the epochs that U.S. History is divided into?"

ON A THURSDAY IN MAY, Bill and five other 8th graders, wearing their most formal clothes, rode the train in to Ione and sat in unfamiliar desks to start a long two days of exams. A member of the County Board of Education came from Newport to conduct the tests. The monitor checked his pocket watch and at precisely 9:00 a.m., as prescribed by the State Board of Education, Bill, his four classmates, and all hopeful 8th graders in the entire State of Washington dipped their pens and began to demonstrate that they were or were not adequately educated to the standards of the State of Washington. Bill's confidence grew as the day went on and only a few trick questions showed up.

In June the entire brand new Pend Oreille County Board of Education as well as County School Superintendent Hester Soules read the exams and determined that William Alvin Wooding and two of his four classmates were now permitted to stop their formal education. They also allowed E. Ray Harting to cover 9th and 10th grade subjects, if there were any students who wanted them.

But other forces were working against Bill. More and more families were homesteading up Tiger Hill, too far to come by foot or horseback daily, and certainly too far to battle through winter snow to the school at

Tiger. The same County Board of Education that had granted Bill's dream now allowed the parents on Tiger Hill theirs: they could have a one-month trial session in early summer to determine if they had enough students for a true school. The families cleaned the packrats out of an abandoned cabin, equipped it with white pine desks and benches built by the families, and a hodgepodge of whatever books those families could come up with. Eleven children religiously attended the school for a month. The County Board declared the experiment satisfactory. Over the rest of the summer the families built the permanent school of peeled logs, and in all ways according to the State Board's specifications. It was Bill who brought by pack train the windows that lined one side of the building, and it was Bill who brought the flattop wood stove for heating it. He didn't know he was ruining his own plans. The pine desks were moved in, and the County Board approved the purchase of textbooks. Things looked good for both schools.

Then, shortly before school opening in October the County Board hired Mrs. Ada M. Cooper for the Tiger School and assigned E. Ray Harting to the Forest Home School. Mrs. Cooper was not qualified to teach any subjects beyond the 8th grade. The last door was closed.

"Bill, I wish it was different," Wes told him. "Before the fire and before Parker Brothers Wholesalers, we could have maybe squeezed out board money. And maybe we can again in a while. But right now it's not a thing we can do."

"I know, Pa. I'll just wait till I'm able to earn it. I can do this by myself, in time.

1912

ON JANUARY 11 the *MINER* announced to the world that Uriah's divorce from Ada was granted *as the plaintiff had prayed*. In his claim filed over a year ago he said she had *deserted without cause* on September 19, 1909, and that he had seen her only twice since then.

"So that explains all her coming and going to Metaline and Blueslide. She wanted a divorce, even if she had to look to be in the wrong to get it. And he's been just as bad, back and forth to Metaline and Seattle, to show he didn't want to be with her either," Wes realized. "Do you think it can be really true that they've only seen each other twice in more than two years?"

He reread "...*as the plaintiff had prayed.....deserted without cause*'! They must know a lot more than I do if they can imply who's in the wrong."

"Yeah. I'm right here and I wouldn't know where to point a finger," she agreed.

"It seems to me hard enough to figure out your own marriage, much less somebody else's."

"What's that supposed to mean?" she flirted.

"Only good things, Girlie. Only good things."

In this present, sad business they couldn't be on either side. They knew Uriah had been high-handed in coming to the Pend d'Oreille. He'd left Ada alone many times when he knew she was frightened in the wilderness. He'd scoffed at her need for company when the girls were all away. When she advertised for a youngster to stay on the ranch with her, he'd refused to pay. He'd ignored her need for the city and its trappings. At the same time, they couldn't think that Ryer should have given up his flair for adventure and gain; these weren't any less admirable aims than Ada's. No doubt her desire for Seattle clothes, Seattle schools for the girls, Seattle excitement and entertainment could never be satisfied. Nor satisfying.

"I think what's wrong," Wes concluded, "is that Uriah thinks just about piling up money for the future. He doesn't live life as it comes along. He just uses the present to get ready for the future. I wonder when he thinks his real life will begin."

Ada and Uriah found themselves in an odd situation. With the divorce granted, he could have evicted her. But he was letting Ada sleep at the homestead in order to have a caretaker, he said, and so that Ethel had someplace to come during school vacations. Ada slept at the homestead and ran the Cottage Hotel; Uriah slept at the Cottage Hotel, and found ways to spend his days anywhere but there. The Cedar Valley Ranch, with its name of bucolic satisfaction, was no longer a ranch or a home, and no longer even had cedar - the beautiful, lacy trees that supported a whole world of ferns and berries and wild ginger had gone three years ago for railroad ties. He was leasing out most of it for pasture, and cows munched around the blackened stumps, right up to the house.

"But, remember. When there were trees around, she was always afraid of what was in them."

The divorce wasn't all his brother's woes that Wes couldn't help. Ryer came back in February from a trip to Seattle with a huge walrus mustache, sideburns that joined a full beard, and his hair longer than he'd ever worn it. "Is that you in there, Ryer?" Uriah confirmed it was, and kept his face averted when he could. Wes let it go at that, but Jennie made it her business to get a better look. She was sure the left side was larger than the right. Clearly he didn't want to answer any questions, and part of her knew she should honor his privacy. But she kept watching. When she saw him go into the hotel dining room at an off hour, she followed him in. She poured herself a cup of coffee, added molasses to taste, and joined him without invitation. Uriah expected no one to be in the dining room in mid-afternoon. Trapped, though, he had to go through with the bowl of oatmeal mush he'd ordered as his main meal of the day.

"Ryer, there's something wrong, ain't there?"

"It's wrong to have somebody watch you eat when you can't use your mouth right."

"Ryer, this is too serious for pride. You can't hardly swallow, right?"

"Okay, Jennie." He managed to get another spoonful into his mouth and down his throat. "There's a big tumor thing on the left side of my head. I had an operation in Seattle in November, and they thought they took it out. But it's as big as ever again. "

"Did you tell that doctor it came back?"

"Nope."

"Ryer, it don't sound like something that oughta be let go."

"That operation cost 20 acres of poles, and I don't much want to do it again. And I don't know what this divorce will cost before it's done. Ada thinks the girls ought to have part of what I've made. And I guess she's right."

"And you don't want to think about it, right? Well, it ain't going away, Ryer." He blinked what she hoped was agreement. She didn't see him again before she heard he'd gone to stay with his father and sister in Seattle.

He came back in March to check on his timber sales. A second surgery had been unsuccessful. How much Ada even knew of his situation Jennie didn't know.

Uriah's greed, whether for a good cause or not, saddened Wes. When three Kalispels in a week came by in rags to beg for tobacco or money, Wes nearly cried. These people who had been so beautiful, so skilled, when he came here just 12 years ago, had lost in that short time their dignity, their health, their culture. They were treated with contempt on all sides. "They had a perfect world," he said. "Then greed sold them whisky, which is poison to their minds and souls. Greed has taken most of their land. You can't live off the land unless you can range a long ways. The caribou and the deer don't line up along the riverbank and wait to be shot. The camas is all fenced in now. Their sacred hills, where they went to get their heads clear, are being logged and mined. They're supposed to live on 4600 acres of flood plain and brushy hillsides, and it can't be done. It makes me sick."

Uriah came through again in April, this time on his way to the Mayo Brothers Clinic clear back in Minnesota. On the train south to Spokane was a party of whores just run out of Ione, singing, sipping from flasks, and showing off. Other passengers chose to be either appalled or amused. Uriah seemed not to know they were there, his thoughts on himself. "Wes, he's spending all he's made in Alaska and all he's made skinning his homestead. And he's not going to survive this. What a waste."

Jennie was right. When he came back, Uriah was beaten. The Mayo Brothers doctors had said the tumor was too close to the jugular vein for surgery. He'd have to die of the tumor or die of the surgery. He stayed at the Cottage Hotel, spending more and more time in his room. The hirsute disguise was thinning; a protruding eye was becoming noticeable. In July, his last attempt at garnering wealth was a trip with George Tiger to Newport to lobby for the Tiger-Colville Road, which might bring some customers for the two men's plats, two neighboring plats so different in purpose.

In the fall, Uriah left Tiger for the last time, going *to the coast to benefit his health*. Jennie knew that meant his father and sister would nurse him to the end. She would have liked to do it herself, but Uriah's pride and vanity wouldn't let him stay among the people for whom he'd played the role of rising rich man, and it certainly wouldn't let him stay where Ada could see his final decline. Already, his food had to be pureed with mortar and pestle and he would eat only in his room alone. Jennie gave him a supply of morphine to take on the train with him. She and Wes saw him off.

1913

AGAIN JENNIE WAS enduring one of those periods of pointless and patternless change. Flora Cross had become Postmaster and Jennie missed Emmanuel Yoder. He might have been foolish, but he was a familiar fool. She missed seeing his blue coat with the brass buttons going down to the riverboat for the "heafy mail." When Emmanuel had first arrived in the Pend d'Oreille he was envious of the uniforms worn by the steamboat crews and commented publicly about them. Eventually a wag visiting to Ohio anonymously sent him a Union Civil War coat. He maintained during his entire postal tenure that "the government" had sent it to him. He always put it on, buttoned it up carefully, donned the campaign cap that came with it, and wore both when he went down the bank to the riverboat, and later to the railroad depot, to pick up the "heafy mail." "I yust go down to get dat heafy mail, Yennie," he'd said to her every post day for the four years they'd shared a building. When Flora Cross took over, the crews broke the tradition of requiring the Tiger Postmaster to carry up the mail bag and brought it themselves into the post office. When she had occasion to meet the train, Jennie always wanted the silly little ceremony to occur, and missed it when it didn't.

It was now that late winter period before planting when she was so restless. After two years the new board house was becoming home, but she kept finding reasons to go back to the old log house: to rechink it, to see if she'd moved all the herbs she wanted, to just sit on the floor of their bedroom and remember. She told herself she had to stop this.

At midday dinner she said to Wes, "What do you say we rent out the old house? I got to get weaned of it some time."

"You're ready, are you, Girlie? Let's jump on it. It'd be a few more dollars a month to give Mike Fox." By the next day a couple who'd sold their claim to the Panhandle for *$1 and considerations* were in the log house.

The rent did help. They were able to chew down a little faster the debt that Mike Fox was holding for them. Through the last two winters Jennie had taken in laundry and ironing at 40 cents a dozen for the loggers and railroad crew in the area. She taught the boys to build traps of the kind she had devised up at Monte Cristo. For most of the winter they sent their peltry to Minneapolis or Chicago. Just before the season ended in the spring, they learned that Denver was paying better prices and they should have been sending them there all along. For one thick bearskin they got $50. For muskrats, mink, weasels, bobcats, lynx, and coyotes they got less, but there was something in their traps almost every day, and the money was significant. After the boys ran the traplines in the morning, Wes, Tom and Bill kept the pole shipments going. They all got a kick out of keeping track of what they owed Mike Fox, and watching the amount go down. In the previous summer and fall Jennie had preserved extra eggs and could sell them at high winter prices to Zimmerman's store. As summer came on, they chewed faster yet. In May, Tom sold fry from Renshaw Creek to the state hatchery. When school was out and the roads opened, Davey joined the workforce. Then another setback.

In late June the river rose above flood level. They were amazed at the power of the deluge and the damage it could do. They tried to pull out of the water what useful items they could on the chance they could return them to their owners, and use them if they couldn't. The flood didn't threaten any buildings on the high bank of Tiger, but when it went back down it left plenty of standing water, and within a month the mosquitoes were so bad the summer logging was suspended because the horses had to stay in the barn. Davey kept the pack train going by starting well before dawn and getting up high early, where they weren't so bad, then hurrying to get back to the barn before the evening droves. The others found a way to make up for the logging they couldn't do. When the county road was being built near their spread Wes, Tom and Bill took advantage of the new practice of landowners being given first dibs on the jobs. "We used to do this for free, and it probably ought to be that way, but we need the money bad enough now I'm not turning it down," Wes said. It was hard ever to inspire enthusiasm in Jasper, but he worked vaguely with his mother in the garden and they put up enough for the winter, as well as several barrels of sauerkraut and many tons of potatoes for sale. This had gone on for two years, and they believed they were going to hang onto the land. "Jennie, we got away with it, I do believe," Wes told her one night when they sat at the round Greenamyer table by lamplight and went over the accounts while the May moths flitted in to look at their lamp.

And they almost did get away with it. But in July Mike Fox's parents in Ohio died within a week of each other and he went back home to take over their farm.

"Sorry, Wes, but I've got to have the money right now to move me and the family and to get the folks's little cabin ready for my wife and kids. I couldn't wait any longer. I've got to leave right now, so I went and got a lien against your 'stead. I hope the two years I gave you helped."

No one could blame anyone. They'd given it their best shot, and circumstances just turned against them. The only thing left to do was sell 40 acres and keep 119. They sold the south 40, the section most thoroughly logged.

"We never use that land anyway, I guess. It just means the boys will get 30 acres apiece instead of 40," Wes allowed. They'd suffered more serious reversals of fortune, and he wasn't much daunted by this one.

Jennie wasn't daunted but she wasn't as cavalier as he was, either. "Eleven years work to lose it ain't as easy to take as you say, Wes. But nothing to do but live with it, I guess."

*****

WHEN FRANK DARROW LOANED THE second volume of Sherlock Holmes stories to George Tiger he didn't expect the tome to break George's foot, threaten his life, fuel a conflagration, and change the business district of the town.

When Darrow came down from his place at Middleport he always brought books to loan to someone. Charles Dickens was most popular, of course, usually going from borrower to borrower without a rest on Darrow's bookshelves. John Renshaw, Wes, and Lee Bilderback enjoyed Upton Sinclair and Frank Norris. Mrs. Parker and her daughters liked Sir Walter Scott and Robert Burns, and Ray Harting liked Charles Darwin. Books never failed to return, though sometimes enriched with tobacco spittle, coffee stains, or bacon grease. Flora Cross at the post office enjoyed John Galsworthy and Jane Austen, and paid her dues by facilitating circulation, Darrow's visits being infrequent. Darrow put the second volume of Sherlock Holmes directly in George's hands himself, though, and chatted outside the post office a while about a mutually favorite story in the first book. Then George went inside to pick up his mail, and came back out with his face undecided between amusement, skepticism and concern. "Frank, I got a blackhand letter! Who'd think it in Tiger? Look here."

Darrow read: "Tiger: Put $250 in cash in the big ceder stump that is betwene yor old empty store bilding and the blacksmith shop. There is a lard buckit there to put it in. If you do not, you are dead. I give you a weak."

"Well, George, that seems kind of far-fetched, but I suppose you ought to talk to B.F. about it. It could be real."

But Sheriff B.F. Gardiner was downriver in Metaline Falls trying to explain to Joe Busta, Holgar Larsen and the group of other immigrants they'd organized to vote, why he had to arrest them for trying to be good, if premature, citizens.

That night George moseyed over to the specified cedar stump and, sure enough, found the lard can, of the kind children carried their lunches to school in, its lid firmly on. He hefted it. Empty.

The next night he went back and this time lifted the lid, thinking there might be a followup note. None. He stayed home the next two nights, enjoying the Sherlock Holmes. When he finished one particular story, "The Adventure of the Empty House," he fell into the mood of amused contempt that Holmes always felt for his miscreants. Not for a moment did George think of actually giving away $250. During some moments, though, he did worry about the letter writer following through with his threat. Now Sir Arthur Conan Doyle had given him a plot for avoiding death while holding the blackhander up for ridicule.

Beginning on the next day at noon, George pulled a rocking chair into the lower level front window of the space in his new building that C.A. Perry rented from him for a mercantile store. There he sat till past dark, reading. For three days he repeated the pattern, ensuring that everyone in town noticed him. He told questioners he was helping Cal keep an eye on the merchandise. He checked the can again on the sixth evening, and found a second note. "You got one mor day, Tiger."

Late that night George fashioned quite a good dummy of himself, complete with his Newport suit and hat, and stuffed with gunny sacks and pillows. He attached cords to the rockers so the chair could be made to rock, even to shift a little from left to right. He experimented with lantern angles until the dummy appeared real enough, and to be comfortably reading. The face had to be kept shaded, George not having Holmes's resource of a master waxworker to construct a realistic face. When Cal closed the store an hour after dark, George had him douse all the lights for a moment while he heaved the dummy into the chair and arranged the lighting as it had been in rehearsal. For an hour the dummy rocked. Then it sat still while George went out the back door, went out of sight over the riverbank, and came up near the cedar stump. The moon was half full, a wind was coming up fast. George placed a note in the lard can and went into the rear of his older, one-story empty building. From there he could see the nearby cottonwood stump with the slab of bark left on for a backrest where Jennie's customers or Wes used to sit to chew the fat. He could also see across the street where he himself appeared to be sitting reading in the storefront of his newer, two-story building. Then a thrill: a man about his own size, the collar of his black canvas coat turned up, approached the cedar stump. A rain was coming down now, the moon was lost in clouds, and a south wind blew cottonwood leaves horizontal, obscuring George's view of the lard can dastard. There wasn't a chance of the man's reading the note in the dark, and his two attempts at lighting a match in the tornado failed. He disappeared, taking the note to a protected spot. When a shot went through the storefront window and into the dummy's head, George knew the extortionist had read "I'm watching you from my old storefront. How about you find some brave woman to escort you over to talk to me." The culprit ran off down a trail toward the sloughs. George stepped into the trail and sent three shots after him. The running target was camouflaged by moving branches and shadows, and the shots didn't stop him. Still watching down the trail, George stepped backward up onto the porch of the old store and went through a rotten board. He felt a sharp wrench, and fell full face on the floor. He disentangled himself, rubbed the foot, and looked down an empty trail. Hoping he had at least wounded the son-of-a-bitch, George knew better than to go hobbling down the trail to find out. There couldn't be a better situation for ambush than the thick stand of hazelnuts and hawthorn where the trail disappeared. Looking back at the dummy with the hole in its hat, he realized too late that the three shots would have told the culprit that the dead man was not George. The foot was drawing his attention more and more. He needed to get off it, and didn't want any more encounters that night. He limped to Blackie King's log house on the river bank and asked to be put up for the night. George had housed Blackie and his wife for two weeks when they first arrived on the boat some years ago but he and Blackie were not especially close, which made Blackie a good choice.

"Well, sure, George. What's wrong with your place?"

George told the story. Blackie wanted to go look for the shooter. "No,

Blackie, it's not the right night. You can't see anything, and with this wind you can't hear anything. If he's serious, he might still be around. But he wouldn't come here - nobody connects us two."

Emma King brought quilts and stirred up the fire in the main room. Already the foot was swollen too much to get the boot off, so Blackie went to the shed for his leather shears.

"Shall I warm some coffee, George? A piece of pie?"

"Nothing, thanks, Emma."

Blackie came back, unlaced the boot, and cut it off. "Sorry, George. These look like mighty fine boots."

"They were, Blackie, but the tradeoff feels good. That foot can grow some more now without making me groan so much. I'll just try to get to sleep here."

It wasn't easy to do. The change from prank to pain took some digesting. He thought back over everything that had happened during the week. He couldn't say he hadn't thought it could turn serious or he wouldn't have had a loaded gun on him. Reading an amusing story was one thing; enacting it was another. The damn foot hurt like Bejesus. This didn't happen to Sherlock Holmes. But Holmes had three policemen, two detectives and Watson when he made the capture. What had made him think he could do this all alone? He could have gone up to The Falls and told B.F. he needed help. Those eager-to-vote immigrants weren't a threat to anybody. He could have rung in old Joe Parker. Wes Wooding's boys would have helped. Hell, so would any one of twenty settlers. Darrow's idea had been right. God damn, that foot hurt. He raised it onto the back of a chair and tried to sleep. He lowered it to the couch and tried to sleep. He sat up in a chair and tried to sleep. He went back to the raised foot position, and finally went into a shallow doze broken every time he moved the foot. In the morning he'd see if Jennie knew anything to do for it.

A half hour later Hy Maggott came pounding on the door for Blackie to come help with the fire. He was surprised to find George there.

"Where's the fire, Hy?"

"Well, George, I'm sorry. I didn't know you was here."

"I'm in a sorry state, Hy. I don't think I can give you a hand. This foot is busted, feels like."

Blackie and Emma came down the ladder from the bedroom. "What is it, Hy?"

"A fire, Blackie. We want to get water on the buildings around it. Bring all the buckets you got. Emma, would you do a spell at the windlass?"

All three were out the door. George used a straight-backed chair to pull himself to the door. When he looked out, his whole body turned damp and his stomach turned. He could tell it was his new building and he could tell it was beyond hope. The flames were still high, and the whole town looked red. Pain or no pain, he hopped with one bare foot into the street with the help of Emma's broom. B.F. Gardiner was there, back in town after all. George headed for the store's back door, thinking to save Cal's accounts for him. Like all country merchants, Cal operated largely on credit. He'd need the accounts to collect. B.F. stopped him. "No good, George. It's gone. The stuff inside's gone. We're just trying to keep it from catching on another building. Jennie saw it when she came back from delivering a baby, but it was already beyond help."

George walked around the building, trying to spot the blackhander in the crowd. He didn't go back to the Kings'. Bill and Tom Wooding made a chair of their arms and took him to their house to see if their mother knew something to do for him. She had him sit with the foot in a bucket of ice. She gave him morphine. She had him sleep with it higher than his head. But she said he had to go to Newport to a doctor. "How's the insurance, George?" Wes asked him gently.

"About half. The building's worth $4,000; it's insured for $2,000. I don't want to rebuild, Wes. I'm tired of trying to build a damn town where nobody needs a town. I'd been thinking we needed a sign on the road. But all that sign needs to say is FOUR MILES TO IONE."

They were the first discouraged words they'd ever heard from George. After they got him on the southbound train, Wes and Jennie talked about it. When the Caribou Lodge folded, he'd laughed it off. He'd been one of the first to bounce back after the forest fires in ought ten. He'd never failed to search out a settler who needed help to get started. He'd done all that platting, given away part of the land, had used his own money to put up a good store and dance hall. What was different this time?

"This time, somebody did him harm on purpose, Jennie. This blackhander focused on George for no other reason than that he imagined George had accumulated a little money. Then when he couldn't get any, he burned his store down just for spite. George thinks only about doing the most good for the most people. This measly little man with his anonymous letter thinks only about what he thinks somebody ought to do for him. George has lived a lot, and done a lot of things, but I don't think he ever understood there are people like that. He takes it personally."

"That's why he never got interested in politics, ain't it, Wes? It didn't occur to him that everybody wasn't working in the same direction anyway, that some people just want to grab what they can for themselves. He thought if he did good he'd get good. Kind of like a child in that way."

1914

WHILE HIS FOOT mended, George stayed in Newport in a boarding house. Wes visited and found him despondent. "Jennie, I wish he'd come home and start getting back to normal. He's always been such a contented guy. Now he seems to think he's unwanted here. His brain knows the town didn't do this to him, but his gut thinks it did." In early January Dr. Rusk said there was no reason George couldn't go back to any regular work. Joe Parker and John Bettencourt went up to accompany him home. They found him down with smallpox and couldn't even visit him; Dr. Rusk had quarantined him in the new Pest House the Newport City Council had bought (over the protests of neighboring families), and George felt more than ever alienated from anything that was important to him.

George finally came home, in February, and while he didn't die, he was changed. He was through with buying and selling. He didn't open his house to travelers. He attended social functions but sat quietly, seeming to think of other times and other places. When he learned that the Cement post office was being closed, a too clear sign that F.G. Jordan's venture would never develop either, he said, "So there's two of us silly fools who tried to overreach ourselves."

******

IT WAS THE SKY THAT finally made Jennie love the new place. The two-story clapboard house sat on the highest knoll on the valley floor of Tiger, high enough that the railroad embankment no longer loomed in their lives. With fields on all sides, she could look out a window in any room and see mountains and sky. There wasn't any configuration of cloud or combination of colors that didn't take her spirit above whatever trouble, confusion or drudgery she might think she had. Looking out the windows helped her curb an irascibility that seemed to be growing in her as the boys grew up, and that she didn't like.

A good thing it was that she was relaxing in her rocker darning, with a chicken roasting in the oven and watching stripes of apricot clouds being stretched across the sky from Huckleberry to Hooknose when Davey and a retinue of a dozen children came down the road.

Davey was bringing in Patience and her daughter Bonnie, following them and waving an unnecessary switch. Jennie hadn't seen him since school was out three hours ago, which hadn't worried her. A program for the end-of-term festivities was in the works, and the lunch-hour practice wasn't always enough, since a couple of children had been late in getting their lines learned, and Mrs. Cooper didn't start rehearsals until all lines were in hand. Likely Davey'd gone from school straight to his chores. So where did this assortment of youngsters come from? She laid down the sock, left her chair and went to a window where she could enjoy the procession. She saw now that Davey was covered with mud and that the children were trailing him, doing a kind of follow-the-leader game and laughing. He was doing a clumsy imitation of the cows, swinging his arms in front of him, swaying his hips exaggeratedly, sometimes raising his head and lowing. Then the collection of children, from all the houses in calling distance, would do their individual versions of the same thing. Davey wove the parade back and forth across the wagon road, almost falling into last year's tawny grass at the edge, then recovering and giving out another bellow as he crossed to the other side. Jennie laughed at their fun, and stepped out onto the porch to better hear their giggles. At the whack of the door closing behind her, every head except Davey's jerked up and turned toward her. When the youngsters saw that it was indeed Aunt Jennie every last one scampered back up the road, squealing as they went. In seconds, all had disappeared. She had expected them to come up to the house and tell her what a funny boy Davey was and how he could make them all laugh and how he'd organized them into a little circus troupe, and what fun Davey always was. Davey gave another bellow, and hearing no echo behind him he turned and found he was alone. He turned a stiff-legged quarter circle, found no one, and repeated this until he'd gone full circle. At the same moment he accepted that his entourage was gone, he saw his mother standing on the porch. He gave a mock-gallant bow and called to her "Hello, Mother Dear." His smart-alecky greeting stiffened her spine and raised her chin. "You come up here, Davey. Pronto."

He grinned again, and raised his chin in mockery of hers. "I think I'll take these ladies to the barn first, Mother Dear."

"No, you won't. You'll get in this house right now." She started down the slope to the road, and he realized he'd better at least start to obey her. He met her half way. With no introduction she cupped his chin in her hand, looked into his droopy eyes, and sniffed his breath. "You're drunk!"

"Only a little, Mother Dear. Mother Dear, you do make the best elderberry blossom wine."

"And who offered you some? And it's all gone anyway, long aga. Where'd you get whatever you've been drinking?"

"I told you, Mother Dear. Elderberry blossom wine. When you sent me to the root cellar after that last cabbage the other night I saw a bottle stashed way back behind the sand box with the carrots in it." His silly grin still held up, but her authority was about to wilt it. "And I went back today and I only drank the whole thing. I didn't think it'd make me drunk, but mayhap it did. Have you ever been drunk, Mother Dear?"

"No, I ain't. And I ain't never seen your Pa drunk. Now I'm seeing the first drunkard in this family. And I ain't very proud of him."

"I'm not a drunkard, Ma." His bravado had crumbled and Mother Dear was gone. She was Ma again.

"Whether you are or you ain't you sure look like one right now. Get in that house." She jerked the switch from his hand, popped his legs once with it, took the cows to the barn, milked, poured the milk into its settling pans, and finally believed her anger was under control enough that she could deal with Davey and drink. She found him sound asleep on the front room floor, mud drying around him. Good enough for the time being. She'd see what Wes and the boys had to say.

They left him asleep on the floor while they discussed what to do with him. Tom and Bill, 20 and 18, took the role of adults. "No supper, and leave him where he is." Jasper was appalled at the story of the neighborhood children laughing at his brother. "He made us all look silly. When they laugh at him, they laugh at us. I'll be ashamed to go to school tomorrow," he said righteously. No one was inclined to indulge his sensitivity. Wes, to no one's surprise, also took things seriously. "Thirteen is old enough to know better. A man's supposed to be in shape to do his work when it needs doing. If he's known to have a taste for liquor at 13, what kind of jobs will people hire him for?"

They did indeed leave him where he was. After they were all in bed, they heard him getting some bread and milk in the kitchen, then cleaning up the mud and taking himself to bed. Everyone pretended to have no interest in him. They continued the silent treatment for the rest of the week, contempt being the worst punishment they could think of. At school, teasing was a different torment. Mrs. Cooper wondered why it seemed to be the joke of the week for someone to bellow out "Moo" whenever Davey Wooding moved from his desk to the blackboard, or to the outhouse, as he needed to do rather frequently for a day or two.

Fortunately for Davey, both family and schoolmates were distracted a few days later when a small herd of elk trailed down over the hill from Stevens County, where they'd been transplanted from Yellowstone Park. It was the game of the day to sic the schoolyard dogs on them, a game sanctioned by all farmers and homesteaders, who hoped the hungry animals would go back to Stevens County, if not clear to Yellowstone. Only Davey welcomed them, as they drew the spotlight of notoriety off him.

****

IN JUNE WES WENT TO Seattle to help nurse Uriah during his last weeks. Ryer now weighed about 75 pounds, Wes wrote, because he couldn't eat anything but beef tea, and needed help with that. A diaper had to be changed frequently and he had to be turned to keep his skin in one piece. Surprisingly he was very accepting of the help from Wes and his father. Uriah, who had been so handsome, and so vain, had one side of his face gone, with dressings that had to be changed every few hours. He was more comfortable with help from the two men than from his sister, who now could concentrate on the cooking and cleaning. In mid-July, Uriah died. The four girls went, but Ada stayed at the hotel and nursed her bitterness.

****

AUGUST BROUGHT BAD FIRES IN the north county. Sawmill operators and timber owners were nervously hiring fighters and guards. Tom, Bill and Jasper all went. Wes knew they had to accept the pay, but he didn't like the smell of that money. It seemed to him that protecting the neighborhood was something people ought to do willingly, as volunteers. The best part was that the fires stayed away from Tiger this time.

Too young to be hired for fire-fighting, Davey ran the pack train every day there was need for it; he found occasional jobs around town, and there was plenty to do on the farm. There was always tack in need of repair, and there was no way to be caught up on weeding. He loved the world of work, but it was made up of things he'd already mastered. With school out, he felt a kind of restlessness that came from his idle mind. Wes fed a similar need by reading. But Davey had more of Jennie in him, and needed to be active while he learned. Wes appreciated Davey's need, and when he saw in the *MINER* an announcement for a county competition for youngsters, he showed it to Davey. "Look at all the categories they have." Davey picked out one he knew a little something about, but not as much as he'd like. From the Domestic Science listing he chose bread baking, deciding to learn something beyond the biscuits he made for occasional hunters he packed in.

After two sessions of bread baking by himself he concluded that learning a skill entirely by trial and error was a slow process, and he looked around for a tutor. Jennie was pretty good at bread, but her product of pride was pies. Besides, she didn't think they could both take time off from work. She gave him free use of the kitchen, on condition that he leave it at least as clean as he found it. "That's as far as I want to go, Davey. It's your set-to, not mine." His Pa and his brothers would only taste the bread and give painfully honest evaluations. The first loaf went to the pigs, with warnings about wasting flour. They ate the second, but were not flattering in their comments. Davey didn't know anyone around who'd qualify as an expert. Even the restaurant at the hotel now had its bread sent up from Krupp's Bakery in Newport on the train twice a week. He started to wonder if maybe baking bread of contest quality was beyond his reach. At a noon break from tying up a raft of logs for the Lucas Brothers, Davey mentioned his problem to George Tiger, who enjoyed sitting on the riverbank watching work done the way it was in the old days.

"Davey, down in Oregon I had a job in a bakery for a while. And after 35 years of batching, I make a pretty good loaf if I do toot my own horn."

George's kitchen was not as well equipped as Jennie's, but though bread took lots of technique, it didn't take much equipment. George set the same standard of cleanliness as Jennie, but beyond that condition, Davey had free rein of the bachelor's cabin. Whenever the pack train didn't go, he worked at the riverbank or wherever there was money to be made; no one was offering to pay for his project, and flour and yeast weren't free. Afternoons George tried to be home to give pointers as Davey made two loaves a day. Between George and the Woodings, they could use that much, and Jennie was pleased to be relieved of a regular chore. "It makes up a little for the time he's taking off work," she said.

Each day Davey's product improved. On the eighth day, the bread was perfect. He was sure he had the craft mastered, and the fair was still two months off. George warned him, though, that consistency was a bigger challenge than one good day. "You can't depend on dumb luck to win a contest." Sure enough, Davey remembered occasional days when Jennie's bread was somewhat dry or slightly gooey or a little dense. "And what you've got to do," George lectured, "is be sure you can do a perfect one on the very day of the fair." So Davey continued, learning to deal with varying humidities and temperatures. He found he couldn't just bring in whatever wood was on top of the pile. For the long rising process, he used cottonwood to keep the warming shelf on the top of George's range just warm enough. When it was time to bake the bread, he let the cottonwood burn down and restocked with tamarack to make a faster, hotter oven. One day he grabbed some aspen, and was amazed to find it could lend a bitter taste to the bread. He got so he could tell with his bare hand when the oven was just right. It turned out George's stove had a better side to the oven. While he needed to make two loaves a day to have dough to knead properly, he determined that the loaf on the north side would be the one to go to the fair and the one on the south side to the table. George said some people opened the oven half way through and reversed the loaves top to bottom and front to back, but Davey's experiments showed him that for that one perfect loaf he wanted, he was better off to give the favored position to the prize loaf all the way through the baking. His brothers could make do with second best for their sandwiches. He learned that both loaves were better if he put a pan of water in the bottom of the oven. He was glad he was earning the money for his ingredients himself. It gave him the independence to put in a little extra sugar and to use cream instead of milk. Jennie wasn't tolerant of extravagance. George taught Davey the perfect way to add milk to make the yeast bubble up just right and he trained Davey's eye to know the exact moment when the kneading should begin. The kneading - the most pleasurable part of the whole process - took even more instruction. For many days neither of them could figure out why Davey couldn't learn to use a light enough touch. At first George put it up to boyish fervor and coached Davey to put less muscle into it. "This isn't the same as cutting shingle bolts, you know." Davey was an earnest apprentice, but he couldn't seem to do what George asked; the bread still came out heavy. Finally George sat back in his rocking chair and gave his best analytic eye to the job. He saw that Davey leaned forward and down to reach the table built to the specifications of a man three inches shorter than himself. When they built a proper kneading table for a boy Davey's height, the bread improved.

By September George said the bread was consistently light enough, sweet enough, tender enough, white enough, and with a crust delicate enough and beautifully brown enough it could have gone to the Lewis and Clark Centennial Exposition in Portland, much less the Pend Oreille Boys' and Girls' Industrial Fair. George allowed the baker boy to fall back to practicing every third day to keep his hand in.

Neither of them wanted to give up the companionable afternoons, though, and they devoted more time than was strictly necessary to producing a framed display of cross-sections of all woods native to Pend Oreille County, accompanied by a live branch with leaves or needles, the latter to be replenished on the morning of the fair. The task was simple enough, but the sad man and the inquisitive boy wanted to stretch the job, so they made a frame, also of native woods, that they sanded and polished to a fare-thee-well. They went together on jaunts to locate woods native to the county but not to their immediate locale. They took horses and went on overnight trips into the high mountains to find alpine fir and white bark pine. They cut branches with bark, and cross-slabs that they sanded and lacquered. They searched through the whole summer for an example of yew, and found it just in time to include. "Used to be lots of that ugly stuff," George complained.

In October The *MINER*'s Tiger reporter reflected the town's pride in Davey for taking second prize in both categories. George, though, took exception with the judging. "That girl who took first place didn't have a bread as good as Davey's, but she put a fancy cut on top of the loaf so she won. The boy they said had the best wood display had fewer woods than Davey, and even had one I've never seen in this county. Where do they get these judges?" But George knew he'd had a first-class summer's enjoyment. His faith in humanity was rebuilt by the earnest boy who'd been so eager to learn from the old settler. "By God, that boy's not one who'll ever burn down somebody's building."

1915

A SKIFF OF tentative fall snow was melting in the late morning sun and Jennie was taking up the last of the potatoes and deciding if she liked the new potato digger when she heard two rifle shots from the direction of the Renshaws. As she bent over and shook the extra dirt from a fine two-pounder and admired it, she reflected that you didn't hear the sounds of hunting as often as you used to. With the valley floor fully settled, hunters had to go farther up the hills. She gave the shots no more thought, but as she continued on down the rows she did think back to the time, with Wes gone to the mines, when she used her big .10 gauge to keep meat on the table for herself and the boys. But the boys had grown up, and for years now she wouldn't deprive them of their manly chore of bringing in the meat. Tom, especially, enjoyed hunting. On Sundays when the St. Regis mill closed and they couldn't haul lumber, he usually knew of some family who could use a deer or a few birds. When Cass Morgan and his oldest boy both died from gases when they went down into their well that had gone dry shortly after Mrs. Morgan died of scarlet fever, everyone else reflected on the horror and the tragedy, but Tom brightened when he observed that the remaining children would surely need a deer that fall.

While she loaded the potatoes into the little garden wagon, Jennie had lots of such memories: of hunting in the A.T. and in the West Sierra and in the Cascades, and easiest of all here in the Pend d'Oreille. Maybe now the game didn't present itself at your door as it did just a few years ago, but an easy jaunt was all it took.

After midday dinner, Jennie saw Nettie Renshaw Lucas coming across the railroad embankment, headed for the Wooding house. Jennie hallooed and Nettie changed direction and joined her in the potato field. "Jennie, I've killed two deer. I hope you can use one."

"So that's what I heard. What'd you kill two for, Nettie?"

"I just couldn't resist. Pa made such a fuss about going out hunting today. It took him all morning to get together his gear, and to choose the right gun and clean it, and to try to remind the dog what hunting was, and to get camp gear together, and to saddle his horse. You'd have thought he had a fort to supply, not just four people. So when I stepped out the door and saw two does grazing about ten steps away, I reached for my gun and I couldn't resist killing them both. I've been working all morning at dressing them out. I want to have it all done when he gets home tomorrow. But I needed a break, and I needed somebody to laugh with about it. Charlie's in the woods. Ma's still back in New York visiting Uncle Homer, and I'm glad. She might not see the fun in it."

Jennie saw the fun all right, and she gave Nettie the laugh she wanted. But then she said, "Nettie, I don't know. If I take your doe, what'll Tom have to do?"

"What'll I do with it all? Thank goodness they were small."

"Thank goodness there wasn't four does standing in your backyard. Give one to Peggy O'Neal. He likely can sell it at the store. He probably won't pay you money for it, but he might butcher them both and let you keep one. The other one'd be off your hands."

"The point is teasing Pa. Wouldn't it be perfect if he came home with nothing?" And exactly that happened. When John got home at blue dusk the next day, Nettie had two does cut into quarters and could ask him where his take was. Of course he had nothing, but John Renshaw could laugh at himself as well as at anyone else. Nettie got her joke. She took one deer to Peggy O'Neal, but he had to turn it down, he said; selling venison was illegal now. Nettie hitched her wagon and took four quarters clear to Ione to give to the preacher at the Congregational Church to distribute where it might be needed. The rest she spent a day canning.

Jennie had good reason to reflect on all this when a week later she went into the post office and walked in on a couple of Kentuckians who's settled around Blueslide, and were now bending Flora Cross's ear.

Jennie greeted them. "What brings you down the river, Whitey? Orvil?"

"Mornin', Aunt Jennie. Want to see if the god-damn game warden is any fairer down here. He's sure enough got it in for Blueslide hunters. Spends most of his time sniffin' around there, and the rest of the country can take all the deer, fish, and bear they want - the way it ought to be anyway."

She should have known she couldn't josh him into a better humor before she said "Whitey, even a bad shot like you can kill more than he can use, though. There needs to be enough to go around, seems like, and more people are moving in all the time."

"Go around, be damned. I moved out to this country because I could take a deer when I wanted and how I wanted. I had my blue heelers sent out on the train. Then they said I couldn't hunt with dogs no more. Now they say I can just shoot in the fall. What's a man supposed to do the rest of the time? What's my old woman supposed to cook?"

Orvil pitched in. "Hey, Whitey, maybe after you got the four measly deer the game warden says you can have, you're supposed to shoot the game warden."

Both men guffawed. Jennie and Flora glanced at each other; both could see there was no chance of civil conversation. Jennie traded some eggs for baking powder and went her way.

Bill and Tom came in late after their last load. Bill came into the house and asked Jennie to heat a few buckets of water so he could soap and rinse some dried lather off the horses. He wanted some of her California ointment, too. "That collar rubbed Star and Kelly. It's not fitting just right." Something about both boys' manner spoke of a stifled anger. They generously curried all four horses and left them in the barn for the night. "They're working awful hard now and it's going to be cold tonight." When they were satisfied that the horses were cared for they brought in two loads of harness to stash behind the stove for the night to keep it soft.

"If you're through pampering those horses, your Ma has dinner ready," Wes said.

Bill looked up. "I guess it does look like pampering. But, Pa, we saw something up the hill that makes you want to treat any live creature right."

Tom was red with anger. "We had a little spill on the way down. I went back in the brush looking for a pry pole, and found something that still makes me sick. A few yards off the road there was a little clearing. Some yahoo shot two yearlings and three does, two of them carrying fawns, and left them there, no effort to dress them out or use them at all. I scared up about thirty ravens and eagles. Good thing there wasn't a cougar or bear around. Who'd expect to run into something like that?"

Wes asked, "Are you sure they were shot? There might still be enough wolves still around here to do something like that."

"I looked. There was enough left so you could find the wounds, and even two bullets."

Davey chipped in. "Pa, who is it you're supposed to tell about something like that? The sheriff? Is there a deputy down here?"

Tom said, "There's a game warden. He lives in Newport, I think."

"I don't know if he'd come down this far, or what he could do if he did. But we can send him a letter on the morning train," Wes promised.

Jennie stayed quiet through the whole exchange, vigorously mashing a pan of potatoes. She would ordinarily have served them plain boiled, but like the boys she needed a way to work off some anger.

While the rest of them cleaned up the kitchen, Wes wrote the letter, with constant input from the other five. They were still upset when they went to bed, and could hear each other rustling the bedclothes for a long time.

A FEW DAYS LATER JENNIE smiled at good memories when she saw Ruby Belle and her babes drive up in a light one-horse carriage. She went out to meet her niece and hitched her gentle Roanie to the rail fence. Ruby Belle handed down five-year-old Myrtle Maude. Jennie was pleased to see the little girl wearing the dress she'd made her. Four-year-old Little Jimmie was in striped dress and long bloomers, also from Jennie's needle. The two of them scampered into the house to see if Aunt Jennie had cookies set out for them. Ruby Belle placed year-old Gladys in Jennie's arms and not too agilely stepped down herself, the fourth baby clearly showing under her dress and coat.

As she did when she had a disappointment or worry, Ruby Belle had come to her Aunt Jennie to commiserate. "Aunt Jennie, I was called to do jury duty, and I can't go!"

"Did you want to?"

"Surely I wanted to. I never knew a woman who did it before, but they're calling more and more. And some are going. With all these game law trials, and people driving cars without getting licenses, they need more juries." She laughed. "Uncle Wes says not enough women are serving, and not enough are voting. He says it's been five years since women could vote in this state, and he hasn't got you out yet."

"I don't understand all the stuff they put in the papers about the candidates, and I ain't going to vote for somebody unless I know for myself what I'm getting into. Anyway, about this jury duty. Why can't you?"

"Because the trial's in two weeks. Gladys is still on the breast, and the new baby could come any time. So they have you fill out a paper if you can't serve, and I've sent it in. But I'd give anything if I could. Wouldn't it be fun to see what everybody says?"

While she made tea for herself and Ruby Belle, and angel tea, mostly milk and sugar, for the tots who now were on their third round of sugar cookies, Jennie asked Ruby Belle if she believed the story Charlie Lucas brought home from a Blueslide trial was true. "Seems the game warden caught a bunch of fellas ice fishin', which they ain't supposed to do on the river no more. So as Charlie tells it Old Man Rummerfield is fast thinkin', and he drops his pole through the hole and there ain't no evidence against him. This makes the game warden mad, and he arrests the other four and suppeenies Old Man Rummerfield so he'll have to testify against 'em. So when they get to court the prosecutor says, what were you doing on such and such a date? Rummerfield says he was settin' on the ice watchin' the boys. The prosecutor says, would that be the defendants in this trial? Yes, that's right. What were these boys doing? I don't believe I remember. This just happened last week, and you don't remember? No, I don't remember. That's a convenient memory you have, Mr. Rummerfield. Perhaps you remember if there were some holes cut in the ice. Yes, I believe there were. Do you happen to know what those holes were for? No, I don't. Do you know just when these holes were cut in the ice? No, I don't have any idea. They might have been cut this winter or they could have been cut last winter."

Ruby Belle whooped along with her aunt. "Aunt Jennie, that's too good to be true. What does Charlie say happened then?"

"Well, I guess everybody in the courtroom howled just like you did, and the judge, that's Lee Bilderback, and he ain't none too religious himself about game laws, acquitted the fishermen and adjourned the court."

"See," said Ruby Belle, "that's just the kind of thing I'd love to be there for. It sounds like real fun, and you're doing your duty."

"Well, I guess seein' to these kiddies is a duty, and mostly it's fun."

"Except I've been doing it for five years. I wouldn't trade them in, you know that, Aunt Jennie. But a break from it wouldn't be bad."

"Well, bring 'em by here now and then. I miss young'uns, and none of my boys show signs of bringin' me any."

AS IT TURNED OUT, EVERYONE was glad Ruby Belle couldn't serve. There were two shooting trials to be heard, one a murder and one an attempted murder, not fun for anyone but especially wrong for someone made tender by making new life. Jennie reflected on whether this was just a tragic coincidence or whether it meant that the Pend Oreille, as it drew more people to its peace, was doomed to violence. This winter brought extra heavy snow, and took her back to that first, snug winter when she was sure she'd left things like murder behind in the outside world. She wanted, as she had then, to keep her thoughts in the bounds of the homestead, to protect her serenity, even if it meant closing out some things. But she was surrounded now by people and by information, and learned of such things whether she wanted to or not.

She especially wished she didn't have to know about Joe Cusick's trial, for instance. In August Joe had shot and killed Harry Kilburn, who used to work for Joe in his tavern. Joe was now on trial and might go to the state penitentiary at Walla Walla, though Joe was said to have bragged that his considerable money could buy freedom one way or another. That attitude had finished any sympathy Wes still had for Joe; he was thoroughly disgusted with him. Jennie wanted to believe the other story, that Joe had not been the same since a sledding accident about eight years ago. He'd hit his head hard in the wreck, and people said that ever since then when he got excited he got too excited. Supposedly when they found him over the dying Harry Kilburn he was dancing around, squealing "I gotsie him with my little gunsie! Betsy dinged him! Betsy dinged him!" Jennie remembered the riverboat captain before his gusto went amok.

Ruby Belle was at Aunt Jennie's kitchen table quite a lot that winter, often reading aloud from the *MINER* so that sometimes Jennie had to hear the news twice. Ruby Belle liked to pretend she was on the jury, and made Jennie her sounding board. "Aunt Jennie, if somebody does something when their head isn't right, like Joe Cusick, do you punish them the same way as you would a sensible person? You know, you don't punish a three-year-old the same way you would an eight-year-old who's supposed to know better. Is there some place to put a deranged killer except in with the purposeful killers?" But the majority of the jury - which included one woman whom Ruby Belle roundly envied - were more in Wes's camp, and Joe did go to Walla Walla.

Wes thought the other trial was more significant, because while one crazy man couldn't ruin a community, determined scofflaws surely could. Didn't she remember what it was like in the A.T., when there was so much robbing and shooting going on that they had to sometimes live inside Fort Scott with the Mormans?

A poaching case had been going on at Blueslide, and this one had ended in the near killing of a decent man, the Prosecutor who was doing his duty and trying to uphold the law for everyone. Also in the near killing of a gabby, resentful, self-centered no-good. It started when the game warden confronted Bill Solomon at the ferry landing at Ruby, being photographed with no fewer than seven deer slung over the rail. Solomon began energetically to cuss out the warden, and soon upgraded to shoving. The warden restrained Solomon by stepping behind him and enclosing the man, arms and all, within his own arms. When a couple of crewmembers guffawed, Solomon's rage turned into a dangerous and icy sullenness. When he was released he went for retribution to a different branch of the law; he charged the game warden with assault. Some didn't think the warrant against Warden Walker should ever have been issued, but Justice Bilderback did, and the charge came to court, though in another jurisdiction, out of his own hearing. In poaching charges a defendant always asked for a jury trial, because he knew it was impossible to find a jury that didn't contain fellow poachers. That insurance might have pertained in this case but the only two witnesses to the shoving incident, while of the poacher persuasion, didn't come to court, not understanding what "change of venue" meant. On hearing this, Poacher Solomon began a long harangue, vilely accusing everyone connected with the court of conspiring against him. Tired of listening, and with no witnesses, Judge Teters threw the case out, and Poacher Solomon was even more infuriated. He was still spouting venom when Judge Teters, followed by everyone else, left the courtroom. Solomon's supporters gathered in a huff outside, promising Solomon they weren't giving up either, and this wasn't over yet. Prosecutor Leavy went directly to the railroad platform, 30 yards from the little all-purpose one-room town hall where trials were held, to catch the southbound train back to Newport. Solomon broke away from his cohorts and followed Leavy to the platform, where he continued to yap at him. Other people waiting for the train drew away, annoyed by Solomon's shrill fury. "You're gonna get yours, Leavy," he shrieked. He'd hardly spouted his threat when, sure enough, a bullet intended for the Prosecutor burst from bushy ambush. The shooter was heard running away up the hill into deep timber. He didn't know until his friends found his hiding place and told him, that he had missed his target and instead hit his friend Solomon directly in the mouth. The bullet had entered one cheek, severed Solomon's tongue, and exited the other cheek. Solomon didn't die, but he wasn't annoying people with his blabber any more.

When Wes read the story aloud to the family, Jennie jumped in before anyone could speak. "Nobody in this room hadn't better laugh." Davey looked puzzled. His Pa explained, "Irony is the word that escapes Mother."

PART III
IT SLIPS AWAY

1916 – 1923

1916

THE FIRST DAY to feel like spring came in mid-February. There'd actually been melt for a week, and now it was seeping into the ground the way it should, readying the soil for an easy tilling. By March the loggers complained they had to use sleighs to bring the logs down, then change to wagons in the bottom, twice the work to get the logs to the mills that now were numerous along the river, or to the river itself for rafting downriver, or to the train to go either direction. The St. Regis Mill kept ten teams hauling and Bill, now 20, thought he saw the door reopening to more school. For five years he'd been saving all he decently could from his wages, and had some in a bank account in his own name. He thought now of a way to build it faster. "Ma, maybe I could buy a team and wagon and sleigh and chains, and haul for St. Regis or any mill that was contracting." Thinking to get around her fear of logging, he threw in, "It wouldn't be as dangerous as logging, where they're falling trees."

Wes came in and changed that tune. "Hauling on a hill as steep as Tiger is about as dangerous as work can get, Bill. I notice bells aren't enough, and you fellas howl all the way down because you can't know what's around the next corner. Ten teams going up and down a one-wagon track makes for a lot of encounters. Every time you get out and pry a wheel out of the mud, you're at the mercy of your team. If your brake lets loose, you can be over the bank in a trice. But aside from that, how much do you need and how much do you have?" Jennie's head jerked up to hear Wes suddenly showing a business sense in his son's affairs when he'd never shown any in his own.

Bill made some sharper inquiries, and found he was $50 short. At the rate he was saving from uncertain work like firefighting, logging and farming, the whole country would be logged before he had a team.

TWO DAYS LATER AT DINNER Bill told them he thought he'd go Out to find work

- maybe Spokane, or planting in the Palouse or maybe mining somewhere. "Oh, yeah, working in a mine's a quick way to get rich," Wes grinned.

"Can I go, Bill?" Jasper threw in at once. "I've got $10 traveling money." Wes said to Jennie later, "At least he's interested in something."

On the first of March the two of them, one as well heeled as the other, took the train to Spokane. Sure they'd find work, they spent freely. It was a letdown, then, to find that jobs weren't posted on every corner. They'd been well warned about the sharks, but they tried the Union halls. The Union halls had no place for inexperienced workers, though, especially 16-year-old Jasper, and Bill knew they couldn't split up. By the time they got to the Palouse the planting was done. They earned their keep with a pack train going to California. They got a week here and a week there in Colorado mines. They found the gypsying as profitable as their parents had; all that came in went out. But they kept at it. In October the bindlestiffs started heading south for warmer weather. Bill and Jasper knew the warmest place would be at Tiger, under their parents' roof and beside their parents' stove. They moved from mine to mine north and west through Nevada, Utah, Idaho. Stories of Jennie's travels with the photographer's wagon came back to them, and stories of Wes's jobs in various mines. They felt they were reliving their parents' failures rather than making their own fortunes. As they moved into Idaho they felt more and more beaten, and more and more embarrassed about dragging their tails home. They tried the Coeur d'Alene Mining District, and the Silver Valley. At Wallace they knew they were going home broke. They sat in on a poker game, thinking the little they had to lose wouldn't make much more difference. But luck finally struck. Between them they came out with $100, the most money they'd seen at one time. Jasper thought at once of making an entrance upon their return home, anything to keep them from going in with their tails between their legs. Bill still had his thoughts on the team and equipment that would set him up in business. They worked out a partnership. They'd spend half the money on dude suits and accouterments to make a splash. They'd keep enough to set Bill up in business, and he'd guarantee Jasper paid work whenever he wanted it.

On a mild day in December Jennie was at the station waiting to load three 50-gallon barrels of sauerkraut onto the northbound train, so she was there to see Bill and Jasper come in dressed, as she later told Wes, like French dancing-masters. She hadn't expected to be so proud of them, but to have Ada and Orla and everyone else who met the train see them come in in a pair of Chicago suits with neckties, stickpins and a pair of straw skimmers, was surprisingly pleasing. Real nabobs accessorized with big cigars; and sure enough, as the boys stepped onto the platform, they postured with a couple of foot-long cheroots. Their mother smiled at their newly-acquired pompousness, forgivable in boys who'd worked since toddlerhood at all the humble tasks of a homestead, plus cutting cordwood for steamboats, running trap lines and packtrains, and logging with horses. They now seemed to gainsay the naysayers, some of whom were gratifyingly present. Jennie remembered Ada saying they'd be back in two weeks, tails between their legs. Hy Maggott on his stump in front of the store had remarked that the hop fields of Yakima wouldn't likely prove any richer than the spud fields of Tiger. Flora Cross at the post office had been kinder; when letters arrived from Provo and Twin Falls, she said she hoped the boys were finding work. Jennie was glad all these folks were there to see the homecoming.

When he stepped down and saw Jennie, Jasper set down his valise, inhaled deeply, and said "Hello, Mother," before exhaling with his chin lifted skyward. Bill hugged her. The train went on north, and the three of them followed it afoot for the hundred yards home.

"Did you miss any meals?"

Bill grinned. "We might have postponed a few."

"How's your shoe leather?"

"Fine, Ma," answered Jasper. That would have been a good time to tell the story of walking from Coeur d'Alene to Wallace with holes in their soles and cardboard inserts only slightly deterring the dampness. But it wasn't part of the main story line, which was of their incredible success at earning money in the larger world.

Wes came home and the ante went up. Their father had behind him several decades of job search and job work, would be even harder to fool about accumulated earnings. Bill tried a couple of times in the name of truth to inject some of the disappointing chapters of their saga, but Jasper wouldn't allow it, butting in with enhanced versions. The packer in Pocatello said they balanced a load better than he did. The miners in Utah said they were mighty fast learners. The sheepmen in Burns wanted them back next summer.

As dinner concluded, Jasper brought out three more cigars. Wes accepted his and settled himself to read the *APPEAL TO REASON*. He had congratulated the boys as much as he thought necessary, and understood more of what was unsaid than Jasper would have liked to know.

While Jennie and Davey finished the dishes and Jasper finished yet another tale of glory, Jennie threatened to pierce his balloon with a direct question. "Well, Jasper, just how much money did you bring home?"

"Enough, Ma. I'm thinking to talk to Lee Jett if he still has that forty to sell."

She was setting up the laundry tubs to soak tomorrow's wash. "Just what part of Utah were you in? I traveled a lot through there as a girl in the old photographer's wagon. How much Mormon moola'd you get your hands on?"

"Ma, maybe I'll get you a ruffler for your sewing machine."

She smiled slyly. "Tom? I don't think he's got no money. Let's search him."

Scuffling was common in the Wooding household, and Tom was glad for a chance to break the tension. Grinning, he laid his cigar on the kitchen counter and moved behind Jasper in position to pin his elbows. "I'll hold him, Ma, and you check his pockets." Jennie moved to Jasper's chest. She saw the familiar wrinkling of his chin as he pursed his mouth and raised his face in the way he did to defy the teasing of his brothers, the kids at school, or even elders who challenged his dignity. She opened her eyes wide and pushed her lips into a fish mouth as if to say "What are you going to do about it?" Tom had pinned Jasper's left arm and was just putting his hand on the right when it thrust forward, the cigar clenched firmly. The arm, the boy, were both beyond stopping and the burning cigar jabbed hard into his mother's naked eye. Her scream was still in the air when Wes leaped toward them. "Jasper, what have you done to Mother?" He lowered her into her sewing rocker. By then Jasper was out of the house. Bill brought water to flush the eye. This brought her out of the chair with another scream. She walked on bouncing tiptoe around the room, trying whether closed or open was worse. She began swinging her shoulders from one side to the other, as if that would bring relief; as she turned each way she uttered a breathless "Ah!" They all were stupefied, terrified of doing something to cause her more pain. The touch of the eyelid on the eyeball was unendurable, and she kept both eyes wide, wide open, repeating the faint "Ah! Ah! Ah!"

Jennie was the first to think of Jasper, what he must be feeling, what he might be doing. "Bill, ...go...get... brother." But at that moment they heard the team and sleigh pull up to the door. Jasper was already there with the team harnessed, ready to take her to the doctor.

Beginning with the laundry the next morning, Jasper did his best at all her work for the two weeks she suffered the worst pain of her life. He could never speak first, went around the house with his chin almost on his chest. He chopped wood and hauled water, he cleaned, he baked, he cooked. He delivered her friend Florence Earley for the daily dressing of the wound, but didn't stay in the room to see the blistered eyeball.

Jennie slept only an hour at a time. A restiveness possessed her, driving her to walk the room constantly, windows darkened against the reflecting snow. Thankfully she was able to knit as she paced. She unraveled old garments, reknit them, and shuffled the ownership. Everyone got new gloves, hats, sweaters, and socks.

Jennie forgave Jasper in the first hour. Whether the fateful thrust had been deliberate cruelty, wild impulse, or sheer accident was never clear to anyone. Jasper didn't know either, but the guilt and the shame were great. When he said he liked the name Jack better than Jasper and would they please call him that from now on, Jennie wondered how long it would be till he forgave himself.

1917

WES ALWAYS REMEMBERED 1917 as the year the draft made everyone peek around the door for Slackers, suspect their lifelong neighbors of treason, and try to compete for being the most patriotic when they didn't much believe in what they were being patriotic about. And it was the year the Wobblies made the most progress for everyone, he said, and thereby made themselves the most hated they had ever been.

In April the country easily allowed Woodrow Wilson to forget he'd ever said there was such a thing as a nation being "too proud to fight," and let him take them into The Great War. There weren't any Civil War veterans living in Tiger but there were others, like Wes, who had been orphaned by it and who were unequivocal pacifists. There were several who had served in the Indian wars, and a couple from the Spanish-American War, and even the most hardened of them had seen what war meant to families as well as to the soldiers themselves. No one had any heart for a war of any kind, and certainly not for one across the water among countries that had no meaning for half of them and to the other half was the place they'd chosen to leave. Apparently this feeling wasn't unique to Tiger, because after about six weeks the voluntary enlistments were so few nationwide that a draft was initiated. This made ammunition for the many anti-war protesters through that summer, who pointed out that if the war was so popular, why was the draft necessary? In June, Wilson signed the Espionage Act, which sounded as if it was supposed to control spies. And it might have, but it was used a lot more - 2,000 times - to jail war protesters, including Elizabeth Gurley Flynn.

Tom and Bill were staying through the work week at Panhandle Camp #2 in the LeClerc Creek Drainage with Bill's new span of American horses when the supply packer brought word that the U.S. had entered the European War. No one was sure what it would mean, but they didn't see how it would affect them very much. Old Ben Hargreaves said war always meant the government needed more of everything, and maybe they'd have to cut trees faster. Oscar Lungren didn't see how that was possible, they were already highballing dark to dark.

Two days later a fellow came up with the packer to try to get recruits for the Army. Nobody was interested, and he went back down with the packer. That night in the outhouse a poem was posted:

I love my flag, I do, I do,
Which floats upon the breeze
I also love my arms and legs,
And neck, and nose and knees.
One little shell might spoil them all
Or give them such a twist,
They would be of no use to me;
I guess I won't enlist.

I love my country, yes, I do
I hope her folks do well.
Without our arms, and leg and things,
I think we'd look like hell.
Young men with faces half shot off
Are unfit to be kissed.
I've read in books it spoils their looks.
I guess I won't enlist.

When men with families nearby went home from the camp on Saturday night some found that their people, if they'd had no need to walk down to the store that week, didn't yet know of the War. Most knew, but didn't see how it would affect them way out West and way Downriver. Those who read the *MINER* or the *SPOKESMAN-REVIEW* were soon being bombarded with the glory and patriotism of it all, but they left the enthusiasm to town people in Newport and Spokane. Wes had too much reading and thinking behind him to believe it wouldn't touch his family. "With four sons, this family has sudden value for the Government. The Fat Cats who talked Wilson into keeping the seas safe for their trade ships by going to war don't mean to go themselves. They mean to send other people to war. And they don't even mean to send their own sons. They mean to send other people's sons while they keep theirs home to handle the extra business the war will bring. It probably won't last long enough to take Davey, and Jack may squeak by, but Tom and Bill are sure bets."

Jennie's sewing rocker went still. When he looked, he saw a face that must have been the one that looked at Naomi and Alma beside the wagon. "God, I'm sorry, Jennie. I didn't mean sure bets to be killed. I meant sure bets to be eligible. They might not get called. I hope to Hell they won't. And if they do, we'll hope they don't have to go where the shooting is." He knelt and put his arms around her. "Jennie, I'm so sorry. My mouth did it again."

No one they knew enlisted. In the towns, though, where people had more free time, jingoism was easier to sell. Young Doctor Wallace of Newport, now Lieutenant Wallace, had joined up before the U.S. even entered. His letters to the *MINER* about how grisly the Balkan front was, and about his homesickness, and the experience and education he was gaining, were lapped up. Ralph Shackelton, 16 years old and in the 9th grade at Newport, enlisted to show he was a man, and the Navy accepted him to show they could sacrifice boys just as well as men. A potential sailor volunteering from Metaline Falls was turned down because his final naturalization papers hadn't come through, but he was later drafted though the papers still hadn't come through.

People were asked to put in more gardens to help with *the country's situation*. Jennie was already farming all she had cleared, but she noted a low spring runoff along Renshaw Creek and crowded in an extra acre of spuds in the flood plain. Asked if this meant she was supporting the War she said, "No, but if they're gonna have the damned thing, I'm gonna do what I can to make people less miserable." Metaline Falls plowed up its ball field to plant potatoes, as well as the strip between the train depot and the business section. They said they'd make it a park in the spring, when the war was over.

The draft didn't make the war popular; being coerced didn't make people more willing to do something they hadn't wanted to do voluntarily. For the rest of the year, Downriver registrations were a sign of how long a man could hold out against the inevitable. The War Department set the county population at 7511, though local estimates were under 6500; the War Department of course used its own number to determine that Pend Oreille County owed them 592 men. A lottery would be used to determine who would go when. Exemptions were sought by men with families, especially heads of farm families. The

Draft Board, made up of town men, didn't have a clear understanding of how essential a farmer's presence was to his family's income. Heinie Anderson at Tiger, with a wife and two children, was exempted, but men with wives and no children were not. The Draft Board must have imagined that that farm wife was accustomed to using her day to tat and give tea parties, and would now find plenty of time to run the farm.

The term *Slacker* was invented, to indicate and humiliate men who hadn't registered or who hadn't shown up for their exam. The term was used to fan a local war. Most energetic in finding Slackers were those who had no eligible soldier in their family. The Draft Board ordered the arrest of 19 men who didn't register. The *MINER* published the names of alleged Slackers, then failed to apologize when it developed that many of those named had already enlisted voluntarily and were in fact in the Army, or were in lumber camps, or picking apples in Wenatchee, or bringing in the crop in the Palouse and hadn't received their notices, or had gone for their exams somewhere besides Newport.

Even in the field of love the divisiveness pertained. Marriage licenses for the year doubled. To some, the numerous weddings showed how much in love the young folks were, and how they wanted to claim their partners before being separated. But the Superpatriots declared these marriages were merely bids for exemptions. There were fights between local boys and soldiers in uniform, the latter having a considerable edge with girls.

By the end of April some town people had formed themselves into a Newport branch of the patriotic "Home Guard," made up of men and boys ineligible for the draft for one reason or another. Just what they were to do was unclear, except to don uniforms and do military-like drills in the street and harass men they branded as Slackers. They were sore insulted when they learned the War Department did not find that work worthy of funding and they had to buy their own uniforms if they wanted them.

Many Kalispels, like Indians across the country, were reluctant to register, because they were sure - with good cause - that their land would be taken while they were away. It had taken until 1914 to get legal status for the Kalispel Reservation, and they didn't yet feel secure with it.

In July one-third of the county's 72 recruits were from Tiger. "They're so busy in Newport calling up farm boys and looking for Slackers, they can't find their own hometown recruits," noted John Renshaw. In August 160 men were called to the draft, and 119 responded. Of the 119, only 28 solid recruits passed the test and had no exemptions. The 28 included William

Norman and William A. Wooding of Tiger. Faced now with the reality, Bill as well as his family knew the only choice was to go, and leave talk of the foolishness of war for another time.

The whimsy of the lottery called up Bill, not Tom. The toe shortened in the woodshed when he was a tad and shot clear off when he was 12 didn't save him; his exam deemed him eligible. Before he left, Bill spent two months working 18-hour days in the woods with his team, trying to fatten what he now thought of as his college fund; the dream had expanded as the years passed. "I'll go to school when I get back."

When the Red Cross and the YMCA both made pitches within a month for donations, Tiger people couldn't send much. But they still understood barter. Jennie spent the two months before Bill left knitting and sewing for him, then organized women from Tiger, Lost Creek and Blueslide to meet in Renshaw Hall to make sweaters, socks, mufflers and wristlets for local boys going to war. Only when the local lads were supplied three times over did she agree to become part of a Red Cross unit that would send the garments, made with yarn, needles and instructions sent by the U.S. Government, to the larger soldiery outside Pend Oreille. When the YMCA had a drive to collect books for the soldiers' canteens, Frank Darrow brought a wagonful. He didn't support the war any more than Wes did, but like Jennie he wanted those who had to go to have what comfort they could, and perhaps keep their minds open.

On a crisp October evening the whole family and several neighbors took the train to Newport to see William and Bill off. The sendoff was exhilarating. There was a procession of the Home Guard, the Red Cross, school children and general citizens. Dozens of torches lighted the streets. The Town Band wore red, white and blue sashes over their uniforms. The new soldiers lined up for handshakes from everyone. Around a gigantic bonfire outside the depot every Pend Oreille soldier was given tobacco or candy or some other such comfort. The three coaches reserved for troops were decorated with bunting and flags, and a banner on each side read "Newport - Trenches - Berlin," the supposed route of the brave boys inside. As the train departed for Camp Lewis, the crowd sang to the tune of "My Country 'Tis of Thee":

God save our splendid men;
Bring them home safe again,
God save our men.

Keep them victorious, patient and chivalrous;
They are so dear to us,
God save our men.

Flora Cross was delighted to hear her birth country's anthem sung by her allies. No one corrected her lyrics when she sang "God Save the King."

The next day the patriotic fervor turned into a hangover. "I guess it greased the wheels a bit so we could stand him going," Jennie opined. "A kind of Dutch courage."

They were soon back in the hatefulness of the local war scene. George House of Tiger was posted as a Deserter, not just a Slacker, for registering but not going for his exam when called. Down in Colfax, patriots made a public list of "wealthy" residents who were assumed *able to buy Liberty bonds but refused to do so.* The blacksmith in Newport threw out of his shop a man he labeled an "anarchist" because he found a point to admire in the Russian revolutionists. Thus, the divisiveness of the war and the divisiveness of political views blended in confusion. Otto Weik, a shoemaker in Colville, was interned by federal officers until after the war for his unspecified *pro-German sympathies.* "Well, wouldn't you think he *would* still love his family over there?" Davey asked. Weik's shop was locked and sealed by the government. "He'll have a lot of rust to clean up," sympathized Jack, whose personal chore was taking care of the family blacksmith tools. All unnaturalized German men over age 24 were required to register. Jennie's comment: "I'm glad Frank Schmaus is gone from here; I'd hate to see any of this slopped on him." At Spirit Lake a vigilante group was formed to keep *enemy propaganda* out of that area. Wes's observation: "Meaning any kind of intelligent discussion of the war." Jennie'd had enough when she got an order from Metaline for two barrels of "liberty cabbage"; when the barrels were ready she had Wes help her with the spelling and painted in four-inch letters on the lid and two sides of each barrel SAUERKRAUT. Wes discouraged her from writing SAUERKRAUT, YOU SONS OF BITCHES!

Wes was sorry to see the country go crazy. "They're using jingoism to shut up people they disagreed with before this war even came up." Flora Cross campaigned for magazines of any kind to be sent to soldiers and sailors in Europe. The Postal Service would send them, regardless of weight, for a penny per copy. Wes was tempted to take her his collections of the *APPEAL TO REASON* and the *INDUSTRIAL WORKER*, but backed off because she was too nice a lady to embarrass just because the President's Cabinet was banning all Socialist literature from the mails. "See what I mean? We were just as Socialist in 1912. But they didn't act against us until there was a war. That way everybody who might object to their highhanded tactics is afraid of looking unpatriotic."

A month after Bill left, they got some reassurance. On his enrollment form Bill had called himself a logger; Tom had called himself a horse packer. Bill was sent with thousands of other Northwest boys to the coast of Oregon, where spruce was being harvested for airplanes and ships. "So the poor lumber barons get a little boost too," said Wes.

"But at least Bill's not being shot at, and he does the same work he did here. And the bunkhouses can't have as many lice, because they're not as old," Tom offered. But Bill's first letter said the coastal fleas were worse than the inland lice, and anyway they had just as many lice too, and he wished the Wobblies would go in the Army so they could clean up conditions there. He had reason to hope, he said, that he'd get sent closer to Pend Oreille. The spruce was running out, and the white pine of the Inland area would have to do. He guessed they'd have to rename the Spruce Squadrons the Pine Platoons.

But the Wobblies weren't likely to help Bill with his fleas. They were busy fighting their own war, declared against them by the United States Department of Justice. "Justice!" Wes spat. "Department of Injustice, I'd say. Anybody who wants justice is either a Union member or he roots for them. If a working man wants a fair shake, he's got to join up with other stiffs. The biggest Union-breaker in this country is Woodrow Wilson. His God-damned Sedition Act and his God-damned Immigration Act, and his God-damned Syndicalism Laws!"

When Bill went away to Camp Lewis, he left his team in the family's care. He encouraged Tom to find work for the horses. "They need to work or they won't be worth a damn when I come back. Go up and talk to Bush Bergren and try to get on at Leach Camp #2. Number four's about finished. It's not worth taking the team across on the ferry, but if you can stay on this side, you should have work through the winter."

"If I don't get called up before then."

"Well, if you do, you do. Then maybe they'd take a chance on Jack or Davey. They're going to be short of men, between the War and the Wobblies."

Tom went up to try at Leach Camp #2, above Blueslide on Lost Creek, and was right back home to get the team. He told his brother, "Jack, their blacksmith quit when his brother-in-law got drafted. He wanted to go home and help his family. If you go right now, they might take a chance on you."

"Strike while the iron's hot, Mr. Blacksmith," Wes instructed. As she always did, Jennie laughed at his joke and they hugged their appreciation of each other's fun. The boys, though, were serious about their sudden induction into the world of salaried work and paid no attention to their playful elders.

"Do I take my own tools?"

"Which you don't own," pointed out Wes. "Those are mine and they aren't leaving the place. There's plenty of gear right here I'll have to keep in shape."

"No, Leach has its own forge and stuff up there. Just pack up a bedroll and let's go. Well, maybe your leather apron. You can even ride up, when the team goes up."

Jennie was sorting out blankets and deciding which she would risk to bunkhouse damp and dirt when Davey came in. "Tom," he asked, "do you think they'd take me?"

"What are you, twelve? I didn't see any little boys up there, no."

"You know I'm sixteen! And you know I can handle horses better'n you can. I don't know logging, maybe, but just maybe I'd learn some, living in a logging camp and all."

"If you want a job, you better lay off the smart talk. Those guys'll send you sliding back down the chute toward home if you sass them. What do you think, Ma? Can you spare the sprout?"

That suddenly, Wes and Jennie were alone in the house. On the third night, when she'd finally pared the size of the dinner down to one-tenth of the usual, which they were amazed to find was all the two of them actually could eat, she told him how she felt. "You'd think after all the gypsying, I'd be used to people coming in and going out from my life. But now it's been 18 years right here, wrapped up in the five of you. When they said they was going I didn't think for a minute I'd have any feelings about it. But I do. I sure do."

"Pretty quiet, huh?"

"And you know, Wes, they'll likely never all live here again. It's time they'll be getting married, or moving away even."

"And we'll be the old folks."

"We are the old folks, Wes."

"I hear old ladies make pretty good pies. What kind you got, Girlie? Okay if I still call you that?"

On Saturday night the boys rode three of the horses down for a day off for laundry. They got home well after dark, and would leave the next afternoon in time to be in camp before dark.

"So what happens to the fellas that don't have horses? There ain't hardly time to walk both ways," Jennie asked.

"They stay up there. And they have to go on paying for the day's mess too, even though they aren't paid for Sunday, of course, 'cause they don't work. So we're kind of lucky," Jack realized.

Tom, more experienced of lumber camps, wasn't as delighted by the whole picture.

"This camp doesn't have any way to do laundry, like #1 did. And no drying space except in the bunkhouse. So if you come in wet, and you mostly do, you eat wet and then hang your duds up by your bunk when you go to bed, and hope they get dried out. You can imagine what it smells like, with 40 guys' sweaty, wet wool drying out all at once. The men who've been there longest get the places nearest the stove." As he told this, Jennie began stringing clothesline from wall to wall and setting up laundry tubs in the kitchen. They all helped to fill them.

Jack and Davey talked only of the big wages they were making. Jack bragged about his $4 a day as blacksmith to Tom's $3.50 as teamster and Davey's $2.50 as flunky and punk.

Tom pointed out, "That may be, but on top of that the team gets $40 a month and free hay and oats while they're up there. All of us got to pay $1 a day for grub." He went out for a load of tamarack to keep the fire going for hot water. When he came back he had a new thought. "If the team's earning $40 a month, how much of that should go into Bill's savings?" They decided the whole forty would go into the college fund since Bill hadn't gone away by choice, and he wasn't exactly off on a joy trip, and he'd worked five years to pay for the team.

"Anyway, two fifty a day's more money than I ever earned before," said Davey. But he fell asleep before it was his turn to scrub his clothes, and had to be wakened. On Sunday afternoon, though, he was eager to go back to where he was counted almost a man. Washing dishes in the cookhouse or clearing brush for a skidroad or shoveling out the horsebarn were glamorous jobs now they were followed by paydays.

When the *MINER* came at midweek, Wes told Jennie the boys didn't know how lucky they were. "These poor bindlestiffs that ride the train from job to job are being dragged off the Great Northern boxcars at Newport and put in jail."

"Ain't that 'cause they ain't got a paid ticket?"

"True. But they've been riding the rails free for years. Most local police didn't see any need to enforce the Railroads' rules. Now all of a sudden with this war craziness the town clowns have decided it's their patriotic duty to make life miserable for the working stiffs. Most of these guys carry Wobbly cards, and the coppers ask to see them. In the Newport court it makes a difference whether they want to stay loyal to their Union. If they do, they get $50 or 30 days. But if they'll tear up their card and stay on *good behavior,* - whatever that is - and promise to *look for work,* - which is what they were doing in the first place - they only get $10. These Superpatriot types have swallowed the line that it's unpatriotic to hold up production during the war, so anybody who believes in the Union and in strikes is 'helping the Kaiser win the war'. And they've got the billy clubs on their side."

"Wes, how does it make you feel when the cops doing this stuff are people you know and have to go on living with?"

She stopped him with that. Slowly, he worked out, "I hate what they do, but I can't let myself hate them. As you say, I have to go on living with them. I don't want to hate the people I live amongst. They were shallow thinking before, and I ignored it. What they're doing now is despicable, but it comes from what they are and were all along. Day by day, I have to swallow some stuff." Then he regained his momentum. "What made me sickest is when Charlie Barker snitched on those Wobblies at Ruby last summer."

"Tell me about that." She knew the story, but he needed to tell it.

"Well, there was a Wobbly Hall at Ruby, a log cabin owned by Clayton Payne. Clate's a Wobbly writer; his stuff goes to Chicago and all over the country in their pamphlets and speeches and books. Organizers could stay at Clate's place. They kept a lot of their literature there to pass out at logging camps all through the area. At a Wobbly Hall the guys can have someplace to send their mail. They can stay dry, live pretty decently, and make plans to get decent living conditions for the men in the camps. And that includes strikes when necessary. Now, I don't think Charlie Barker is especially opposed to the Union or to strikes. He's not particularly on the side of the Bosses. But it's just like this war craziness. Charlie wants to be in with the upper crust in the county, and he saw a way to look good to the Newport crowd. He has a place at Ruby too, so like everybody else there he knew all about the Wobbly Hall, which had been there for a long time. Always before, if cops came around, the boys in the hall would learn about it ahead of time, and they could all go hide in the woods till the coast was clear. See, Clate's had this place at Ruby for about 12 years. He works as a carpenter, and they say he's good at it, and he has a good reputation as an honest man. He's been a Wobbly since 1907, and nobody bothered him about it. Charlie Barker sure never did.

"But this time Charlie and another scissorbill from Ruby who works for the county went to the sheriff in Newport. He made them deputies, and they rode the train down with him. They got off two miles south of Ruby and walked the tracks, so nobody saw them come in on the train. They sneaked through the brush to the Wobbly Hall, and found two men there and arrested them. Of course they put up no resistance anyway, but all three of the coppers pulled guns on them. It seems five more men were swimming in the river, with their clothes on the bank. So they arrested them one at a time as they came out of the water."

"Couldn't they just swim across? Somebody on the other side'd help 'em out, I bet. Why'd they come out if they knew the cops was there?"

"They couldn't do anything else but come out; the water's fast there, out from shore; that's why the ferry's there, the current'll power it. So all seven men went to jail and all their stuff was taken as evidence. The sheriff found all kinds of the Wobbly literature; they called it *inflaming circulars*. Those men are still sitting in jail waiting for trials."

ON SATURDAY NIGHT TOM, JACK and Davey came home again. They brought their bedrolls to the porch. "Ma, there's a little problem with these. What do you know about lice?"

"I know them damn bedrolls ain't coming in the house till we've treated 'em." With five lanterns for the examination, they took the bundles to the woodshed and unrolled them. "It's worse than lice," she diagnosed. "It's lice and bedbugs. Bedbugs are lots worse to get rid of. And I know, too, you don't have either one of them if you keep things clean. Those blankets was unsullied when they went up there 10 days ago, don't think they wasn't."

"We know, Ma." They could see they stood in danger of being held accountable for the vermin, so Tom spoke for them all. "But they're surely sullied now. What can we do about it? Itching all day is one more way to be uncomfortable. Cold and wet and tired and sleepy and sometimes sore are about all I can handle."

"Well, we can't wash these blankets and have them dry by tomorrow, but thank goodness for this cold streak, and we can hang them out overnight. Maybe we'll freeze some of the little buggers. And we'll shake the bejesus out of the blankets tomorrow and pick them over in daylight."

"Thanks, Ma."

"There's lots of onions in the root cellar. Take a bag of those up with you. Eat all you can. Bugs don't like the smell of 'em coming out of your pores. It might help. Can't hurt."

"Thanks, Ma."

"Now, start spending some time on your housekeeping. When you get up there tomorrow, take everything off of the bed and wipe it all down with turpentine. Take some tin cans back up with you and set each leg of the bed in a can, and pour some coal oil in the cans. Take the mattress apart, burn the old straw, get some fresh straw from the horse barn, wash the ticking....."

They all three burst into laughter. "Ma, I don't think we can do that in a logging camp. There just isn't extra room to lay everything out. Or extra hot water to wash all that stuff. If we were the only ones who did it, that's three wet ticks and nowhere to dry them. That bunkhouse is really crowded. And it isn't exactly beds, anyway. It's a rack of bunks nailed to the wall and the floor."

"Well, how do the rest of them do it?"

They were astounded to realize she thought they were the only ones with lice and bedbugs in their gear. "Ma, that's most of the problem. Everybody has the bugs, and even if you were speckless and spotless you'd catch them right off. That's what happened to us. Ma, we work 12 to 16 hours. Plus we need time to eat three meals. By the time you come in at night and go to the cookhouse, there's not time to take a bath, even if they had a bathhouse, which they don't. This is my third camp, Ma, and it's the dirtiest I've seen. Some of the men take time to oil their boots at night. But that's about all the time there is for taking care of your stuff. At #5 they can't even do that, because they aren't allowed to use lanterns at night so they won't read Wobbly literature and sing Wobbly songs."

Wes chipped in. "That's what this eight-hour-day campaign is about. The anti-Union people want you to believe it's because Wobblies are lazy. People understand when the Union asks for fair living conditions like bathhouses and laundry sheds and decent food. But they're not so supportive of shorter hours. They forget that some time at the end of the day to keep yourself clean is part of decent living."

AS HE HAD WITH THE miners ten years ago, Wes found himself divided. He knew the Union movement was right. He knew Solidarity was the only way to get a better life for people. But he couldn't bring himself to back some of the tougher practices he'd heard about. In bed that night, he reflected. "Strikes are okay. Work slowdowns are okay. 'A dishonest day's work for a dishonest day's pay,' as they say. But sabotage is out." He rolled over toward her. "Jennie, I don't know if I'm all that principled or if I'm just cowardly. Sometimes I wish I was made of the kind of stuff that can go all the way with this movement. People like Big Bill Haywood don't ever seem to doubt themselves. Here we stay comfortable and let them fight the battles for us."

"Or Gurley Flynn," she recalled. "You and me're the kind that stays with our family and swallows what we have to. I admire them folks for giving up their lives for what they believe in, but for myself I prize you and the boys and our place more. Maybe we're namby-pambies. I hope that ain't it."

In November when Wobblies were assumed to be the ones who cut the airhoses on 70 cars in the Great Northern yard at Newport, Wes wasn't heard to make his usual daily pro-Wobbly remarks at the Tiger Store. But he did go to Ione in support two weeks later when crowds of Wobblies showed up to see the Sheriff take Morris Levine by train to Newport. Morris Levine, like Clayton Payne, was a Wobbly of national importance. He was a newspaperman who saw the world's future in the policies of the IWW. He'd given up his career in journalism to spread the word. He'd been working at the Bilin camp on Winchester Creek and had come Downriver to organize at the Timblin camp northwest of Ione. There were federal charges against him, and at the personal request of Big Bill Haywood Levine had turned himself in to the town marshal without resistance Though Levine had surrendered, the marshal was uneasy when he saw crowds of resentful men coming from the Timblin camp. He deputized 15 townsmen and shackled Levine. The crowd might have turned violent at that had not some saner heads than either the Deputies' or the Wobblies' prevailed. The Wobblies far outnumbered the Deputies, and there was muttered talk about freeing Levine. Wes, standing among the Wobblies, found himself saying "Boys, these deputies are being shits, but they're our neighbors, and if we hurt them today we're going to be sick about it tomorrow."

Just as Wes was wondering whether he was wise or just chicken-hearted, John Renshaw's two chestnuts brought his buggy around the corner of the station. Charlie Lucas was driving, and John's mandolin was already sounding when they reached the platform. Nettie jumped out with her banjo, and her mother followed with her tambourine. Still tying up the chestnuts, Charlie started the singing to the tune of "John Brown's Body."

When the Union's inspiration through the workers' blood shall run,

At the end of one line Wes stepped onto the platform and added his voice.

There can be no power greater anywhere beneath the sun;

By the end of the second line everyone realized what was happening, and began joining in.

Yet what force on earth is weaker than the feeble strength of one?
But the Union makes us strong.

The train started up, and the entourage boarded it. By the time they reached the chorus, a hundred voices were singing goodbye to Morris Levine and the 16 lawmen guarding him.

Solidarity forever, Solidarity forever.
Solidarity forever, For the Union makes us strong.

It took four verses to move the train down the track toward Tiger and Newport, and Wes was sure, at least for that day, that the power of song was better than the power of fists.

1918

BILL WROTE OFTEN, and Jennie's progress as a reader had its best year. Bill wrote large, thinking of his father's eyes. Also, he knew his mother wouldn't be satisfied with one reading, would want to unfold the letter and reread it while she was waiting for the stove to heat or the fish to bite, so he wrote in a style he thought would be easier for her, imagining this would be something like the early readers he'd had when he was small.

THESE SPRUCES ARE NOT AS HARD AS PINES ARE, AND THEY DO NOT WORK US AS LONG AS THEY DO AT PANHANDLE OR LEACH. I HAVE TIME TO READ, AND THE YMCA HAS LOTS OF BOOKS FOR US. I THINK MORE AND MORE ABOUT GOING TO COLLEGE WHEN I GET OUT OF THE ARMY. MA, MAKE SURE JACK AND DAVEY TAKE CARE OF THE TEAM. WHEN I AM HOME I WILL GET SOME LOG CONTRACTS. I WILL SAVE FOR A YEAR AND THEN GO TO COLLEGE. A FELLOW HERE WAS GOING TO COTNER UNIVERSITY IN BETHANY, BACK IN NEBRASKA. HE SAYS MAYBE WE COULD ROOM TOGETHER THERE. I TOLD HIM I STILL HAVE TO SAVE UP BEFORE I CAN TRY IT. HE SAYS OK ANYWAY. MA, I WANT MORE THAN ANYTHING TO GO TO COLLEGE. I WANT TO GET SOMEWHERE. SAY HELLO TO EVERYBODY AT TIGER. LOVE, BILL

"Why would he want to go to Nebraska? Ain't there colleges closer to home? And he ain't done with high school anyway, is he?" she asked Wes.

"Maybe if he's going to go away from home he'd like to be with somebody he knows. When I left Kansas I ended up in Arizona just because there was a young fellow from home there and I went where he was. I didn't even care a whole lot about him, but he was familiar."

"Or maybe this fella he knows has got a sister. Well, it's a long way down the road. I ain't gonna worry about it now." Every letter was proof, at least, that he hadn't yet been sent from the safety of the Oregon woods to the war in Europe.

What she did have to worry about was illness in Pend Oreille. It was a bad winter for chickenpox and smallpox. Dr. Hiatt from Ione had gone in the Army, and Jennie and Christina Carpenter were again the medical staff for the area.

In January Newport had 50 cases of smallpox, but the schools remained open. Like most school boards, Newport's was reluctant to pay teachers for days when they didn't teach. "So the poor little kids have to just take their chances," she said. "Let's just hope nothing worse than chickenpox and smallpox comes along." She was glad when the boys came home to find work closer to home, away from lumber camp infestations.

IN JUNE CAME DIFFERENT FEARS. Tom was called up, sent briefly to Camp Lewis, and given orders for France. It seemed packers were in great demand in France. He wrote that he guessed the Army had heard of his experience in the Tiger Cedar Swamp, and thought he could handle any mud Europe could churn up. He assured her, from his nonexistent store of war lore, that packers were among the safest soldiers, because they didn't have to stay where the fighting was, and were too badly needed to be put in danger.

He was gone before letters could cross back across the state, and the next missive was a printed card filled out in his own good handwriting:

THE SHIP ON WHICH I SAILED HAS ARRIVED SAFELY OVERSEAS

Thos. A. Wooding

Co K 157th Inf. 40th Div.

AMERICAN EXPEDITIONARY FORCES

There was no date. Jennie gazed at and caressed the handwritten part of the note, remembering the days when he walked the trail through the hawthorns to the log school and learned his letters. From the first he had been proud to learn them, proud of how he could form them, prouder to read from his own writing than from printed books. To think of him a soldier, in a uniform, sitting in a tent way over the water, and still writing the same letters he'd learned here at Tiger in the school his own ma got going. She marveled at the clarity and the strength of his hand, her own readable but sketchy.

In another month, a letter came telling them all in his buoyant tone that his career as a packer had "lasted quick." "It turns out they use mostly mules in the Army, and I convinced them that experience with horses didn't count much with mules. Now, my real reason was that I found out it isn't so that the packers don't go to the Front. They're maybe not in the trenches, but they're mighty close to them, because their job is to take supplies to the men who are in the trenches. And some say the enemy likes to bombard the pack trains because being short of supplies is how he likes to see us.

"Well, it seems they were short of cooks in this area. So when they asked for volunteers, I spoke up. When they asked about experience, I gave them a story about how packers have to cook for the people they're moving. And I said I'd cooked in lumber camps. That's almost true, because I did help the cook out at Muddy Creek #2 once when his flunky stayed drunk overnight and couldn't do breakfast. So don't worry, Ma, I'm safe as anybody here. Our cook tents are a long way behind the front line trench, and I haven't seen anybody get hurt here, ever."

But that was the last letter, and they were left with only that piece of dubious reassurance to sustain them for a year.

WES ACCUSED JENNIE OF TURNING into a Superpatriot when her fervor for food conservation and preservation heightened to finger pointing. Last fall she'd taken the Food Conservation Pledge, as had most families in the county. He'd asked how she thought she could conserve any more than she already did. But he soon found out, when she went back to chicory root coffee. Herbert Hoover, the administrator of the war food program, asked for one wheatless meal daily, and potato flour all but replaced wheat at the Wooding house, Jack and Davey forced to steam the potatoes, mill them with the mortar and pestle, and spread them to dry on screens above the stove. "With five acres of potatoes, we can let all the wheat go to the

Boys Over There. And I notice you can't tell a potato roll from a wheat roll." Hoovering demanded two meatless meals each day, so trout replaced bacon on the morning table. When they thought of complaining, she said "Do you think it does Tom and Bill any good to complain?" Tuesday was to be meatless altogether, but at the Woodings' this was joined by meatless Monday through Sunday, if you counted only store meat. Jennie didn't buy meat again till a year after the Armistice; she could supply her table and two or three neighbors' tables with her .10 gauge and fishlines. Wednesday was supposed to be entirely wheatless; easy for Jennie. Porkless Sunday was easy enough to observe; once again neighbors shared a bear and hardly noticed the difference. The Woodings went onto War Rations like the most patriotic family in Spokane. The more home produce Jennie traded to Peggy O'Neal at the store, the more would be saved for the big suppliers to sell to the Army. When Wes asked if she minded stinting herself to help the capitalist farmers, she said she only cared that the Boys Over There have enough to eat. When the Food Administration repeated their threat to make the regulations mandatory if people didn't observe them voluntarily, Jennie Wooding had nothing to worry about.

In May came a request for women to preserve eggs all month against shortages in the coming fall. The Food Administration suggested the water glass method, but said any way would do. Jennie's choice was to bring the eggs straight from the nest still warm and to grease each egg all over with lard, careful not to miss a spot. Poor Davey was sent hourly to the nests. The greased eggs were stored in a keg. She kept a pan with lard and a clean white rag to make adding eggs convenient. Jennie read that mashed carrots could replace eggs in most recipes, but her experiments weren't encouraging. "Do you think they try out all these ideas they send out?" she asked.

Shortly after Tom's departure in June, the Pend Oreille County Food Administrators sent letters asking 35 residents of the county to explain their apparently excessive flour purchases in the past six weeks. Jennie went berserk. The *MINER* didn't print the names of the miscreants, and Wes had to restrain her from going to Newport to demand a list in order to publicly shame the criminals. "How are they any different than the Slackers? No, they're worse! They stay home safe and sound, and don't even want to give up their precious white cakes. If anybody's a traitor, it's them with their stuffed pantries."

JENNIE AND RUBY BELLE WERE seated at the kitchen table with cups of mint tea and some dried apples. Ruby Belle asked, "Aunt Jennie, do you have any sugar for this tea?"

"I got a little sugar, yeah, but I'm saving it for a Thanksgiving pie. I brought in some honey, though. Here."

Ruby Belle smiled. "Aunt Jennie, you surely do support the War Effort."

"The War Effort, yep. The War, nope."

"What's the difference?"

"I don't for a minute think this war is going to make life better for one single country that's in it. That's hooey. But War Effort that will keep our Boys safe and healthy, I'll support that all the way. I hate the war and I love the soldiers. And I don't see nothing hard to understand about that."

"Aunt Jennie, Barton Brawley's home from the war because he lost his right arm. Barton says a lot of the men have been dying of the influenza."

"I don't see how that can be. I've known a few people to die of the flu, but it's usually babies and old folks and the sickly who had something else wrong with them already."

"Barton says the government doesn't tell us much about it because they think it will hurt morale. They think people are better off not knowing too much."

Jennie hit the ceiling. " 'Not knowing too much!' Are we children? Hellfire, I don't even believe in treating children that way. They need to know all they can about the world, good and bad. And the grownups - and especially the ones who're supposed to take care of the sick - oughta know all there is to know about a sickness, and how to ward it off. Boy, that burns me up!" She picked up a burlap-wrapped brick and scrubbed with both hands at the stove top.

"Barton says it's been around since March, but I've never read anything about it in the paper."

As if Jennie's outrage was what the War Department had needed to bring them to honesty, that week's *MINER* ran an article on the *influenza epidemic.* An official policy of secrecy apparently had not been an effective cure, and admission of the seriousness was finally being made public. The epidemic had become so bad that even though the war continued, there would be no inductions for that month because of the influenza in the camps. Jennie began to shake when Wes read the news to her. "Bill's in one of them camps over there on the Coast." She tried to recover: "He's strong and healthy, though. It shouldn't hit him too bad."

The next week's paper explained, however, that unlike any previous influenza, this one hit healthy young men the hardest. She was desperate. "And what about Tom? Wes, do they have it in France too?"

He wanted to be gentle but saw no way. "It's all around the world, Jennie."

Before worry could entirely consume her, Jennie found a place to direct her energy and help with her version of the War Effort. It was reported that fruit pits and nut shells were used in the making of gas masks. The Food Administration requested that everyone save, clean, and dry the pits and shells and deliver them to local schools where they would be collected and passed on to the Red Cross. Jennie regretted that the request came after the fall canning, but she donned gloves and went through the compost pile to pick out the prune pits that she knew were only a little ways down. She used her school board influence to organize the school children to go each afternoon for two weeks to harvest wild hazelnuts. "Even if you know they're wormy, bring 'em in," she directed. No complaining about prickly husks was allowed. Even the littlest had to save their tears till they were home with their mothers.

Jennie ate her strong words about truth-telling when little Nola Mae Hines asked what a gas mask was. Jennie explained, "The soldiers wear them so they won't breathe the mustard gas."

Nola May persisted, "What's mustard gas?"

"It makes them sick."

"What kind of sick, Aunt Jennie? Like when I ate the bad cottage cheese?"

Jennie wasn't prepared to tell a six-year-old that a soldier might get bad skin blisters, or might go blind, or might cough up his bronchial tubes for six weeks while he was tied to his bed because of the pain, and that then he might choke to death. She told Nola May evasively, "Even sicker than that. So that's why we're getting all the nuts we can. Now run help Daisy and Harriet over there."

She admitted to Nettie, in charge of the older children who were taking the prickly green husks off the brown little nuts, "I guess there's a limit to how honest I can be. But it ain't no excuse for the President's Cabinet keeping secrets from grownups."

The shipment of nut shells had just gone off on the train when the influenza came to the Pend Oreille. The towns Upriver were hit the hardest. The scariest story was of a girl in Priest River who was dead 72 hours after she first got sick. Jennie hoped the Downriver area would be protected by distance. But as the railroad brought freight faster, it also brought the sickness faster. By the next week two of the county's six deaths were Downriver and hardly a family was without one or more cases. By Halloween there was an epidemic warning for the county, and public meetings were banned in Newport. The State Board of Health fought the epidemic by encouraging sleeping with the windows open and thorough handwashing. In November the Army resumed inductions, but had the Men Going Away to War wear gas masks as soon as they stepped on the train in Newport, and ordered them to spread out among several cars. Jennie told Christina Carpenter, "But what when they get there? Won't they have to sleep in barracks together? Their methods are okay, but they ain't enough. The War puts so many people together, and that's where it spreads. I wish all the Boys could go home to their families and get some good home nursing."

There were fewer cases in the countryside, but there were also fewer nurses to go around. For a week Jennie slept in her clothes, moving from family to family on old Shorty, seldom sleeping at home. Drowsing home on horseback one night, Jennie relived the routine of 14 years ago, when some of the children with the scarlet fever were her own. She jerked awake on the memory of switching Jasper for not taking his medicine.

1919

JENNIE AMAZED WES one morning in mid January by waking him to say she needed a doctor. He thought she was joking. She hadn't seen a doctor for her own needs in her entire life. "Flu?" he asked.

"No, the doctor couldn't do nothing for that that I can't do. I got a bad pain right here on my side and kind of to the back. Fever. Just plain miserable sick. "

"Appendix?"

"More likely gall bladder, and I ain't gonna take that out myself."

She packed a bag, Wes harnessed the team, and she rode in jostled misery lying down in the back of the wagon for the four miles to Ione. Dr. Haitt, home now from the War, confirmed her diagnosis, and she took the train straight from Ione to Spokane, lying on a stretcher in the baggage car.

The motorized cab from the train station to Sacred Heart Hospital was en eye-opener for both of them. The ride was considerably smoother than that in the wagon, and even sitting up she was more comfortable in the mild air of the closed car. "I feel like I'm already in the hospital," she told him. For a while, Wes was more interested in the automobile than in her condition. He asked the driver about shock absorbers and suspension systems and windshields. She was surprised that he could sound as if he knew what he was talking about, he who had never ridden in a car before either. "Where'd you learn all that?" she whispered.

"At the Tiger Store. Everybody wants to sound like an expert, and you pick up stuff in spite of yourself."

She'd known enough not to eat or drink since the night before, and expected the surgery to be done in the morning, as she and Dr. Haitt had concurred. But the Spokane surgeon gave little respect to the country doctor, less to the midwife. After all, he'd had almost two years of medical school.

He was cautious; he would do tests and he would "observe." Her pain would be a good guide to his diagnosis, he said, so it was necessary to withhold any painkiller, even laudanum, and to jab around in her abdomen twice a day. "I'm glad he ain't around full time," she told the nurse. The nurse was devoid of humor in regard to "Doctor," and sniffed at Jennie's lack of appreciation for the great man. Wes thought to phone Flora Cross with an update, and ask her to send Jack and Davey to Spokane to be with their mother. "Wes, I ain't gonna die from this, for Pete's sake. Somebody's got to stay with the animals. Let 'em go on with their work." The nurse asked about the rest of the family, and suggested the "soldier boy" on the Coast ask his company commander for leave to see his sick mother. Jennie knew that was unnecessary, but a chance to see Bill was not to be passed up, even if the grounds were dubious. "I guess they wouldn't send Tom home from France, would they?"

"I'm sure the observation won't go on long enough for him to come this far," the nurse answered humorlessly. It seemed it would, to Jennie in pain and to Wes stashed in a boarding house.

Finally the doctor was satisfied, and a week later removed Jennie's gall bladder. In the meantime, the waiting had made her sicker, and the recuperation would be longer. Altogether she was in the hospital three weeks, and except for the trainride back to Tiger, in bed for two months. Bill was allowed only a token visit, and his single day with her was the day of the surgery, so the visit was practically nonexistent from her point of view.

SHE WAS BARELY OFF PAP and interested in some grouse and spuds when the *MINER* ran on the front page, as if it could be taken seriously, a proposal to divert the entire Pend Oreille River in order to irrigate the Columbia Basin desert land. From that time, Wes considered her on her own to recover her health, and spent his time giving speeches and writing letters to the *MINER*.

> *Once again, those who have shaped this country and tamed it and used it for wholesome lives are beneath consideration. Those of us who use it in a way that lets it be useful forever are to be written off. Some Capitalists who will be able to sell the water to small farmers and lure them into slavery that'll end up with the farmers' lives broken, the land full of weeds and the barns empty don't care one bit what misery they cause both in the Pend d'Oreille Valley and in the Columbia Basin, so long as they make*

*enough to have Crab Louis at the Davenport Hotel and drive
there in their Cadillacs and Oldsmobiles.*

Jennie pretended to dismiss the idea of the river being moved away as too silly to consider, though she knew the Owens River, where she grew up, had been taken away to give water to Los Angeles. She went about the planting - this year accepting plenty of help from Jack and Davey. In fact, they were all three on their hands and knees planting onion sets between the cabbages, when the 11:30 northbound train came into the station. After nine years of living within shouting distance of the tracks and looking distance of the depot, they didn't bother to raise their heads. They were moving in a broad row, going from east to west, with the tracks behind them. The softspoken stranger had time to leave the tracks and approach within ten feet. "Hi, Ma." The voice wasn't quite right, and she looked around in curiosity at this greeting. But it was indeed Tom. She covered her mouth with one hand and clutched with the other for her walking stick to help her rise to a walking position. Her mind stumbled ahead of the joy and the welcome to inventory the changes in him. The voice, for one thing. And the simple, direct greeting in place of a tease or a jest. The set of his mouth, the focus of his eyes. The stoop of his shoulders. He was a different man, an older one, a gentler one, a quieter one, a sadder one. The two boys and the dog got to him before she did because they had no subtle confusion to slow them. By the time she reached him, the three brothers were locked in a mass hug, Rover standing quietly on Tom's shoes. There was no noise, no thumping of shoulders. Tom's quiet radiated so clearly to them that they did none of the boyish back-whacking or noisy joshing they would have done two springs ago, before the oldest brother went away and came back a different man. Rover, he who yipped himself into a frenzy when Shorty came back from just one day on range, was subdued and silent. Jennie recognized in Tom the deepest pain, the pain that can be kept in check only by quiet and calm. She saw there was no physical maiming, and knew it was the worse pain, the agony of mind that is harder to live with. Jack and Davey moved away for her, and she held onto him a long, long time, saying nothing. Finally Davey asked, "Are you home for good, Tom?"

"Oh, yes, Davey, it's for good. To be home is very, very good."

They started to the house, Jennie holding one arm, Jack carrying Tom's duffle bag and walking close beside him and holding onto the other arm. Davey picked up the dog and followed behind. They left their tools in the field and went to their home. Jennie went straight to the stove to stir the fire and start some biscuits. The midday meal was ordinarily cold, but she had to mark the homecoming. Tom went to the rocker where his mother sat to sew or knit, and where his father had held one boy or another on his lap to read to them all; Tom rocked so gently his movement was evident only by matching the chairback to the pattern on the wall behind him. Davey stepped out to pump water and Jack went to the pole yard to find Wes and bring him home. "How's some ham and gravy and biscuits, Tommie?"

"Fine, Ma. Just fine." His tone told her that the food of home can never be found anywhere else, that it is the food of the soul. That anything that came from that gorgeous black iron stove would nourish him deeply. That he never wanted to leave this place again. That these people were the only ones he wanted to see ever again. That he had never known how much he loved them. That this Tiger homestead was the center of the universe. And she caught every word.

For a month Tom stayed very close to the house. He took over the food, always cooking too much for a family of just five. His own appetite was much smaller than before he went away, but his brothers, at 18 and 20, could put away plenty, and the rest went into lunch buckets the next day. Tom liked seasonings, and cooking for hundreds of men with different backgrounds had meant leaving everything bland. No one disliked it too much, but no one liked it very much. Now he was free to experiment with Jennie's herbs, to try different combinations, to use her many pickles, preserves and relishes. The speed and the skills he'd picked up in the Army cook tents now were directed toward pleasing those he loved.

Though Jennie could have used extra help in the garden and fields that time of year, Tom preferred to be in the house. When he couldn't spend all his waking hours cooking, he found improvements to make. He built more and better shelves in the kitchen. He sanded, stained, waxed and buffed every piece of furniture. He took over the housecleaning. When Wes asked if he was ready to get back to logging, he said "Pa, for now I like it under a roof."

Wes and Jennie talked that remark over in the bed that night. They reflected that for both of them life had been largely lived out of doors, the house merely necessary protection from weather and darkness. They were outside far more than they were in. They saw that for Tom things had changed, and the house was necessary protection against something in the outside world that he hadn't described to them. "Let's give him the time he needs. Remember, when the girls died, nothing was any good for us except to just live it out."

"But it's been a month. Wes, maybe I can at least get him into the garden. I can truly use help there anyhow. That operation wasn't so very long ago, you know." The next day she drew Tom out to weed the herb garden around the door. When she came back from the big garden in the bottom, the little one around the porch was weed-free, and he'd separated the chives and the garlic and cut back the sage. He'd dug out the excess horseradish and put it in the burn pile. He was back in the house, putting the finish on three gooseberry pies.

****

JENNIE MIGHT HAVE STRATEGIZED TO lure him farther and farther from the house, but in May a school event distracted her. Of eight eighth graders, only Bluebelle Kramer passed her exams. Parents clamored for the teacher's dismissal. Jennie had been watching all year as the young girl, who was all that was left to teach the school, lost control of the group of children who were losing control of themselves as first the war and then the epidemic made their lives unsteady and made them take out their hurt on the least secure adult in their world. When the Directors met to discuss the teacher for next year's session, Jennie had a list of the 8th graders.

1. Emil Benson had moved in in February after being out of school since the previous May.
2. Mae Mummson had never been bright, and no one expected her to pass.
3. Ditto for Mae's brother Jumbo, already in his second year of 8th grade.
4. Tillie Burdette's brother had been buried at Thiencourt, France, in March.
5. Lloyd Freemyer had barely survived the flu, and hadn't been in school a total of two months.
6. Mabel Hupp had nursed her parents and three siblings through the flu and had gone for as long as a week without being out of her clothes, never mind attending school.
7. Clarence Barnett had been needed at home, his three older brothers all being in the services, and had hardly attended since the week he was put on the roll.
8. Only Bluebelle Kramer's family had been here all year, had had no one in the war, and had escaped the flu.

"I know this teacher's new, but it's just too easy to put the blame on that. I don't think anybody could have brought them kids through this year." But the other two directors weren't willing to take a chance on a second year of failure and Jennie, weakened herself by her own illness and Tom's sadness, wasn't up to a fight. She did manage to get the girl a letter of recommendation that shouldn't keep her from getting another position.

BY THIS TIME THE EARLY harvesting was upon them, and she was grateful for Tom's help with the canning. It became clearer, though, that he was reluctant to talk to anyone outside his family. He did not offer to make trips to the store for the mail or provisions. If someone stopped by the house his exchange was brief, then he found work to do upstairs. He continued to run the household, now including the milking and care of the animals.

Wes used the time to keep an eye on what the *MINER* called a *building boom*. Bob Cross was installing an up-to-date gasoline tank with a pump so that he wouldn't have to roll the gas in barrels from the train, dip it out in a can and pour it into the cars' tanks with a funnel. Dan Spencer was building a pool hall, and Frank Gillis was putting up a blacksmith shop. Not to be left out, Wes began a small cottage over on the main street. Wes's eyes were bad that whole year, and Jennie warned the boys to keep him safe. He enjoyed the building, working some himself, and looking forward to the rent it would bring in. "Or maybe one of the boys will want to live in it."

In July Wes astonished everyone, family and town alike, by buying a Nash Rambler. He was the last person they'd expected to fall for the new foolishness. Wes had agreed with Hy Maggott many a time that "if you hear 'em, they're stuck, and if you don't hear 'em they're broke down." Wes was married to the best hostler in the country, and they were never short of transportation or labor. "Maybe it's something Tom'll get interested in," he defended.

Jennie saw no use for a family car. "It ain't big enough for hauling or pulling, Wes. What do we need an automobile for just to ride in? Who wants to go that fast anyway? I can walk most places I want to go, and I can ride Shorty otherwise. It was nice when I was sick, and so was the hospital. But I ain't sick now." It was a month before she even agreed to take a ride, and then just one. "Rushing around like a Gilly Glue Bird! You can't see what's growing, you can't hear the birds, you can't smell nothing but the car, you can't tell how much the wind's blowing. I'll pass, Wes."

By August Tom had scoured and furbished every inch of the house and finally found an outdoor job. He delighted the town by whitewashing the outside of the house. The two-story lumber house sat just yards from the north-south road, on a knoll, and was visible for a mile coming either direction. The Tiger Town columnist to the *MINER* remarked that *if everyone would follow his example it would brighten the district quite a bit."* Tom was pleased by the notice people took, but he wasn't yet ready to spend time with them.

BILL'S TRAIN GOT INTO NEWPORT on September 2. Thinking to scope out potential hauling contracts before he went on home, he went to the *MINER* office to ask what notices there were. He met there Miss Cecil Stoll, newly arrived that summer from Wisconsin and working wherever she was needed at the newspaper office, mostly with local advertising, and today at the front desk. When he told her his purpose, she was helpful and friendly. Reading through notices for timber and lumber haulers, he learned that Jack was working the team at the Fidelity Mill in Albeni Falls, on the Idaho side. He looked again at the slight, brown-haired girl with the quick brown eyes and decided she was more interesting than drayage. When he asked her if he could come back when she was off work and take her to supper at Kelly's Bar, she accepted. Over plates of lima beans and ham hocks, Bill learned she was here without family and staying in a rented room on Fourth Avenue. "What brought you way out West?" Bill asked. She said she had had to leave home, but offered no explanation. Her approach to the lima beans made him think that her acceptance of his invitation had more to do with the free food than with his company. But he knew hunger could be satisfied, and then she might notice him. He asked her to dinner and a movie the next day. They talked so long over that dinner they never went to the movie. It seems she came from a little backwater town under some bluffs on the Mississippi River, Nelson, Wisconsin. Her mother had died bearing her first child, who was Cecil. Her father gave her the boy's name because he knew there'd never be a son. He was a gloomy man, Cecil said, who used the death of his wife to never have another good day. He lived only for the duty he begrudgingly fulfilled. If he didn't exactly raise her, in any parental way, he supported the little girl by shoveling manure in dairy barns around the area until she, Cecil, was old enough to go to work in the local cheese factory. Then he quit working, citing rheumatism. He didn't work again, and became gloomier and gloomier. Cecil's memories of the evenings of her life were of her father sitting in a chair and staring into his lap. He spoke to her only about the practicalities of life. They went nowhere except she to school and he to work. He didn't believe in church, he didn't drink. "Thank god for school, or I would have ended up as crazy as he is. I met other people there, and got an idea my life wasn't the way a life was supposed to be. I thought about failing my 8th grade exams on purpose, so I could have another year. But nobody would have believed it, and my schoolwork was the only thing I'd ever had to be proud of."

Small for 13, Cecil was given half wages for milking, on the assumption that she couldn't be as valuable as a grown woman. When she turned 16 the injustice was too appalling, and the women in the barn spoke up for her to the barn manager. She got the raise, but life didn't change much, because her father still collected her money and put it in an old churn to save, for what he didn't say. He allowed her to do nothing after work except maintain the two-room house, put repetitious meals on the table, and watch him brood. He would hear nothing of her finding her own life beyond the house. "It's a wonder I grew up sane enough to see straight. But I had enough sense to know to get out. So when Dad went to bed one night I put all my clothes in a cheese bag I'd brought from work, took my money from the churn, walked to the river, borrowed a boat, and rowed over to Wabasha, on the Minnesota side, where the Great Northern ran. I had to wait till about noon the next day for a train, and I was terrified Dad would figure out where I was. I don't know why I thought he'd know where to look, but I stayed in the depot ladies' room almost the whole time." She went west because that was where the first train through was going. She got off at Newport because that was how much money she could spend on a ticket.

Pretty resourceful, thought Bill. He imagined her to be like his mother, able to build her own life, able to work round the clock, competent enough to let a man have a little independence, perky enough to be some fun. And she did herself up prettier than the girls at Tiger.

His family didn't know exactly when to expect him, so Bill took a room at the Antler Hotel and dug in for whatever time it would take. It didn't take much; they were married the following week at the home of the Justice of the Peace. They spent a night in Bill's room, then took the train to Tiger.

Someone in the family had met every train from the south ever since Bill's letter had arrived; this time it was Wes. His eyes were bad that week, but loved ones' ways of moving let them be picked out of a much bigger crowd than the one detraining at Tiger, Washington, in 1919. The young man he was watching turned to help a fellow passenger, a small woman, off the train. Wes took his son's hand, searched his face, saw it was still Bill, and embraced him in relief. The woman didn't move away. He supposed she was coming to visit relatives and didn't know where they were. "Can I help you find somebody, Miss?"

Wes thought he was prepared for anything, but a bride hadn't entered his mind. More astonishing than the fact of her was the confidence with which she bore herself. It was not toughness, he didn't think, and not worldly experience, but there was none of the apprehension or shyness to be expected of most girls under such circumstances. By the time they had walked to the house, her absence of coyness had spread to him so that his entrance words were "Look what Bill brought home from the War!"

The new little house on main street wasn't ready for tenants, so Bill and Cecil went into the old homestead house, Hawthorn Lodge: a blessing, Jennie was sure, for their marriage. Full of his new status as head of household, Bill went back to Newport the next day to help Jack finish up the logging contract he had there with Bill's team. It didn't occur to him that a new bride might want to be with the bridegroom.

In the time she spent alone with Cecil, Jennie began to realize that the girl's unexpected poise didn't cover mature strength so much as cold disregard. She told Wes, "I reckon if her upbringing was the way Bill tells it, she can't all of the sudden have the feelings normal people have. If she comes from a place where there wasn't any real living, she'll have to learn it before she's all there." As she helped Cecil settle into the old Hawthorn Lodge, she tried to resurrect for her the years of raising the boys there and building the place she loved so much. Cecil seemed not to hear. The warmth of the close family that had lived there meant nothing to her, was beyond her experience and her understanding. When Jennie shyly disclosed that the late winter moon peeked at the bed, Cecil looked at her as if she were odd. Wes delivered the box Bill had made when he was nine and in which he kept his treasures. He thought about the good hour Cecil had ahead when Bill recited the history of each item; but she took it without a word and stuffed it brusquely under the bed.

The most exciting event of Cecil's week was not Bill's return on Saturday, but the chivaree given on that third day of her marriage. It was clear that it had been planned for another new couple, the Henricksons, and that the Woodings were a tack-on. But it was the first festive acknowledgment of Cecil in any capacity in her life, and she made the most of it. As the revelers went back and forth between the two houses, Cecil went with them, not asking Bill if he cared to accompany her. Charlie Lucas and old Andy Graupner spelled each other at the calling, and Cecil danced every dance, sometimes with Bill but often not.

WES AND JENNIE, WITH HELP from Jack and Davey, put the new household together, with little interest shown by the bride. Knowing Cecil's background, Ruby Belle expected she would attach herself to Aunt Jennie, as she herself had done as a girl when Ada had closed in on herself. But once Jennie had finished furnishing the house, sewn new curtains for the main room and the larger bedroom, and had naively refurbished the old herb garden at the front door, Cecil had no more use for her.

The minimal cleaning and cooking Cecil did left her with plenty of free time. It was a busy time of year for Jennie and she could have used help with the harvesting, especially after using up a precious week helping the newlyweds. Thinking that perhaps Cecil was shy to insert herself into the elder Woodings' affairs, she went over one morning to take a big cabbage and to ask for help with the sauerkraut the next day. Cecil was absent. Jennie walked on to the store to get pickling salt, and found Cecil there, seated near the stove with four men who liked to spend their mornings there with chewing tobacco and gab. In her years of running the store, Jennie had seen women stop to chat, but they always remained standing. Cecil, seated like a crony, was a surprise. Jennie exchanged a look with Flora Cross. Cecil caught the look, interpreted it correctly, and knew she should leave. She picked up two books from FrankDarrow's lending library and went home, not waiting to walk with Jennie.

The Woodings' preoccupation with their new daughter-in-law was broken the next week when Davey drew their attention to himself. On a particular afternoon, Davey found himself alone. Wes had taken the train to Newport on business, Bill and Jack were far up Tiger Hill with the team, and Tom and Jennie were immersed in canning. Davey thought it a good time to "try out the Rambler," he said, as if he had ever driven another car, and as if it were not his driving skill that needed "trying." The car was parked at the depot, far enough from the house to be unobserved. At first Davey only sat in the driver's seat, fantasizing about driving the car down to Ione or up to Lost Creek. That was as far as his imaginings would have gone, except that Cecil came by just then, going to the store to see if they had canned salmon. She saw him first. "Whacha doing, Davey? Keeping the seat warm for your dad?"

"Nah. He told me it isn't running just right, and maybe I'd give it a test run and see what I think's wrong. Maybe I'll fix it for him."

"You keep his car running for him?"

"Me and my brothers. We all do some. Pa didn't grow up with cars, and he doesn't take to 'em too well. Then, too, he can't see the parts real well."

"So where are you going to take it on this test run?"

"Over to the Landing, I guess, and back a few times."

She went on to the store, saving him the embarrassment of making his first try at starting the car in front of her. He got out, cranked it as he had done for Bill and jumped back in. He released the hand break, let out the clutch ever so slowly, and the car moved just as slowly toward the Landing. As he went by the Store, he peeked in to see if Cecil was watching. She had her back to him, but Flora Cross jerked her head up, startled. When he reached the Landing, no other cars or wagons were around, so there was room to make a slow and careful circle and head back to the depot. This time Cecil was watching and waved. Davey was ten feet tall. At the depot he stopped, found the reverse gear and did a neat backup and turn, and started back toward the Store and the Landing. This time she was on the porch. He coolly brought the car to a halt. Then the fateful words: "Want to come along?"

"Sure, Davey. I've never ridden in a car. My town, Nelson, isn't much different from Ione and Tiger. Just the doctor and a couple of other rich guys have 'em."

He was afraid to get out and open the door for her, not knowing for sure if he could put the car in neutral. She didn't seem to expect it, though, and sat on the edge of the seat beaming, hoping someone was noticing. He started again, slowly, again made his circle at the Landing, and headed back to the depot. Now an accomplished motorman, he accelerated, pretending his fine mechanic's ear needed to hear the engine at different speeds. Again he managed reverse and headed for the third time for the Landing. This time, though, when he approached his turnaround circle at a still higher speed, he found Guy Gale's wagon and team crosswise in the space he needed. It took several seconds for his foot to leave the gas pedal, and far too many more for his foot to find the brake and clutch pedals. There was no way the car would stop before it hit Guy's old Candy and Mavis. He veered enough to the right to avoid the horses, but was now headed for the riverbank. The car was at last slowing, but not enough. Laughing hilariously, Cecil jumped out, landed on her feet, and ran some steps to maintain her footing. Davey couldn't see the bottom of the bank, where there might be half a dozen men working on a log raft right in the Nash's path. He jerked the wheel still harder to the right, directed the car toward an old-growth bull pine to stop it, turned off the switch, and jumped clear. If the bull pine had been a second-growth, or if it had not been down a long slope that let the car pick up speed, the Rambler might have fared better. As it was, the tin fenders sitting six inches above the hard rubber tires crumpled back on themselves, exposing the big round headlights that exploded on impact, lending an alarming sound of danger to the event. The radiator crunched in, and the hood opened up from the left side and slammed against the tree trunk. The windshield was knocked into the steering wheel, shattering glass all over the seat and slashing it in a dozen places. The front tires, up off the ground a foot and a half, continued to spin. Steam poured from the defunct radiator, decorating the pathetic wreck that was Wes's Rambler. By now half a dozen people were running from the Store. Cecil was no longer laughing; she was seated pale-faced against a cedar stump. Davey was beet red and trying hard not to weep in front of her. The car wheezed and went still.

There was a strong sense of fairness among those who ran to the rescue. They couldn't be called bystanders or onlookers, because they were, in a true meaning of the word, participants. They'd seen Jennie by the sweat of her brow support the family and Wes earn the money for this toy. They didn't begrudge Wes the car, because he worked hard too, much harder than a man with his vision handicap might have been expected to. A few of them owned cars, and understood the weakness that made him buy it. And they loved Davey too. One or two went to check Cecil; most went to make sure Davey wasn't hurt. The physical threat out of the way, they began to realize the trouble Davey was in, and what this would mean to Jennie and Wes. As far as they knew, Jennie'd never blamed Wes a whit for his lack of business sense, but this would be a test. They would both be pretty hard on Davey. A man of 60 might be indulged a $900 car, but when it was just two months old an 18-year-old boy had no business teaching himself to drive on it. Among several of the witnesses there was suspicion, correct, that the girl was at least part of the cause of this mishap. Not that Davey couldn't make a fool of himself without help, but it did seem that usually he had an audience.

Wes and Jennie surprised the boys by not being as agitated as they expected. They'd seen more property than this come and go with much direr effects. Davey himself told them of the wreck, so that they could see, before they might have misheard the news, that he was unhurt. Beyond that, they saw little cause for grief. When the next week's *MINER* teased about Davey's *joy ride* Jennie and Wes smiled with their neighbors. The Rambler was pulled into the barn next to the blacksmith shop, and Davey was assigned to fix it, to earn the money for parts, and to spend his wages on no other thing until the job was done. Bill was not to hire him or let him share in the earnings from the team. He was to earn this money without family support. Not even family tools were to be lent. "You're not gonna wear out my axe paying me back money you owe me," Wes affirmed.

That left him just jobs where the tools were provided. Till Thanksgiving he made posts for Charlie Youngreen. Then he cut a cord of wood in a week for U.S. Anderson. That job let him buy an axe, and he cut firewood for another week. Then he was kept employed cutting rickwood for the Ione Market, walking the 8 miles round trip on the train tracks. After hours, by lantern light, he reshaped the fenders and hood in the blacksmith shop. This revealed that the right running board was also pushed back and he removed, reshaped, and reattached that. His wages went for a new windshield, two new tires, and a radiator. The four broken wooden spokes from the front wheels he could reconstruct himself. He put all this together, somewhat like new. The motor was little damaged, the Rambler having failed to hit the bull pine head on. The last week of his "slave wages" went for some black paint, and the job was done and Davey back in good graces by Christmas.

USING THE MONEY HE'D SAVED in the Army, Bill sold his two-horse team and bought four big Percherons, in fact Dominick deCarlo's complete logging outfit, and began hauling again for the St. Regis Lumber Company. He was able to be home nights, but they were very short nights, and Cecil was left alone too much of the time. She did not develop the interest in homemaking that Bill had taken for granted, so the hours were very long. Daily she made two trips to the Store, once to get the mail and once to buy some canned pork and beans or canned salmon to put on the table as a dinner. The two chores could well have been done in one trip, of course, but the chance to chat with Flora Cross and whoever else might be available was the real reason for going. If she needed to exchange the books she read most of the day, that could make a reason for a third trip. Few of Frank Darrow's books were of interest to her, but there was little else. Wes's magazines and newspapers weren't much better, except for the society items in the *MINER* which made her dream of moving to that big town. Occasionally she'd even recognize names she'd learned in the weeks she'd lived there, and imagine that she'd been acquainted with the people who were going to touring plays, to church, to birthday parties, and to meetings of all kinds while she was cooped up in a little log shack beside the railroad track, with nowhere to go except to another little log shack that passed as a store. This surely wasn't what she'd left Wisconsin for.

******

JACK HAD RECENTLY BEEN HELPING Frank Gillis in his blacksmith shop over on the Tiger main street, where he was sometimes thrown into company with Frank's daughter Lillian. He remembered Lillian from school, though not as an important person in his life. In fact, it was hard to know just who were the important people in Jack's life, or in Lillian's. What they had in common was that they lived within a quarter mile of each other and they both had a sort of vagueness about them. But that might bond two people as well as any other trait. If Jack came into the smithy to find Lillian sitting by the fire watching the sparks, unaware that they were sometimes landing on her loose, frizzled brown hair, it didn't alarm him any more than it did her. If her father assigned her to organizing the dozens of horse shoes hanging from nails on the rafters, and if she spent her time gazing at the rhythm of the pattern they made there, Jack understood perfectly. If she came in and found him knocking a pole against the lengths of chain hanging on the wall just to see them wave, she wasn't surprised. If he began to gaze at the light coming through the window and making a haze of motes and smoke in the dim air, she might join him. When Frank was present they stayed largely on course, and he never complained of Jack's work or seemed to expect more of Lillian. In fact, Frank talked increasingly of opening a blacksmith shop in Metaline Falls and finding someone to run the one in Tiger.

When Jack told Jennie and Wes that he and Lillian were going to be married in December, they were astonished. As was everyone in both families and in the town. "Guess there's been more going on in there than shoeing," Hy Maggott cracked.

Jennie took it more seriously. Bill's marriage was looking more and more unfortunate, and she wasn't ready for another mistake. "Wes, they're old enough in years, but you'd think they was half what the calendar says. How can they make a family?"

"Same way everybody else does, Girlie. Everybody figures it out some way."

"Like Cora and Willard Nesbit with their little Boyd?"

"But these kids have you and me and the Gillises to help them while they need it. And whatever they might be, they aren't lazy. Just occasionally.... beguiled."

It didn't occur to Jack and Lillian to wait for anybody's approval, and they were married in the Congregational Church in Ione on Christmas Eve.

1920

THE HEAVY SNOW of that winter began on New Year's Day, so that folks began to leave the party at the Tiger School early. There never was a winter thaw, and soon the accumulation was four feet on the level, and keeping paths open was difficult even for the tallest man. Children couldn't see the landscape as they trudged to school through white alleys. There was a maze from the Wooding house to the barn to the outhouse to the woodshed to the road. Jennie looked out the kitchen window one noon to see Wes squinting at the five-way intersection near the porch, apparently not knowing which way he should go. She knew an attack of sore-eye was coming on. Any eyestrain at all provoked it, and the constant white glare on all sides was plenty to make him half blind.

The day after New Year's Tom went across the border into British Columbia, into the caribou country. "Ma, maybe I'd come out of this if I spent some time truly alone. Maybe I'd come back glad to see people." So he took the train to Metaline Falls and went north on snowshoes with a pack to spend the winter in an old Hudson's Bay cabin doing some trapping, and a little hunting for his own table. She hoped it was the right idea.

Wes and Jennie were living alone in the house, with Bill and Jack gone to their own homes and Dave staying at the St. Regis #3 bunkhouse. As the snow deepened, Bill and Jack also stayed up at the bunkhouse and fought the snow to come down only once a week. Cecil was alone in the Hawthorn Lodge. Lillian was ostensibly living in the new little house on mainstreet, but she spent much of each day and most nights at her parents' house.

Wes had cleared the snow off his own roof and off Lillian's. Most years this job was unnecessary, but the daily snowfall showed no sign of stopping. He explained to Cecil that it needed to be removed before a thaw came and added so much wet weight it would break rafters. Cecil had no interest in roof construction or weather changes, and thought of an excuse to go to the store. Wes had finished half her roof and was inching toward the ladder to go down and move it to the other side. Sweating and stiff, he backed over the edge of the roof, put one foot on the ladder and was off balance for the moment it took to bring the other leg down onto the top rung. His attention on stabilizing himself, he didn't see that he was bringing the leg down outside the ladder rail. He shifted his weight, thinking both feet were in place, and fell to the ground head first, his head and shoulders going not into a soft pile of new snow, but onto an iced-over mound harder than bare ground. He lay there for an hour before Cecil came back from the store and found him. She stopped short when she saw him and ran the quarter of a mile back to the store for help, not even checking to see if he was breathing, much less what she could do for him; her only concern was for herself and the terrible event she was thrown into. Flora Cross sent Hy Maggott to get Jennie, while Bob and two other men went to Cecil's house to help Wes. The men took a horse and sleigh, and got there before Jennie, who couldn't go directly across the unbroken field and the tracks, but had to ride Shorty a frustrating half mile south to the railroad crossing and then a half mile back north to get to the Hawthorn Lodge. Wes was half conscious by then, and the men were moving him into the sleigh. Cecil was standing on the porch, helping in no way, but composing in her head the tale she would tell of her own terror and her race for rescue. Knowing the one thing Cecil could handle was a trip to the store, Jennie sent her to have Flora call for the doctor to come from Ione. Shorty was tied on behind and Jennie rode in the sleigh with Wes's head on her lap. At home, she had them move him onto a pallet she fixed in the kitchen, near water and the stove; she put cool cloths on his head. The doctor affirmed there were no broken bones, and he approved her plan to keep Wes's head up on three pillows and to keep him awake through the night. They agreed there was no point in his going to the new hospital in Ione; Jennie could give just as good care at home, probably better.

Wes stayed on the pallet for most of a week, day and night, his head throbbing only a little less each day. He could see Jennie moving around, and tell the approximate time of day by the light at the windows. But he couldn't read without severe pain in his head and soreness in his eyes. That was the hardest part, lying there with nothing to occupy body or mind. George Tiger was away and couldn't help, and most people were busy shoveling snow and skidding logs. John Renshaw and Joe Parker were good to come when they could to visit and do most of the talking. After 34 years, Jennie and Wes still found plenty to talk about. But all his conversationalists had other things to do. A use was finally found for Cecil. It turned out she was an excellent reader, and though she had little interest in politics, she could keep Wes up to date through the *APPEAL* and the *MINER*. It helped.

But after three days, Cecil was bored and needed a change. Adding to her itch, Bill and Jack brought their pay envelopes down on Saturday and left them with their wives. For the first time in her life Cecil had in hand money that wasn't assigned to some immediate use. It didn't go into an old churn; it didn't have to go for room and board by tomorrow morning. Cecil herself could decide what to do with it. With the Hawthorn Lodge provided free, and plenty of table food coming from Jennie's supply, and even with her own wasteful ways, Cecil could have put most of the money into Bill's college fund, as he expected. That plan didn't have a chance.

Cecil found that she needed new shoes, and right now. She couldn't wait for shipment from Chicago. She couldn't, of course, find any suitable ones at the Tiger Store, and even Ione's and Newport's weren't worth trying. Only Spokane would have the kind of shoes Cecil suddenly needed. She enticed Lillian to go with her on the train to Spokane. They would have to stay overnight in a hotel and eat in a restaurant, the train coming only once a day now. They would do some shopping and see a movie. Lillian had never known she wanted to go shopping and see a movie, but Cecil swept her along. "I guess so," she agreed. But Lillian came back alone the next day, saying that Cecil had bought some shoes that needed reshaping, so she was going to stay an extra day. Lillian didn't talk about her outing to either Jennie or her own mother, but she did confide some things to Ruby Belle. "Ruby Belle, it sounds like it'd be fun, but it really wasn't. Everything's so different, and so noisy, and so confusing. Cecil likes seeing new things and talking to strangers. But I'm not like her. I never knew what I was supposed to be doing, or how to act. I just wanted to be back home. And the prices! Imagine a slice of roast beef for fifty cents, and you pay extra for every single thing you have with it. Can you think of paying fifteen cents for a helping of spuds? A dime for a single slice of bread? I'm eating at home!"

Cecil came tripping back the next day with not one but two pairs of shoes, three new waists, and a new hat she was wearing as she stepped off the train. She went straight to Lillian's house to show her the tube of very red lipstick she'd bought. "I don't dare wear it around town, but when Bill comes home I'm going to wear it for him. I'll have to do something to make him happy after he finds out how much of last week's pay is left." She laughed as she told it.

After a week Wes didn't need the cold cloths any more, and at the end of the second week he insisted on going to the pole yard to work. He got in two weeks before the flu hit half the people in Tiger, including him. No one's life was threatened by this milder strain, but Jennie was kept busy again going from house to house. In the midst of it came a letter from her sister Ella telling her that their father had died. He had been living with Ella, and Jennie could imagine how cantankerous he would have been in his last years, unable to herd horses, useless to everyone around him, demanding service from everyone and infuriated when he saw himself losing the power to dictate to them. Jennie's brow wrinkled as the realization hit her that she and Wes were now of the oldest generation, would doubtless soon be grandparents. And the fall from the ladder, the worsening eyesight, and now the flu were telling them that they needed to think about their closing years. What if she herself fell off a ladder or got sick? Maybe they couldn't take care of each other if they were both ailing. But Wes got well, went back again to the pole yard, and things seemed normal again.

In March, Jack's father-in-law arranged for the young people to buy 10 acres from Nettie Lucas. Again with a prod from the elders, Jack began building a house for himself and Lillian a half mile north toward Ione on the county road. "But Wes, Lillian just takes it all for granted. I'd think she'd be thrilled to her eyeteeth, but she just goes about her business like nothing was happening. She's like a little girl, thinking that's what grownups are for, to take care of her."

"Jennie, just wait. She'll grow up, and so will he. Everybody doesn't do it at the same rate."

Jennie threw herself a party for her 50th birthday. Through the evening 60 people managed to crowd into the house to enjoy a marble cake Ora made for her and to dance to the music of the Renshaws. The guests were gone by midnight in deference to Wes's recuperation, and he and Jennie were just settling into bed when there was a quick knock and someone came up the stairs. Bill knocked a second time at their bedroom, and they called him in. He stood at the door and looked around them, but not at them. He seemed choked, unable to talk. At Wes's invitation he finally sat on the edge of their bed, but looked at the walls, and told them that Cecil was going back East "for an operation," and she'd be leaving the next day. He said he couldn't afford to go with her, with a new two-year contract in his pocket to log cedar over by Aladdin. He went back to the Hawthorn Lodge, never having looked at them straight on. They knew they didn't have the whole story. Cecil was gone the next day without coming by to say goodbye.

"What do you think of that operation story?" Wes didn't answer, which was answer enough.

"Well, it ain't entirely a tragedy," she went on.

"No," Wes agreed, "but it's hard for Bill."

It was very hard for Bill. So hard that he couldn't talk to Wes and Jennie about how he felt or what he meant to do next. He left just one day later for Aladdin, talking only about the horses and the logging contract, as if Cecil had never happened.

In April Tom came back from the caribou country and moved back into the house with Jennie and Wes. He seemed ready now to be himself, to talk to folks, to mix as normal. In fact, he began calling the dances at the Tiger School.

"Wes," Jennie asked, "do you think Aladdin will do for Bill what Canada did for Tom?"

It did not. In May Bill came home to put the Percherons again in Tom's care. He'd sold the contract, he said, to a logger in Marcus. He was still stolid, still explained nothing. He packed as if he would be staying away and left on the train in two days. They got one terse letter with a Wisconsin postmark. *No luck. She hasn't been here. Her dad's about the way she described him. I guess I've lost her.* There was no return address.

Wes and Jennie didn't hear from Bill again for almost three years.

When Dave went to Oroville, half way across the state in the Okanogan Valley, for some sheepherding, he said it would be for the summer. But after two weeks he was back, after Tom wrote him that there was probably money to be made poisoning ground squirrels for farmers. He came back for the demonstration given by the county agent, but soon felt dissatisfied again.

The *MINER* reported that he was again on his way back to the Okanogan, quoting Dave as saying *the Pend Oreille water did not agree with him.* Jennie puzzled at the remark, and the boys didn't tell her that in the Okanogan Dave was freer to drink illegal booze.

ON A JUNE DAY THAT changed every few minutes between rain and sun, and left rising plumes of mist all across the valley, Jennie went up Tiger Hill to Thomas Lake and delivered what would be her last baby, Doris June Trimble. Coming off the trail onto the Tiger-Colville Road, she met Deputy Black and Prosecutor Rochford with 44 pints of homebrew they'd found cached in the brush at Paddy Johnson's cabin on Lost Creek. They'd also found in the house a fine batch in process, and a large quantity of malt, hops, and syrup. They had Paddy in the wagon too, and were taking him and the abundant evidence to the Justice of the Peace at Lost Creek. "Tell Wes we've got a sure one this time," said Rochford, who'd been sorely frustrated at his inability to convict bootleggers. But the MINER reported the next week that His Honor had dismissed the charges on the grounds that someone else could have planted the evidence. Rochford was furious. He found cause to disqualify the J.P. and reopen the case with another magistrate. "We've got him this time, Wes," he said at the Tiger Store. But it would be 18 months before the case could be heard, and then it was dismissed again because the only remaining evidence, the 44 pints of beer Jennie had seen up Tiger Hill, had exploded in the sheriff's vault. Wes was disgusted.

THINGS SEEMED NORMAL THROUGH THE summer, but in September Wes had another siege of sore eye. Insisting he could at least do the home chores, he put the axe deeply into his left foot while splitting wood. Jennie stitched it up and again made the pallet for him downstairs. This time he could read, at least, and enjoyed watching the People's Party gain strength in Ione. "It's not as good as if they were Socialists, but it sure beats Republicans, like it usually is." He especially watched the growing Prohibition campaign, eager for the New Year when he was sure there'd be fewer little home stills and less booze sold to the working man to keep his mind off his low wages and bad conditions.

In October came an event that eclipsed any of Wes's other interests. Jack and Lillian named their baby Frank Wesley. There was nothing else of importance in the world, then, for Wes. Jennie admired and loved the baby, but it was Wes who found reason several times a day to walk the half mile to baby Wes's house. Lillian took his help for granted when he walked little Frank around over his shoulder or rocked him while she napped. Though everyone else called the infant Frankie, they took it in stride when his grandpa always called him Wes.

Jack and Lillian were in the fairly sturdy two-story log house Jack had built them. Her parents, sensing the vagueness in the young people's plans for their future, offered to have him take over her father's blacksmith shop on the Tiger main street, complete with the tools and tack. There was now a one-way dirt road clear through from Colville to Tiger, passable with a wagon most of the time from July through September, and occasionally during the rest of the year. It was a good place and time for a blacksmith shop. Lee Jett had a dairy north of Tiger Town and delivered milk by wagon to the whole area. There was someone mining hopefully for oil and gas at Tiger, with lots of equipment. The teams hauling up and down Tiger Hill for St. Regis and for Lost Creek Cedar Company had equipment that had to be kept working. Everyone else's business depended on Jack's, and he was finding success in spite of himself.

"Wes, they do seem hellish young, but they ain't doing too bad. Between us and the Gilleses, maybe we'll raise 'em yet. You know, after he had that fever when he was five, he fought me on everything that came up."

"I was thinking. Did you notice when that changed?"

She hadn't thought about it. "When?"

"When he put that cigar in your eye. After that, it was as if he wasn't his own self anymore. He never bucked anybody again. To this day I don't think he's made a decision of any kind. He just lets other people lead him around. That'll be okay if it's good people leading him, if he never has a test. But I shudder to think what will happen to him if he ever has to leave this little world of Tiger."

1921

WITH MARCH GROUND fog all around, Jennie was in the woodshed splitting kindling when she heard the train whistle. She stuck the hatchet in the chopping block and walked toward the depot in hopes this year's shipment of government seed had come in. It was shortly afterwards that she first learned there were people in this world who made a living by running away from reality, who even worked hard at producing illusion rather than fuel and food.

The first of the movie people to find Tiger was Bert Van Tuyle, director, scout, and lover to the famous Nell Shipman. VanTuyle stepped off the northbound train and Jennie watched him spend several minutes gazing at the main street, as if to appraise it for purchase. But VanTuyle wasn't looking to make a purchase; he was looking to make a movie. In Van Tuyle's eyes Renshaw Hall would play perfectly the role of an Alaskan dance hall, and the various houses and cabins scattered about clearly suggested Sourdoughs and Gold Prospectors. All the buildings were a similar shade of gray weathered cedar, some of log, some of board and batten, and some of clapboard. The sidewalks running between the businesses, and from each building to its outhouse, were made of fir, and were only slightly grayer than the buildings. Fortunately the Wooding house, which Tom had whitewashed during his despondency, was out of eye's range. What VanTuyle found was exactly the movie set he'd been looking for through Idaho and Washington: a representation of an Alaskan village with the buildings straightforward but tentative, with a look of frontier about them, and doorways tall enough for Nell, at five foot eleven, to enter without stooping. The late winter sky drizzled on dirty snowbanks, and the effect was complete.

VanTuyle stepped with a distinct limp into the store and post office, where as always a panel of four was seated at the stove. VanTuyle imagined he was talking only to Flora Cross behind the counter, and was taken aback to find himself fielding questions and comments from the council. He had no idea how clearly his expensive black wool coat over a heavy cable-knit Irish sweater, his high-laced custom-made White boots from Spokane, his astrakhan hat and his fur-lined leather gloves marked him as an outsider. He was right to consider his garb practical for spending the winter in primitive living conditions in the north, but he didn't know that no actual locals could afford what he was wearing - or that if they could, they chose suits and ties to make clear their status.

Apparently it was customary for visitors to explain themselves and their mission to those who belonged here. Before long they knew not only who VanTuyle was, but who Nell Shipman, "The Queen of the Dogsleds," was, and that she was planning the last scenes of her artistic masterpiece "The Grub Stake," a film requiring rustic buildings, drifts of snow, and if possible ice cakes in the river and some people who were used to handling animals. VanTuyle hoped to find all this in one place, along with housing for 15 people through what remained of the winter. Incidentally, these 15 people proposed to bring with them two teams of sled dogs, several bears, three deer, two elk, four coyotes, two wolves, one cougar, two caribou, two bobcats, and miscellaneous raccoons, skunks, eagles, owls, porcupines, beavers, badgers, marmots and muskrats.

"You can save yourself a fair amount of freight costs, Mister. We got all them here except maybe the marmots, and them they've got in Spokane. No need to drag yours up here from California," Joe Parker offered helpfully.

Van Tuyle explained that for movie-making it was necessary to have animals that were, if not exactly trained, at least accustomed to the demands of life around a film set: traveling frequently in small cages, letting themselves be guided where the humans wanted them to go, living in close quarters with other animals, many of whom were not their natural companions, and being not too inclined to bite, claw or maul. And above all, they must be available on cue; a movie company could not wait around for an elk or bear to wander into their scene. Also, he clarified, the animals were not in California; they had been living for two years just over the mountains in the Idaho Panhandle, on the upper reaches of Priest Lake. It was the company's intention to bring the animals over the mountains in cages.

"So you'd be bringing this here zoo over in July," assumed Hy Maggott.

"Why do you say July?"

"I mean after the snow's off the pass."

"What we're actually after is the winter scenery. It's winter scenes in Alaska that we're shooting. By my map it's only about 20 miles over here as the crow flies, and we figure we can manage that."

"But you're not moving crows. You're moving big-ass bears and elk and such. And with switchbacks you've got a long, long road to slog," Bob Cross pointed out.

"Maybe you'd want to take them down on the Idaho side to Newport, and then up here on the train," suggested George Tiger. "Could be a lot of trouble coming through 20 feet of snow."

VanTuyle seemed averse to following that line of conversation, and asked where he might find some available horses and some people accustomed to handling animals.

"Try the Woodings."

"Jennie Wooding."

"Them Wooding boys. They know what there is to know about freighting."

"Might be some Woodings who could go."

"I'd try Woodings. They've got them big grays."

Jennie was back home with her seed shipment, and rounding up her less-used pans and crockery for seed-starting containers to go in the south windows. Van Tuyle's knock stopped her work for a time, while she and Wes heard his outrageous proposal; and besides wranglers he was looking for pack horses. Jennie admitted, "We got four Perch'ons and five cayuses. They can't all be let go, but the winter logging's about done, and I guess we could do without the Perch'ons. They're no use for farm work anyway. Can you find lumber sleighs over there on the other side? You could put quite a few animal cages on one of them."

"Mrs. Wooding, I'll be honest with you. We've run up a lot of debt around the Priest Lake. I'd like that not to get around over here, if you don't mind. Now, we've come up with a fairly small stake to do these Pend Oreille scenes, but if they know over there that we've got some money, they'll want it to go on the debts. Also, they'll expect us to pay the high, high rates we did back when we had generous cash. That's the reason we can't use the train, and the reason we aren't doing any more business over there than we can help. As far as sleighs go, they'd have to go round trip whichever side we get them on, so we'd rather get them here. And we'd like to pay whatever's the going rate in Tiger, not the exorbitant rates people sometimes imagine Hollywood is used to."

She was sorry Wes was present. His soft spot for debtors had cost them 40 acres, and she was sure she'd learned more from that experience than he had. He'd doubtless be glad to go into a business contract with people who had already admitted nobody would trust them in their own neighborhood.

But as usual she ended up going along with Wes's romantic enthusiasm and when Dave and Tom came in, Wes encouraged them to accept VanTuyle's offer. "To help out," their pa put it, apparently not caring if the boys were paid well, poorly, or at all, as long as they could help needy wayfarers. Fortunately Tom knew enough about packing rates to be able to set a fair price, and Dave and Tom took on the most unlikely contract they'd ever encountered.

Van Tuyle stayed at Velma Coleman's boarding house for two days while he scouted for the scenes he needed to accommodate. There'd be some shots on the Tiger main street and of the exterior of Renshaw Hall. He needed reliable ice for the sled dog scenes - the ice on Priest Lake was spotty at any time, and spring was not far off.

Tom spoke up. "Heritage Lake has solid ice for another two months. And there's a bunch of cabins up there to put up your people. It's west of here about seven miles, mostly up.

Van Tuyle asked, "Is there a big falls up there? There's this canoe disaster scene. The reason I came over here is because I heard about your big river."

"Nothing up there like that."

Wes had a better idea. "The scariest falls on this river is Metaline Falls, the Big Falls, some call it. It isn't just one big drop - it rolls like it's turning over, and it goes on and on like you see in pictures of the Niagara Falls. There's a good place to put in at, close by at Metaline. And there's a new concrete toll bridge there. That bridge is going to save you barging all those animals across the river. Be thankful you aren't trying to do this a year ago."

"You'll be taking the train in the morning, Mr. Van Tuyle?" asked Tom.

"Frankly, I'd like to save that return fare. I'd just as well go along with you, and ride on the load."

Felix LaSota had come into the Tiger Store and heard of the movie adventure. He came to the Wooding house to put in his two cents worth. Felix had been on the surveying crew for the Washington-Idaho line, and he knew the Pass Creek area well. Felix also had a well-developed sense of adventure and mischief. Tom took him to the barn, out of VanTuyle's hearing.

"What do you think, Felix?"

"I think you won't get there as soon as you wish you could. It's March and you'll have the whole winter's snowfall still sitting there. There've been some thaws; a lot of the way you'll have ice on top. But if you do fall through, you'll have a long way down. You won't have any less than 20 feet of snow up top. I could give you a lot of horror stories, but from what I hear of you Wooding boys, you'll make it over there. Now, coming back with a zoo, I don't know. It's the damnedest thing I ever heard of, but I'd love to see you try it."

"Would you love to try it yourself?"

Felix chuckled. "Not likely. Not now that I'm married. I like my evenings home with Winnie. I'll just hear about it when you get back. How long do you think it'll take you to get over there?

"We figure four days."

"And coming back?"

"What would you think? Six?"

"Take food for fourteen."

The road to Metaline Falls was passable year round now, with people using the new bridge and keeping the snow packed down. At Metaline Falls they mounted the huge covered flume that served as a roadway between Metaline Falls and the mill pond below Sullivan Lake. They unharnessed and strung out the horses so as to reduce the weight on the high flume. There was ice on much of it, but Jack had put spiked winter shoes on the four horses, and there were no mishaps. At the end of the flume, they loaded the wagons with bales of hay from the Prouty farm. The Proutys had for years run pack trains up the way they were going, and were astounded to hear their plan, but like Felix LaSota they were too amused by the idea to discourage them.

The party took far more hay than was needed to cross the mountains one way. Beginning just above Sullivan Lake, they left a cache of hay every ten miles for the return trip. The sleighs lightened as they progressed.

"This is almost too easy," Dave remarked.

Their good fortune continued, since loggers had been able to work all winter, and the trail was open clear to the top of Pass Creek Pass. Beyond there, though, the Forest Service was not selling any of the people's timber to logging companies, as Wes would have said, and they finally had to break their own trail down the east side to Priest Lake, a distance of about 25 miles. Bill's Percherons were a godsend, pushing through the four feet of new snow on the trail. The lead span was rotated frequently.

"Van Tuyle, do you think we can start back soon enough to take advantage of this trail we're breaking?"

"Let's hope so. Nell should have everything ready. The crew will have the cages ready."

The deep snow slowed them, but only by a day. They reached the movie compound, Lionhead Lodge, after dark on the fifth day. "See those Perch'ons? That's why Bill bought grays, so you could see them in the dusk. If you're doing winter logging on days with just eight hours of daylight, you need all the help you can get."

The Nell Shipman Motion Picture Company had a lease from the state of Idaho on 103 acres of wooded land on the north end of Priest Lake. Nell, the only actual actor left, plus Bert Van Tuyle, cinematographers, carpenters, grips and animal handlers, had already been there two years shooting animal shorts and scenes for "The Grub Stake," and had built cages out of six-inch pines and animal wire, cabins out of the bigger timber. They had not scalped the area, as so many settlers did, but had scattered the cabins and cages among firs, tamaracks and cedars; windbreak against the lake, they might say, but the beauty of the plan was clearly intentional. It was exactly the atmosphere Nell wanted to show in her back-to-nature films.

Before coming to Idaho, they'd shot all the interior scenes on a professional movie stage in Spokane, housing cast and crew for six months at the posh Davenport Hotel. The interior scenes for "The Grub Stake" done, most of the cast and crew were sent back to Hollywood, and a much slimmer budget, truly a mere grub stake by now, paid for shipping the skeleton crew, the zoo and the filming equipment by truck and barge to this remote spot that looked idyllic to Nell Shipman when she found it. She called it "the nethermost reaches of Nowhere." It still did look idyllic, and Nell's enthusiasm for her art was not diminished after two years of doing the cooking herself for the company and for the zoo - hundred-pound batches of dog biscuits at a time -, reddening her knuckles by laundering for them all, managing the whole company on the deficient budget, and making films when she could. "Now, there's one woman who could meet Ma's muster,'" Dave whispered to Tom. "She's bigger'n Ma, too. But even in those britches she doesn't look a bit like a man, does she?"

To Dave's surprise, Tom blushed heavily and looked away.

"What's that about, Big Brother?"

"Dave, I just recognized her. When I was in the Army at Camp Lewis, waiting to go to France, some of us went in to Tacoma and saw a movie some guys said would have a nude scene in it. They called it "Back to God's Country." It was filmed somewhere like this, I guess. It was about this lady out in the woods with ferns and stuff all around her, and a couple of bears. It went by real fast, and she had a lot of leaves all around her, but it's true she wasn't wearing any clothes. Dave, that's her!"

Dave stifled a hoot.

"Don't you dare let on. And when we get back home you won't tell anybody. Hear me?"

Dave didn't promise, but by the time he knew Nell better, he would have done nothing to embarrass her, in spite of the fun it would have been to smoke Tom, and he never did tell.

Bert VanTuyle having got a taste of the difficulty of crossing the Selkirk Range in March, he and Nell Shipman spent a long evening in conference, reconsidering the scenes on their agenda, and paring the cast list of animals down from the 200 in residence at Lionhead Lodge. They would make do with only two bears, one cougar, one owl, one eagle, two deer, one coyote and a pair of beavers. The sixteen sled dogs would of course work their way across the pass. It was already the practice to supplement the cast with crew members. One carpenter had to date played 23 different roles, six of them in one picture. There was no way, however, to reduce the weight from the cameras, costumes, and props; they were already so bare-boned that no further cuts could be made. The bark canoe needed for the tragedy at the falls wouldn't take up extra space, since it would be packed full of equipment. Rations for animals and people would be carried on the lumber sleighs with the bedrolls, animal crates, cameras, costumes and props. The Percherons would be harnessed as two two-horse teams. Snowshoes were checked carefully the night before; one pair per person and six extra pairs were roped on the sides of the dogsleds. Van Tuyle rode in one sled under a wrap of furs, Nell standing behind him and driving. The other was filled with rations, and one of the roustabouts drove.

Dave marveled, "That movie star lady can go all that way standing up?"

"Don't worry about her," a prop man assured him. "She can do whatever the trek calls for, and look beautiful when she gets there."

The roustabout, who had made many supply runs down and up the lake in VanTuyle's company, added, "Usually Van Tuyle rides, though. That foot of his got frostbit when they was making a film up in north Alberta. He don't take the cold very good. Has to keep it dry. I believe what she likes best about him is looking after him."

The first several miles of the trail were familiar, since the company had been shooting pictures up that way; they started before dawn. Weather had been clear and dry and in the mid-twenties for several days, and the Woodings were much encouraged by the mild temperatures and by the ease of their trip over from Tiger.

But ease was behind them.

On the first afternoon the temperature began dropping, and by morning it was below zero. It continued to drop the next day, and by the second morning it was 40 below. Both nights it was necessary to pitch tents in order to keep falling ice crystals off their faces so they could get any sleep at all. The trip was slowed by setup and takedown. All the animals as well as the humans were going through food faster than they had expected. Felix LaSota's advice was proving good; if they hadn't brought twice the food they had at first planned, they would be in trouble.

"Well, there's lots worse things than cold," Dave told his brother. "We aren't likely to get snow this way, and what could be better than open trail all the way across?" It was the last good moment they had.

The dogsleds came around a bend to a north face and stopped to wait for the lumber sleighs. They heard the bells, and were just starting out when they heard a growl above them. Hackles rose on all 16 sled dogs and they turned their heads from side to side, looking for the source of the threat, suspecting each other of devilment. The dogsled drivers had to stop to keep from being overturned. The growl came again.

Nell and VanTuyle carried only small sidearms. In their two years at Lionhead Lodge they had used them only to dispatch three sled dogs who were terminally injured in a mass dogfight when they were first put into their strange pen. One of the crew, he who kept the table supplied, always went armed with a long-barreled .32 caliber, model 94 rifle, but at age 70 he was thought better suited to standing by at the lodge than to traipsing through the winter Selkirks. Cameramen and prop men did not expect to be called to defend the party. In short, all they could do was hope that whatever was causing the disturbance would not attack.

The dogs continued their frenzy. VanTuyle jumped up from his seat, but snapping jaws discouraged him from any attempt at either unharnessing or quieting the dogs. He could only helplessly swear and try to steady one and then the other sled.

For Nell the event brought another kind of excitement. She got a glimpse of brown fur wriggling just over the rim of an indentation in the snow. She was sure it was a marten, an animal she not only didn't own, but had never seen in the wild. She would have given anything to touch one, perhaps to capture one, and she was convinced beyond doubt that that was what was making the sound. Bent over a pair of lead dogs, VanTuyle didn't see Nell leave the trail and climb the ice-covered snow on the edge of the road. By the time he looked up, Nell was 20 feet up the hillside, her head down looking for footholds and her vision limited by her wolf-fur hood. Above her about 50 yards Van Tuyle saw a starved-looking grizzly sow standing in front of the depression where a small furry creature wriggled.

"Nell! Nell! Come back! Nell!"

She didn't even turn her head toward him. "It's okay, Bert. I'm wearing my heavy gloves."

The dogs by now were hopelessly tangled and starting to nip at each other. He couldn't let another all-out fight develop. But he couldn't leave Nell to investigate a grizzly den, either. Before he could figure out a course of action, he heard the bells of the first sleigh, and saw it come around the corner with Dave Wooding atop the 15-foot load. Dave saw the whole scene clearly, but no more than VanTuyle did he know anything helpful to do. The six men scattered among the boxes and bales of the load could see nothing outside the small nests they had constructed for themselves. They heard VanTuyle yell, "Wooding, have you got a gun?"

"You don't want a gun, Mr. VanTuyle. The only thing you could have worse than that grizzly is a wounded grizzly. And we don't want to set off an avalanche either. Just hope one or the other of 'em turns back."

Through the clear air, Nell heard what he said, and finally looked up to see the towering, defensive mother grizzly above her. From Nell's position the bear looked to be 60 feet tall. Without hesitating, Nell dropped instantly to a sitting position, pushed off, and slid on her behind the whole distance down to the dogsled.

The grizzly wagged her head back at the cub, then turned again and peered toward the hazy conglomeration below her. She repeated this three times. Everyone below her remained frozen and silent. Even the dogs miraculously quieted. As Nell reached the road, the mother bear went back to the edge of the den, looked once more toward the odd creatures below her, then she and the small fur ball disappeared.

Everyone would have liked to move on at top speed but they spent another hour, nervous eyes on the den, untangling and reharnessing the dogs. Finally they moved on, more nervous now about the woods around them.

By the time the train came to a place where they could do a thorough rearrangement it was dark, and they stopped for the night. Beginning that night, and for the remainder of the trip, they kept the fire big and bright through the night. When they started out the next morning they revised the travel plan and decided there would be more safety in numbers, and the dogsleds and horse-drawn lumber sleighs would stay together. There was some relief, too, from the bitter cold. It was around zero, and they were starting to feel more comfortable.

About two hours later, Tom saw a man on the sleigh ahead of him throw off the blanket he'd been wrapped in. Soon another took off his outer coat, and Tom realized the temperature was rapidly rising. When he saw Dave himself, exposed to wind on top of the load, do the same, he realized they had trouble coming. Snow would start soon. He whistled the signal, it was passed on, and all four rigs stopped.

"We're in for it. We don't have many more hours of open trail. Next time we find a place where we can get those dogs off the road, let's move the horses ahead where they can break trail when it gets deep. We'll eat there, and then I think we ought to keep moving as long as we can before we camp, even after dark, if the dogs and horses can take it."

"It hasn't even started to snow yet," VanTuyle protested.

As he spoke, the first large flakes came down, covering the road and the loads with unbelievable speed. By the time they climbed back aboard and moved on, everything was white.

In the next hour no really broad spots offered themselves, so they unharnessed the dogs in the road, carried their harness and even the sleds by hand on the up-slope side of the road, and moved the dogsleds to the rear. For another couple of hours the mighty Percherons pushed on as the snow deepened. Then Tom called another halt and they reharnessed the horses with just two in the front.

"We'll run poles between the two horses and let them break trail. We'll have to rotate 'em every half hour, but we'll get there." They continued past dark with lanterns, making about a mile an hour. They couldn't go on as long as Tom had wanted, because both horses and dogs needed rest. They stopped for the night, and again thanked Felix LaSota for the extra food.

The next day went just the same, the snow unremitting. By night they'd reached the top, Pass Creek Pass, and could cheer an accomplishment, though they were a scant half way to Sullivan Lake. For the dogs, things would be easier now on the downhill route, but the horses were in for another kind of trouble. The two horses in front were slowed by the snow. But the rear horses now had the hazard of an icy, steep descent. Tom had brought rough-locks for both sleighs, a heavy chain to drag behind the trailbreaking pair to roughen the ice for those behind. His concern was for the Percherons' knees, and the rotations couldn't help that. "I'm not giving these horses back to Bill lame," Tom said. "We'll take all the breaks we need to rest 'em. They're too fine of animals to be ruined for some storytelling. I don't care how beautiful Nell Shipman is."

Dave was surprised. "What's that got to do with anything?"

"Well, just in case you thought it did."

On the sixth day the snow stopped and the sun came out. This added the problem of melting and refreezing ice, but the rough-locks and the spiked shoes helped the horses. Now it was the dogs who suffered. They were allowed to stop every few minutes to lick off the ice that built up between their toes.

A few miles below Sullivan Lake they came to the mill pond where the big flume began. It could not accommodate the harnessed horses and loaded sleighs, and they would have to use the road, still not broken after the gigantic storm. The flume proved unusable for the dogs, too, covered with sheet ice as it was. They were given another ten miles - another day - of arduous trailbreaking. "But at least we never had to use all those snowshoes. The horses brought us through," Tom told Nell.

"Those Percherons are the most valiant animals I've ever seen," Nell stated. Tom glowed as if he had developed the breed himself.

At the nooning, Nell took out of her pack mascara, rouge and lip rouge. She put on a sable dress and coat, a gigantic broad-brimmed ermine hat, and changed her boots for soft reindeer-hide mukluks. When she came onto the main street of Metaline Falls after nine days on the trail, she looked as if she'd crossed the mountains in her private railroad car. For the final mile VanTuyle took over the second sled and, dogs yipping with tails wagging, they came into town looking like a million dollars. Nell put them all up at the Washington Hotel. "We've got to act like motion picture stars, or they won't believe we are," she said. "I know we can't afford it, but it's part of what's expected. If you start acting cheap, the whole house of cards falls in."

Bert VanTuyle went at once to locate the smallest boat with the strongest motor in the area. The next day the whole town turned out to watch Nell not go over the falls. The cinematographers were ecstatic to find the bridge was just yards upstream of the big, broad Metaline Falls. They could place their cameras on the bridge and at the mouth of Sullivan Creek where it emptied into the river. Nell got into the canoe, paddled herself downstream, lost her paddle, added frenzied gestures of fear, and approached the roaring waterfall. At the last minute the strong little launch *METALINE*, she who had once maneuvered through the perilous Box Canyon, pulled on the ropes attached to the canoe, and hauled Nell safe and sound to shore. Then the same canoe, with a dummy made by Nell's own hands, and who had made the crossing of the Selkirks waiting for her moment of fame, sacrificed her life by actually going over the Falls.

The crowd cheered Nell and the crowd cheered the crew of the *METALINE*, and the crowd cheered the cougar that waited on one side of the river and the bear that waited on the other side for the beautiful lady to meet her doom. The wranglers out of sight in the brush got no cheer.

After the second night at the Washington Hotel, the Nell Shipman Motion Picture Company moved on to Tiger, and right up the hill to Heritage Lake. For the month that they stayed in the area, Tom hoped he would again be necessary to Nell, but he understood when she said that she was embarrassed to hire him for more work when she hadn't paid him yet for what he had done.

It took perhaps a month for Tom to come back to reality, for life at Tiger to be the true one, for the events on Pass Creek Pass to become a memory, and for him to laugh at Nell's line "It's okay, Bert, I'm wearing my heavy gloves," when she met the grizzly.

****

IN JULY JENNIE'S SISTER AND husband, Ella and Berch Fine, her brother Harry, and Ella's two daughters came to visit from California. Jennie had last seen them when she made her visit in '09, when both their parents were alive. She was surprised at the comfortable kind of love they brought with them. She hadn't realized the fatigue that came with being the matriarch. Watching out for Wes's health, wondering about Bill's absence, worrying about Dave's drinking, straining to help Jack and Lillian grow up, all made her the spar tree, the one that supported the whole operation. With the dear old siblings from California she became a youngster again, loved from all sides for who she was, not expected to provide or produce anything. They stayed up late into the evenings, drinking Jennie's red elderberry wine and remembering the times as children in the Owens Valley.

"Remember when Archie and Harry captured four horned toads and played like they was working them for horses?"

Ella remembered that Jennie was considered the prettiest one in the family. This went to Jennie's head one time so that when their mother sent her for a bucket of water Jennie turned to Emma and said "Em, you get it. I am the prettiest; everyone says so."

"Yes," said Jennie, "and about then I thought I was the smartest, the way my backside smarted after Mother got through putting the ding bats on me."

They remembered driving the horses to thresh grain on the tramping floor in the shed behind the house in the greasewood south of Bishop. "That doesn't sound so hard, watching horses go around and around," Dave offered.

His Aunt Ella upbraided him. "You had to manage two horses on the front of the wagon and six or eight tied on behind it. You had to be there every minute to turn the grain over so the horses would step on it and grind it out. When it was all shelled out and the straw was all lifted off, then you'd fan out the chaff and dust with a hand mill. With the heat and dust of the Owens Valley, don't tell me it wasn't hard work."

"That heat and dust was why I never could stay around the Owens Valley," said Wes. "I couldn't see anything when I was there. That's how your mother snared me; I couldn't see what she looked like." Jennie snapped the back of his neck with a dishtowel.

"And why did Ma put up with Pa, the way he was?" Ella asked. "Boys, I've got to tell you one story about your Grandpa Allison that pretty much sums him up." They refilled their glasses and cups and settled closer to Ella. "This is when we was living on another broken down rental, around Black Rock. Now, Ma had a pretty good setup for her laundry, that she carried in the wagon from house to house as we moved. She had two sawhorses and a couple of planks nailed together so the buckets were up where she didn't have to bend too bad. And she had fairly good buckets and tubs that she kept trading up on when she got a chance. And she had all us kids to haul the water from the Owens River for her and to gather wood to heat it; and there was lots of cottonwood to burn down to charcoal to make good lye for soap. It was a good layout. But what she didn't have was a washboard, which is why her knuckles burned all the time, especially in hot water. So on top of doing the wash for the twenty grownups and children of us on the place, she took in from Mrs. Hall for a few months and earned fifty cents. She had that earmarked for the price of a new washboard.

"Well, one day Pa said he was going to town, which was about eight or nine miles through heavy sand, and he thought he needed four horses to pull the wagon. So he took us kids, like always, to make a long line to help him catch the horses, which was still pretty wild. That can get right vigorous, and blamed if he didn't lose his pocket knife in the sand. He made us look and look, but we didn't find it, and he finally said he guessed he'd go without it. I hated to see Ma give him the fifty cents for the washboard; I saw his nature clearer than she did. But she did, and while he was gone she told us girls she'd make a new dress for the one that found the knife. We spent all day at it, and Jennie was the one that found it. So when Pa came home the next day all us kids ran to the wagon like wild Apaches and jumped all around him to show the knife. But he pulled out a new pocket knife that he'd of course spent Ma's fifty cents on. I thought we'd top him still, and I said I'd ride back on old Clinker to change the knife for a washboard at Snedens' General Store. But he was too tickled, and he went off cackling that now he had a knife for each pocket. He never offered to tell her he was sorry or anything. I don't know when she ever got a washboard. Ma continued to stick it out, but us kids always got out as fast as we could."

Berch Fine remembered a later time, when the three sisters were married and the six of them and their babes lived on the west side of the Sierra, above Visalia and Dinuba. They all remembered the birth of Billie in the gunny sack house. Jennie and Ella teased Wes and Berch again about how the women kept finding more gold than the men. "We all lived in a 30-foot dugout with redwood supports," Jennie told the youngsters. "I know how long it was, because I helped dig the dirt and carry it out in buckets."

After another week, the California relatives entrained for their five-day trip home, and Jennie cried at the departure. "That was some fun, Wes. I just wish they wasn't so far away. Do you think I'll see them again?"

Tom and Dave went through the summer fighting fire, often sleeping in the camps. Jack didn't go back after that week of emergency around Muddy Creek and Ione; the firefighters needed a blacksmith more than they needed one more recruit. "And Lillian likes me home, Ma."

"Wes," Jennie said that night, "I'm glad for them that they can keep the family together. But I'll tell you just between you and me and the gatepost that not many women get the chance I did to hold down the home front by themselves. I did things in those years I never had dreamed I could do."

"Pretty proud of yourself, Girlie."

"I am, and then some. I love you, Wes! I love that we done this together." She rolled over against him and squeezed him very tight.

****

ON A FOGGY MORNING IN late September, Wes announced he was going to work at the pole yard. "There's a big backlog waiting for a crew to load them. Even this late a fire could come down to the log deck, and we need to get them out of here."

"How well are you seeing, Pa?"

"Well enough, Tom. I'll keep my hat off so I can see what's coming at me. "

"Ok, Pa. But I'm coming along, and I want to work alongside you."

So Tom was there to see one-armed Lefty Benson, with an axe he carried under his stump, climb to the top of a flatbed railroad car loaded with cedar logs, cut off some rough butts of branches that a sloppy logger had left on, and then toss the axe down to the ground. Tom saw it coming, and yelled at his Pa. Wes heard him, but didn't know which way to duck. He didn't see the axe coming, even without his hat. And without the hat the wound was greater. The good luck was that the blade was turned up when the axe struck, but the butt end hit the top of his head, knocking a gash that took Jennie 24 stitches to close. He was again in bed for a month, back to the routine of cold cloths, darkened room, pain and boredom.

This time Jennie's fear was realized: they were both down at the same time. All through October and into November her belly was hurting her. Stumped, she tried Dr. Corbett in Ione. After a few weeks he sent her to a doctor in Spokane. Lillian accompanied her on the train, this time with a box lunch she had prepared for the two of them; no more restaurants for Lillian. Neither doctor came up with much. "Wes, I think it's an ulcer. There's a little blood in my stool, and my stomach hurts. It's true I've been worrying more than I ought to about these kids."

"What can you do for it?"

"Well, stop thinking they're kids, for one thing. They're grownups, and I got to let them be that. If Bill wants to go off and disappear, I don't have to think we did something wrong. If Dave wants to drink hisself to grief, I got to let him. If Jack and Lillian are still kids, it just ain't for me to cure. Everybody gets to make their own damn-fool mistakes."

"Oh. Well. I meant is there any medicine for an ulcer?"

"Quinine seems to be helping. And I'm going to give up so much pepper and garlic and onions. I'll drink a lot of milk."

"Do I have to give up good stuff too?"

She laughed. "Not unless your stomach hurts. I think I can figure out a way to get the pepper on your spuds without so much on mine."

By Halloween they were both well enough to go to the party at the Tiger School. Jennie sewed them costumes; Wes played 500 rummy through the evening dressed as Lazarus, and she was Clara Barton. Restraint was new to them both, but she denied herself bobbing for raw apples, and they danced only five of the slower numbers. "Guess it's cards for us for a while, Girlie."

1922

JANUARY OPENED WITH the appointment of a new Justice of the Peace and a new Constable, both declared by the Tiger Town correspondent to believe in law and order. What did the other ones believe in, asked Charlie Lucas over cards at the Renshaws'. Wes speculated that they believed in the same thing, but maybe the new ones would not just believe in it so much as they might chase down a few bootleggers or gamblers.

Neither of the new lawmen was local; they'd been appointed in Newport, and they aroused considerable curiosity in Tiger. George Tiger had had a trip to the Newport Courthouse and brought back with him news about the new J.P. "This John Irving Mitcham applied, and they couldn't say no because he was so qualified. Seems he's not just new to us, he's new to the State of Washington. He had all kinds of important positions over in Idaho. He was a mayor, and a state senator, on the city council of one town and their mayor twice, he was a police judge for four years and a justice of the peace for six years."

Jennie calculated. "He ain't young, is he?"

"Truly not. I understand he was in the Idaho Territorial Legislature, before Statehood. You'll like this, Jennie: he's a great champion of education, and was important in getting the state university started."

George meant only kindness in grouping the reluctant member of the Tiger School Board with the Founder from the University of Idaho, but it made Jennie feel like a fraud, and she ducked her head.

Wes jumped in with a diversion. "How'd you learn all this on a trip to get new boots, George?"

"Well, I went by to check to see if they were recording my plat sales right, and you can't go in that courthouse without catching a lot of gossip. They say he's a staunch Republican." A general groan met that tidbit.

"And the new Constable?"

"Not much about him, except he's supposed to be hard-nosed. Which makes him a good match for this John Irving Mitcham, because Mitcham's an ordained minister in the United Brethren."

"Coo!" said Flora Cross. "What has he not done?"

"Is he bringing a family?"

"A wife, name of Arizona. And there's a grown daughter, name of Mary. About your age, I think, Nettie."

Frank Darrow chuckled. "I don't know how much you folks know about the United Brethren. Ever run into any?"

Wes remembered a missionary who'd passed through, unsuccessfully, back in '03. "I believe that's the brand he was."

"Well, if this Mitcham was a preacher for them, he agrees with you Socialists on women's suffrage and temperance. There's to be no liquor, tobacco or gambling. Maybe he took this job as a mission, because there's plenty of all three in the Hills of Tiger. Also, as a minister for the United Brethren, he's not supposed to jest, or to preach loud and long."

"Well, that last is to their credit," John Renshaw observed.

"They don't believe in picnics, fairs, cakewalks, fancy dress, or jewelry."

"Whoa!" Jennie interrupted. "There's a lot of range there. We run cakewalks at the school programs, but on the other hand, I might agree with them that the world don't need jewelry," said Jennie.

"Nevertheless, all those things are legal," said John Renshaw. "I trust this Mitcham doesn't mean to use his position to promote his own personal views. But if he can close up some of these stills, more power to him. Working men don't need Capitalist temptations so close to hand when they get their paychecks."

They all found reasons to be near the train depot when the newcomers came in. The white-haired gentleman with the full suit, celluloid collar and beard reaching to the second button of his vest was clearly John Irving Mitcham. His was only the second beard in Tiger at this time, and would make him recognizable if the stiff spine and suit didn't. The lady with him matched him in propriety, dressed for the streets of Boise or Spokane in a gray wool traveling suit and a veiled hat, skirts brushing the platform, all of a style suggesting she might have worn them in the days of the Idaho Territorial Legislature. The younger woman, though, was a surprise. Her clothes were plainer than Nettie's own, her skirts were at a sensible three inches above her ankle, and her boots were the kind homesteading women wore. Something about the way she moved told Jennie she knew horses. The man who had to be the new Constable was also a surprise - he was stout. "He'll be good in the Fat Man Race on the Fourth of July," said John Renshaw, "but can he run fast enough to catch a moonshiner?"

"Maybe he's good on the trigger," said Nettie ruthlessly.

Surprises were still ahead of them. Judge Mitcham was much as they had expected and hoped. He did not brook foolishness from miscreants, especially from bootleggers, moonshiners and gamblers. No one ever found out if the Constable could shoot straight, because just the rumor that he could prevented anyone's testing him. Any evidence he brought in resulted in a conviction, and the team of new law enforcers worked like clockwork.

But there were continuing rumors of moonshine still reliably available up Tiger Hill in the area beyond the St. Regis mill. It was Dave, who had a few shady acquaintances himself, who learned the whole story and was much too waggish to keep it to himself. He told Jack, Jack told Tom, and Tom told Wes who, in outrage, shared it broadly.

It seems that Tiger Mary, as Judge Mitcham's daughter was now known in certain circles, was an entrepreneur. Out of a one-horse buckboard with a canvas-covered bed she was operating a fully portable still.

Again at an evening of cards, this time at the Crosses', Dave speculated, "That's why she brought such a good horse with her. No little cayuse for her. All that equipment can be pretty heavy, and one strong horse is cheaper to feed than two measly ones. And she's got one of those spotted coach dogs, like a pointer..."

"Dalmatian," Orla supplied.

"...and he's a great watchdog, I guess, and they're something to see together, him running along between the horse's hooves and never getting in the way."

"So she knew before she came here what she was going to be doing, and brought the right horse and dog."

"Maybe so. Anyway, she does pretty well, they say. At packing, I mean. She's got a good copper kettle and coil - nobody'll get poisoned from her stuff. And a fifty-gallon oak barrel, and a whole bunch of 10-gallon ones, small enough that she can handle them herself. She's got a half-dozen buckets, and a hose and pump. She can pack in a good pile of dry wood - she doesn't want to be starting with wet wood and making unnecessary smoke."

"All of that in one wagon?"

"More. She takes the bags of sugar and mash up too."

"Can she unload all that? How does she cook it?"

"I don't know. Maybe she's got a portable forge under the kettle."

"Could be, I guess. Pretty brave woman, isn't she?"

"Brave how?"

"Well, all kinds of laws are against it now. And some of these moonshiners are going to jail since the federal law came in."

"Think about it. Who's her dad?"

"Do you mean a Man of the Lord would adjust the law to his own ends like that?"

"Maybe he wouldn't. But I think that fat little Constable would. And if he thinks the Justice of the Peace would be pained to see his own daughter hauled in, I guess he wouldn't do it."

"So you're saying Judge Mitcham might not even know about it?"

"It's possible."

They didn't learn the answer to that just then. But the next thing they knew the buckboard with the horse and the dog trotting out front was showing up at sawmills, especially at the Panhandle Mill in Ione, on paydays.

"A good clientele there, I suppose," Frank Darrow said.

"Just what I've been preaching about since the county went dry in '09. We don't want somebody following up our workingman for his money," said Wes. "Every law they pass against it seems to make it more available to them. And now here this Tiger Mary is chasing them from mill to mill and payday to payday."

"That's not the worst of it, Wes," reported Charlie Lucas. "Now she's got a three-card monte game going out of the back of the wagon."

"With complete immunity from the law, from what I hear."

"Though that can get complicated. Up there in her stomping ground, it's hard to tell sometimes where the county line is. Apparently a couple of weeks ago a Pend Oreille sheriff's deputy - working without help from our Constable - came across her and tried to arrest her. She convinced him she was on the Stevens County side of the line. So he came back down to Tiger and phoned the Stevens County sheriff. By the time Stevens County could get a deputy up there, she'd moved the whole shebang and was in Pend Oreille County again."

At the next card game at the Renshaw house, Wes was on a tirade about the Mitchams' racket and their Republican beliefs. "The thing about unrestricted Capitalism is that the Capitalist never thinks about what's good for anybody but himself. He doesn't care what he does to the people around him, so long as he turns a dollar."

"Or in this case, She," Frank Darrow interposed.

Nettie arranged her hand. "What if she hasn't thought of it that way?"

"What do you have in mind, Nettie?" asked her mother, who knew something of the way Nettie's mind worked.

"I think Jennie or somebody - maybe not Wes while he's so mad - could point out to her what the harm is in it. Maybe she'd change her way of doing business."

Charlie disagreed with his wife. "I'm not sure she could change her stripes that much. She still wants to make money."

"If that's all she cares about, the way Wes says, maybe we could suggest something else. I hear Fred Jeannot's getting ready to move on, and his building's going to be for sale. Could it be a saloon and hotel?"

Charlie choked on a laugh.

"I mean a respectable one, of course. Sure, there'd be illegal liquor sold here in town, and we'd have to call it something besides 'saloon,' but it'd be easier to keep an eye on the liquor as well as on the customers if it was right here on main street. She wouldn't be so literally 'following up the working man'."

In six months of running the rolling still and monte game, Tiger Mary had made enough to afford Jennie's proposal. "Hell, yes, Jennie. I didn't know you all felt that way. It's sure no fun for me dragging my butt and that god damned wagon from Hell to Breakfast. Long as I can figure out a way to make it look to my dad like I'm selling root beer, it's a go."

So they did finally learn that the notorious Tiger Mary was enough afraid of her parents that she protected the righteous ideals of John Irving Mitcham and his wife Arizona. And that she was, as Jennie reported, "generous to a fault," and didn't mind reducing her revenues a little if it made the town happy.

Over dinner one night Dave asked the family, "Do you think it's true what they say, that she's been married seven times?"

Jennie snapped. "Now, that is sure as Hell none of my business, and I ain't gonna stick my nose in it for all the Socialist ideals in the Pend Oreille."

****

FOR THREE MONTHS THEY'D BEEN waiting for a decision from Washington, D.C., on the diversion of the Pend Oreille River for the irrigating of the Columbia Basin. Could that be possible? Would they really move a great river that people had lives built on? Jennie dreamed at night of the empty riverbed, slimy weed spread over damp rocks and gravel, the island off Tiger's Landing a misplaced hill, the banks crumbling along the edge with no water to support them.

Finally in March the decision came, and the fear was over - it wouldn't be done because the agricultural powers were outplayed by the hydroelectric interests. It had nothing to do with what was best for the folks who'd been homesteading for 20 years on the river, but in any case their life would continue.

"What hydroelectric interests would that be?" asked Charlie Lucas.

"The ones that some damn Capitalist plans to make a fortune on to take out of the country," answered Wes. "When they say 'agricultural powers' you know they don't mean some poor 'steader trying to raise hay for a few cattle. They mean the big guys. For now, we've got them held off. Maybe the 'hydroelectric interests' will lose interest before they figure out a way to harness Box Canyon and Z Canyon. Anyway, we'll be dead by then." But Jennie's bad dreams didn't stop at once, just because the threat was gone.

SHORTY CONTINUED TO WORRY HER too. She knew he was going, and spent extra time with him, stroking his face, brushing him down, feeding him slices of dried apples. "If Rover was still alive, maybe Shorty might show more spunk," she told Wes. The temperatures were mild now, but Shorty seemed cold all the time. When she went out to the barn one morning, he was wheezing and lying on his side. "Old Fellow, we've had a good lot of years together. There's only one horse like you in a person's lifetime. I'll never regret putting up with your nonsense." She told Wes she knew she should put him down, but it was like losing a piece of herself. "I don't know what all puts a life together, but I know Shorty's been a part of mine."

There was some cheer to be found in the coming of Jack's second baby. Lillian would have two in diapers come June, and Jennie made stacks of flannel diapers and pair after pair of all-purl soakers, in all the colors that scrap yarn would provide. Some special striped ones used up the tiniest scraps and gave her a chuckle when she thought of showing them to Ada.

The summer fires weren't as bad as last year's, but there was plenty of firefighting work for Tom. He refused jobs that kept him from sleeping at home, though, wanting to be nearer his parents; Wes's mishaps and Jennie's stomach pains worried him.

No letter came from Bill, and somehow all the losses mixed in Jennie's dreams. She'd see 15-year-old Bill diving into the river to save red-headed Ethel Honsinger, and all the water suddenly draining out and leaving a bottom of muck and slime that they both sank down into. On one horrible night, that dream recurred and Naomi and Alma were in the center of the slick river bottom in a rowboat, their heads bloodied, and no one able to move the boat.

****

IN OCTOBER TOM TOOK HIS summer's money and sowed the first and last wild oats of his life. He bought a Model T Ford. The *MINER* exaggerated things considerably when it reported him *jazzing around* in it.

"For a family with two cars, four horses and five cayuses, we don't get around much," Wes observed.

"I'm afraid one of those cayuses ain't going to travel much more, either. Old Shorty's reaching the end, I think, Wes. He just stands at that fence and looks at the ground. He's been a good old friend. I hate to see him go."

Tom was able to enjoy his car until past Thanksgiving, then he put it up on blocks for the winter, along with Wes's. Just before Christmas he took the train to Spokane, giving no explanation. That wasn't surprising, given the time of year; perhaps he wanted to buy some secret gifts. But his return was truly a surprise. He brought Bill with him.

Tom had heard from Bill a few times during the two and a half years he'd been gone, but at Bill's insistence had not told the family his whereabouts. He felt terribly guilty about contributing to his parents' worry, but a brother's confidence had to be respected. In fact, Bill's whereabouts were very changeable. He'd gone to Wisconsin looking for Cecil but hadn't found her. He'd tried that college in Nebraska but left there, again broken-hearted, this time over one Ruth Olson. Then he'd tried mining in several spots in South America, but found himself too prone to illnesses and infections. "Something about my blood that doesn't fight stuff off so well." For six months now he had been in California, moving from job to job and missing the family sadly. "But I'm still ashamed about that Cecil business. I don't see how I could do such a bad job of judging somebody. I wish I could come home with a good job and a good woman." When Tom urged at least a Christmas visit, he came. They decided to make it a surprise, and Jennie and Wes both cried when they saw him. He brought with him a crate of oranges, and they had a gladsome week squeezing juice and candying the peels. Jennie had no nightmares the whole time. Bill was still embarrassed about his local history, and stayed close to the house, which was just fine with them all.

****

ON THE FRIDAY AFTER CHRISTMAS Jennie was digging a snow tunnel on the north side of the root cellar, where she meant to stash some smelt. Flora Cross had taken up a subscription order for some to be sent from the coast as soon as the run started. They were a favorite of Wes's, but the order didn't materialize every year. Word was, though, that now, early as it was in the season, they were on their way from Newport. She wanted to keep them a surprise from Wes until they appeared on the table. For a boy from Kansas, Wes had a good taste for fish from the sea, and for him this annual smelt harvest was even better than the New Year's oysters.

Her head and shoulders were inside the tunnel and she didn't hear the alarm bell at first. Then as she backed out to give her spine a rest, she realized that she was supposed to respond to that bell, dinner treat or no. She brushed off her skirt, ran to the house for her nursing bag, and headed for the pole yard.

As she approached the siding she saw a group of men around a man on the ground. Their manner told her it was serious. Then one of them looked at her, said something to the others, and three men came toward her, meaning to stop her. As they reached her and kept her from continuing on, she realized what that meant: one of hers was on the ground. "Who is it?" she yelled.

"Jennie, it's Wes," Charlie Lucas whispered.

She began to scream and continued to scream until she had twisted from them and run the rest of the distance to the pole yard, where Wes lay on the ground, his head split wide, his eyes finally, totally and permanently blind. In a bizarre resume , she screeched at the circle of men, "Three, it's a curse! Three, it's a curse! Three, it's a curse!"

"What's she mean?" Charlie Lucas asked.

"He's hurt his head three times in the last year," offered George Tiger, who'd come to investigate the bell.

Tom knew more. "And my two sisters died of smashed heads, and now this is the third one."

Tom had been with his Pa when the hook came loose from the cedar pole and the chain fell off and the pole fell straight down. He'd yelled, and Wes had taken a step backward, directly into the path of the log.

Now Tom saw to his horror that Jennie was free of all restraint and had Wes's head in her lap. She was trying once again, as at the roadside in California almost 30 years ago, to stuff brain back into skull. By now the other boys had been summoned from the barn and the blacksmith shop. Only they had the authority to force her from her crazed doctoring and to put her in the arms of John Renshaw and George Tiger. But she was still in charge, and she ordered them to take Wes home.

They made a litter of a tarpaulin someone brought from the caboose, and the four sons raised their Pa shoulder high and carried him home. Jennie walked behind.

1923

FIRST COMING OUT of deep sleep, Jennie had the same feeling of weight on her chest, of being in a void, not in the bed or the blankets, but in an empty space with something keeping her lungs from expanding, from letting in air and life. The next thought was: what's wrong? what's missing? where am I supposed to be? can I move? Her eyes opened in the dark. Then it came back: Wes wasn't just up earlier than she was. Wes was dead. She lay back and let that sink in. This was the fourth morning of such wakenings, and her deepest mind still didn't know Wes would not be back in the bed, Wes would not roll against her again, Wes would not wake her with his arms wrapping her against him. She put her face under the quilts in an attempt to crawl back into herself and him. The smell under the covers was a comfort, a relief. Her own sleep scent was there, familiar and welcome. And so was Wes's, because the flannel sheets still held some of it, and because she had slept each night with the clothes she had taken off his body after the boys carried him home. His hat and his coat she'd had Jack burn outside because of the blood, and his boots went at once to Bill, whose own were growing leaks, but the rest of the clothes she'd rolled into a ball and slipped under the quilts on Wes's side of the bed. She could hug them when she went to sleep, she could smell them in her sleep, and on waking she could bring him back a little.

She lay with all she could of him until she heard the boys stirring downstairs, Dave starting the fire, Bill starting breakfast, Tom putting away their bedrolls. In a few more minutes Jack arrived from his own house, needing to be with her and his brothers more than with his own wife and babies. Still she clung to the upstairs nest that had held her and Wes for so long. The sounds down below were familiar, but with a strangeness; usually she was the one down there starting the day. Now she was the indulged one, her grown sons the protectors and caretakers.

IN THESE FOUR DAYS SHE'D come to realize the boys really were grown up. They had their own grief and shock - especially Tom, who'd been with his Pa when it happened - but very soon they'd drawn around their Ma, shielding her from the helpful neighbors and from those, like Ada, who just wanted to become important by being part of the tragedy. The boys fed her and themselves, managed all the chores of the place, made the plans for the funeral.

Jennie knew she should get up, try to get herself and the boys through this day of the funeral. She'd just as well dress for it now; it was to be at 10 in the morning, and there wasn't much point in changing clothes in a short while.

To leave the clothes was hard, but she got out of bed, still holding the bundle, and separated the garments. She removed her nightgown and pulled Wes's union suit onto her own body. The smell of it was the dear smell of his body, his sweat, his sawdust, his tobacco, the cayuse he rode, a trace of Friday morning's gizm, the last there would be. No one else would notice she wore man's underwear, covered by her own petticoats and dress, and she would be comforted all through this day of the funeral. She put on two flannel petticoats, the darkest flannel blouse and skirt she had, laced up her boots, and went downstairs. On a nail she found Wes's old blue sweater, and put that on. Any time she ducked her head into her chest that day she would be able to smell Wes.

The boys were more than competent with the breakfast. She let them carry the load, and sat in Wes's chair, a rocker he'd made when they first came to the Pend d'Oreille. Its arms were a comfort to her, another embrace from Wes. The boys marked the specialness of the day with huckleberry syrup for the pancakes instead of the everyday serviceberry syrup. The bacon was more of Wes's presence - three months ago he had butchered and cured it for winter use. Dave poured the coffee, and they were ready for one more ritual - the Funeral Breakfast. Jennie felt Wes being taken away from her. The ceremonies that were supposed to help would mark the end, the parting. She would rather have had a private burial here at the place for just the family. But Flora Cross and George Tiger, and even Nettie Lucas, said that the town deserved to be part of the farewell, and she'd feel better for sharing it with them. Maybe so; anyway, she'd gone along.

Tomorrow Jennie would get back in harness; today she let the boys do the dishes while she sat in the rocker and rubbed Spot's silky ear between two fingers when he laid it on her knee. She gazed at the walls of the house, remembering the building of it, not just once but twice, after the forest fire burned it before they could move in.

Through these four days Jennie had been as dead as Wes, though she still had to walk around. Her feeling about food could hardly be called an appetite, but somehow the body took care of itself - and her sanity - by taking in the nourishment. The boys ate along with her this morning, then did the cleanup and headed for the barn. Dave brought Kit and Kelly from their stalls, harnessed them, and held them while his brothers brought the low lumber sleigh out. He put the two horses into the traces, and Wes's hearse was ready. The four of them brought Wes, now in the coffin the four of them had built over the past four days.

Jack had worked alone in the smithy, making black hinges and straps; it was suitable that Wes's accouterments be originals, the product of this family's hands. None of them had ever examined a coffin, not in such a way as to remember how to duplicate one. Tom had gone to George Tiger. One of the strange but helpful notions of the Odd Fellows, of which George was one, was that they should "bury the dead" for the community. It would be George's last favor to his friend to go to the head man, the Noble Grand, and get drawings for Wes's last home. Tom felled specially for this job a cedar that grew between the house and the old house and had overlooked their 23 years of homebuilding. At George Tiger's old sawmill they cut the boards to protect Wes. Bill planed and shaped the lumber, Tom mitered the joints.

Laying Pa in was the hardest part. There was nowhere to go for instructions on how to touch their father's remains with both reverence and purpose. Bill and Tom at the shoulders, Jack and Dave at the legs, they hefted on Tom's "now" and put Pa into the box, his head at the broad end. They were struck now by the harshness of the unprotected body bumping against the wood walls of the coffin. They felt dumb, not having foreseen this. They couldn't carry him thumping and banging around inside there. They set the coffin back down and didn't need to speak the problem.

Tom asked, "Did George's Head Fellow say anything about that?"

"Nothing in the drawings," said Bill. "But seems like some packing or something is asked for."

"Well, we don't want to go ask Ma for blankets or anything, not right now."

"Wood chips," said Tom. Their silence showed concurrence, and Bill went off to his planing site with a barrel and shovel.

Dave wasn't satisfied. "We gonna just lay him on chips? Ma or somebody's gonna want to look at him a last time, and we don't want him with chips stuck in his hair and gettin' in his eyes." They thought a while. He tried again, "Shall I go ask Flora or one of the ladies for something? Something fancy?"

Tom thought not. "This is ours to do."

"There's a fair amount of tanned hide at the smithy. How's about we take him out, put the chips in, and cover them with leather? Then we try him again. Bet he won't bump then." And Dave was the man who could implement the idea with finesse, one wall at a time, stitching the seams almost invisibly, using the largest pieces where the viewer would see the most. On the bottom, Pa would cover up most of the bedding, and the smaller, more flawed pieces went there.

Jack found a busted traveling trunk in the shed and spent two hours prying out the fancy-headed nails that held its metal straps on. These he burnished and used around the top to hold the casket lining to the walls.

Through the four days, the boys had taken turns dragging the road north toward the cemetery. The trip from Tiger would be about two miles, and the sixteen inches of snow that had come down since Friday night would have prevented Wes's neighbors from getting to the graveyard. Kit and Kelly were harnessed to the log-and-chain drag and slowly plodded the distance to and from the cemetery hour after hour to firm it down. Packed hard, it would allow the sled runners to move easily along, more easily than wheels in the spring's mud or the summer's dust. As soon as they'd finish the job, more snow would come down. The four of them traded off shifts for hours each day and night, any time they weren't preparing the coffin or running the place. George Tiger said the Odd Fellow would take care of opening the road from Ione, so that friends there could come by sleigh. If Wes had lived his normal span, people could have come in automobiles on plowed roads, but not in 1923 in winter in the Pend Oreille.

The Odd Fellows managed the grave, and their understanding of frozen ground dictated the day of the funeral. Starting an hour after the death on Friday, a fire was laid over the grave site. It was tended steadily, kept burning through the night, and in the morning the few inches of thawed earth were dug out. The fire was relaid in the hole, and the process repeated until by Tuesday morning the hole was the prescribed six feet deep. They'd sent word that they could hurry the schedule some by using blasting powder. Hurry was the last thing Jennie wanted, and forcing their way into the earth didn't seem appropriate for the burying of Wes Wooding. She hadn't thought of it when she said no to the blasting, but she saw on Tom's relieved face that explosions and holes in the ground still had a context of horror for her war veteran. Putting Wes in the ground should be a tender event.

Jennie did indeed want a last look at Wes, and went out to the shed to talk to him where he was already lying on the lumber sleigh. Touched by the boys' work, she smiled and told him, "They're good boys, Wes. That's something we did right for sure. They don't do one whit of all this for show, for respectability. They do it for love of us. I love them so much. And I don't know as I deserve them. I think they're better people than you and me was, Wes. I recall all our sternness, maybe our stinginess. I was always holding back, saving, stinting. They don't. I know Jack had all this tanned hide ready for a couple of smithy aprons. I probably would've kept it for that, if it was me. He gave it to you, and no begrudging. Maybe he's got more of you in him. Anyway, those boys are the best thing we made, Wes.

"I'm gonna spend a lot of time looking back now, I guess. That feels kinda odd. You and me was always looking ahead, at what we was gonna do, gonna make, gonna build. Now I can't think of a thing I want to build alone. But believe me, Wes, there's a lot to look back on. Guess I'll just do that for a while, and that'll keep you here some more."

The limbs of the cedar tree that had come down to make Wes's coffin lay on the ground outside the barn. To crown the boys' work, she took the little bow saw and trimmed fronds to a size to wreathe the coffin. The boys hefted it onto the sleigh, and she put the branches in place. "We're ready, Wes."

She went out to Dave, hitching the horses. "Let's go, then." He called for the others. Tom brought the stool that each of them in turn had used to climb up onto rigs too high for them. There was no real reason Jennie needed it - she could move as well as any man, skirts or no. But it seemed an honorary thing, and she took his hand and stepped up onto the lumber sleigh. She sat flat on the floor on one side of the coffin; Bill sat beside her. Jack and Dave took the other side. Tom as eldest took the reins. He clucked the cayuses off and the hearse with casket and mourners aboard started up. At once Bill yelled to his brother to stop, jumped down, and ran back into the house to get a blanket. He'd felt her shiver. Whether it was from cold or grief, the blanket would help. The Kalispel women who rode their horses on the back side of the river always wore them, and looked dignified doing it. Jennie looked the same. She was not a huddled mass of grief supported by her sons; she was the head of a family, the full and surviving partner of the man they were transporting.

This time it was Jack who stopped the sleigh. He ran clear back to the barn and came back with a set of bells that were sometimes rented out to night travelers. He attached them to Kit and Kelly's harness, and they were off in grandeur. The ring that could denote festivity and fun on a crisp winter dance night now proclaimed pride in the family that was Wooding. Their chief might be dead, but he was with them and they were a force.

They headed off. In respect, no one had taken the road ahead of them but as they proceeded, one family or one bachelor and then another took the road behind them. Each road they passed, whether from the river side or the hill side, brought more mourners.

Ada, when she and Ethel saw them, declared, "My Heavens, she looks like a squaw! They surely could have afforded to rent a second rig. That woman hasn't gained an ounce of style. Ethel, you must have known they were going to do this - why didn't you stop it?"

Frank Darrow coming down off Tiger Hill told his horse Altgeld, "That woman has more class than anyone I know. They look like a Norse funeral barge, fronds and bells and all." He galloped to catch up, and became an honor guard behind the lumber sleigh.

When they came to the cemetery there were already a dozen rigs and saddle horses tied to trees outside the entrance, their owners still with them, waiting for the Wooding sleigh to be the first to enter. As they reached the wooden cattleguard at the entrance to the cemetery, Jennie removed her blanket and folded it. They drove on to the gravesite, from which they could glimpse the river through a fringe of cedars.

Jennie remembered the day 17 years ago when she and the boys had come to this place with most of the women and children from Cement to Yocum to clear brush to make the proud Odd Fellows' Cemetery. It was before they'd had the first cayuse, and they walked the distance with the first dog, Si, hauling the little wagon with their tools, and on the way home the sleeping four-year-old Davey. There'd been a lot of discussion at the time about whether to leave a windbreak over the river. Some thought it would be nice to have more sun and a view of the river and the meadow on the other side and all the mountains to the east. Another faction thought the windbreak would be better and would keep the wooden gravemarkers upright longer. Jennie saw it both ways, and hadn't said much. Today, she was glad the trees had stayed. Wind off the river would have made her even more tense than she was. Now a principal in the function of this graveyard, Jennie found her attention was on the hole in the ground, not on the scenery.

That hole was where Wes would go now, away from her and to where she could never see him again. With both hands she grasped the edge of the coffin, her hands acting of themselves to hold onto him, to keep him from the icy ground. The heap of frozen brown dirt, dusted but not hidden by some new snow, had a harsh look, a rawness that made the hole forbidding. Bill helped her to rise, an assistance she'd never needed before in her life. Standing, she could look down into the hole and see that someone had lined it, sides and bottom, with budless red willow branches. The effect was of a nest, of a sanctuary, almost of a cottage. Someone among those Odd Fellows understood the brutality of putting a loved one into the hard frozen ground and had tried to soften it for those who loved him.

They hadn't thought to bring chairs - when had any of them needed to sit down? But now they felt the need for one, at least, for Jennie. John Mitcham, erstwhile preacher, remembered how draining this exercise could be, and had brought in his wagon a half dozen chairs, collected from his house and his neighbors'. As she stepped toward the hole, Jennie saw him arranging them at the edge. She was bewildered at first, but a weakness in her legs made her understand Mitcham's gesture and she let Bill guide her into one. The boys were not sure it was manly for them to sit, but then they saw that she needed them near her. Dave sat at her left, Jack at her right. Tom and Bill stood behind, leaning more on the chairback than was usual for them. People were gathering on three sides of the hole and behind Jennie and the boys.

From somewhere appeared a group of eight men in black coats, with bare heads, and with wide orange silk scarves around their collars and down their fronts to below their waists. George Tiger was one of them, and she recognized a few others, men who must have had some business dealings with Wes, but were hardly close friends. Why would they have such an intimate part in his leaving, when they'd had so little part in his living? A meanness came up in her, a scoffing that they just wanted to be important, to dress up in their silk scarves and play officialdom. But then she sensed their genuine solemnity, their dread of their own turn in the hole, and their awkwardness at moving in a formal procession. There was no harm in what they were doing, and it did seem as if there had to be a ritual of some kind. This was as good as any, and she felt an appreciation for the men who had left their familiar and comfortable pursuits, to come here and do what they saw as needing doing. She would have a warm spot for them ever afterward, whenever she saw them on the street in Ione or in their various workplaces.

One of them carried what appeared to be a Bible, probably planning to mutter some things she wouldn't be able to listen to, her mind staying with Wes, who was now being lowered into the willow nest.

Some curiosity, a remnant from her normal living self, made her look to see how that was done. Thankfully these helpful Odd Fellows were doing that too; her boys would be spared that. She watched the arrangement of leather straps and 2x6's. Frank Darrow, knowing how cruel the shovels of frozen dirt would sound on the cold wooden box, moved the cedar boughs from the sleigh to cover the coffin.

Everything was in place now, and Fellow #7 stepped forward. The choice of the song, "In the Sweet Bye and Bye," was innocent. Not one Fellow, from One to Eight, had understood anything about the Wobbly movement except that their little town newspaper, organ of the Main Street business interests and thereby of the Lumber and Railroad barons, hated it. The Fellows couldn't know that for Wes Wooding the true words were the ones Tom and Bill brought home from the lumber camps.

The Fellows sang:
    IN THE SWEET BY AND BY
    WE SHALL MEET ON THAT BEAUTIFUL SHORE
    IN THE SWEET BY AND BY
    WE SHALL MEET ON THAT BEAUTIFUL SHORE.

The Woodings and half their friends heard:
    YOU WILL EAT BY AND BY
    IN THAT GLORIOUS LAND ABOVE THE SKY
    WORK AND PRAY, LIVE ON HAY
    YOU'LL GET PIE IN THE SKY WHEN YOU DIE.
    (THAT'S A LIE!)

Listening to the singing, Jennie was sure some people were singing the cynical words, but no one acknowledged hearing them. It was just as well Wes wasn't there, as he might well have drowned out the Fellows, letting his love of music and love of fun override decorum.

Time now for some words. The eighth Odd Fellow, apparently the Top Fellow, read something from the book. Jennie didn't mind, though Wes might have. He for sure would have objected to prayer. But here it came. When the Top Fellow closed the book, bowed his head, and waited for the others to do the same, Jennie saw Frank Darrow's head erect, as well as John Renshaw's. Others of the old Socialists managed an in-between posture that made it unclear whether they were praying, or just resting their necks. Jennie emulated them. As the prayer began, over Wes's dead body, a bunch of over-wintering geese took off from the river below, squawking instructions to each other and drowning out the Top Fellow's piousness. The geese's timing was so appropriate to Wes's attitude that Jennie couldn't help a small smile, which the boys sensed and echoed. The first joke since Wes died brought him back to them in a flash; the wave of love, the remembrance of quirks, was a comfort. Jennie hoped any observers thought they were smiling for the comfort of the prayer, not the aspersions of the geese. It was clear now that Wes's memory, Wes's presence, wasn't going into the hole with his body. The rest of the funeral was easier to bear.

At the end, the Next to the Top Fellow brought a shovel toward them. Jennie was ready to tell him it wasn't theirs, that somebody else brought it. Then he put it into Tom's hands, clearly expecting something. Tom was as stumped as she was. John Mitcham took a step forward and whispered to Wes's bereaved that the eldest son should put a ceremonial shovel of dirt in the hole. Tom looked at her to see if she encouraged this. She topped him. Jennie rose, took the shovel from Tom, moved heavily to the pile of dirt, and heaped the shovel. She dropped the soil slowly onto the cedar boughs, her goodbye to Wes's body easier than she had thought it would be. She passed the spade to Tom, and the boys one by one repeated the farewell. John Renshaw took the shovel from Dave, Joe Parker from him, George Tiger from him, and other men in turn. With Jennie's example other women, Ora Renshaw and Nettie Lucas, then Flora Cross and Tiger Mary, stepped forward. The filling continued as Jennie and the boys headed for the wagon.

This next wrench caught her off guard. Back on the sleigh, she looked back toward the grave and realized they were leaving Wes here. He wasn't going back home. Tears were pushing their way out now, a wind coming up to encourage them. Jennie held composure for everybody's sake. She hung on until they were home and she was back in bed. Then she howled and sobbed and swore; she'd take up her life tomorrow, but not yet, not now.

****

MAINTAINING THE COMPOSURE BECAME A habit, but at great cost to herself. She didn't want the boys or the neighbors to see her weeping. Weeping was a strange experience for Jennie, but now every small thing could bring the tears, and they sometimes became uncontrollable so that she'd have to go upstairs or into the brush to keep people from seeing how unsteady she really was. The things that would set her off were many. Everything connected with her life was connected with Wes. They'd dug this well together, they'd built this root cellar together and roofed it together. They'd slept in this bed together, first in the old house and now in the new house, for 23 years, not to mention 14 before that on miscellaneous pallets and pads, cushions and mattresses. The pan she took to fry potatoes in was the one he'd fought with her about for washing it too often and not letting the bacon grease cure it to his taste. The eggs that went into it reminded her of when they'd laughed all one afternoon when they rebuilt the pole fence around the chicken yard. But she kept these things to herself.

BILL STAYED LONGER THAN THE Christmas visit Tom had arranged, but after two weeks he was ready to go back to California. Over some bedtime pie with them all, he asked about his Percherons. "Coming back here reminds me of what I said I was going to do when I left. I'm thinking to go back to college," he said. "If I sold the team, I'd have enough to set me up pretty well. Would it hurt your situation, Ma? You've had 'em quite a while, and they've earned more than their keep. How about if I sold them before I go?"

They all still wanted to help Bill with his dream of being a schoolteacher. No one objected. Dave started doing extra grooming, getting the big grays ready to look their best. Jack put word out at the Tiger Store. Tom passed the word among all the gyppo loggers he knew. Within a week Bill had a price that astonished them all, and the brave Percherons that had hauled Nell Shipman and her zoo over Pass Creek Pass became a family legend. Bill was gone in two days, all of them promising it wouldn't be so long this time.

DAVE AND TOM WERE STILL on the place, but they were gone so much Jennie was left to herself with Shorty, Spot and the other animals for company. If a place could be a comfort and a blessing, she found now it could also be a torture. She had more sympathy for Ryer in the old days being forever off somewhere, anywhere except at the place that had gone so sour.

In February she went in desperation to Newport for a month to stay with the Braddocks, old friends from Tiger, also with an interest in photography.

She'd work in the bakery there. Jennie enjoyed her vacation, but after a month she knew she had to go back to see about the animals and get ready for planting. Surely she could live with the pain now, surely it would be less sharp now. And it was less sharp now, but deeper, as her body came to know this was forever. It wasn't just something to be endured for a while; it was forever.

When she came home, she found Shorty still older. His eyes were glazed over, and it was clear how important Rover's work as guide dog for the old cayuse had been. Shorty had to be kept in the corral now; he hated it, wanted to be loose and free. But the other horses made his life miserable; they knew he was no longer top horse and they took every opportunity to nip him, kick at him, even chase him. He was better off alone, even if he thought he was in prison. As a farm horse Shorty was worth nothing now, and Tom asked whether she was sure she didn't mind feeding him good hay. She answered, "The range'll be open soon, and he'll eat for free."

Tom didn't say that Shorty's days on range were over, that he didn't have the teeth to tear and chew the wild grass. "And next winter?"

"That might solve itself, Tom."

On a foggy morning in June she took Shorty out of the barn and led her near-blind old friend to the edge of the garden where she was working. She saw that the Renshaws had put barbed wire where there used to be rails around their garden. She went in for lunch, leaving Shorty standing looking at the ground. When she came back he was tangled in the wire, and thrashing with more energy than he'd shown in a couple of years. But it was self-destructive energy. He was cutting gashes across his shoulders and face. She got him untangled and calmed, and took him back to the barn and cleaned the cuts. The next morning the gashes were red. She went to the barn to get some of the California Liniment. The bottle was empty; Dave had had to do plenty of doctoring during the month she was gone. The second morning there was pus. "He's just too old to fight stuff off," she told Dave.

"Ma, I think you're going to have to put him down."

Three days later she accepted that it had to happen. Putting Shorty down meant a shot to his head. With the experience of Wes's ruined brain so raw, she could not do it herself. To have a loved one torn away was the limit of human endurance anyway; you could not be expected to send him away by your own hand. Her four little boys had grown up with Shorty, and she would not ask any of them. She needed someone who cared for Shorty, but not as much as all the Woodings did. And she needed a good gunman who'd make it one clean shot. Bob Cross came from the store with his old Winchester. The boys used the old fresno to deepen a depression beside the tracks where the railroad had taken out gravel when they built the roadbed. Dave led Shorty down into the hole and left him dimly watching the ground. Then Tom, Jack, Dave and Jennie walked toward the house. As they rounded the corral they heard the shot. They broke step, but kept moving. Tom went back later and covered Shorty over. Plenty of gravel was still there to stave off coyotes and ravens.

Good old Shorty was gone now too.

SHE GOT A GARDEN IN, but a fraction the usual size. Well, she told herself, she surely didn't need as much food for herself and two boys who were gone half the time with their meals coming from a cookhouse or a restaurant. There were plenty of other farmers now to keep the boardinghouses and work camps going. In July Tom and Dave were suddenly out of work when the St. Regis millpond washed out and the mill closed down. Dave went to Montana to see what the sheepherding was like there, Tom to Oregon for the same reason.

"Ain't there sheep here to herd? The train's been bringin' 'em in in them double-decker cars for a week now, to eat cheap off government land."

"They bring their own herders, Ma. They're all set for the summer. I don't want to go Out, but there's nothing here right now."

Jack and Lillian and the babies were next door, just a half mile away, and Jennie found some relief in visiting there. It was her personal secret challenge to keep the babies' bottoms free of rashes, something Lillian couldn't seem to remember to do. But the babies' relief lasted longer than Jennie's; when she came back home there were the emptiness, the heaviness, the bleakness, all waiting for her.

Most years, after the little plants got past the dangers of their infancy, as the garden grew and she could see food forming itself, her confidence, her faith in herself and the soil, increased. This year was different. Her sadness deepened as the garden matured, and she came to see no point in harvesting it. It was hard to think ahead, to plan. The thought of being alone in the coming winter was crushing.

"I've got to shake out of this," she told Ora Renshaw. "Maybe the old gypsying would work. I know moving around don't bring happiness, but at least it keeps your mind off of your misery some of the time. Here, every single thing I look at makes me want to bawl."

One night she fixed a good dinner, something she'd got out of the habit of doing, and asked Jack's family over. When she'd put out the jelly roll she told them, "I believe I'll go to California to visit my sister Ella Fine. I ain't had a really good trip in years." She hadn't meant to add "Who wants to go?"

Lillian surprised them. She'd never had a trip of any kind, she said, except that silly one to Spokane with Cecil, and she thought another one sounded like a good idea to take the bad taste out of her mouth. She thought with Jennie and Jack along she wouldn't be so afraid. Jack wanted to indulge her. It would be his chance to show off as the world traveler, to show her places he'd already been, and tell her his personal version of his adventures the time he and Bill went to find their fortunes. He and Lillian could be useful, he said, and Ma wouldn't have any fun traveling alone. And she didn't want to leave Frankie and Virginia, did she?

Jennie'd been talking to Wes lately when she was alone in the bed, and that night she told him, "I'm glad they want to go, but don't it seem kind of like children to leave a home and a business and go traveling? I hope them two are more sensible than I think they are. But one good thing, I can keep them baby butts dry if they come along."

She wired the plan to Dave and Tom. After the wire got to Paradise, Montana, it was more than two weeks till the supply man hauled it with Dave's rations, along with fresh books and magazines, up to the mountain camp where he was living with no one except 2,000 sheep. He asked the camp man to wire back that he couldn't leave the job, but he'd meet them in California after he took the sheep down to their winter pens, probably in early November. He didn't say so in the wire, but Dave's own version of the grief was lessened by being away from people. He took no booze up to the camp, and didn't let the supply man leave any.

Tom was working in the little town of Prineville, Oregon, building sheep pens for the winter. He wasn't critical to the job, and he thought he could be home in five days. He was.

"Ma, what happens to the place if we all leave? I never thought about you not being here."

"Well, I don't see you staying put much," she snapped.

He could see she needed to go right now, and arrangements to leave a functioning farm and a flourishing blacksmith business didn't happen overnight. Tom would stay on the place and run the farm and the smithy, with help from Lillian's father, until Dave got home in the fall. He'd see to the harvesting and sell what he could of the produce. He'd keep in touch with them and with Bill and Dave, and they would all meet up in California somewhere by Christmas.

"Train, Gramma?" asked Frank when he overheard the talk.

She spoke to them all when she said, "Frankie, I guess I ain't thought about that part. But I know it won't be on the damned train. It's dirty, it don't go where you want, and it costs too much." That's all she said then, gave herself a day to mull it over. I guess, she told herself, I thought I was going off in a wagon with a horse or two. That's really what was kind of in my head when I'd picture it. But that, too, is gone for good. I think I've figured out why people have to die - they really like the past best. And the past ain't going to stay around. It's time for things the way they are to move on, so there has to be new people to move on with the new things. Now, we'd look pretty silly going down one of them California highways in the old farm wagon. That's really the best way to travel, though - you can see things better, and you got time to think about what you're seeing. The way people rush around nowadays - like Gilly Glue Birds -don't give them time to figure out what it all means. But you can't just decide you'll be different, you'll be the slow one. You might want to be the big rock in the stream with the water separating around you and rushing on downstream. That big rock looks mighty strong and wise. But a person ain't like that. Instead of a big rock, you're a stick-in-the-mud. And the big stick-in-the-mud don't look wise - she looks like she can't figure things out no more. So the big rock is just a big rock - too big to move, and a lot of trouble to everybody. So I guess this big rock had better act like she's part of the new times.

When she took a box of canning jars over to Lillian, she picked up with Frank as if they were continuing a conversation. "Frankie, we'll go in your Uncle Tom's Model T. Grandpa's Rambler's more apt to break down. And we don't say so around your Uncle Dave, but since he wrecked it that time it leans kind of funny on corners, if you're going to the right. Your Uncle Tom's Model T is a coupe, but really it's got about as much room inside as the Rambler. The Rambler just looks big 'cause it's got that great big hood out in front. And the best thing is, the Model T's got windshields all around. Setting out in September, we'll be going through some rain, and likely even snow when we get to the mountains. The Rambler's good if you want folks to see you, but give me the Tin Lizzie for being comfy."

******

JENNIE WAS SEATED AT THE kitchen table with Alice and Ruby Belle while their children played in the creek. "Aunt Jennie, when're you coming back?"

"I don't know, Ruby Belle. I'm right now just looking to see if there's something I want to do or someplace I want to be. I just know it ain't here. Not right now."

"But you're not selling the place?"

"Not now. Tom's going to find me somebody to lease it, somebody that'll take animals and all. That'll give me money to live on. In the mean time, me and Jack and Lillian'll take what jobs we can, and work our way to California."

"What kind of work do you think you want?"

"Whatever shows up. We're heading first for the Yakima Valley. Some apples might be ready, the hops will for sure. The three of us can do that for a while, and maybe make enough to pay for our food and gas to get on to the next leg."

The girls came by again to see them off, on September 6. Jack drove and Lillian sat in the front beside him. Jennie was in the back, with Baby Virginia on the seat beside her in a padded box her daddy had made her, content to sleep or look around or play face and finger games with Jennie. Under Jennie's feet and piled in every empty space were boxes and bags of their clothes and their camping and cooking gear. Frank would have his third birthday on the road; he was passed back and forth from mother to grandmother as he became restless.

Alice and Ruby Belle pretended to push the Ford to get it started while Tom cranked it, and they were on their way, everybody yelling goodbyes, wiping their eyes, and laughing at the babies, to keep from thinking about what was happening. As they went onto the main street, George Tiger waved his hat from the Landing before the morning river fog hid him. Ada came out onto the porch of the hotel, saw them, waved a dishtowel, shook her head, and went back in. They bumped over the railroad crossing, passed through the pole yard, and headed south.

THANKS

To Bill Kittredge, Molly Gloss, Debra Earling, Jack Shoemaker, and Suzanne and Tony Bamonte for encouragement.

To the Wooding family members who gave not only permission to do this, but much help in filling in the blanks: Diana Wooding Miller, who preserved Jennie's memoir and her photographs; Jack Wooding, Ellene Wooding Tebb, Patricia Wooding Niven, Virginia Wooding Durr, and Bertha Wells.

To Al Six for everything, including fun on the road from Washington to Arizona to Montana, chasing Jennie's rainbows.

To these readers who checked for historical accuracy: Sue Armitage, John Ogmundson, Faith McClenny, Bill Piper, Winnie Sundseth and Anne Geaudreau. Thanks to the Pend Oreille County Historical Society for their excellent archives and their help, to the *Newport Miner,* to Lee Stark and the Tiger Museum, and again to Tony and Suzanne Bamonte for their *History of Pend Oreille County.*

To these who read it and made most useful suggestions: Maggie Ryland, Patty White, Becky Clarke, Amanda Six, Kristen Six, Alta Thompson, Joanne Samaradoff, Jack Wooding, Gene Adams, Nolan Lewis, Anne Williams, Mike Kyle, Peggy Thomas, and Kirsten Redinger.

To these one-time or present Pend Oreille residents who added much: Cliff and Carol Collinge, Bede Jordan, John and Lila Middleton, Donna Jean Davis, Patty Martin, Pat Kinney, Phyllis Johnston, Shannon Haney, Anne and Jere Dennis, Millie Rader, Monte Coleman, and John Kinney.

For whatever errors and missteps may still survive, only I am responsible. I apologize to anyone I've forgotten to thank.

Eva Gayle Six